NEIL GAIMAN . . .

**"IS A TREASURE HOUSE OF STORY,
AND WE ARE LUCKY TO HAVE HIM."**
STEPHEN KING

FRAGILE THINGS

"Neil Gaiman wants to tell you a story—thirty-one of them, actually. . . . No Gaiman fan can be without it. . . . These are not children's stories, by any stretch of the imagination—and stretching your imagination is exactly what Gaiman sets out to do. If you've never encountered Gaiman's unique voice before, this volume is an excellent introduction. . . . You may find yourself gorging at this narrative feast, not stopping until you've read two or three or even half a dozen at a time."
St. Louis Post-Dispatch

"[Gaiman's] a one-man story engine. . . . *Fragile Things* is a delightful compendium . . . a fine sample of the author's versatility. Gaiman writes in different registers: comedy, satire, pastiche, deadpan, lyrical, or whimsical, but almost invariably dark."
Chicago Sun-Times

"A hodgepodge of material, containing everything from a pastiche of both Arthur Conan Doyle and H.P. Lovecraft to a shared-world story based on the first *Matrix* movie. Gaiman's literary interests and influences are wide-ranging, and he indulges them prodigiously. . . . Those with a taste for inventive idiosyncrasy will find themselves amply rewarded."
San Francisco Chronicle

"[A] stellar short story collection . . . Neil Gaiman travels from whimsy to fantasy to horror and back in *Fragile Things*. . . . Fans of Gaiman's work will find much to enjoy in the tales presented here."

The Oklahoman (Oklahoma City)

"Opening a book of short works by Neil Gaiman is like tearing into a box full of wrapped presents, confident and expectant that peeling away the paper from each gift will reveal something wonderful and unexpected and rewarding. . . . [He] spins out thought-provoking fictions that yank the reader out of complacency while never failing to entertain. . . . The author's darkly upbeat humor makes some of his stories funny and frightening all at once. . . . A true pleasure."

Denver Post

"Gaiman is a fabulous writer in every sense of the word. . . . *Fragile Things* . . . [is] a hodgepodge of styles, genres, and tones. There are many wondrous, unsettling, and otherwise utterly Gaiman-esque things to be found within its covers, and fans of his work should absolutely not pass it by. . . . Brilliant . . . For any reader who likes thoughtful, imaginative, and entertaining fiction, it's made to order."

Madison Capital Times (Wisconsin)

"*Fragile Things* is a powerful and oddly unified collection, a perfect introduction to Gaiman's work for new readers and a thrilling reminder to his long-time fans. . . . Gaiman is a visionary storyteller. . . . The shorter prose form allows Gaiman a greater freedom of whimsy and provocation than even his graphic work, with stunning results. . . . Active, involving, reader-pleasing short fiction."

Toronto Star

"Neil Gaiman's *Fragile Things* is a beautiful book . . . there are some wonderful stories inside."
The Times (London)

"Gaiman at his best is terrific. . . . Good, gruesome, and filled with ironic touches . . . These very disparate tales . . . all come from the realm of the deeply dark . . . Gaiman has that same ability [as Ray Bradbury] to move from one genre-within-a-genre to another and not leave the reader who prefers horror to sci-fi, fantasy to realism, in the dust. There is a commingling of styles and outre vignettes in *Fragile Things* that demands that the reader try yet another, then another, like alien canapés at a Trekkie party. These are gothic tales of high caliber."
Baltimore Sun

"Gaiman takes a widely varied approach to his stories, defying anyone who tries slapping his book with a genre label. . . . For all their fantastic, amazing, or horrifying trappings, these are stories about people. . . . Also here and there and in some unexpected places, we read about ourselves. . . . If you find yourself wondering why a comic book and fantasy writer keeps stirring up such a fuss in literary circles, pick up a copy of *Fragile Things*."
Lexington Herald Leader (Kentucky)

"Gaiman follows no overarching theme, but that is what makes these stories charming, at times creepy, and good fun. They read like dreams and meditations, with a stream-of-consciousness quality to their presentation. . . . Well worth adding to any collection; highly recommended."
Library Journal

"This really creepy collection of stories shows that Gaiman may be the heir to Stephen King's Evil Empire."
Newsweek

"He's so good. . . . There's not one piece of prose or poetry in *Fragile Things* that won't repay re-reading. . . . Words, when they're as well-chosen and deftly arranged as those in this book, can perform miracles of strength, staying with their audience long after the breath and ink that gave them birth have vanished."
Seattle Times

"In Neil Gaiman's short stories, fantasy and realism are old friends, keen to embellish each other's best anecdotes. *Fragile Things* confirms Gaiman's reputation as an ingenious teller of sinister tales, whose whimsical and fine writing, at its best, equals . . . Edgar Allan Poe . . . The fictions [are] marvelous in every sense."
The Observer (London)

"Gaiman's talents and interests lend themselves—perfectly, in fact—to the short form and there are gems in this collection. . . . These stories run from light-as-a-feather whimsy to the very dark and the deeply disturbing. . . . Brilliantly unsettling."
Miami Herald

"Neil Gaiman is an admired writer because he can create a fantasy world and convince you, through his graceful prose and sharp descriptions, that it is real. And he has done so again with *Fragile Things*. . . . Gaiman's words are as enjoyable as ever."
Boston Globe

"**O**ne delight after another."
Booklist (* Starred Review *)

"[**G**aiman] loves to surprise his readership in as many ways as possible, and *Fragile Things* delivers a barrage of offbeat narrative blindsides. . . . Gaiman chills and disturbs with so much of *Fragile Thing*s that the humor is absolutely essential. . . . The form and content of the collection varies wildly from tale to tale . . . but nearly all of them show off Gaiman's consistent and considerable craft, along with his contagious enthusiasm for storytelling itself."
Fort Lauderdale Sun-Sentinel

"*Fragile Things* represents the fantasy author at his best."
Cleveland Plain Dealer

"**R**esurrection and rebirth, iterations and overlappings of tales and characters—these are the features of a place we can call Neil Gaiman Land. And if you've never met its gods and humans, ghosts and zombies, consider a trip....This enchanting anthology gathers the wide-ranging output of a productive writer."
Toronto Globe and Mail

"**T**he wide variety of selections shows Gaiman's influences and his amazing range as one of the world's most popular fantasy writers. Some stories are frightening; a couple are laugh-out-loud funny; some are downright strange . . . I hope Gaiman has room on his shelf for a few more trophies. Readers will be hard-pressed to find a better collection this year."
Rocky Mountain News (Denver, CO)

Books by Neil Gaiman

Novels and Collections
THE OCEAN AT THE END OF THE LANE
STORIES • ANANSI BOYS • AMERICAN GODS
STARDUST • SMOKE AND MIRRORS • NEVERWHERE
GOOD OMENS *(with Terry Pratchett)* • FRAGILE THINGS

For Children
THE DAY I SWAPPED MY DAD FOR TWO GOLDFISH
THE WOLVES IN THE WALLS
(both illustrated by Dave McKean)
CORALINE

Graphic Novels (with Dave McKean)
VIOLENT CASES • SIGNAL TO NOISE • MR. PUNCH

Other
MIRRORMASK *(with Dave McKean)*

Sandman
PRELUDES & NOCTURNES • THE DOLL'S HOUSE
DREAM COUNTRY • SEASON OF MISTS • A GAME OF YOU
FABLES AND REFLECTIONS • BRIEF LIVES • WORLDS' END
THE KINDLY ONES • THE WAKE

Death
THE HIGH COST OF LIVING • THE TIME OF YOUR LIFE

Miscellaneous Graphic Novels
THE BOOKS OF MAGIC • MIRACLEMAN: THE GOLDEN AGE
BLACK ORCHID

Nonfiction
MAKE GOOD ART
DON'T PANIC!
GHASTLY BEYOND BELIEF *(with Kim Newman)*

ATTENTION: ORGANIZATIONS AND CORPORATIONS
HarperCollins books may be purchased for educational, business, or sales promotional use. For information, please e-mail the Special Markets Department at SPsales@harpercollins.com.

NEIL GAIMAN

FRAGILE
SHORT FICTIONS AND WONDERS
THINGS

HARPER

An Imprint of HarperCollinsPublishers

This book was originally published in hardcover October 2006 by William Morrow and in trade paperback October 2007 by Harper Perennial, both Imprints of HarperCollins Publishers.

Pages 341–344 constitute an extension of this copyright page.

Frontispiece illustration: A panel from the comic strip "Little Nemo in Slumberland" by Winsor McCay, the *New York Herald*, September 29, 1907.

This is a collection of fiction. Names, characters, places, and incidents are products of the author's imagination or are used fictitiously and are not to be construed as real. Any resemblance to actual events, locales, organizations, or persons, living or dead, is entirely coincidental.

HARPER

An Imprint of HarperCollins*Publishers*
195 Broadway
New York, NY 10007

Copyright © 2006 by Neil Gaiman
Excerpt from *Anansi Boys* copyright © 2005 by Neil Gaiman
ISBN 978-0-06-051523-2

All rights reserved. No part of this book may be used or reproduced in any manner whatsoever without written permission, except in the case of brief quotations embodied in critical articles and reviews. For information address Harper paperbacks, an Imprint of HarperCollins Publishers.

First Harper paperback printing: February 2010
First Harper Perennial trade paperback printing: October 2007
First William Morrow hardcover printing: October 2006

HarperCollins® and Harper® are registered trademarks of HarperCollins Publishers.

Printed in the United States of America

Visit Harper paperbacks on the World Wide Web at
www.harpercollins.com

20 19 18 17 16 15 14 13 12 11

If you purchased this book without a cover, you should be aware that this book is stolen property. It was reported as "unsold and destroyed" to the publisher, and neither the author nor the publisher has received any payment for this "stripped book."

For Ray Bradbury and Harlan Ellison,
and the late Robert Sheckley,
masters of the craft

CONTENTS

INTRODUCTION

"I think . . . that I would rather recollect a life mis-spent on fragile things than spent avoiding moral debt." The words turned up in a dream and I wrote them down upon waking, uncertain what they meant or to whom they applied.

My original plan for this book of tales and imaginings, some eight years ago, was to create a short story collection that I would call *These People Ought to Know Who We Are and Tell That We Were Here,* after a word balloon in a panel from a *Little Nemo* Sunday page (you can now find a beautiful color reproduction of the page in Art Spiegelman's book *In the Shadow of No Towers*), and every story would be told by one of a variety of dodgy and unreliable narrators as each explained their life, told us who they were and that, once, they too were here. A dozen people, a dozen stories. That was the idea; and then real life came along and spoiled it, as I began to write the short stories you'll find in here, and they took on the form they needed to be told in, and while some were told in the first person and were slices of lives, others simply weren't. One story refused to take shape until I gave it to the months of the year to tell, while another did small, efficient things with identity that meant it had to be told in the third person.

Eventually I began to gather together the material of this book, puzzling over what I should call it now that the previous title seemed no longer to apply. It was then that the One Ring Zero CD *As Smart as We Are* arrived, and I heard them sing the lines I had brought back from a dream, and I wondered just what I had meant by "fragile things."

It seemed like a fine title for a book of short stories. There are so many fragile things, after all. People break so easily, and so do dreams and hearts.

"A STUDY IN EMERALD"

This was written for the anthology my friend Michael Reaves edited with John Pelan, *Shadows Over Baker Street.* The brief from Michael was "I want a story in which Sherlock Holmes meets the world of H. P. Lovecraft." I agreed to write a story but suspected there was something deeply unpromising about the setup: the world of Sherlock Holmes is so utterly rational, after all, celebrating solutions, while Lovecraft's fictional creations were deeply, utterly irrational, and mysteries were vital to keep humanity sane. If I was going to tell a story that combined both elements there had to be an interesting way to do it that played fair with both Lovecraft and with the creations of Sir Arthur Conan Doyle.

As a boy I had loved Philip José Farmer's Wold Newton stories, in which dozens of characters from fiction were incorporated into one coherent world, and I had greatly enjoyed watching my friends Kim Newman and Alan Moore build their own Wold Newton–descended worlds in the *Anno Dracula* sequence and *The League of Extraordinary Gentlemen,* respectively. It looked like fun. I wondered if I could try something like that.

The ingredients of the story I had in the back of my head combined in ways that were better than I had hoped when I began. (Writing's a lot like cooking. Sometimes the cake won't rise, no matter what you do, and every now and again the cake tastes better than you ever could have dreamed it would.)

"A Study in Emerald" won the Hugo Award in August 2004 as Best Short Story, something that still makes me intensely proud. It also played its part in my finding myself, the following year, mysteriously inducted into the Baker Street Irregulars.

"THE FAIRY REEL"
Not much of a poem, really, but enormous fun to read aloud.

"OCTOBER IN THE CHAIR"
Written for Peter Straub, for the remarkable volume of *Conjunctions* that he guest-edited. It began some years earlier, at a convention in Madison, Wisconsin, at which Harlan Ellison had asked me to collaborate with him on a short story. We were placed inside a rope barrier, Harlan at his typewriter, me at my laptop. But before we could start the short story, Harlan had an introduction to finish, so while he finished his introduction I started this story and showed it to him. "Nope. It reads like a Neil Gaiman story," he said. (So I put it aside and started another story, which Harlan and I have now been collaborating on ever since. Bizarrely, whenever we get together and work on it, it gets shorter.) So I had part of a story sitting on my hard drive. Peter invited me into *Conjunctions* a couple of years later. I wanted to write a story about a dead boy and a living one, as a sort of dry run for a book for children I had decided to write (it's called *The Graveyard Book,* and I am writing it right now). It took me a little while to figure out how the story worked, and when it was done, I dedicated it to Ray Bradbury, who would have written it much better than I did.

It won the 2003 Locus Award for Best Short Story.

"THE HIDDEN CHAMBER"
Began with a request from two editors, the Nancys Kilpatrick and Holder, to write something "gothic" for

their anthology, *Outsiders*. It seems to me that the story of Bluebeard and its variants is the most gothic of all stories, so I wrote a Bluebeard poem set in the almost empty house I was staying in at the time. *Upsettling* is what Humpty Dumpty called "a portmanteau word," occupying the territory between *upsetting* and *unsettling*.

"FORBIDDEN BRIDES OF THE FACELESS SLAVES IN THE SECRET HOUSE OF THE NIGHT OF DREAD DESIRE"

I started writing this story in pencil one windy winter's night in the waiting room between platforms five and six of East Croydon railway station. I was twenty-two, going on twenty-three. When it was done I typed it up and showed it to a couple of editors I knew. One sniffed, told me it wasn't his kind of thing and he didn't honestly think it was actually anybody's kind of thing, while the other read it, looked sympathetic, and gave it back explaining that the reason it would never be printed was that it was facetious nonsense. I put it away, glad to have been saved the public embarrassment of having more people read it and dislike it.

The story stayed unread, wandering from folder to box to tub, from office to basement to attic, for another twenty years, and when I thought of it, it was only with relief that it had not been printed. One day I was asked for a story for an anthology called *Gothic!* and I re-membered the manuscript in the attic and went up to find it, to see if there was anything in it that I could rescue.

I started reading "Forbidden Brides," and as I read it I smiled. Actually, I decided, it *was* pretty funny, and it was smart, too; a good little story—the clumsinesses were mostly the sort of things you'd find in journeyman work, and all of them seemed easily fixable. I got out the computer and did another draft of the story, twenty years after the first, shortened the title to its present form, and sent it off to the editor. At least one reviewer felt it was facetious nonsense, but that seemed to be a minority opinion, as "Forbidden Brides" was picked up by several "best-of-the-year" anthologies and was voted Best Short Story in the 2005 Locus Awards.

I'm not sure what we can learn from that. Sometimes you just show stories to the wrong people, and nobody's going to like everything. From time to time I wonder what else there is in the boxes in the attic.

"THE FLINTS OF MEMORY LANE,"
"GOOD BOYS DESERVE FAVORS"
One story was inspired by a Lisa Snellings-Clark statue of a man holding a double bass, just as I did when I was a child; the other was written for an anthology of real-life ghost stories. Most of the other authors managed tales that were rather more satisfying than mine, although mine had the unsatisfying advantage of being perfectly true. These stories were first collected in *Adventures in the Dream Trade*, a miscellany published by NESFA Press in 2002, which collected lots of introductions and oddments and such.

"CLOSING TIME"
Michael Chabon was editing a book of genre stories to demonstrate how much fun stories are and to raise funds for 826 Valencia, which helps children to write. (The book was published as *McSweeney's Mammoth Treasury of Thrilling Tales*.) He asked me for a story, and I asked if there was any particular genre he was

missing. There was—he wanted an M. R. James–style ghost story.

So I set out to write a proper ghost story, but the finished tale owes much more to my love of the "strange stories" of Robert Aickman than it does to James (however, it also, once it was done, turned out to be a club story, thus managing two genres for the price of one). The story was picked up by some "best-of-the-year" anthologies, and took the Locus Award for Best Short Story in 2004.

All the places in this story are true places, although I have changed a few names—the Diogenes Club was really the Troy Club in Hanway Street, for example. Some of the people and events are true as well, truer than one might imagine. As I write this I find myself wondering whether that little playhouse still exists, or if they knocked it down and built houses on the ground where it waited, but I confess I have no desire actually to go and find out.

"GOING WODWO"

A *wodwo,* or *wodwose,* was a wild man of the woods. This was written for Terri Windling and Ellen Datlow's anthology *The Green Man.*

"BITTER GROUNDS"

I wrote four short stories in 2002, and this was, I suspect, the best of the lot, although it won no awards. It was written for my friend Nalo Hopkinson's anthology *Mojo: Conjure Stories.*

"OTHER PEOPLE"

I don't remember where I was or when on the day I came up with this little Mobius story. I remember jot-

ting down the idea and the first line, and then wondering if it was original—was I half remembering a story
I'd read as a boy, something by Fredric Brown or Henry
Kuttner? It felt like someone else's story, too elegant and
edgy and complete an idea, and I was suspicious of it.

A year or so later, bored on a plane, I ran across my
note about the story and, having finished the magazine I
was reading, I simply wrote it—it was finished before
the plane landed. Then I called a handful of knowledge-
able friends and read it to them, asking if it seemed familiar, if anyone had read it before. They said no. Normally
I write short stories because someone has asked me to
write a short story, but for once in my life I had a short
story nobody was waiting for. I sent it to Gordon Van
Gelder at the *Magazine of Fantasy and Science Fiction,*
and he accepted and retitled it, which was fine by me.
(I'd called it "Afterlife.")

I do a lot of writing on planes. When I began writing
American Gods I wrote a story on a plane to New York
that would, I was certain, wind up somewhere in the
fabric of the book, but I could never find anywhere in
the book it wanted to go. Eventually, when the book
was finished and the story wasn't in it, I made it into a
Christmas card and sent it out and forgot about it. A
couple of years later Hill House Press, who publish extremely nice limited editions of my books, sent it out to
subscribers as a Christmas card of their own.

It never had a title. Let's call it,

THE MAPMAKER

One describes a tale best by telling the tale. You see?
The way one describes a story, to oneself or to the
world, is by telling the story. It is a balancing act and it
is a dream. The more accurate the map, the more it re-
sembles the territory. The most accurate map possible

would be the territory, and thus would be perfectly accurate and perfectly useless.

The tale is the map which is the territory.

You must remember this.

There was an emperor of China almost two thousand years ago who became obsessed by the notion of mapping the land that he ruled. He had China re-created in miniature on an island which he had constructed at great expense and, incidentally, a certain amount of loss of life (for the waters were deep and cold) in a lake in the imperial estates. On this island each mountain was become a molehill, and each river the smallest rivulet. It took fully half an hour for the emperor to walk around the perimeter of his island.

Every morning, in the pale light before dawn, a hundred men would wade and swim out to the island and would carefully repair and reconstruct any feature of the landscape which had been damaged by the weather or by wild birds, or taken by the lake; and they would remove and remodel any of the imperial lands that had been damaged in actuality by floods or earthquakes or landslides, to better reflect the world as it was.

The emperor was contented by this, for the better part of a year, and then he noticed within himself a growing dissatisfaction with his island, and he began, in the time before he slept, to plan another map, fully one one-hundredth the size of his dominions. Every hut and house and hall, every tree and hill and beast would be reproduced at one one-hundredth of its height.

It was a grand plan, which would have taxed the imperial treasury to its limits to accomplish. It would have needed more men than the mind can encompass, men to map and men to measure, surveyors, census-takers, painters; it would have taken model-makers, potters, builders, and craftsmen. Six hundred professional dreamers would have been needed to reveal the nature of things hidden beneath the roots of trees, and in the deepest mountain caverns, and in the depths of the sea, for the map, to be worth anything, needed to contain both the visible empire and the invisible.

This was the emperor's plan.

His minister of the right hand remonstrated with him one night, as they walked in the palace gardens, under a huge, golden moon.

"You must know, Imperial Majesty," said the minister of the right hand, "that what you intend is. . . ."

And then, courage failing him, he paused. A pale carp broke the surface of the water, shattering the reflection of the golden moon into a hundred dancing fragments, each a tiny moon in its own right, and then the moons coalesced into one unbroken circle of reflected light, hanging golden in water the color of the night sky, which was so rich a purple that it could never have been mistaken for black.

"Impossible?" asked the emperor, mildly. It is when emperors and kings are at their mildest that they are at their most dangerous.

"Nothing that the emperor wishes could ever conceivably be impossible," said the minister of the right hand. "It will, however, be costly. You will drain the imperial treasury to produce this map. You will empty cities and farms to make the land to place your map upon. You will leave behind you a country that your heirs will be too poor to govern. As your advisor, I would be failing in my duties if I did not advise you of this."

"Perhaps you are right," said the emperor. "Perhaps. But if I were to listen to you and to forget my map world, to leave it unconsummated, it would haunt my world and my mind, and it would spoil the taste of the food on my tongue and of the wine in my mouth."

And then he paused. Far away in the gardens they could hear the sound of a nightingale. "But this map land," confided the emperor, "is still only the beginning. For even as it is being constructed, I shall already be pining for and planning my masterpiece."

"And what would that be?" asked the minister of the right hand, mildly.

"A map," said the emperor, "of the Imperial Dominions, in which each house shall be represented by a life-sized house, every mountain shall be depicted by a mountain, every tree by a tree of the same size and type, every river by a river, and every man by a man."

The minister of the right hand bowed low in the moonlight, and he walked back to the Imperial Palace several respectful paces behind the emperor, deep in thought.

It is recorded that the emperor died in his sleep, and that is true, as far as it goes—although it could be remarked that his death was not entirely unassisted; and his oldest son, who became emperor in his turn, had little interest in maps or mapmaking.

The island in the lake became a haven for wild birds and all kinds of waterfowl, with no man to drive them away. They pecked down the tiny mud mountains to build their nests, and the lake eroded the shore of the island, and in time it was forgotten entirely, and only the lake remained.

The map was gone, and the mapmaker, but the land lived on.

"KEEPSAKES AND TREASURES"

This story, subtitled "A Love Story," began life as a comic, or part of it did, written for Oscar Zarate's noir collection, *It's Dark in London,* illustrated by Warren Pleece. Warren did an excellent job, but I was dissatisfied with the story, and I wondered what had made the man who called himself Smith what he was. Al Sarrantonio asked me for a story for his 999 anthology, and I decided it would be interesting to revisit Smith and Mr. Alice and their story. They also turn up in another tale in this collection.

I think there are more stories about the unpleasant Mr. Smith to be told, particularly the one in which he and Mr. Alice come to a parting of the ways.

"THE FACTS IN THE CASE OF THE DEPARTURE OF MISS FINCH"

This story began when I was shown a Frank Frazetta painting of a savage woman flanked by tigers and asked to write a story to accompany it. I couldn't think of a story, so I told what happened to Miss Finch instead.

"STRANGE LITTLE GIRLS"

. . . is really a set of twelve very short stories, written to accompany Tori Amos's CD *Strange Little Girls*. Inspired by Cindy Sherman and by the songs themselves, Tori created a persona for each of the songs, and I wrote a story for each persona. It's never been collected anywhere, although it was published in the tour book, and lines from the stories were scattered throughout the CD booklet.

"HARLEQUIN VALENTINE"

Lisa Snellings-Clark is a sculptor and artist whose work I have loved for years. There was a book called *Strange Attraction,* based on a Ferris wheel Lisa had made; a number of fine writers wrote stories for the passengers in the cars. I was asked if I would write a story inspired by the ticket-seller, a grinning harlequin.

So I did.

On the whole, stories don't write themselves, but for this one all I really remember making up was the first sentence. After that it was a lot like taking dictation as

Harlequin gleefully danced and tumbled through his Valentine's Day.

Harlequin was the trickster figure of the commedia dell'arte, an invisible prankster with his mask and magical stick, his costume covered with diamond shapes. He loved Columbine, and would pursue her through each entertainment, coming up against such stock figures as the doctor and the clown, transforming each person he encountered on the way.

"LOCKS"

"Goldilocks and the Three Bears" was a story by the poet Robert Southey. Or rather, it wasn't—his version told of an old woman and the three bears. The form of the story and what happened was right, but people knew that the story needed to be about a little girl rather than an old woman, and when they retold it, they put her in.

Of course, fairy tales are transmissible. You can catch them, or be infected by them. They are the currency that we share with those who walked the world before ever we were here. (Telling stories to my children that I was, in my turn, told by my parents and grandparents makes me feel part of something special and odd, part of the continuous stream of life itself.) My daughter Maddy, who was two when I wrote this for her, is eleven, and we still share stories, but they are now on television or films. We read the same books and talk about them, but I no longer read them to her, and even that was a poor replacement for telling her stories out of my head.

I believe we owe it to each other to tell stories. It's as close to a *credo* as I have or will, I suspect, ever get.

"THE PROBLEM OF SUSAN"

The doctor the hotel had called told me the reason my neck hurt so badly, that I was throwing up and in pain and confused, was flu, and he began to list painkillers and muscle relaxants he thought I might appreciate. I picked a painkiller from the list and stumbled back to my hotel room, where I passed out, unable to move or think or hold my head up straight. On the third day my own doctor from home called, alerted by my assistant, Lorraine, and talked to me. "I don't like to make diagnoses over the phone, but you have meningitis," he said, and he was right, I did.

It was some months before I could think clearly enough to write, and this was the first piece of fiction I attempted. It was like learning to walk all over again. It was written for Al Sarrantonio's *Flights*, an anthology of fantasy stories.

I read the Narnia books to myself hundreds of times as a boy, and then aloud as an adult, twice, to my children. There is so much in the books that I love, but each time I found the disposal of Susan to be intensely problematic and deeply irritating. I suppose I wanted to write a story that would be equally problematic, and just as much of an irritant, if from a different direction, and to talk about the remarkable power of children's literature.

"INSTRUCTIONS"

Although I put several poems into *Smoke and Mirrors,* my last collection, I had originally planned that this collection would be prose only. I eventually decided to put the poems in anyway, mostly because I like this one so much. If you're one of the people who doesn't like poems, you may console yourself with the knowledge that they are, like this introduction, free. The book would cost you the same with or without them, and nobody pays me anything extra to put them in. Sometimes it's nice to have something short to pick up and read and put down again, just as sometimes it's interesting knowing a little about the background of a story, and you don't have to read it, either. (And while I've spent weeks cheerfully agonizing about what order to put this collection into, how best to shape and order it, you can—and should—read it in any way that strikes your fancy.)

Quite literally, a set of instructions for what to do when you find yourself in a fairy tale.

"HOW DO YOU THINK IT FEELS?"

I was asked for a story for an anthology themed about gargoyles, and, deadline approaching, found myself feeling rather blank.

Gargoyles, it occurred to me, were placed upon churches and cathedrals to protect them. I wondered if a gargoyle could be placed on something else to protect it. Such as, for example, a heart. . . .

Having just reread it for the first time in eight years, I found myself mildly surprised by the sex, but that's probably just general dissatisfaction with the story.

"MY LIFE"

This odd little monologue was written to accompany a photograph of a sock monkey in a book of two hundred photographs of sock monkeys called, not surprisingly, *Sock Monkeys,* by photographer Arne Svenson. The sock monkey in the photo I was given looked like he'd had a hard sort of life, but an interesting one.

An old friend of mine had just started writing for the *Weekly World News,* and I'd had much fun making up stories for her to use. I started wondering whether there was, somewhere out there, someone who had a *Weekly World News* sort of a life. In *Sock Monkeys* it was printed as prose, but I like it better with the line breaks. I have no doubt that, given enough alcohol and a willing ear, it could go on forever. (Occasionally people write to me at my Web site to find out if I would mind if they use this, or other bits of mine, as audition pieces. I don't mind.)

"FIFTEEN PAINTED CARDS FROM A VAMPIRE TAROT"

There are seven stories still to go in the Major Arcana, and I've promised artist Rick Berry that I'll write them one day, and then he can paint them.

"FEEDERS AND EATERS"

This story was a nightmare I had in my twenties.

I love dreams. I know enough about them to know that dream logic is not story logic, and that you can rarely bring a dream back as a tale: it will have transformed from gold into leaves, from silk to cobwebs, on waking.

Still, there are things you can bring back with you from dreams: atmosphere, moments, people, a theme. This is the only time I can remember bringing back a whole story, though.

I first wrote it as a comic, illustrated by the multitalented Mark Buckingham, and then later tried reimagining it as an outline for a pornographic horror film I'd never make (a story called "Eaten: Scenes from a Moving Picture"). A few years ago editor Steve Jones asked me if I would like to resurrect an unjustly forgotten story of mine for his *Keep Out the Night* anthology, and I remembered this story and rolled up my sleeves and started to type.

Shaggy inkcaps are indeed wonderfully tasty mushrooms, but they do deliquesce into an unpleasant, black, inky substance shortly after you've picked them, which is why you will never see them in shops.

"DISEASEMAKER'S CROUP"

I was asked to write an entry in a book of imaginary diseases (*The Thackery T. Lambshead Pocket Guide to Eccentric and Discredited Diseases,* edited by Jeff Vander-Meer and Mark Roberts). It seemed to me that an imaginary disease about making imaginary diseases might be interesting. I wrote it with the aid of a long-forgotten computer program called Babble and a dusty, leather-bound book of advice to the home physician.

"IN THE END"

I was trying to imagine the very last book of the Bible.

And on the subject of naming animals, can I just say how happy I was to discover that the word *yeti,* literally translated, apparently means "that thing over there." ("Quick, brave Himalayan Guide—what's that thing over there?"

"Yeti."

"I see.")

"GOLIATH"

"They want you to write a story," said my agent, some years ago. "It's to go on the Web site of a film that hasn't come out yet, called *The Matrix.* They're sending you a script." I read the film script with interest, and wrote this story, which went up onto the Web a week or so before the film came out, and is still there.

"PAGES FROM A JOURNAL FOUND IN A SHOEBOX LEFT IN A GREYHOUND BUS SOMEWHERE BETWEEN TULSA, OKLAHOMA, AND LOUISVILLE, KENTUCKY"

This was written for my friend Tori Amos's *Scarlet's Walk* tour book, several years ago, and it made me extremely happy when it was picked up for a "best-of-the-year" anthology. It's a story inspired very loosely by the music of *Scarlet's Walk.* I wanted to write something about identity and travel and America, like a tiny companion piece to *American Gods,* in which everything, including any kind of resolution, hovered just out of reach.

"HOW TO TALK TO GIRLS AT PARTIES"

The process of writing a story fascinates me as much as the outcome. This one, for example, began life as two different (failed) attempts to write an account of a tourist holiday on Earth, intended for Australian critic and editor Jonathan Strahan's upcoming anthology *The Starry Rift.* (The story is not in there. This is the first time it's appeared in print. I'm going to write another story for Jonathan's book instead, I hope.) The tale I had in mind wasn't working; I just had a couple of fragments that didn't go anywhere. I was doomed and had started sending e-mails to Jonathan telling him that there wasn't going to be a story, at least, not one from me. He wrote back telling me he'd just got an excellent story in from an author I admired, and she wrote it in twenty-four hours.

So, nettled, I took an empty notebook and a pen and I went down to the gazebo at the bottom of the garden and during the course of the afternoon I wrote this story. I got to read it aloud for the first time a few weeks later at a benefit at the legendary CBGBs. It was the best possible location to read a story about punk and 1977, and it made me feel very happy.

"THE DAY THE SAUCERS CAME"

Written in a hotel room in New York the week I read the audio book of my novel *Stardust,* while waiting for a car to come and take me away, for editor and poet Rain Graves, who had asked me for a couple of poems for her Web site at www.spiderwords.com. I was happy to discover that it worked when read before an audience.

"SUNBIRD"

My oldest daughter, Holly, told me exactly what she wanted for her eighteenth birthday. "I want something nobody else could ever give me, Dad. I want you to write me a short story." And then, because she knows me well, she added, "And I know you're always late, and I don't want to stress you out or anything, so as long as I get it by my nineteenth birthday, you're fine."

There was a writer from Tulsa, Oklahoma (he died in 2002), who was, for a little while in the late 1960s and early 1970s, the best short story writer in the world. His name was R. A. Lafferty, and his stories were unclassifiable and odd and inimitable—you knew you were reading a Lafferty story within a sentence. When I was young I wrote to him, and he wrote back.

"Sunbird" was my attempt to write a Lafferty story, and it taught me a number of things, mostly how much harder they are than they look. Holly didn't get it until her nineteen-and-a-halfth birthday, when I was in the middle of writing *Anansi Boys* and decided that if I didn't finish writing something—anything—I would probably go mad. With her permission it was published in a book with an extremely long title, often abbreviated to *Noisy Outlaws, Unfriendly Blobs, and Some Other Things That Aren't As Scary . . .* , as a benefit for the literacy program 826 NYC.

Even if you have this book, you might still want to pick up a copy of the book with the extremely long title, because it has Clement Freud's story "Grimble" in it.

"INVENTING ALADDIN"

One thing that puzzles me (and I use *puzzle* here in the technical sense of *really, really irritates me*) is reading, as from time to time I have, learned academic books on folktales and fairy stories that explain why nobody wrote them and which go on to point out that looking for authorship of folktales is in itself a fallacy; the kind of books or articles that give the impression that all stories were stumbled upon or, at best, reshaped, and I think, Yes, but they all started *somewhere,* in someone's head. Because stories start in minds—they aren't artifacts or natural phenomena.

One scholarly book I read explained that any fairy story in which a character falls asleep obviously began life as a dream that was recounted on waking by a primitive type unable to tell dreams from reality, and this was the starting point for our fairy stories—a theory which seemed filled with holes from the get-go, because stories, the kind that survive and are retold, have narrative logic, not dream logic.

Stories are made up by people who make them up. If they work, they get retold. There's the magic of it.

Scheherazade as a narrator was a fiction, as was her sister and the murderous king they needed nightly to placate. *The Arabian Nights* are a fictional construct, assembled from a variety of places, and the story of Aladdin is itself a late tale, folded into the *Nights* by the French only a few hundred years ago. Which is another way of saying that when it began, it certainly didn't begin as I describe. And yet. And still.

"THE MONARCH OF THE GLEN"

A story that began with, and exists because of, my love of the remoter parts of Scotland, where the bones of the Earth show through, and the sky is a pale white, and it's all astoundingly beautiful, and it feels about as remote as any place can possibly be. It was good to catch up with Shadow, two years after the events in my novel *American Gods.*

Robert Silverberg asked me for a novella for his second *Legends* collection. He didn't mind if I wrote a *Neverwhere* novella or an *American Gods* novella. The *Neverwhere* novella I began had some technical troubles (it was called "How the Marquis Got His Coat Back" and I shall finish it one day). I began writing "The Monarch of the Glen" in a flat in Notting Hill, where I was directing a short film called "A Short Film about John Bolton," and finished it in one long mad winter's dash in the cabin by the lake where I'm currently typing this introduction. My friend Iselin Evensen from Norway first told me tales of the *huldra,* and she corrected my Norwegian. Like "Bay Wolf" in *Smoke and Mirrors,* this was influenced by *Beowulf,* and by the time I wrote it I was certain that the script for *Beowulf* that I had written for and with Roger Avary would never be made. I was of course wrong, but I enjoy the gulf between Angelina Jolie's portrayal of Grendel's mother in the Robert Zemeckis film and the version of the character that turns up here.

I want to thank all the editors of the various volumes in which these stories and poems first appeared, and particularly to thank Jennifer Brehl and Jane Morpeth, my editors in the U.S. and U.K., for their help and assistance and, particularly, their patience, and my literary agent, the redoubtable Merrilee Heifetz, and her gang around the world.

As I write this now, it occurs to me that the peculiarity of most things we think of as fragile is how tough they truly are. There were tricks we did with eggs, as children, to show how they were, in reality, tiny load-bearing marble halls; while the beat of the wings of a butterfly in the right place, we are told, can create a hurricane across an ocean. Hearts may break, but hearts are the toughest of muscles, able to pump for a lifetime, seventy times a minute, and scarcely falter along the way. Even dreams, the most delicate and intangible of things, can prove remarkably difficult to kill.

Stories, like people and butterflies and songbirds' eggs and human hearts and dreams, are also fragile things, made up of nothing stronger or more lasting than twenty-six letters and a handful of punctuation marks. Or they are words on the air, composed of sounds and ideas—abstract, invisible, gone once they've been spoken—and what could be more frail than that? But some stories, small, simple ones about setting out on adventures or people doing wonders, tales of miracles and monsters, have outlasted all the people who told them, and some of them have outlasted the lands in which they were created.

And while I do not believe that any of the stories in this volume will do that, it's nice to collect them together, to find a home for them where they can be read, and remembered. I hope you enjoy reading them.

Neil Gaiman
On the first day of Spring 2006

A STUDY IN EMERALD

I. The New Friend

FRESH FROM THEIR STUPENDOUS EUROPEAN TOUR,
WHERE THEY PERFORMED BEFORE SEVERAL OF THE
CROWNED HEADS OF EUROPE, GARNERING THEIR
PLAUDITS AND *PRAISE* WITH *MAGNIFICENT DRAMATIC
PERFORMANCES*, COMBINING BOTH COMEDY AND
TRAGEDY, THE *STRAND PLAYERS* WISH TO MAKE IT
KNOWN THAT THEY SHALL BE APPEARING AT THE *ROYAL
COURT THEATRE, DRURY LANE*, FOR A LIMITED EN-
GAGEMENT IN APRIL, AT WHICH THEY WILL PRESENT
MY LOOK-ALIKE BROTHER TOM!, *THE LITTLEST
VIOLET-SELLER* AND *THE GREAT OLD ONES COME*
(THIS LAST AN HISTORICAL EPIC OF PAGEANTRY AND
DELIGHT); EACH AN *ENTIRE PLAY* IN ONE ACT! TICKETS
ARE AVAILABLE NOW FROM THE BOX OFFICE.

It is the immensity, I believe. The hugeness of things below. The darkness of dreams.

But I am woolgathering. Forgive me. I am not a literary man.

I had been in need of lodgings. That was how I met
him. I wanted someone to share the cost of rooms with
me. We were introduced by a mutual acquaintance, in
the chemical laboratories of St. Bart's. "You have been
in Afghanistan, I perceive," that was what he said to me,
and my mouth fell open and my eyes opened very wide.

"Astonishing," I said.

"Not really," said the stranger in the white lab-coat, who was to become my friend. "From the way you hold your arm, I see you have been wounded, and in a particular way. You have a deep tan. You also have a military bearing, and there are few enough places in the Empire that a military man can be both tanned and, given the nature of the injury to your shoulder and the traditions of the Afghan cave-folk, tortured."

Put like that, of course, it was absurdly simple. But then, it always was. I had been tanned nut-brown. And I had indeed, as he had observed, been tortured.

The gods and men of Afghanistan were savages, unwilling to be ruled from Whitehall or from Berlin or even from Moscow, and unprepared to see reason. I had been sent into those hills, attached to the ——th Regiment. As long as the fighting remained in the hills and mountains, we fought on an equal footing. When the skirmishes descended into the caves and the darkness then we found ourselves, as it were, out of our depth and in over our heads.

I shall not forget the mirrored surface of the underground lake, nor the thing that emerged from the lake, its eyes opening and closing, and the singing whispers that accompanied it as it rose, wreathing their way about it like the buzzing of flies bigger than worlds.

That I survived was a miracle, but survive I did, and I returned to England with my nerves in shreds and tatters. The place that leech-like mouth had touched me was tattooed forever, frog-white, into the skin of my now-withered shoulder. I had once been a crack-shot. Now I had nothing, save a fear of the world-beneath-the-world akin to panic, which meant that I would gladly pay sixpence of my army pension for a Hansom cab rather than a penny to travel underground.

Still, the fogs and darknesses of London comforted me, took me in. I had lost my first lodgings because I screamed in the night. I had been in Afghanistan; I was there no longer.

"I scream in the night," I told him.

"I have been told that I snore," he said. "Also I keep irregular hours, and I often use the mantelpiece for target practice. I will need the sitting room to meet clients. I am selfish, private, and easily bored. Will this be a problem?"

I smiled, and I shook my head, and extended my hand. We shook on it.

The rooms he had found for us, in Baker Street, were more than adequate for two bachelors. I bore in mind all my friend had said about his desire for privacy, and I forbore from asking what it was he did for a living. Still, there was much to pique my curiosity. Visitors would arrive at all hours, and when they did I would leave the sitting room and repair to my bedroom, pondering what they could have in common with my friend: the pale woman with one eye bone-white, the small man who looked like a commercial traveler, the portly dandy in his velvet jacket, and the rest. Some were frequent visitors, many others came only once, spoke to him, and left, looking troubled or looking satisfied.

He was a mystery to me.

We were partaking of one of our landlady's magnificent breakfasts one morning, when my friend rang the bell to summon that good lady. "There will be a gentleman joining us, in about four minutes," he said. "We will need another place at table."

"Very good," she said, "I'll put more sausages under the grill."

My friend returned to perusing his morning paper. I waited for an explanation with growing impatience. Finally, I could stand it no longer. "I don't understand. How could you know that in four minutes we would be receiving a visitor? There was no telegram, no message of any kind."

He smiled, thinly. "You did not hear the clatter of a brougham several minutes ago? It slowed as it passed us—obviously as the driver identified our door, then it sped up and went past, up into the Marylebone Road. There is a crush of carriages and taxicabs letting off passengers at the railway station and at the waxworks, and it is in that crush that anyone wishing to alight without being observed will go. The walk from there to here is but four minutes. . . ."

He glanced at his pocket watch, and as he did so I heard a tread on the stairs outside.

"Come in, Lestrade," he called. "The door is ajar, and your sausages are just coming out from under the grill."

A man I took to be Lestrade opened the door, then closed it carefully behind him. "I should not," he said. "But truth to tell, I have not had a chance to break my fast this morning. And I could certainly do justice to a few of those sausages." He was the small man I had observed on several occasions previously, whose demeanor was that of a traveler in rubber novelties or patent nostrums.

My friend waited until our landlady had left the room before he said, "Obviously, I take it this is a matter of national importance."

"My stars," said Lestrade, and he paled. "Surely the word cannot be out already. Tell me it is not." He began to pile his plate high with sausages, kipper fillets, kedgeree, and toast, but his hands shook, a little.

"Of course not," said my friend. "I know the squeak of your brougham wheels, though, after all this time: an oscillating G sharp above high C. And if Inspector Lestrade of Scotland Yard cannot publicly be seen to come into the parlor of London's only consulting detective, yet comes anyway, and without having had his breakfast, then I know that this is not a routine case. Ergo, it involves those above us and is a matter of national importance."

Lestrade dabbed egg yolk from his chin with his napkin. I stared at him. He did not look like my idea of a police inspector, but then, my friend looked little enough like my idea of a consulting detective—whatever that might be.

"Perhaps we should discuss the matter privately," Lestrade said, glancing at me.

My friend began to smile, impishly, and his head moved on his shoulders as it did when he was enjoying a private joke. "Nonsense," he said. "Two heads are better than one. And what is said to one of us is said to us both."

"If I am intruding—" I said, gruffly, but he motioned me to silence.

Lestrade shrugged. "It's all the same to me," he said, after a moment. "If you solve the case then I have my job. If you don't, then I have no job. You use your methods, that's what I say. It can't make things any worse."

"If there's one thing that a study of history has taught us, it is that things can always get worse," said my friend. "When do we go to Shoreditch?"

Lestrade dropped his fork. "This is too bad!" he exclaimed. "Here you were, making sport of me, when you know all about the matter! You should be ashamed—"

"No one has told me anything of the matter. When a police inspector walks into my room with fresh splashes of mud of that peculiar mustard-yellow hue on his boots and trouser legs, I can surely be forgiven for presuming that he has recently walked past the diggings at Hobbs Lane, in Shoreditch, which is the only place in London that particular mustard-colored clay seems to be found."

Inspector Lestrade looked embarrassed. "Now you put it like that," he said, "it seems so obvious."

My friend pushed his plate away from him. "Of course it does," he said, slightly testily.

We rode to the East End in a cab. Inspector Lestrade

had walked up to the Marylebone Road to find his brougham, and left us alone.

"So you are truly a consulting detective?" I said.

"The only one in London, or perhaps, the world," said my friend. "I do not take cases. Instead, I consult. Others bring me their insoluble problems, they describe them, and, sometimes, I solve them."

"Then those people who come to you—"

"Are, in the main, police officers, or are detectives themselves, yes."

It was a fine morning, but we were now jolting about the edges of the rookery of St. Giles, that warren of thieves and cutthroats which sits on London like a cancer on the face of a pretty flowerseller, and the only light to enter the cab was dim and faint.

"Are you sure that you wish me along with you?"

In reply my friend stared at me without blinking. "I have a feeling," he said. "I have a feeling that we were meant to be together. That we have fought the good fight, side by side, in the past or in the future, I do not know. I am a rational man, but I have learned the value of a good companion, and from the moment I clapped eyes on you, I knew I trusted you as well as I do myself. Yes. I want you with me."

I blushed, or said something meaningless. For the first time since Afghanistan, I felt that I had worth in the world.

2. The Room

VICTOR'S *VITAE!* AN ELECTRICAL FLUID! DO YOUR LIMBS AND NETHER REGIONS LACK LIFE? DO YOU LOOK BACK ON THE DAYS OF YOUR YOUTH WITH ENVY? ARE THE PLEA- SURES OF THE FLESH NOW BURIED AND FORGOT? VIC- TOR'S *VITAE* WILL BRING LIFE WHERE LIFE HAS LONG BEEN LOST: EVEN THE OLDEST WARHORSE CAN BE A PROUD STALLION ONCE MORE! BRINGING LIFE TO THE

DEAD: FROM AN OLD FAMILY RECIPE AND THE BEST OF
MODERN SCIENCE. TO RECEIVE SIGNED ATTESTATIONS OF
THE EFFICACY OF VICTOR'S *VITÆ* WRITE TO THE V. VON
F. COMPANY, 1B CHEAP STREET, LONDON.

It was a cheap rooming house in Shoreditch. There was
a policeman at the front door. Lestrade greeted him by
name and made to usher us in, and I was ready to enter,
but my friend squatted on the doorstep, and pulled a
magnifying glass from his coat pocket. He examined the
mud on the wrought iron boot-scraper, prodding at it
with his forefinger. Only when he was satisfied would he
let us go inside.

We walked upstairs. The room in which the crime had
been committed was obvious: it was flanked by two
burly constables.

Lestrade nodded to the men, and they stood aside. We
walked in.

I am not, as I said, a writer by profession, and I hesitate to describe that place, knowing that my words cannot do it justice. Still, I have begun this narrative, and I
fear I must continue. A murder had been committed in
that little bedsit. The body, what was left of it, was still
there, on the floor. I saw it, but, at first, somehow, I did
not see it. What I saw instead was what had sprayed
and gushed from the throat and chest of the victim: in
color it ranged from bile-green to grass-green. It had
soaked into the threadbare carpet and spattered the
wallpaper. I imagined it for one moment the work of
some hellish artist who had decided to create a study in
emerald.

After what seemed like a hundred years I looked down
at the body, opened like a rabbit on a butcher's slab, and
tried to make sense of what I saw. I removed my hat,
and my friend did the same.

He knelt and inspected the body, examining the cuts
and gashes. Then he pulled out his magnifying glass,

and walked over to the wall, examining the gouts of drying ichor.

"We've already done that," said Inspector Lestrade.

"Indeed?" said my friend. "What did you make of this, then? I do believe it is a word."

Lestrade walked to the place my friend was standing, and looked up. There was a word, written in capitals, in green blood, on the faded yellow wallpaper, some little way above Lestrade's head. "R-A-C-H-E . . . ?" said Lestrade, spelling it out. "Obviously he was going to write 'Rachel,' but he was interrupted. So—we must look for a woman. . . ."

My friend said nothing. He walked back to the corpse and picked up its hands, one after the other. The fingertips were clean of ichor. "I think we have established that the word was not written by His Royal Highness—"

"What the Devil makes you say—?"

"My dear Lestrade. Please give me some credit for having a brain. The corpse is obviously not that of a man—the color of his blood, the number of limbs, the eyes, the position of the face, all these things bespeak the blood royal. While I cannot say *which* royal line, I would hazard that he is an heir, perhaps . . . no, second in line to the throne . . . in one of the German principalities."

"That is amazing." Lestrade hesitated, then he said, "This is Prince Franz Drago of Bohemia. He was here in Albion as a guest of Her Majesty Victoria. Here for a holiday and a change of air. . . ."

"For the theaters, the whores, and the gaming tables, you mean."

"If you say so." Lestrade looked put out. "Anyway, you've given us a fine lead with this Rachel woman. Although I don't doubt we would have found her on our own."

"Doubtless," said my friend.

He inspected the room further, commenting acidly

several times that the police, with their boots, had obscured footprints and moved things that might have been of use to anyone attempting to reconstruct the events of the previous night.

Still, he seemed interested in a small patch of mud he found behind the door.

Beside the fireplace he found what appeared to be some ash or dirt.

"Did you see this?" he asked Lestrade.

"Her Majesty's police," replied Lestrade, "tend not to be excited by ash in a fireplace. It's where ash tends to be found." And he chuckled at that.

My friend took a pinch of the ash and rubbed it between his fingers, then sniffed the remains. Finally, he scooped up what was left of the material and tipped it into a glass vial, which he stoppered and placed in an inner pocket of his coat.

He stood up. "And the body?"

Lestrade said, "The palace will send their own people."

My friend nodded at me, and together we walked to the door. My friend sighed. "Inspector. Your quest for Miss Rachel may prove fruitless. Among other things, *Rache* is a German word. It means 'revenge.' Check your dictionary. There are other meanings."

We reached the bottom of the stair and walked out onto the street. "You have never seen royalty before this morning, have you?" he asked. I shook my head. "Well, the sight can be unnerving, if you're unprepared. Why my good fellow—you are trembling!"

"Forgive me. I shall be fine in moments."

"Would it do you good to walk?" he asked, and I assented, certain that if I did not walk then I would begin to scream.

"West, then," said my friend, pointing to the dark tower of the palace. And we commenced to walk.

"So," said my friend, after some time. "You have never

had any personal encounters with any of the crowned heads of Europe?"

"No," I said.

"I believe I can confidently state that you shall," he told me. "And not with a corpse this time. Very soon."

"My dear fellow, whatever makes you believe—?"

In reply he pointed to a carriage, black-painted, that had pulled up fifty yards ahead of us. A man in a black top hat and a greatcoat stood by the door, holding it open, waiting, silently. A coat of arms familiar to every child in Albion was painted in gold upon the carriage door.

"There are invitations one does not refuse," said my friend. He doffed his own hat to the footman, and I do believe that he was smiling as he climbed into the box-like space and relaxed back into the soft, leathery cushions.

When I attempted to speak with him during the journey to the palace, he placed his finger over his lips. Then he closed his eyes and seemed sunk deep in thought. I, for my part, tried to remember what I knew of German royalty, but, apart from the Queen's consort, Prince Albert, being German, I knew little enough.

I put a hand in my pocket, pulled out a handful of coins—brown and silver, black and copper-green. I stared at the portrait stamped on each of them of our Queen, and felt both patriotic pride and stark dread. I told myself I had once been a military man and a stranger to fear, and I could remember when this had been the plain truth. For a moment I remembered a time when I had been a crack-shot—even, I liked to think, something of a marksman—but my right hand shook as if it were palsied, and the coins jingled and chinked, and I felt only regret.

3. The Palace

At Long Last Doctor Henry Jekyll is proud to announce the general release of the world-renowned "Jekyll's Powders" for popular consumption. No longer the province of the privileged few. *Release the Inner You!* For Inner and Outer Cleanliness! TOO MANY PEOPLE, both men and women, suffer from CONSTIPATION OF THE SOUL! Relief is immediate and cheap—with Jekyll's Powders! (Available in Vanilla and Original Mentholatum Formulations.)

The Queen's consort, Prince Albert, was a big man with an impressive handlebar mustache and a receding hairline, and he was undeniably and entirely human. He met us in the corridor, nodded to my friend and to me, did not ask us for our names or offer to shake hands.

"The Queen is most upset," he said. He had an accent. He pronounced his Ss as Zs: *Mozt. Upzet.* "Franz was one of her favorites. She has so many nephews. But he made her laugh so. You will find the ones who did this to him."

"I will do my best," said my friend.

"I have read your monographs," said Prince Albert. "It was I who told them that you should be consulted. I hope I did right."

"As do I," said my friend.

And then the great door was opened, and we were ushered into the darkness and the presence of the Queen.

She was called Victoria, because she had beaten us in battle, seven hundred years before, and she was called Gloriana, because she was glorious, and she was called the Queen, because the human mouth was not shaped to say her true name. She was huge, huger than I had imagined possible, and she squatted in the shadows staring down at us, without moving.

Thizsz muzzst be zsolved. The words came from the shadows.

"Indeed, ma'am," said my friend.

A limb squirmed and pointed at me. *Zstepp forward.*

I wanted to walk. My legs would not move.

My friend came to my rescue then. He took me by the elbow and walked me toward Her Majesty.

Isz not to be afraid. Isz to be worthy. Isz to be a companion. That was what she said to me. Her voice was a very sweet contralto, with a distant buzz. Then the limb uncoiled and extended, and she touched my shoulder. There was a moment, but only a moment, of a pain deeper and more profound than anything I have ever experienced, and then it was replaced by a pervasive sense of well-being. I could feel the muscles in my shoulder relax, and, for the first time since Afghanistan, I was free from pain.

Then my friend walked forward. Victoria spoke to him, yet I could not hear her words; I wondered if they went, somehow, directly from her mind to his, if this was the Queen's Counsel I had read about in the histories. He replied aloud.

"Certainly, ma'am. I can tell you that there were two other men with your nephew in that room in Shoreditch, that night. The footprints were, although obscured, unmistakable." And then, "Yes. I understand. . . . I believe so. . . . Yes."

He was quiet when we left the palace, and said nothing to me as we rode back to Baker Street.

It was dark already. I wondered how long we had spent in the palace.

Fingers of sooty fog twined across the road and the sky.

Upon our return to Baker Street, in the looking-glass of my room, I observed that the frog-white skin across my shoulder had taken on a pinkish tinge. I hoped that I was not imagining it, that it was not merely the moon-light through the window.

4. The Performance

LIVER COMPLAINTS?! BILIOUS ATTACKS?! NEUR-ASTHENIC DISTURBANCES?! QUINSY?! ARTHRI-TIS?! THESE ARE JUST A HANDFUL OF THE *COMPLAINTS* FOR WHICH A PROFESSIONAL EXSANGUINATION CAN BE THE *REMEDY*. IN OUR OFFICES WE HAVE SHEAVES OF TES-TIMONIALS WHICH CAN BE INSPECTED BY THE PUBLIC *AT ANY TIME*. DO NOT PUT YOUR HEALTH IN THE HANDS OF *AMATEURS!!* WE HAVE BEEN DOING THIS FOR A VERY LONG TIME: V. TEPES—PROFESSIONAL EXSANGUI-NATOR. (REMEMBER! IT IS PRONOUNCED *TZSEP-PESH!*) ROMANIA, PARIS, LONDON, WHITBY. *YOU'VE TRIED THE REST—NOW TRY THE BEST!!*

That my friend was a master of disguise should have come as no surprise to me, yet surprise me it did. Over the next ten days a strange assortment of characters came in through our door in Baker Street—an elderly Chinese man, a young roué, a fat, red-haired woman of whose former profession there could be little doubt, and a venerable old buffer, his foot swollen and ban-daged from gout. Each of them would walk into my friend's room, and, with a speed that would have done justice to a music-hall "quick-change artist," my friend would walk out.

He would not talk about what he had been doing on these occasions, preferring to relax, staring off into space, occasionally making notations on any scrap of paper to hand, notations I found, frankly, incomprehen-sible. He seemed entirely preoccupied, so much so that I found myself worrying about his well-being. And then, late one afternoon, he came home dressed in his own clothes, with an easy grin upon his face, and he asked if I was interested in the theater.

"As much as the next man," I told him.

"Then fetch your opera glasses," he told me. "We are off to Drury Lane."

I had expected a light opera, or something of the kind, but instead I found myself in what must have been the worst theater in Drury Lane, for all that it had named itself after the royal court—and to be honest, it was barely in Drury Lane at all, being situated at the Shaftesbury Avenue end of the road, where the avenue approaches the rookery of St. Giles. On my friend's advice I concealed my wallet, and, following his example, I carried a stout stick.

Once we were seated in the stalls (I had bought a threepenny orange from one of the lovely young women who sold them to the members of the audience, and I sucked it as we waited), my friend said, quietly, "You should only count yourself lucky that you did not need to accompany me to the gambling dens or the brothels. Or the madhouses—another place that Prince Franz delighted in visiting, as I have learned. But there was nowhere he went to more than once. Nowhere but—"

The orchestra struck up, and the curtain was raised. My friend was silent.

It was a fine enough show in its way: three one-act plays were performed. Comic songs were sung between the acts. The leading man was tall, languid, and had a fine singing voice; the leading lady was elegant, and her voice carried through all the theater; the comedian had a fine touch for patter songs.

The first play was a broad comedy of mistaken identities: the leading man played a pair of identical twins who had never met, but had managed, by a set of comical misadventures, each to find himself engaged to be married to the same young lady—who, amusingly, thought herself engaged to only one man. Doors swung open and closed as the actor changed from identity to identity.

The second play was a heartbreaking tale of an orphan girl who starved in the snow selling hothouse violets—her grandmother recognized her at the last, and swore that she was the babe stolen ten years back by bandits, but it was too late, and the frozen little angel breathed her last. I must confess I found myself wiping my eyes with my linen handkerchief more than once.

The performance finished with a rousing historical narrative: the entire company played the men and women of a village on the shore of the ocean, seven hundred years before our modern times. They saw shapes rising from the sea, in the distance. The hero joyously proclaimed to the villagers that these were the Old Ones whose coming was foretold, returning to us from R'lyeh, and from dim Carcosa, and from the plains of Leng, where they had slept, or waited, or passed out the time of their death. The comedian opined that the other villagers had all been eating too many pies and drinking too much ale, and they were imagining the shapes. A portly gentleman playing a priest of the Roman God told the villagers that the shapes in the sea were monsters and demons, and must be destroyed.

At the climax, the hero beat the priest to death with his own crucifer, and prepared to welcome Them as They came. The heroine sang a haunting aria, whilst, in an astonishing display of magic-lantern trickery, it seemed as if we saw Their shadows cross the sky at the back of the stage: the Queen of Albion herself, and the Black One of Egypt (in shape almost like a man), followed by the Ancient Goat, Parent to a Thousand, Emperor of all China, and the Czar Unanswerable, and He Who Presides over the New World, and the White Lady of the Antarctic Fastness, and the others. And as each shadow crossed the stage, or appeared to, from out of every throat in the gallery came, unbidden, a mighty "Huzzah!" until the air itself seemed to vibrate. The moon rose in the painted sky, and then, at its height, in one final moment of theatrical magic, it turned from a pallid yellow, as it was in the old tales, to the comforting crimson of the moon that shines down upon us all today.

The members of the cast took their bows and their curtain calls to cheers and laughter, and the curtain fell for the last time, and the show was done.

"There," said my friend. "What did you think?"

"Jolly, jolly good," I told him, my hands sore from applauding.

"Stout fellow," he said, with a smile. "Let us go backstage."

We walked outside and into an alley beside the theater, to the stage door, where a thin woman with a wen on her cheek knitted busily. My friend showed her a visiting card, and she directed us into the building and up some steps to a small communal dressing room.

Oil lamps and candles guttered in front of smeared looking glasses, and men and women were taking off their makeup and costumes with no regard to the proprieties of gender. I averted my eyes. My friend seemed unperturbed. "Might I talk to Mr. Vernet?" he asked, loudly.

A young woman who had played the heroine's best friend in the first play, and the saucy innkeeper's daughter in the last, pointed us to the end of the room. "Sherry! Sherry Vernet!" she called.

The young man who stood up in response was lean; less conventionally handsome than he had seemed from the other side of the footlights. He peered at us quizzically. "I do not believe I have had the pleasure . . . ?"

"My name is Henry Camberley," said my friend, drawling his speech somewhat. "You may have heard of me."

"I must confess that I have not had that privilege," said Vernet.

My friend presented the actor with an engraved card.

The man looked at the card with unfeigned interest. "A theatrical promoter? From the New World? My, my. And this is . . . ?" He smiled at me.

"This is a friend of mine, Mister Sebastian. He is not of the profession."

I muttered something about having enjoyed the performance enormously, and shook hands with the actor.

My friend said, "Have you ever visited the New World?"

"I have not yet had that honor," admitted Vernet, "although it has always been my dearest wish."

"Well, my good man," said my friend, with the easy informality of a New Worlder. "Maybe you'll get your wish. That last play. I've never seen anything like it. Did you write it?"

"Alas, no. The playwright is a good friend of mine. Although I devised the mechanism of the magic-lantern shadow show. You'll not see finer on the stage today."

"Would you give me the playwright's name? Perhaps I should speak to him directly, this friend of yours."

Vernet shook his head. "That will not be possible, I am afraid. He is a professional man, and does not wish his connection with the stage publicly to be known."

"I see." My friend pulled a pipe from his pocket and put it in his mouth. Then he patted his pockets. "I am sorry," he began. "I have forgotten to bring my tobacco pouch."

"I smoke a strong black shag," said the actor, "but if you have no objection—"

"None!" said my friend, heartily. "Why, I smoke a strong shag myself," and he filled his pipe with the actor's tobacco, and the two men puffed away, while my friend described a vision he had for a play that could tour the cities of the New World, from Manhattan Island all the way to the furthest tip of the continent in the distant south. The first act would be the last play we had seen. The rest of the play might perhaps tell of the dominion of the Old Ones over humanity and its gods, perhaps telling what might have happened if people had had no Royal Families to look up to—a world of barbarism and darkness—"But your mysterious professional man would be the play's author, and what occurs would be his alone to decide," interjected my friend. "Our drama would be his. But I can guarantee you audiences beyond your imaginings, and a significant share of the takings at the door. Let us say fifty per-cent!"

"This is most exciting," said Vernet. "I hope it will not turn out to have been a pipe-dream!"

"No sir, it shall not!" said my friend, puffing on his own pipe, chuckling at the man's joke. "Come to my rooms in Baker Street tomorrow morning, after breakfast-time, say at ten, in company with your author friend, and I shall have the contracts drawn up and waiting."

With that the actor clambered up onto his chair and clapped his hands for silence. "Ladies and gentlemen of the company, I have an announcement to make," he said, his resonant voice filling the room. "This gentleman is Henry Camberley, the theatrical promoter, and he is proposing to take us across the Atlantic Ocean, and on to fame and fortune."

There were several cheers, and the comedian said, "Well, it'll make a change from herrings and pickled-cabbage," and the company laughed.

And it was to the smiles of all of them that we walked out of the theater and onto the fog-wreathed streets.

"My dear fellow," I said. "Whatever was—"

"Not another word," said my friend. "There are many ears in the city."

And not another word was spoken until we had hailed a cab, and clambered inside, and were rattling up the Charing Cross Road.

And even then, before he said anything, my friend took his pipe from his mouth, and emptied the half-smoked contents of the bowl into a small tin. He pressed the lid onto the tin, and placed it in his pocket.

"There," he said. "That's the Tall Man found, or I'm a Dutchman. Now, we just have to hope that the cupidity and the curiosity of the Limping Doctor proves enough to bring him to us tomorrow morning."

"The Limping Doctor?"

My friend snorted. "That is what I have been calling him. It was obvious, from footprints and much else besides, when we saw the prince's body, that two men had been in that room that night: a tall man, who, unless I miss my guess, we have just encountered, and a smaller man with a limp, who eviscerated the prince with a professional skill that betrays the medical man."

"A doctor?"

"Indeed. I hate to say this, but it is my experience that when a doctor goes to the bad, he is a fouler and darker creature than the worst cut-throat. There was Huston, the acid-bath man, and Campbell, who brought the procrustean bed to Ealing . . ." and he carried on in a similar vein for the rest of our journey.

The cab pulled up beside the curb. "That'll be one and tenpence," said the cabbie. My friend tossed him a florin, which he caught and tipped to his ragged tall hat. "Much obliged to you both," he called out, as the horse clopped into the fog.

We walked to our front door. As I unlocked it, my friend said, "Odd. Our cabbie just ignored that fellow on the corner."

"They do that at the end of a shift," I pointed out.

"Indeed they do," said my friend.

I dreamed of shadows that night, vast shadows that blotted out the sun, and I called out to them in my desperation, but they did not listen.

5. The Skin and the Pit

THIS YEAR, STEP INTO THE SPRING—WITH A SPRING IN
YOUR STEP! JACK'S. BOOTS, SHOES AND BROGUES. SAVE
YOUR SOLES! HEELS OUR SPECIALITY. JACK'S. AND DO
NOT FORGET TO VISIT OUR NEW CLOTHES AND FITTINGS
EMPORIUM IN THE EAST END—FEATURING EVENING
WEAR OF ALL KINDS, HATS, NOVELTIES, CANES, SWORD-
STICKS &C. JACK'S OF PICCADILLY. IT'S ALL IN THE
SPRING!

Inspector Lestrade was the first to arrive.

"You have posted your men in the street?" asked my
friend.

"I have," said Lestrade. "With strict orders to let anyone in who comes, but to arrest anyone trying to leave."

"And you have handcuffs with you?"

In reply, Lestrade put his hand in his pocket, and jan-
gled two pairs of cuffs, grimly.

"Now sir," he said. "While we wait, why do you not
tell me what we are waiting for?"

My friend pulled his pipe out of his pocket. He did
not put it in his mouth, but placed it on the table in
front of him. Then he took the tin from the night before,
and a glass vial I recognized as the one he had had in the
room in Shoreditch.

"There," he said. "The coffin-nail, as I trust it shall
prove, for our Master Vernet." He paused. Then he took
out his pocket watch, laid it carefully on the table. "We
have several minutes before they arrive." He turned to
me. "What do you know of the Restorationists?"

"Not a blessed thing," I told him.

Lestrade coughed. "If you're talking about what I
think you're talking about," he said, "perhaps we should
leave it there. Enough's enough."

"Too late for that," said my friend. "For there are those
who do not believe that the coming of the Old Ones was

the fine thing we all know it to be. Anarchists to a man, they would see the old ways restored—mankind in control of its own destiny, if you will."

"I will not hear this sedition spoken," said Lestrade. "I must warn you—"

"I must warn you not to be such a fathead," said my friend. "Because it was the Restorationists that killed Prince Franz Drago. They murder, they kill, in a vain effort to force our masters to leave us alone in the darkness. The Prince was killed by a *rache*—it's an old term for a hunting dog, Inspector, as you would know if you had looked in a dictionary. It also means 'revenge.' And the hunter left his signature on the wallpaper in the murder room, just as an artist might sign a canvas. But he was not the one who killed the Prince."

"The Limping Doctor!" I exclaimed.

"Very good. There was a tall man there that night—I could tell his height, for the word was written at eye level. He smoked a pipe—the ash and dottle sat unburnt in the fireplace, and he had tapped out his pipe with ease on the mantel, something a smaller man would not have done. The tobacco was an unusual blend of shag. The footprints in the room had, for the most part, been almost obliterated by your men, but there were several clear prints behind the door and by the window. Someone had waited there: a smaller man from his stride, who put his weight on his right leg. On the path outside I had several clear prints, and the different colors of clay on the bootscraper gave me more information: a tall man, who had accompanied the Prince into those rooms, and had, later, walked out. Waiting for them to arrive was the man who had sliced up the Prince so impressively. . . ."

Lestrade made an uncomfortable noise that did not quite become a word.

"I have spent many days retracing the movements of His Highness. I went from gambling hell to brothel to dining den to madhouse looking for our pipe-smoking man and his friend. I made no progress until I thought to check the newspapers of Bohemia, searching for a clue to the Prince's recent activities there, and in them I learned that an English Theatrical Troupe had been in Prague last month, and had performed before Prince Franz Drago. . . ."

"Good Lord," I said. "So that Sherry Vernet fellow—"

"Is a Restorationist. Exactly."

I was shaking my head in wonder at my friend's intelligence and skills of observation, when there was a knock on the door.

"This will be our quarry!" said my friend. "Careful now!"

Lestrade put his hand deep into his pocket, where I had no doubt he kept a pistol. He swallowed, nervously.

My friend called out, "Please, come in!"

The door opened.

It was not Vernet, nor was it a Limping Doctor. It was one of the young street Arabs who earn a crust running errands—"in the employ of Messrs. Street and Walker," as we used to say when I was young. "Please sirs," he said. "Is there a Mister Henry Camberley here? I was asked by a gentleman to deliver a note."

"I'm he," said my friend. "And for a sixpence, what can you tell me about the gentleman who gave you the note?"

The young lad, who volunteered that his name was Wiggins, bit the sixpence before making it vanish, then told us that the cheery cove who gave him the note was on the tall side, with dark hair, and, he added, he had been smoking a pipe.

I have the note here, and take the liberty of transcribing it.

My Dear Sir,

    I do not address you as Henry Camberley, for it is a name to which you have no claim. I am surprised that you did not announce yourself under your own

*name, for it is a fine one, and one that does you
credit. I have read a number of your papers, when I
have been able to obtain them. Indeed, I
corresponded with you quite profitably two years ago
about certain theoretical anomalies in your paper on
the Dynamics of an Asteroid.*

*I was amused to meet you, yesterday evening. A
few tips which might save you bother in times to
come, in the profession you currently follow. Firstly,
a pipe-smoking man might possibly have a brand-
new, unused pipe in his pocket, and no tobacco, but it
is exceedingly unlikely—at least as unlikely as a
theatrical promoter with no idea of the usual
customs of recompense on a tour, who is accompanied
by a taciturn ex-army officer (Afghanistan, unless I
miss my guess). Incidentally, while you are correct
that the streets of London have ears, it might also
behoove you in future not to take the first cab that
comes along. Cab drivers have ears too, if they choose
to use them.*

*You are certainly correct in one of your
suppositions: it was indeed I who lured the half-blood
creature back to the room in Shoreditch.*

*If it is any comfort to you, having learned a little
of his recreational predilections, I had told him I had
procured for him a girl, abducted from a convent in
Cornwall where she had never seen a man, and that
it would only take his touch, and the sight of his face,
to tip her over into a perfect madness.*

*Had she existed, he would have feasted on her
madness while he took her, like a man sucking the
flesh from a ripe peach leaving nothing behind but
the skin and the pit. I have seen them do this. I have
seen them do far worse. And it is not the price we pay*

for peace and prosperity. It is too great a price for that.

The good doctor—who believes as I do, and who did indeed write our little performance, for he has some crowd-pleasing skills—was waiting for us, with his knives.

I send this note, not as a catch-me-if-you-can taunt, for we are gone, the estimable doctor and I, and you shall not find us, but to tell you that it was good to feel that, if only for a moment, I had a worthy adversary. Worthier by far than inhuman creatures from beyond the Pit.

I fear the Strand Players will need to find themselves a new leading man.

I will not sign myself Vernet, and until the hunt is done and the world restored, I beg you to think of me simply as,

Rache.

Inspector Lestrade ran from the room, calling to his men. They made young Wiggins take them to the place where the man had given him the note, for all the world as if Vernet the actor would be waiting there for them, a-smoking of his pipe. From the window we watched them run, my friend and I, and we shook our heads.

"They will stop and search all the trains leaving London, all the ships leaving Albion for Europe or the New World," said my friend, "looking for a tall man, and his companion, a smaller, thickset medical man, with a slight limp. They will close the ports. Every way out of the country will be blocked."

"Do you think they will catch him, then?"

My friend shook his head. "I may be wrong," he said, "but I would wager that he and his friend are even now only a mile or so away, in the rookery of St. Giles, where the police will not go except by the dozen. And they will hide up there until the hue and cry have died away. And then they will be about their business."

"What makes you say that?"

"Because," said my friend, "if our positions were reversed, it is what I would do. You should burn the note, by the way."

I frowned. "But surely it's evidence," I said.

"It's seditionary nonsense," said my friend.

And I should have burned it. Indeed, I told Lestrade I *had* burned it, when he returned, and he congratulated me on my good sense. Lestrade kept his job, and Prince Albert wrote a note to my friend congratulating him on his deductions, while regretting that the perpetrator was still at large.

They have not yet caught Sherry Vernet, or whatever his name really is, nor was any trace found of his murderous accomplice, tentatively identified as a former military surgeon named John (or perhaps James) Watson. Curiously, it was revealed that he had also been in Afghanistan. I wonder if we ever met.

My shoulder, touched by the Queen, continues to improve, the flesh fills and it heals. Soon I shall be a deadshot once more.

One night when we were alone, several months ago, I asked my friend if he remembered the correspondence referred to in the letter from the man who signed himself Rache. My friend said that he remembered it well, and that "Sigerson" (for so the actor had called himself then, claiming to be an Icelander) had been inspired by an equation of my friend's to suggest some wild theories furthering the relationship between mass, energy, and the hypothetical speed of light. "Nonsense, of course," said my friend, without smiling. "But inspired and dangerous nonsense nonetheless."

The palace eventually sent word that the Queen was pleased with my friend's accomplishments in the case, and there the matter has rested.

I doubt my friend will leave it alone, though; it will not be over until one of them has killed the other.

I kept the note. I have said things in this retelling of events that are not to be said. If I were a sensible man I would burn all these pages, but then, as my friend taught me, even ashes can give up their secrets. Instead, I shall place these papers in a strongbox at my bank with instructions that the box may not be opened until long after anyone now living is dead. Although, in the light of the recent events in Russia, I fear that day may be closer than any of us would care to think.

> S—— M—— *Major (Ret'd)*
> *Baker Street,*
> *London, New Albion, 1881*

THE FAIRY REEL

If I were young as once I was, and dreams
  and death more distant then,
I wouldn't split my soul in two, and keep
  half in the world of men,
So half of me would stay at home, and
  strive for Fäerie in vain,
While all the while my soul would stroll up
  narrow path, down crooked lane,
And there would meet a fairy lass and
  smile and bow with kisses three,
She'd pluck wild eagles from the air and
  nail me to a lightning tree
And if my heart would run from her or
  flee from her, be gone from her,
She'd wrap it in a nest of stars and then
  she'd take it on with her
Until one day she'd tire of it, all bored
  with it and done with it
She'd leave it by a burning brook, and off
  brown boys would run with it.
They'd take it and have fun with it and
  stretch it long and cruel and thin,
They'd slice it into four and then they'd
  string with it a violin.
And every day and every night they'd
  play upon my heart a song

So plaintive and so wild and strange that
    all who heard it danced along
And sang and whirled and sank and trod and
    skipped and slipped and reeled and rolled
Until, with eyes as bright as coals, they'd
    crumble into wheels of gold. . . .

But I am young no longer now; for sixty
    years my heart's been gone
To play its dreadful music there, beyond
    the valley of the sun.
I watch with envious eyes and mind, the
    single-souled, who dare not feel
The wind that blows beyond the moon,
    who do not hear the Fairy Reel.
If you don't hear the Fairy Reel, they will
    not pause to steal your breath.
When I was young I was a fool. So wrap
    me up in dreams and death.

OCTOBER IN THE CHAIR

October was in the chair, so it was chilly that evening, and the leaves were red and orange and tumbled from the trees that circled the grove. The twelve of them sat around a campfire roasting huge sausages on sticks, which spat and crackled as the fat dripped onto the burning apple-wood, and drinking fresh apple cider, tangy and tart in their mouths.

April took a dainty bite from her sausage, which burst open as she bit into it, spilling hot juice down her chin. "Beshrew and suck-ordure on it," she said.

Squat March, sitting next to her, laughed, low and dirty, and then pulled out a huge, filthy handkerchief. "Here you go," he said.

April wiped her chin. "Thanks," she said. "The cursed bag-of-innards burned me. I'll have a blister there to-morrow."

September yawned. "You are *such* a hypochondriac," he said, across the fire. "And such *language*." He had a pencil-thin mustache and was balding in the front, which made his forehead seem high and wise.

"Lay off her," said May. Her dark hair was cropped short against her skull, and she wore sensible boots. She smoked a small brown cigarillo that smelled heavily of cloves. "She's sensitive."

"Oh puh*lease*," said September. "Spare me."

October, conscious of his position in the chair, sipped

his apple cider, cleared his throat, and said, "Okay. Who wants to begin?" The chair he sat in was carved from one large block of oakwood, inlaid with ash, with cedar, and with cherrywood. The other eleven sat on tree stumps equally spaced about the small bonfire. The tree stumps had been worn smooth and comfortable by years of use.

"What about the minutes?" asked January. "We always do minutes when I'm in the chair."

"But you aren't in the chair now, are you, dear?" said September, an elegant creature of mock solicitude.

"What about the minutes?" repeated January. "You can't ignore them."

"Let the little buggers take care of themselves," said April, one hand running through her long blonde hair. "And I think September should go first."

September preened and nodded. "Delighted," he said.

"Hey," said February. "Hey-hey-hey-hey-hey-hey-hey. I didn't hear the chairman ratify that. Nobody starts till October says who starts, and then nobody else talks. Can we have maybe the tiniest semblance of order here?" He peered at them, small, pale, dressed entirely in blues and grays.

"It's fine," said October. His beard was all colors, a grove of trees in autumn, deep brown and fire-orange and wine-red, an untrimmed tangle across the lower half of his face. His cheeks were apple-red. He looked like a friend; like someone you had known all your life. "September can go first. Let's just get it rolling."

September placed the end of his sausage into his mouth, chewed daintily, and drained his cider mug. Then he stood up and bowed to the company and began to speak.

"Laurent DeLisle was the finest chef in all of Seattle, at least, Laurent DeLisle thought so, and the Michelin stars on his door confirmed him in his opinion. He was a remarkable chef, it is true—his minced lamb brioche had won several awards; his smoked quail and white truffle ravioli had been described in the *Gastronome* as 'the tenth wonder of the world.' But it was his wine cellar . . . ah, his wine cellar . . . that was his source of pride and his passion.

"I understand that. The last of the white grapes are harvested in me, and the bulk of the reds: I appreciate fine wines, the aroma, the taste, the aftertaste as well.

"Laurent DeLisle bought his wines at auctions, from private wine lovers, from reputable dealers: he would insist on a pedigree for each wine, for wine frauds are, alas, too common, when the bottle is selling for perhaps five, ten, a hundred thousand dollars, or pounds, or euros.

"The treasure—the jewel—the rarest of the rare and the *ne plus ultra* of his temperature-controlled wine cellar was a bottle of 1902 Château Lafitte. It was on the wine list at one hundred and twenty thousand dollars, although it was, in true terms, priceless, for it was the last bottle of its kind."

"Excuse me," said August, politely. He was the fattest of them all, his thin hair combed in golden wisps across his pink pate.

September glared down at his neighbor. "Yes?"

"Is this the one where some rich dude buys the wine to go with the dinner, and the chef decides that the dinner the rich dude ordered isn't good enough for the wine, so he sends out a different dinner, and the guy takes one mouthful, and he's got, like, some rare allergy and he just dies like that, and the wine never gets drunk after all?"

September said nothing. He looked a great deal.

"Because if it is, you told it before. Years ago. Dumb story then. Dumb story now." August smiled. His pink cheeks shone in the firelight.

September said, "Obviously pathos and culture are not to everyone's taste. Some people prefer their barbecues and beer, and some of us like—"

February said, "Well, I hate to say this, but he kind of does have a point. It has to be a new story."

September raised an eyebrow and pursed his lips. "I'm done," he said, abruptly. He sat down on his stump.

They looked at one another across the fire, the months of the year.

June, hesitant and clean, raised her hand and said, "I have one about a guard on the X-ray machines at La-Guardia Airport, who could read all about people from the outlines of their luggage on the screen, and one day she saw a luggage X-ray so beautiful that she fell in love with the person, and she had to figure out which person in the line it was, and she couldn't, and she pined for months and months. And when the person came through again she knew it this time, and it was the man, and he was a wizened old Indian man and she was pretty and black and, like, twenty-five, and she knew it would never work out and she let him go, because she could also see from the shapes of his bags on the screen that he was going to die soon."

October said, "Fair enough, young June. Tell that one."

June stared at him, like a spooked animal. "I just did," she said.

October nodded. "So you did," he said, before any of the others could say anything. And then he said, "Shall we proceed to my story, then?"

February sniffed. "Out of order there, big fella. The man in the chair only tells his story when the rest of us are through. Can't go straight to the main event."

May was placing a dozen chestnuts on the grate above the fire, deploying them into patterns with her tongs. "Let him tell his story if he wants to," she said. "God knows it can't be worse than the one about the wine. And I have things to be getting back to. Flowers don't bloom by themselves. All in favor?"

"You're taking this to a formal vote?" February said.

"I cannot believe this. I cannot believe this is happening." He mopped his brow with a handful of tissues, which he pulled from his sleeve.

Seven hands were raised. Four people kept their hands down—February, September, January, and July. ("I don't have anything personal on this," said July, apologetically. "It's purely procedural. We shouldn't be setting precedents.")

"It's settled then," said October. "Is there anything anyone would like to say before I begin?"

"Um. Yes. Sometimes," said June, "sometimes I think somebody's watching us from the woods, and then I look and there isn't anybody there. But I still think it."

April said, "That's because you're crazy."

"Mm," said September to everybody. "That's our April. She's sensitive, but she's still the cruelest."

"Enough," said October. He stretched in his chair. He cracked a cobnut with his teeth, pulled out the kernel, and threw the fragments of shell into the fire, where they hissed and spat and popped, and he began.

There was a boy, *October said,* who was miserable at home, although they did not beat him. He did not fit well, not his family, his town, nor even his life. He had two older brothers, who were twins, older than he was, and who hurt him or ignored him, and were popular. They played football: some games one twin would score more and be the hero, and some games the other would. Their little brother did not play football. They had a name for their brother. They called him the Runt.

They had called him the Runt since he was a baby, and at first their mother and father had chided them for it.

The twins said, "But he *is* the runt of the litter. Look at *him.* Look at *us.*" The boys were six when they said this. Their parents thought it was cute. A name like the Runt can be infectious, so pretty soon the only person who called him Donald was his grandmother, when she telephoned him on his birthday, and people who did not know him.

Now, perhaps because names have power, he was a runt: skinny and small and nervous. He had been born with a runny nose, and it had not stopped running in a decade. At mealtimes, if the twins liked the food, they would steal his; if they did not, they would contrive to place their food on his plate and he would find himself in trouble for leaving good food uneaten.

Their father never missed a football game, and would buy an ice cream afterward for the twin who had scored the most, and a consolation ice cream for the other twin, who hadn't. Their mother described herself as a newspaperwoman, although she mostly sold advertising space and subscriptions: she had gone back to work full-time once the twins were capable of taking care of themselves.

The other kids in the boy's class admired the twins. They had called him Donald for several weeks in first grade, until the word trickled down that his brothers called him the Runt. His teachers rarely called him anything at all, although among themselves they could sometimes be heard to say that it was a pity the youngest Covay boy didn't have the pluck or the imagination or the life of his brothers.

The Runt could not have told you when he first decided to run away, nor when his daydreams crossed the border and became plans. By the time that he admitted to himself he was leaving he had a large Tupperware container hidden beneath a plastic sheet behind the garage containing three Mars bars, two Milky Ways, a bag of nuts, a small bag of licorice, a flashlight, several comics, an unopened packet of beef jerky, and thirty-seven dollars, most of it in quarters. He did not like the taste of beef jerky, but he had read that explorers had survived for weeks on nothing else; and it was when he put the packet of beef jerky into the Tupperware box and pressed the lid down with a pop that he knew he was going to have to run away.

He had read books, newspapers, and magazines. He knew that if you ran away you sometimes met bad people who did bad things to you; but he had also read fairy tales, so he knew that there were kind people out there, side by side with the monsters.

The Runt was a thin ten-year-old, small, with a runny nose and a blank expression. If you were to try and pick him out of a group of boys, you'd be wrong. He'd be the other one. Over at the side. The one your eye slipped over.

All through September he put off leaving. It took a really bad Friday, during the course of which both of his brothers sat on him (and the one who sat on his face broke wind and laughed uproariously), for him to decide that whatever monsters were waiting out in the world would be bearable, perhaps even preferable.

Saturday, his brothers were meant to be looking after him, but soon they went into town to see a girl they liked. The Runt went around the back of the garage and took the Tupperware container out from beneath the plastic sheeting. He took it up to his bedroom. He emptied his schoolbag onto his bed, filled it with his candies and comics and quarters and the beef jerky. He filled an empty soda bottle with water.

The Runt walked into town and got on the bus. He rode west, ten-dollars-in-quarters' worth of west, to a place he didn't know, which he thought was a good start, then he got off the bus and walked. There was no sidewalk now, so when cars came past he would edge over into the ditch, to safety.

The sun was high. He was hungry, so he rummaged in his bag and pulled out a Mars bar. After he ate it he found he was thirsty, and he drank almost half of the water from his soda bottle before he realized he was going to have to ration it. He had thought that once he got out of the town he would see springs of fresh water everywhere, but there were none to be found. There was a river, though, that ran beneath a wide bridge.

The Runt stopped halfway across the bridge to stare down at the brown water. He remembered something he had been told in school: that, in the end, all rivers flowed into the sea. He had never been to the seashore. He clambered down the bank and followed the river. There was a muddy path along the side of the riverbank, and an occasional beer can or plastic snack packet to show that people had been that way before, but he saw no one as he walked.

He finished his water.

He wondered if they were looking for him yet. He imagined police cars and helicopters and dogs, all trying to find him. He would evade them. He would make it to the sea.

The river ran over some rocks, and it splashed. He saw a blue heron, its wings wide, glide past him, and he saw solitary end-of-season dragonflies, and sometimes small clusters of midges, enjoying the Indian Summer. The blue sky became dusk-gray, and a bat swung down to snatch insects from the air. The Runt wondered where he would sleep that night.

Soon the path divided, and he took the branch that led away from the river, hoping it would lead to a house or to a farm with an empty barn. He walked for some time, as the dusk deepened, until at the end of the path he found a farmhouse, half tumbled-down and unpleasant-looking. The Runt walked around it, becoming increasingly certain as he walked that nothing could make him go inside, and then he climbed over a broken fence to an abandoned pasture, and settled down to sleep in the long grass with his schoolbag for his pillow.

He lay on his back, fully dressed, staring up at the sky. He was not in the slightest bit sleepy.

"They'll be missing me by now," he told himself. "They'll be worried."

He imagined himself coming home in a few years' time. The delight on his family's faces as he walked up the path to home. Their welcome. Their love. . . .

He woke some hours later, with the bright moonlight in his face. He could see the whole world—as bright as day, like in the nursery rhyme, but pale and without colors. Above him, the moon was full, or almost, and he imagined a face looking down at him, not unkindly, in the shadows and shapes of the moon's surface.

A voice said, "Where do you come from?"

He sat up, not scared, not yet, and looked around him. Trees. Long grass. "Where are you? I don't see you."

Something he had taken for a shadow moved, beside a tree on the edge of the pasture, and he saw a boy of his own age.

"I'm running away from home," said the Runt.

"Whoa," said the boy. "That must have taken a whole lot of guts."

The Runt grinned with pride. He didn't know what to say.

"You want to walk a bit?" said the boy.

"Sure," said the Runt. He moved his schoolbag so it was next to the fence post, so he could always find it again.

They walked down the slope, giving a wide berth to the old farmhouse.

"Does anyone live there?" asked the Runt.

"Not really," said the other boy. He had fair, fine hair that was almost white in the moonlight. "Some people tried a long time back, but they didn't like it, and they left. Then other folk moved in. But nobody lives there now. What's your name?"

"Donald," said the Runt. And then, "But they call me the Runt. What do they call you?"

The boy hesitated. "Dearly," he said.

"That's a cool name."

Dearly said, "I used to have another name, but I can't read it anymore."

They squeezed through a huge iron gateway, rusted part open, part closed, and they were in the little meadow at the bottom of the slope.

"This place is cool," said the Runt.

There were dozens of stones of all sizes in the small meadow. Tall stones, bigger than either of the boys, and small ones, just the right size for sitting on. There were some broken stones. The Runt knew what sort of a place this was, but it did not scare him. It was a loved place.

"Who's buried here?" he asked.

"Mostly okay people," said Dearly. "There used to be a town over there. Past those trees. Then the railroad came and they built a stop in the next town over, and our town sort of dried up and fell in and blew away. There's bushes and trees now, where the town was. You can hide in the trees and go into the old houses and jump out."

The Runt said, "Are they like that farmhouse up there? The houses?" He didn't want to go in them, if they were.

"No," said Dearly. "Nobody goes in them, except for me. And some animals, sometimes. I'm the only kid around here."

"I figured," said the Runt.

"Maybe we can go down and play in them," said Dearly.

"That would be pretty cool," said the Runt.

It was a perfect early October night: almost as warm as summer, and the harvest moon dominated the sky. You could see everything.

"Which one of these is yours?" asked the Runt.

Dearly straightened up proudly and took the Runt by the hand. He pulled him to an overgrown corner of the field. The two boys pushed aside the long grass. The stone was set flat into the ground, and it had dates carved into it from a hundred years before. Much of it was worn away, but beneath the dates it was possible to make out the words

DEARLY DEPARTED
WILL NEVER BE FORG

"Forgotten, I'd wager," said Dearly.

"Yeah, that's what I'd say, too," said the Runt.

They went out of the gate, down a gully, and into what remained of the old town. Trees grew through houses, and buildings had fallen in on themselves, but it wasn't scary. They played hide and seek. They explored. Dearly showed the Runt some pretty cool places, including a one-room cottage that he said was the oldest building in that whole part of the county. It was in pretty good shape, too, considering how old it was.

"I can see pretty good by moonlight," said the Runt. "Even inside. I didn't know that it was so easy."

"Yeah," said Dearly. "And after a while you get good at seeing even when there ain't any moonlight."

The Runt was envious.

"I got to go to the bathroom," said the Runt. "Is there somewhere around here?"

Dearly thought for a moment. "I don't know," he admitted. "I don't do that stuff anymore. There are a few outhouses still standing, but they may not be safe. Best just to do it in the woods."

"Like a bear," said the Runt.

He walked out the back, into the woods that pushed up against the wall of the cottage, and went behind a tree. He'd never done that before, in the open air. He felt like a wild animal. When he was done he wiped himself off with fallen leaves. Then he went back out the front. Dearly was sitting in a pool of moonlight, waiting for him.

"How did you die?" asked the Runt.

"I got sick," said Dearly. "My maw cried and carried on something fierce. Then I died."

"If I stayed here with you," said the Runt, "would I have to be dead, too?"

"Maybe," said Dearly. "Well, yeah. I guess."

"What's it like? Being dead?"

"I don't mind it," admitted Dearly. "Worst thing is not having anyone to play with."

"But there must be lots of people up in that meadow," said the Runt. "Don't they ever play with you?"

"Nope," said Dearly. "Mostly, they sleep. And even when they walk, they can't be bothered to just go and see stuff and do things. They can't be bothered with me. You see that tree?"

It was a beech tree, its smooth gray bark cracked with age. It sat in what must once been the town square, ninety years before.

"Yeah," said the Runt.

"You want to climb it?"

"It looks kind of high."

"It is. Real high. But it's easy to climb. I'll show you."

It was easy to climb. There were handholds in the bark, and the boys went up the big beech like a couple of monkeys or pirates or warriors. From the top of the tree one could see the whole world. The sky was starting to lighten, just a hair, in the east.

Everything waited. The night was ending. The world was holding its breath, preparing to begin again.

"This was the best day I ever had," said the Runt.

"Me too," said Dearly. "What you going to do now?"

"I don't know," said the Runt.

He imagined himself going on across the world, all the way to the sea. He imagined himself growing up and growing older, bringing himself up by his bootstraps. Somewhere in there he would become fabulously wealthy. And then he would go back to the house with the twins in it, and he would drive up to their door in his wonderful car, or perhaps he would turn up at a football game (in his imagination the twins had neither aged nor grown) and look down at them, in a kindly way. He would buy them all, the twins, his parents, a meal at the finest restaurant in the city, and they would tell him how badly they had misunderstood him and mistreated him. They apologized and wept, and through it all he said nothing. He let their apologies wash over him. And then he would give each of them a gift, and afterward he would leave their lives once more, this time for good.

It was a fine dream.

In reality, he knew, he would keep walking, and be found tomorrow or the day after that, and go home and be yelled at, and everything would be the same as it ever was, and day after day, hour after hour until the end of time he'd still be the Runt, only they'd be mad at him for having dared to walk away.

"I have to go to bed soon," said Dearly. He started to climb down the big beech tree.

Climbing down the tree was harder, the Runt found. You couldn't see where you were putting your feet and had to feel around for somewhere to put them. Several times he slipped and slid, but Dearly went down ahead of him and would say things like "A little to the right, now," and they both made it down just fine.

The sky continued to lighten, and the moon was fading, and it was harder to see. They clambered back through the gully. Sometimes the Runt wasn't sure that Dearly was there at all, but when he got to the top, he saw the boy waiting for him.

They didn't say much as they walked up to the meadow filled with stones. The Runt put his arm over Dearly's shoulder, and they walked in step up the hill.

"Well," said Dearly. "Thanks for coming over."

"I had a good time," said the Runt.

"Yeah," said Dearly. "Me too."

Down in the woods somewhere a bird began to sing.

"If I wanted to stay—?" said the Runt, all in a burst. Then he stopped. *I might never get another chance to change it,* thought the Runt. He'd never get to the sea. They'd never let him.

Dearly didn't say anything, not for a long time. The world was gray. More birds joined the first.

"I can't do it," said Dearly, eventually. "But they might."

"Who?"

"The ones in there." The fair boy pointed up the slope to the tumbledown farmhouse with the jagged, broken windows, silhouetted against the dawn. The gray light had not changed it.

The Runt shivered. "There's people in there?" he said. "I thought you said it was empty."

"It ain't empty," said Dearly. "I said nobody lives there. Different things." He looked up at the sky. "I got to go now," he added. He squeezed the Runt's hand. And then he just wasn't there any longer.

The Runt stood in the little graveyard all on his own, listening to the birdsong on the morning air. Then he made his way up the hill. It was harder by himself.

He picked up his schoolbag from the place he had left it. He ate his last Milky Way and stared at the tumbledown building. The empty windows of the farmhouse were like eyes, watching him.

It was darker inside there. Darker than anything.

He pushed his way through the weed-choked yard. The door to the farmhouse was mostly crumbled away. He stopped at the doorway, hesitating, wondering if this was wise. He could smell damp, and rot, and something else underneath. He thought he heard something move, deep in the house, in the cellar, maybe, or the attic. A shuffle, maybe. Or a hop. It was hard to tell.

Eventually, he went inside.

* * *

Nobody said anything. October filled his wooden mug with apple cider when he was done, and drained it, and filled it again.

"It was a story," said December. "I'll say that for it." He rubbed his pale blue eyes with a fist. The fire was almost out.

"What happened next?" asked June, nervously. "After he went into the house?"

May, sitting next to her, put her hand on June's arm. "Better not to think about it," she said.

"Anyone else want a turn?" asked August. There was silence. "Then I think we're done."

"That needs to be an official motion," pointed out February.

"All in favor?" said October. There was a chorus of "Ayes." "All against?" Silence. "Then I declare this meeting adjourned."

They got up from the fireside, stretching and yawning, and walked away into the wood, in ones and twos and threes, until only October and his neighbor remained.

"Your turn in the chair next time," said October.

"I know," said November. He was pale and thin-lipped. He helped October out of the wooden chair. "I like your stories. Mine are always too dark."

"I don't think so," said October. "It's just that your nights are longer. And you aren't as warm."

"Put it like that," said November, "and I feel better. I suppose we can't help who we are."

"That's the spirit," said his brother. And they touched hands as they walked away from the fire's orange embers, taking their stories with them back into the dark.

FOR RAY BRADBURY

THE HIDDEN CHAMBER

Do not fear the ghosts in this house; they
    are the least of your worries.
Personally I find the noises they make reassuring,
The creaks and footsteps in the night,
their little tricks of hiding things,
    or moving them, I find
endearing, not upsettling. It makes the place
    feel so much more like home.
Inhabited.
Apart from ghosts nothing lives here
    for long. No cats,
no mice, no flies, no dreams, no bats. Two days ago
I saw a butterfly,
a monarch I believe, which danced
    from room to room
and perched on walls and waited near to me.
There are no flowers in this empty place,
and, scared the butterfly would starve,
    I forced a window wide,
cupped my two hands around her fluttering self,
feeling her wings kiss my palms so gentle,
and put her out, and watched her fly away.

I've little patience with the seasons here, but
your arrival eased this winter's chill.
Please, wander round. Explore it all you wish.

I've broken with tradition on
    some points. If there is
one locked room here, you'll never know.
    You'll not find
in the cellar's fireplace old bones or
    hair. You'll find no blood.
Regard:
just tools, a washing machine, a dryer, a
    water heater, and a chain of keys.
Nothing that can alarm you. Nothing dark.

I may be grim, perhaps, but only just as grim
as any man who suffered such affairs. Misfortune,
carelessness or pain, what matters
    is the loss. You'll see
the heartbreak linger in my eyes, and dream
of making me forget what came
    before you walked
into the hallway of this house.
    Bringing a little summer
in your glance, and with your smile.

While you are here, of course, you will hear
    the ghosts, always a room away,
and you may wake beside me in the night,
knowing that there's a space without a door
knowing that there's a place that's locked
    but isn't there. Hearing
them scuffle, echo, thump and pound.

If you are wise you'll run into the night,
    fluttering away into the cold
wearing perhaps the laciest of shifts.
    The lane's hard flints
will cut your feet all bloody as you run,
so, if I wished, I could just follow you,

tasting the blood and oceans of your
    tears. I'll wait instead,
here in my private place, and soon I'll put
a candle
in the window, love, to light your way back home.
The world flutters like insects. I think this
    is how I shall remember you,
my head between the white swell of your breasts,
listening to the chambers of your heart.

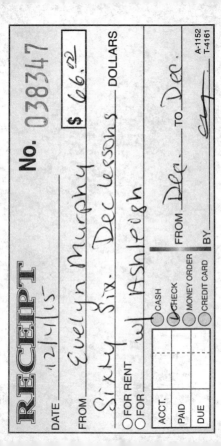

RECEIPT

No. 038347

DATE 12/4/15

FROM Evelyn Murphy $ 66.⁰⁰

Sixty Six Dec lessons DOLLARS

○ FOR RENT
○ FOR w/ Ashleigh

FROM Dec. TO Dec.

○ CASH
○ CHECK
○ MONEY ORDER
○ CREDIT CARD

BY ____

ACCT.	
PAID	
DUE	

A-1152
T-4161

FORBIDDEN BRIDES OF THE FACELESS SLAVES IN THE SECRET HOUSE OF THE NIGHT OF DREAD DESIRE

I.

Somewhere in the night, someone was writing.

II.

Her feet scrunched the gravel as she ran, wildly, up the tree-lined drive. Her heart was pounding in her chest, her lungs felt as if they were bursting, heaving breath after breath of the cold night air. Her eyes fixed on the house ahead, the single light in the topmost room drawing her toward it like a moth to a candle flame. Above her, and away in the deep forest behind the house, night-things whooped and skrarked. From the road behind her, she heard something scream briefly—a small animal that had been the victim of some beast of prey, she hoped, but could not be certain.

She ran as if the legions of hell were close on her heels, and spared not even a glance behind her until she reached the porch of the old mansion. In the moon's pale light the white pillars seemed skeletal, like the bones of a great beast. She clung to the wooden doorframe, gulping air, staring back down the long driveway, as if she were waiting for something, and then she rapped on the door—timorously at first, and then harder. The rapping echoed through the house. She imagined, from the echo that came back to her that, far away, someone was knocking on another door, muffled and dead.

"Please!" she called. "If there's someone here—anyone— please let me in. I beseech you. I implore you." Her voice sounded strange to her ears.

The flickering light in the topmost room faded and vanished, to reappear in successive descending windows. One person, then, with a candle. The light vanished into the depths of the house. She tried to catch her breath. It seemed like an age passed before she heard footsteps on the other side of the door and spied a chink of candle-light through a crack in the ill-fitting doorframe.

"Hello?" she said.

The voice, when it spoke, was dry as old bone—a desiccated voice, redolent of crackling parchment and musty grave-hangings. "Who calls?" it said. "Who knocks? Who calls, on this night of all nights?"

The voice gave her no comfort. She looked out at the night that enveloped the house, then pulled herself straight, tossed her raven locks, and said in a voice that, she hoped, betrayed no fear, " 'Tis I, Amelia Earnshawe, recently orphaned and now on my way to take up a position as a governess to the two small children—a boy and a girl—of Lord Falconmere, whose cruel glances I found, during our interview in his London residence, both repellent and fascinating, but whose aquiline face haunts my dreams."

"And what do you do here, then, at this house, on this night of all nights? Falconmere Castle lies a good twenty leagues on from here, on the other side of the moors."

"The coachman—an ill-natured fellow, and a mute, or so he pretended to be, for he formed no words, but made his wishes known only by grunts and gobblings—reined in his team a mile or so back down the road, or so I judge, and then he shewed me by gestures that he would go no further, and that I was to alight. When I did refuse to do so, he pushed me roughly from the carriage to the cold earth, then, whipping the poor horses into a frenzy, he clattered off the way he had come, taking my several bags and my trunk with him. I called after him, but he did not return, and it seemed to me that a deeper darkness stirred in the forest gloom behind me. I saw the light in your window and I . . . I . . ." She was able to keep up her pretense of bravery no longer, and she began to sob.

"Your father," came the voice from the other side of the door. "Would he have been the Honorable Hubert Earnshawe?"

Amelia choked back her tears. "Yes. Yes, he was."

"And you—you say you are an orphan?"

She thought of her father, of his tweed jacket, as the maelstrom seized him and whipped him onto the rocks and away from her forever.

"He died trying to save my mother's life. They both were drowned."

She heard the dull chunking of a key being turned in a lock, then twin booms as iron bolts were drawn back. "Welcome, then, Miss Amelia Earnshawe. Welcome to your inheritance, in this house without a name. Aye, welcome—on this night of all nights." The door opened.

The man held a black tallow candle; its flickering flame illuminated his face from below, giving it an unearthly and eldritch appearance. He could have been a jack-o'-lantern, she thought, or a particularly elderly axe-murderer.

He gestured for her to come in.

"Why do you keep saying that?" she asked.

"Why do I keep saying what?"

"'*On this night of all nights.*' You've said it three times so far."

He simply stared at her for a moment. Then he beckoned again, with one bone-colored finger. As she entered, he thrust the candle close to her face and stared at her with eyes that were not truly mad but were still far from sane. He seemed to be examining her, and eventually he grunted, and nodded. "This way," was all he said.

She followed him down a long corridor. The candle-flame threw fantastic shadows about the two of them, and in its light the grandfather clock and the spindly chairs and table danced and capered. The old man fumbled with his keychain and unlocked a door in the wall beneath the stairs. A smell came from the darkness beyond, of must and dust and abandonment.

"Where are we going?" she asked.

He nodded, as if he had not understood her. Then he said, "There are some as are what they are. And there are some as aren't what they seem to be. And there are some as only seem to be what they seem to be. Mark my words, and mark them well, Hubert Earnshawe's daughter. Do you understand me?"

She shook her head. He began to walk and did not look back.

She followed the old man down the stairs.

III.

Far away and far along the young man slammed his quill down upon the manuscript, spattering sepia ink across the ream of paper and the polished table.

"It's no good," he said, despondently. He dabbed at a circle of ink he had just made on the table with a delicate forefinger, smearing the teak a darker brown, then, unthinking, he rubbed the finger against the bridge of his nose. It left a dark smudge.

"No, sir?" The butler had entered almost soundlessly.

"It's happening again, Toombes. Humor creeps in. Self-parody whispers at the edges of things. I find myself guying literary convention and sending up both myself and the whole scrivening profession."

The butler gazed unblinking at his young master. "I believe humor is very highly thought of in certain circles, sir."

The young man rested his head in his hands, rubbing his forehead pensively with his fingertips. "That's not the point, Toombes. I'm trying to create a slice of life here, an accurate representation of the world as it is, and of the human condition. Instead, I find myself indulging, as I write, in schoolboy parody of the foibles of my fellows. I make little jokes." He had smeared ink all over his face. "Very little."

From the forbidden room at the top of the house an eerie, ululating cry rang out, echoing through the house. The young man sighed. "You had better feed Aunt Agatha, Toombes."

"Very good, sir."

The young man picked up the quill pen and idly scratched his ear with the tip.

Behind him, in a bad light, hung the portrait of his great-great-grandfather. The painted eyes had been cut out most carefully, long ago, and now real eyes stared out of the canvas face, looking down at the writer. The eyes glinted a tawny gold. If the young man had turned around and remarked upon them, he might have thought them the golden eyes of some great cat or of some misshapen bird of prey, were such a thing possible. These were not eyes that belonged in any human head. But the young man did not turn. Instead, oblivious, he reached for a new sheet of paper, dipped his quill into the glass inkwell, and commenced to write:

IV.

"Aye . . ." said the old man, putting down the black tallow candle on the silent harmonium. "He is our master, and we are his slaves, though we pretend to ourselves that it is not so. But when the time is right, then he demands what he craves, and it is our duty and our compulsion to provide him with . . ." He shuddered, and drew a breath. Then he said only, "With what he needs."

The bat-wing curtains shook and fluttered in the glassless casement as the storm drew closer. Amelia clutched the lace handkerchief to her breast, her father's monogram upward. "And the gate?" she asked, in a whisper.

"It was locked in your ancestor's time, and he charged, before he vanished, that it should always remain so. But there are still tunnels, folk do say, that link the old crypt with the burial grounds."

"And Sir Frederick's first wife . . . ?"

He shook his head, sadly. "Hopelessly insane, and but a mediocre harpsichord player. He put it about that she was dead, and perhaps some believed him."

She repeated his last four words to herself. Then she looked up at him, a new resolve in her eyes. "And for myself? Now I have learned why I am here, what do you advise me to do?"

He peered around the empty hall. Then he said, urgently, "Fly from here, Miss Earnshawe. Fly while there is still time. Fly for your life, fly for your immortal aagh."

"My what?" she asked, but even as the words escaped her crimson lips, the old man crumpled to the floor. A silver crossbow quarrel protruded from the back of his head.

"He is dead," she said, in shocked wonderment.

"Aye," affirmed a cruel voice from the far end of the hall. "But he was dead before this day, girl. And I do think that he has been dead a monstrous long time."

Under her shocked gaze, the body began to putresce. The flesh dripped and rotted and liquified, the bones revealed crumbled and oozed, until there was nothing but a stinking mass of foeter where once there had been a man.

Amelia squatted beside it, then dipped her fingertip into the noxious stuff. She licked her finger, and she made a face. "You would appear to be right, sir, whoever you are," she said. "I would estimate that he has been dead for the better part of a hundred years."

V.

"I am endeavoring," said the young man to the chambermaid, "to write a novel that reflects life as it is, mirrors it down to the finest degree. Yet as I write it turns to dross and gross mockery. What should I do? Eh, Ethel? What should I do?"

"I'm sure I don't know, sir," said the chambermaid, who was pretty and young, and had come to the great house in mysterious circumstances several weeks earlier. She gave the bellows several more squeezes, making the heart of the fire glow an orange-white. "Will that be all?"

"Yes. No. Yes," he said. "You may go, Ethel."

The girl picked up the now empty coal scuttle and walked at a steady pace across the drawing room.

The young man made no move to return to his writing-desk; instead he stood in thought by the fireplace, staring at the human skull on the mantel, at the twin crossed swords that hung above it upon the wall. The fire crackled and spat as a lump of coal broke in half.

Footsteps, close behind him. The young man turned. "You?"

The man facing him was almost his double—the white streak in the auburn hair proclaimed them of the same blood, if any proof were needed. The stranger's eyes were dark and wild, his mouth petulant yet oddly firm.

"Yes—I! I, your elder brother, whom you thought dead these many years. But I am not dead—or, perhaps, I am no longer dead—and I have come back—aye, come back from ways that are best left untraveled—to claim what is truly mine."

The young man's eyebrows raised. "I see. Well, obviously all this is yours—if you can prove that you are who you say you are."

"Proof? I need no proof. I claim birth-right, and blood-right—and death-right!" So saying, he pulled both the swords down from above the fireplace, and passed one, hilt first, to his younger brother. "Now guard you, my brother—and may the best man win."

Steel flashed in the firelight and kissed and clashed and kissed again in an intricate dance of thrust and parry. At times it seemed no more than a dainty minuet, or a courtly and deliberate ritual, while at other times it seemed pure savagery, a wildness that moved faster than the eye could easily follow. Around and around the room they went, and up the steps to the mezzanine, and down the steps to the main hall. They swung from drapes and from chandeliers. They leapt up on tables and down again.

The older brother obviously was more experienced, and, perhaps, was a better swordsman, but the younger man was fresher and he fought like a man possessed, forcing his opponent back and back and back to the roaring fire itself. The older brother reached out with his left hand and grasped the poker. He swung it wildly at the younger, who ducked, and, in one elegant motion, ran his brother through.

"I am done for. I am a dead man."

The younger brother nodded his ink-stained face.

"Perhaps it is better this way. Truly, I did not want the house, or the lands. All I wanted, I think, was peace." He lay there, bleeding crimson onto the gray flagstone. "Brother? Take my hand."

The young man knelt, and clasped a hand that already, it seemed to him, was becoming cold.

"Before I go into that night where none can follow, there are things I must tell you. Firstly, with my death, I truly believe the curse is lifted from our line. The second . . ." His breath now came in a bubbling wheeze, and he was having difficulty speaking. "The second . . . is . . . the . . . the thing in the abyss . . . beware the cellars . . . the rats . . . the—*it follows!*"

And with this his head lolled on the stone, and his eyes rolled back and saw nothing, ever again.

Outside the house, the raven cawed thrice. Inside, strange music had begun to skirl up from the crypt, signifying that, for some, the wake had already started.

The younger brother, once more, he hoped, the rightful possessor of his title, picked up a bell and rang for a servant. Toombes the butler was there in the doorway before the last ring had died away.

"Remove this," said the young man. "But treat it well. He died to redeem himself. Perhaps to redeem us both."

Toombes said nothing, merely nodded to show that he had understood.

The young man walked out of the drawing room. He entered the Hall of Mirrors—a hall from which all the mirrors had carefully been removed, leaving irregularly shaped patches on the paneled walls—and, believing himself alone, he began to muse aloud.

"This is precisely what I was talking about," he said. "Had such a thing happened in one of my tales—and such things happen all the time—I would have felt myself constrained to guy it unmercifully." He slammed a fist against a wall, where once a hexagonal mirror had hung. "What is wrong with me? Wherefore this flaw?"

Strange scuttling things gibbered and cheetled in the black drapes at the end of the room, and high in the gloomy oak beams, and behind the wainscoting, but they made no answer. He had expected none.

He walked up the grand staircase and along a dark-
ened hall, to enter his study. Someone, he suspected,
had been tampering with his papers. He suspected that
he would find out who later that evening, after the Gathering.

He sat down at his desk, dipped his quill pen once
more, and continued to write.

VI.

Outside the room the ghoul-lords howled with frustra-
tion and hunger, and they threw themselves against the
door in their ravenous fury, but the locks were stout,
and Amelia had every hope that they would hold.

What had the woodcutter said to her? His words came
back to her then, in her time of need, as if he were standing close to her, his manly frame mere inches from her
feminine curves, the very scent of his honest laboring
body surrounding her like the headiest perfume, and she
heard his words as if he were, that moment, whispering
them in her ear. "I was not always in the state you see me
in now, lassie," he had told her. "Once I had another
name, and a destiny unconnected to the hewing of cords
of firewood from fallen trees. But know you this—in the
escritoire there is a secret compartment, or so my great-
uncle claimed, when he was in his cups. . . ."

The escritoire! Of course!

She rushed to the old writing desk. At first she could
find no trace of a secret compartment. She pulled out
the drawers, one after another, and then perceived that
one of them was much shorter than the rest, which seeing she forced her white hand into the space where formerly the drawer had been, and found, at the back, a
button. Frantically, she pressed it. Something opened,
and she put her hand on a tightly rolled paper scroll.

Amelia withdrew her hand. The scroll was tied with a

dusty black ribbon, and with fumbling fingers she untied the knot and opened the paper. Then she read, trying to make sense of the antiquated handwriting, of the ancient words. As she did so, a ghastly pallor suffused her handsome face, and even her violet eyes seemed clouded and distracted.

The knockings and the scratchings redoubled. In but a short time they would burst through, she had no doubt. No door could hold them forever. They would burst through, and she would be their prey. Unless, unless . . .

"Stop!" she called, her voice trembling. "I abjure you, every one of you, and thee most of all, O Prince of Carrion. In the name of the ancient compact between thy people and mine."

The sounds stopped. It seemed to the girl that there was shock in that silence. Finally, a cracked voice said, "The compact?" and a dozen voices, as ghastly again, whispered "The compact," in a susurrus of unearthly sound.

"Aye!" called Amelia Earnshawe, her voice no longer unsteady. "The compact."

For the scroll, the long-hidden scroll, had been the compact—the dread agreement between the Lords of the House and the denizens of the crypt in ages past. It had described and enumerated the nightmarish rituals that had chained them one to another over the centuries—rituals of blood, and of salt, and more.

"If you have read the compact," said a deep voice from beyond the door, "then you know what we need, Hubert Earnshawe's daughter."

"Brides," she said, simply.

"The brides!" came the whisper from beyond the door, and it redoubled and resounded until it seemed to her that the very house itself throbbed and echoed to the beat of those words—two syllables invested with longing, and with love, and with hunger.

Amelia bit her lip. "Aye. The brides. I will bring thee brides. I shall bring brides for all."

She spoke quietly, but they heard her, for there was only silence, a deep and velvet silence, on the other side of the door.

And then one ghoul voice hissed, "Yes, and do you think we could get her to throw in a side order of those little bread roll things?"

VII.

Hot tears stung the young man's eyes. He pushed the papers from him and flung the quill pen across the room. It spattered its inky load over the bust of his great-great-great-grandfather, the brown ink soiling the patient white marble. The occupant of the bust, a large and mournful raven, startled, nearly fell off, and only kept its place by dint of flapping its wings several times. It turned, then, in an awkward step and hop, to stare with one black bead eye at the young man.

"Oh, this is intolerable!" exclaimed the young man. He was pale and trembling. "I cannot do it, and I shall never do it. I swear now, by . . ." and he hesitated, casting his mind around for a suitable curse from the extensive family archives.

The raven looked unimpressed. "Before you start cursing, and probably dragging peacefully dead and respectable ancestors back from their well-earned graves, just answer me one question." The voice of the bird was like stone striking against stone.

The young man said nothing, at first. It is not unknown for ravens to talk, but this one had not done so before, and he had not been expecting it to. "Certainly. Ask your question."

The raven tipped its head to one side. "Do you *like* writing that stuff?"

"Like?"

"That life-as-it-is stuff you do. I've looked over your shoulder sometimes. I've even read a little here and there. Do you enjoy writing it?"

The young man looked down at the bird. "It's literature," he explained, as if to a child. "Real literature. Real life. The real world. It's an artist's job to show people the world they live in. We hold up mirrors."

Outside the room lightning clove the sky. The young man glanced out of the window: a jagged streak of blinding fire created warped and ominous silhouettes from the bony trees and the ruined abbey on the hill.

The raven cleared its throat. "I said, do you enjoy it?"

The young man looked at the bird, then he looked away and, wordlessly, he shook his head.

"That's why you keep trying to pull it apart," said the bird. "It's not the satirist in you that makes you lampoon the commonplace and the humdrum. Merely boredom with the way things are. D'you see?" It paused to preen a stray wing-feather back into place with its beak. Then it looked up at him once more. "Have you ever thought of writing fantasy?" it asked.

The young man laughed. "Fantasy? Listen, I write literature. Fantasy isn't life. Esoteric dreams, written by a minority for a minority, it's—"

"What you'd be writing if you knew what was good for you."

"I'm a classicist," said the young man. He reached out his hand to a shelf of the classics—*Udolpho*, *The Castle of Otranto*, *The Saragossa Manuscript*, *The Monk*, and the rest of them. "It's literature."

"Nevermore," said the raven. It was the last word the young man ever heard it speak. It hopped from the bust, spread its wings, and glided out of the study door into the waiting darkness.

The young man shivered. He rolled the stock themes of fantasy over in his mind: cars and stockbrokers and commuters, housewives and police, agony columns and commercials for soap, income tax and cheap restaurants, magazines and credit cards and streetlights and computers . . .

"It is escapism, true," he said, aloud. "But is not the highest impulse in mankind the urge toward freedom, the drive to escape?"

The young man returned to his desk, and he gathered together the pages of his unfinished novel and dropped them, unceremoniously, in the bottom drawer, amongst the yellowing maps and cryptic testaments and the documents signed in blood. The dust, disturbed, made him cough.

He took up a fresh quill; sliced at its tip with his penknife. In five deft strokes and cuts he had a pen. He dipped the tip of it into the glass inkwell. Once more he began to write:

VIII.

Amelia Earnshawe placed the slices of wholewheat bread into the toaster and pushed it down. She set the timer to dark brown, just as George liked it. Amelia preferred her toast barely singed. She liked white bread as well, even if it didn't have the vitamins. She hadn't eaten white bread for a decade now.

At the breakfast table, George read his paper. He did not look up. He never looked up.

I hate him, she thought, and simply putting the emotion into words surprised her. She said it again in her head. *I hate him.* It was like a song. *I hate him for his toast, and for his bald head, and for the way he chases the office crumpet—girls barely out of school who laugh at him behind his back, and for the way he ignores me whenever he doesn't want to be bothered with me, and for the way he says "What, love?" when I ask him a simple question, as if he's long ago forgotten my name. As if he's forgotten that I even* have *a name.*

"Scrambled or boiled?" she said aloud.

"What, love?"

George Earnshawe regarded his wife with fond affection, and would have found her hatred of him astonishing. He thought of her in the same way, and with the same emotions, that he thought of anything which had been in the house for ten years and still worked well. The television, for example. Or the lawnmower. He thought it was love. "You know, *we* ought to go on one of those marches," he said, tapping the newspaper's editorial. "Show we're committed. Eh, love?"

The toaster made a noise to show that it was done. Only one dark brown slice had popped up. She took a knife and fished out the torn second slice with it. The toaster had been a wedding present from her uncle John. Soon she'd have to buy another, or start cooking toast under the grill, the way her mother had done.

"George? Do you want your eggs scrambled or boiled?" she asked, very quietly, and there was something in her voice that made him look up.

"Any way you like it, love," he said amiably, and could not for the life of him, as he told everyone in the office later that morning, understand why she simply stood there holding her slice of toast or why she started to cry.

IX.

The quill pen went *scritch scritch* across the paper, and the young man was engrossed in what he was doing. His face was strangely content, and a smile flickered between his eyes and his lips.

He was rapt.

Things scratched and scuttled in the wainscot but he hardly heard them.

High in her attic room Aunt Agatha howled and yowled and rattled her chains. A weird cachinnation came from the ruined abbey: it rent the night air, ascending into a peal of manic glee. In the dark woods beyond the great house, shapeless figures shuffled and loped, and raven-locked young women fled from them in fear.

"Swear!" said Toombes the butler, down in the butler's pantry, to the brave girl who was passing herself off as chambermaid. "Swear to me, Ethel, on your life, that you'll never reveal a word of what I tell you to a living soul . . ."

There were faces at the windows and words written in blood; deep in the crypt a lonely ghoul crunched on something that might once have been alive; forked lightnings slashed the ebony night; the faceless were walking; all was right with the world.

THE FLINTS OF MEMORY LANE

I like things to be story-shaped.

Reality, however, is not story-shaped, and the eruptions of the odd into our lives are not story-shaped either. They do not end in entirely satisfactory ways. Recounting the strange is like telling one's dreams: one can communicate the events of a dream but not the emotional content, the way that a dream can color one's entire day.

There were places I believed to be haunted, as a child, abandoned houses and places that scared me. My solution was to avoid them: and so, while my sisters had wholly satisfactory tales of strange figures glimpsed in the windows of empty houses, I had none. I still don't.

This is my ghost story, and an unsatisfactory thing it is too.

I was fifteen.

We lived in a new house, built in the garden of our old house. I still missed the old house: it had been a big old manor house. We had lived in half of it. The people who lived in the other half had sold it to property developers, so my father sold our half-a-house to them as well.

This was in Sussex, in a town that was crossed by the zero meridian: I lived in the Eastern Hemisphere, and went to school on the Western Hemisphere.

The old house had been a treasure trove of strange things: lumps of glittering marble and glass bulbs filled with liquid mercury, doors that opened onto brick walls; mysterious toys; things old and things forgotten.

My own house—a Victorian brick edifice, in the middle of America—is, I am told, haunted. There are few people who will spend the night here alone anymore—my assistant tells of her nights on her own here: of the porcelain jester music box that spontaneously began to play in the night, of her utter conviction that someone was watching her. Other people have complained of similar things, following nights alone.

I have never had any unsettling experiences here, but then, I have never spent a night here alone. And I am not entirely sure that I would wish to.

"There is no ghost when I am here," I said once, when asked if my house was haunted. "Perhaps it is you who haunt it, then," someone suggested, but truly I doubt it. If we have a ghost here, it is a fearful creature, more afraid of us than we are of it.

But I was telling of our old house, which was sold and knocked down (and I could not bear to see it empty, could not stand to see it being torn apart and bulldozed: my heart was in that house, and even now, at night, before I sleep, I hear the wind sighing through the rowan tree outside my bedroom window, twenty-five years ago). So we moved into a new house, built, as I said, in the garden of the old one, and some years went by.

Then, the house was halfway down a winding flint road, surrounded by fields and trees, in the middle of nowhere. Now, I am certain, were I to go back, I would find the flint road paved, the fields an endless housing estate. But I do not go back.

I was fifteen, skinny and gawky and wanting desperately to be cool. It was night, in autumn.

Outside our house was a lamppost, installed when the house was built, as out of place in the lampless countryside as the lamppost in the Narnia stories. It was a sodium light, which burned yellow, and washed out all other colors, turning everything yellow and black.

She was not my girlfriend (my girlfriend lived in Croydon, where I went to school, a gray-eyed blonde of unimaginable beauty who was, as she often complained to me, puzzled, never able to figure out why she was going out with me), but she was a friend, and she lived about a ten-minute walk away from me, beyond the fields, in the older part of the town.

I was going to walk over to her house, to play records, and sit, and talk.

I walked out of our house, ran down the grass slope to the drive, and stopped, dead, in front of a woman, standing beneath the streetlamp, staring up at the house.

She was dressed like a gypsy queen in a stage play, or a Moorish princess. She was handsome, not beautiful. She has no colors, in my memory, save only shades of yellow and black.

And, startled to find myself standing opposite someone where I had expected no one, I said, "Hello."

The woman said nothing. She looked at me.

"Are you looking for anyone?" I said, or something of the sort, and again she said nothing.

And still she looked at me, this unlikely woman, in the middle of nowhere, dressed like something from a dream, and still she said nothing at all. She began to smile, though, and it was not a nice smile.

And suddenly I found myself scared: utterly, profoundly scared, like a character in a dream, and I walked away, down the drive, heart thudding in my chest, and around the corner.

I stood there, out of sight of the house, for a moment, and then I looked back, and there was no one standing in the lamplight.

I was fifty paces from the house, but I could not, would not, turn around and go back. I was too scared.

Instead I ran up the dark, tree-lined flint lane and into the old town, and up another road and down the road to my friend's house, and got there speechless, breathless, jabbering and scared, as if all the hounds of hell had chased me there.

I told her my story, and we phoned my parents, who told me there was no one standing under the streetlight, and agreed, a little reluctantly, to come and drive me home, as I would not walk home that night.

And that is all there is to my story. I wish there was more: I wish I could tell you about the gypsy encampment that was burned down on that site two hundred years earlier—or anything that would give some sense of closure to the story, anything that would make it story-shaped—but there was no such encampment.

So, like all eruptions of the odd and strange into my world, the event sits there, unexplained. It is not story-shaped.

And, in memory, all I have is the yellow-black of her smile, and a shadow of the fear that followed.

CLOSING TIME

There are still clubs in London. Old ones, and mock-old, with elderly sofas and crackling fireplaces, news-papers, and traditions of speech or of silence, and new clubs, the Groucho and its many knockoffs, where actors and journalists go to be seen, to drink, to enjoy their glowering solitude, or even to talk. I have friends in both kinds of club, but am not myself a member of any club in London, not anymore.

Years ago, half a lifetime, when I was a young journalist, I joined a club. It existed solely to take advantage of the licensing laws of the day, which forced all pubs to stop serving drinks at eleven PM, closing time. This club, the Diogenes, was a one-room affair located above a record shop in a narrow alley just off the Tottenham Court Road. It was owned by a cheerful, chubby, alcohol-fueled woman called Nora, who would tell anyone who asked and even if they didn't that she'd called the club the Diogenes, darling, because she was still looking for an honest man. Up a narrow flight of steps, and, at Nora's whim, the door to the club would be open, or not. It kept irregular hours.

It was a place to go once the pubs closed, that was all it ever was, and despite Nora's doomed attempts to serve food or even to send out a cheery monthly newsletter to all her club's members reminding them that the club now served food, that was all it would ever be. I was saddened several years ago when I heard that Nora had died; and I was struck, to my surprise, with a real sense of desolation last month when, on a visit to England, walking down that alley, I tried to figure out where the Diogenes Club had been, and looked first in the wrong place, then saw the faded green cloth awnings shading the windows of a tapas restaurant above a mobile phone shop, and, painted on them, a stylized man in a barrel. It seemed almost indecent, and it set me remembering.

There were no fireplaces in the Diogenes Club, and no armchairs either, but still, stories were told.

Most of the people drinking there were men, although women passed through from time to time, and Nora had recently acquired a glamorous permanent fixture in the shape of a deputy, a blonde Polish emigrée who called everybody "darlink" and who helped herself to drinks whenever she got behind the bar. When she was drunk, she would tell us that she was by rights a countess, back in Poland, and swear us all to secrecy.

There were actors and writers, of course. Film editors, broadcasters, police inspectors, and drunks. People who did not keep fixed hours. People who stayed out too late or who did not want to go home. Some nights there might be a dozen people there, or more. Other nights I'd wander in and I'd be the only person around—on those occasions I'd buy myself a single drink, drink it down, and then leave.

That night, it was raining, and there were four of us in the club after midnight.

Nora and her deputy were sitting up at the bar, working on their sitcom. It was about a chubby-but-cheerful woman who owned a drinking club, and her scatty deputy, an aristocratic foreign blonde who made amusing English mistakes. It would be like *Cheers,* Nora used to tell people. She named the comical Jewish landlord after me. Sometimes they would ask me to read a script.

There was an actor named Paul (commonly known as

Paul-the-actor, to stop people confusing him with Paul-the-police-inspector or Paul-the-struck-off-plastic-surgeon, who were also regulars), a computer gaming magazine editor named Martyn, and me. We knew each other vaguely, and the three of us sat at a table by the window and watched the rain come down, misting and blurring the lights of the alley.

There was another man there, older by far than any of the three of us. He was cadaverous and gray-haired and painfully thin, and he sat alone in the corner and nursed a single whiskey. The elbows of his tweed jacket were patched with brown leather, I remember that quite vividly. He did not talk to us, or read, or do anything. He just sat, looking out at the rain and the alley beneath, and, sometimes, he sipped his whiskey without any visible pleasure.

It was almost midnight, and Paul and Martyn and I had started telling ghost stories. I had just finished telling them a sworn-true ghostly account from my school days: the tale of the Green Hand. It had been an article of faith at my prep school that there was a disembodied, luminous hand that was seen, from time to time, by unfortunate schoolboys. If you saw the Green Hand you would die soon after. Fortunately, none of us were ever unlucky enough to encounter it, but there were sad tales of boys from before our time, boys who saw the Green Hand and whose thirteen-year-old hair had turned white overnight. According to school legend they were taken to the sanatorium, where they would expire after a week or so without ever being able to utter another word.

"Hang on," said Paul-the-actor. "If they never uttered another word, how did anyone know they'd seen the Green Hand? I mean, they could have seen anything."

As a boy, being told the stories, I had not thought to ask this, and now it was pointed out to me it did seem somewhat problematic.

"Perhaps they wrote something down," I suggested, a bit lamely.

We batted it about for a while, and agreed that the Green Hand was a most unsatisfactory sort of ghost. Then Paul told us a true story about a friend of his who had picked up a hitchhiker, and dropped her off at a place she said was her house, and when he went back the next morning, it turned out to be a cemetery. I mentioned that exactly the same thing had happened to a friend of mine as well. Martyn said that it had not only happened to a friend of his, but, because the hitchhiking girl looked so cold, the friend had lent her his coat, and the next morning, in the cemetery, he found his coat all neatly folded on her grave.

Martyn went and got another round of drinks, and we wondered why all these ghost women were zooming around the country all night and hitchhiking home, and Martyn said that probably living hitchhikers these days were the exception, not the rule.

And then one of us said, "I'll tell you a true story, if you like. It's a story I've never told a living soul. It's true—it happened to me, not to a friend of mine—but I don't know if it's a ghost story. It probably isn't."

This was over twenty years ago. I have forgotten so many things, but I have not forgotten that night, or how it ended.

This is the story that was told that night, in the Diogenes Club.

I was nine years old, or thereabouts, in the late 1960s, and I was attending a small private school not far from my home. I was only at that school less than a year—long enough to take a dislike to the school's owner, who had bought the school in order to close it and to sell the prime land on which it stood to property developers, which, shortly after I left, she did.

For a long time—a year or more—after the school closed the building stood empty before it was finally demolished and replaced by offices. Being a boy, I was also a burglar of sorts, and one day before it was knocked down, curious, I went back there. I wriggled through a half-open window and walked through empty classrooms that still smelled of chalk dust. I took only one thing from my visit, a painting I had done in Art of a little house with a red door knocker like a devil or an imp. It had my name on it, and it was up on a wall. I took it home.

When the school was still open I walked home each day, through the town, then down a dark road cut through sandstone hills and all grown over with trees, and past an abandoned gatehouse. Then there would be light, and the road would go past fields, and finally I would be home.

Back then there were so many old houses and estates, Victorian relics that stood in an empty half-life awaiting the bulldozers that would transform them and their ramshackle grounds into blandly identical landscapes of desirable modern residences, every house neatly arranged side by side around roads that went nowhere.

The other children I encountered on my way home were, in my memory, always boys. We did not know each other, but, like guerillas in occupied territory, we would exchange information. We were scared of adults, not each other. We did not have to know each other to run in twos or threes or in packs.

The day that I'm thinking of, I was walking home from school, and I met three boys in the road where it was at its darkest. They were looking for something in the ditches and the hedges and the weed-choked place in front of the abandoned gatehouse. They were older than me.

"What are you looking for?"

The tallest of them, a beanpole of a boy, with dark

hair and a sharp face, said, "Look!" He held up several ripped-in-half pages from what must have been a very, very old pornographic magazine. The girls were all in black-and-white, and their hairstyles looked like the ones my great-aunts had in old photographs. Fragments of it had blown all over the road and into the abandoned gatehouse front garden.

I joined in the paper chase. Together, the three of us retrieved almost a whole copy of *The Gentleman's Relish* from that dark place. Then we climbed over a wall, into a deserted apple orchard, and looked at what we had gathered. Naked women from a long time ago. There is a smell, of fresh apples and of rotten apples moldering down into cider, which even today brings back the idea of the forbidden to me.

The smaller boys, who were still bigger than I was, were called Simon and Douglas, and the tall one, who might have been as old as fifteen, was called Jamie. I wondered if they were brothers. I did not ask.

When we had all looked at the magazine, they said, "We're going to hide this in our special place. Do you want to come along? You mustn't tell, if you do. You mustn't tell anyone."

They made me spit on my palm, and they spat on theirs, and we pressed our hands together.

Their special place was an abandoned metal water tower in a field by the entrance to the lane near to where I lived. We climbed a high ladder. The tower was painted a dull green on the outside, and inside it was orange with rust, which covered the floor and the walls. There was a wallet on the floor with no money in it, only some cigarette cards. Jamie showed them to me: each card held a painting of a cricketer from a long time ago. They put the pages of the magazine down on the floor of the water tower, and the wallet on top of it.

Then Douglas said, "I say we go back to the Swallows next."

My house was not far from the Swallows, a sprawling manor house set back from the road. It had been owned, my father had told me once, by the Earl of Tenterden, but when he had died his son, the new earl, had simply closed the place up. I had wandered to the edges of the grounds, but had not gone further in. It did not feel abandoned. The gardens were too well-cared-for, and where there were gardens there were gardeners. Somewhere there had to be an adult.

I told them this.

Jamie said, "Bet there's not. Probably just someone who comes in and cuts the grass once a month or something. You're not scared, are you? We've been there hundreds of times. Thousands."

Of course I was scared, and of course I said that I was not. We went up the main drive until we reached the main gates. They were closed, and we squeezed beneath the bars to get in.

Rhododendron bushes lined the drive. Before we got to the house there was what I took to be a grounds-keeper's cottage, and beside it on the grass were some rusting metal cages, big enough to hold a hunting dog, or a boy. We walked past them, up to a horseshoe-shaped drive and right up to the front door of the Swallows. We peered inside, looking in the windows but seeing nothing. It was too dark inside.

We slipped around the house, through a rhododendron thicket and out again, into some kind of fairyland. It was a magical grotto, all rocks and delicate ferns and odd, exotic plants I'd never seen before: plants with purple leaves, and leaves like fronds, and small half-hidden flowers like jewels. A tiny stream wound through it, a rill of water running from rock to rock.

Douglas said, "I'm going to wee-wee in it." It was very matter-of-fact. He walked over to it, pulled down his shorts, and urinated in the stream, splashing on the rocks. The other boys did it, too, both of them pulling out their penises and standing beside him to piss into the stream.

I was shocked. I remember that. I suppose I was shocked by the joy they took in this, or just by the way they were doing something like that in such a special place, spoiling the clear water and the magic of the place; making it into a toilet. It seemed wrong.

When they were done, they did not put their penises away. They shook them. They pointed them at me. Jamie had hair growing at the base of his.

"We're cavaliers," said Jamie. "Do you know what that means?"

I knew about the English Civil War, Cavaliers (wrong but romantic) versus Roundheads (right but repulsive), but I didn't think that was what he was talking about. I shook my head.

"It means our willies aren't circumcised," he explained. "Are you a cavalier or a roundhead?"

I knew what they meant now. I muttered, "I'm a roundhead."

"Show us. Go on. Get it out."

"No. It's none of your business."

For a moment, I thought things were going to get nasty, but then Jamie laughed, and put his penis away, and the others did the same. They told dirty jokes to each other then, jokes I really didn't understand, for all that I was a bright child, but I heard and remembered them, and several weeks later was almost expelled from school for telling one of them to a boy who went home and told it to his parents.

The joke had the word *fuck* in it. That was the first time I ever heard the word, in a dirty joke in a fairy grotto.

The principal called my parents into the school, after I'd got in trouble, and said that I'd said something so bad they could not repeat it, not even to tell my parents what I'd done.

My mother asked me, when they got home that night.
"Fuck," I said.

"You must never, ever say that word," said my mother.
She said this very firmly, and quietly, and for my own
good. "That is the worst word anyone can say." I promised her that I wouldn't.

But after, amazed at the power a single word could
have, I would whisper it to myself, when I was alone.

In the grotto, that autumn afternoon after school, the
three big boys told jokes and they laughed and they
laughed, and I laughed, too, although I did not understand any of what they were laughing about.

We moved on from the grotto. Into the formal gardens
and over a small bridge that spanned a pond; we crossed
it nervously, because it was out in the open, but we could
see huge goldfish in the blackness of the pond below,
which made it worthwhile. Then Jamie led Douglas and
Simon and me down a gravel path into some woodland.

Unlike the gardens, the woods were abandoned and
unkempt. They felt like there was no one around. The
path was grown over. It led between trees and then,
after a while, into a clearing.

In the clearing was a little house.

It was a playhouse, built perhaps forty years earlier
for a child, or for children. The windows were Tudor
style, leaded and crisscrossed into diamonds. The roof
was mock Tudor. A stone path led straight from where
we were to the front door.

Together, we walked up the path to the door.

Hanging from the door was a metal knocker. It was
painted crimson and had been cast in the shape of some
kind of imp, some kind of grinning pixie or demon, cross-
legged, hanging by its hands from a hinge. Let me see . . .
how can I describe this best? It wasn't a *good* thing. The
expression on its face, for starters. I found myself wondering what kind of a person would hang something like
that on a playhouse door.

It frightened me, there in that clearing, with the dusk gathering under the trees. I walked away from the house, back to a safe distance, and the others followed me.

"I think I have to go home now," I said.

It was the wrong thing to say. The three of them turned and laughed and jeered at me, called me pathetic, called me a baby. *They* weren't scared of the house, they said.

"I dare you!" said Jamie. "I dare you to knock on the door."

I shook my head.

"If you don't knock on the door," said Douglas, "you're too much of a baby ever to play with us again."

I had no desire ever to play with them again. They seemed like occupants of a land I was not yet ready to enter. But still, I did not want them to think me a baby.

"Go on. *We're* not scared," said Simon.

I try to remember the tone of voice he used. Was he frightened, too, and covering it with bravado? Or was he amused? It's been so long. I wish I knew.

I walked slowly back up the flagstone path to the house. I reached up, grabbed the grinning imp in my right hand, and banged it hard against the door.

Or rather, I tried to bang it hard, just to show the other three that I was not afraid at all. That I was not afraid of anything. But something happened, something I had not expected, and the knocker hit the door with a muffled sort of a thump.

"Now you have to go inside!" shouted Jamie. He was excited. I could hear it. I found myself wondering if they had known about this place already, before we came. If I was the first person they had brought there.

But I did not move.

"*You* go in," I said. "I knocked on the door. I did it like you said. Now *you* have to go inside. I dare you. I dare *all* of you."

I wasn't going in. I was perfectly certain of that. Not

then. Not ever. I'd felt something move, I'd felt the knocker *twist* under my hand as I'd banged that grinning imp down on the door. I was not so old that I would deny my own senses.

They said nothing. They did not move.

Then, slowly, the door fell open. Perhaps they thought that I, standing by the door, had pushed it open. Perhaps they thought that I'd jarred it when I knocked. But I hadn't. I was certain of it. It opened because it was ready.

I should have run then. My heart was pounding in my chest. But the devil was in me, and instead of running I looked at the three big boys at the bottom of the path, and I simply said, "Or are you scared?"

They walked up the path toward the little house.

"It's getting dark," said Douglas.

Then the three boys walked past me, and one by one, reluctantly perhaps, they entered the playhouse. A white face turned to look at me as they went into that room, to ask why I wasn't following them in, I'll bet. But as Simon, who was the last of them, walked in, the door banged shut behind them, and I swear to God I did not touch it.

The imp grinned down at me from the wooden door, a vivid splash of crimson in the gray gloaming.

I walked around to the side of the playhouse and peered through all the windows, one by one, into the dark and empty room. Nothing moved in there. I wondered if the other three were inside hiding from me, pressed against the wall, trying their damnedest to stifle their giggles. I wondered if it was a big-boy game.

I didn't know. I couldn't tell.

I stood there in the courtyard of the playhouse, while the sky got darker, just waiting. The moon rose after a while, a big autumn moon the color of honey.

And then, after a while, the door opened, and nothing came out.

Now I was alone in the glade, as alone as if there had never been anyone else there at all. An owl hooted, and I realized that I was free to go. I turned and walked away, following a different path out of the glade, always keeping my distance from the main house. I climbed a fence in the moonlight, ripping the seat of my school shorts, and I walked—not ran, I didn't need to run—across a field of barley stubble, and over a stile, and into a flinty lane that would take me, if I followed it far enough, all the way to my house.

And soon enough, I was home.

My parents had not been worried, although they were irritated by the orange rust dust on my clothes, by the rip in my shorts. "Where were you, anyway?" my mother asked.

"I went for a walk," I said. "I lost track of time."

And that was where we left it.

It was almost two in the morning. The Polish countess had already gone. Now Nora began, noisily, to collect up the glasses and ashtrays and to wipe down the bar. "*This* place is haunted," she said, cheerfully. "Not that it's ever bothered me. I like a bit of company, darlings. If I didn't, I wouldn't have opened the club. Now, don't you have homes to go to?"

We said our good nights to Nora, and she made each of us kiss her on her cheek, and she closed the door of the Diogenes Club behind us. We walked down the narrow steps past the record shop, down into the alley and back into civilization.

The underground had stopped running hours ago, but there were always night buses, and cabs still out there for those who could afford them. (I couldn't. Not in those days.)

The Diogenes Club itself closed several years later, finished off by Nora's cancer and, I suppose, by the easy availability of late-night alcohol once the English licensing laws were changed. But I rarely went back after that night.

"Was there ever," asked Paul-the-actor, as we hit the street, "any news of those three boys? Did you see them again? Or were they reported as missing?"

"Neither," said the storyteller. "I mean, I never saw them again. And there was no local manhunt for three missing boys. Or if there was, I never heard about it."

"Is the playhouse still there?" asked Martyn.

"I don't know," admitted the storyteller.

"Well," said Martyn, as we reached the Tottenham Court Road and headed for the night bus stop, "I for one do not believe a word of it."

There were four of us, not three, out on the street long after closing time. I should have mentioned that before. There was still one of us who had not spoken, the elderly man with the leather elbow patches, who had left the club with the three of us. And now he spoke for the first time.

"I believe it," he said mildly. His voice was frail, almost apologetic. "I cannot explain it, but I believe it. Jamie died, you know, not long after Father did. It was Douglas who wouldn't go back, who sold the old place. He wanted them to tear it all down. But they kept the house itself, the Swallows. They weren't going to knock *that* down. I imagine that everything else must be gone by now."

It was a cold night, and the rain still spat occasional drizzle. I shivered, but only because I was cold.

"Those cages you mentioned," he said. "By the driveway. I haven't thought of them in fifty years. When we were bad he'd lock us up in them. We must have been bad a great deal, eh? Very naughty, naughty boys."

He was looking up and down the Tottenham Court Road, as if he were looking for something. Then he said, "Douglas killed himself, of course. Ten years ago. When

I was still in the bin. So my memory's not as good. Not as good as it was. But that was Jamie all right, to the life. He'd never let us forget that he was the oldest. And you know, we weren't ever allowed in the playhouse. Father didn't build it for us." His voice quavered, and for a moment I could imagine this pale old man as a boy again. "Father had his own games."

And then he waved his arm and called "Taxi!" and a taxi pulled over to the curb. "Brown's Hotel," said the man, and he got in. He did not say good night to any of us. He pulled shut the door of the cab.

And in the closing of the cab door I could hear too many other doors closing. Doors in the past, which are gone now, and cannot be reopened.

GOING WODWO

Shedding my shirt, my book, my coat, my life
Leaving them, empty husks and fallen leaves
Going in search of food and for a spring
Of sweet water.

I'll find a tree as wide as ten fat men
Clear water rilling over its gray roots
Berries I'll find, and crabapples and nuts,
And call it home.

I'll tell the wind my name, and no one else.
True madness takes or leaves us in the wood
halfway through all our lives. My skin will be
my face now.

I must be nuts. Sense left with shoes and house,
my guts are cramped. I'll stumble through the green
back to my roots, and leaves and thorns and buds,
and shiver.

I'll leave the way of words to walk the wood
I'll be the forest's man, and greet the sun,
And feel the silence blossom on my tongue
like language.

BITTER GROUNDS

1. *"Come back early or never come"*

In every way that counted, I was dead. Inside some-where maybe I was screaming and weeping and howling like an animal, but that was another person deep in-side, another person who had no access to the face and lips and mouth and head, so on the surface I just shrugged and smiled and kept moving. If I could have physically passed away, just let it all go, like that, without doing anything, stepped out of life as easily as walking through a door, I would have done. But I was going to sleep at night and waking in the morning, disappointed to be there and resigned to existence.

Sometimes I telephoned her. I let the phone ring once, maybe even twice, before I hung up.

The me who was screaming was so far inside nobody knew he was even there at all. Even I forgot that he was there, until one day I got into the car—I had to go to the store, I had decided, to bring back some apples—and I went past the store that sold apples and I kept driving, and driving. I was going south, and west, be-cause if I went north or east I would run out of world too soon.

A couple of hours down the highway my cell phone started to ring. I wound down the window and threw the cell phone out. I wondered who would find it, whether they would answer the phone and find themselves gifted with my life.

When I stopped for gas I took all the cash I could on every card I had. I did the same for the next couple of days, ATM by ATM, until the cards stopped working.

The first two nights I slept in the car.

I was halfway through Tennessee when I realized I needed a bath badly enough to pay for it. I checked into a motel, stretched out in the bath and slept in it until the water got cold and woke me. I shaved with a motel courtesy kit plastic razor and a sachet of foam. Then I stumbled to the bed, and I slept.

Awoke at 4:00 AM, and knew it was time to get back on the road.

I went down to the lobby.

There was a man standing at the front desk when I got there: silver-gray hair although I guessed he was still in his thirties, if only just, thin lips, good suit rumpled, saying "I *ordered* that cab an *hour* ago. One *hour* ago." He tapped the desk with his wallet as he spoke, the beats emphasizing his words.

The night manager shrugged. "I'll call again," he said. "But if they don't have the car, they can't send it." He dialed a phone number, said, "This is the Night's Out Inn front desk again. . . . Yeah, I told him. . . . Yeah, I told him."

"Hey," I said. "I'm not a cab, but I'm in no hurry. You need a ride somewhere?"

For a moment the man looked at me like I was crazy, and for a moment there was fear in his eyes. Then he looked at me like I'd been sent from Heaven. "You know, by God, I do," he said.

"You tell me where to go," I said. "I'll take you there. Like I said, I'm in no hurry."

"Give me that phone," said the silver-gray man to the night clerk. He took the handset and said, "You can *cancel* your cab, because God just sent me a Good Samaritan. People come into your life for a reason. That's right. And I want you to think about that."

He picked up his briefcase—like me he had no luggage—and together we went out to the parking lot.

We drove through the dark. He'd check a hand-drawn map on his lap, with a flashlight attached to his key ring, then he'd say, *left here,* or *this way.*

"It's good of you," he said.

"No problem. I have time."

"I appreciate it. You know, this has that pristine urban legend quality, driving down country roads with a mysterious Samaritan. A Phantom Hitchhiker story. After I get to my destination, I'll describe you to a friend, and they'll tell me you died ten years ago, and still go round giving people rides."

"Be a good way to meet people."

He chuckled. "What do you do?"

"Guess you could say I'm between jobs," I said. "You?"

"I'm an anthropology professor." Pause. "I guess I should have introduced myself. Teach at a Christian college. People don't believe we teach anthropology at Christian colleges, but we do. Some of us."

"I believe you."

Another pause. "My car broke down. I got a ride to the motel from the highway patrol, as they said there was no tow truck going to be there until morning. Got two hours of sleep. Then the highway patrol called my hotel room. Tow truck's on the way. I got to be there when they arrive. Can you believe that? I'm not there, they won't touch it. Just drive away. Called a cab. Never came. Hope we get there before the tow truck."

"I'll do my best."

"I guess I should have taken a plane. It's not that I'm scared of flying. But I cashed in the ticket. I'm on my way to New Orleans. Hour's flight, four hundred and forty dollars. Day's drive, thirty dollars. That's four hun-

dred and ten dollars' spending money, and I don't have
to account for it to anybody. Spent fifty dollars on the
motel room, but that's just the way these things go. Academic conference. My first. Faculty doesn't believe in
them. But things change. I'm looking forward to it. Anthropologists from all over the world." He named several names that meant nothing to me. "I'm presenting a
paper on the Haitian coffee girls."

"They grow it, or drink it?"

"Neither. They sold it, door-to-door in Port-au-Prince,
early in the morning, in the early years of the last century."

It was starting to get light now.

"People thought they were zombies," he said. "You
know. The walking dead. I think it's a right turn here."

"Were they? Zombies?"

He seemed very pleased to have been asked. "Well,
anthropologically, there are several schools of thought
about zombies. It's not as cut-and-dried as popularist
works like *The Serpent and the Rainbow* would make it
appear. First we have to define our terms: are we talking
folk belief, or zombie dust, or the walking dead?"

"I don't know," I said. I was pretty sure *The Serpent
and the Rainbow* was a horror movie.

"They were children, little girls, five to ten years old,
who went door-to-door through Port-au-Prince selling the
chicory coffee mixture. Just about this time of day, before
the sun was up. They belonged to one old woman. Hang
a left just before we go into the next turn. When she died,
the girls vanished. That's what the books tell you."

"And what do you believe?" I asked.

"That's my car," he said, with relief in his voice. It was
a red Honda Accord, on the side of the road. There was
a tow truck beside it, lights flashing, a man beside the tow
truck smoking a cigarette. We pulled up behind the tow
truck.

The anthropologist had the door opened before I'd
stopped; he grabbed his briefcase and was out of the car.

"Was giving you another five minutes, then I was going to take off," said the tow truck driver. He dropped his cigarette into a puddle on the tarmac. "Okay, I'll need your triple-A card and a credit card."

The man reached for his wallet. He looked puzzled. He put his hands in his pockets. He said, "My wallet." He came back to my car, opened the passenger-side door and leaned back inside. I turned on the light. He patted the empty seat. "My wallet," he said again. His voice was plaintive and hurt.

"You had it back in the motel," I reminded him. "You were holding it. It was in your hand."

He said, "God *damn* it. God fucking *damn* it to Hell."

"Everything okay there?" called the tow truck driver.

"Okay," said the anthropologist to me, urgently. "This is what we'll do. You drive back to the motel. I must have left the wallet on the desk. Bring it back here. I'll keep him happy until then. Five minutes, it'll take you five minutes." He must have seen the expression on my face. He said, "Remember. People come into your life for a reason."

I shrugged, irritated to have been sucked into someone else's story.

Then he shut the car door and gave me a thumbs-up.

I wished I could just have driven away and abandoned him, but it was too late, I was driving to the hotel. The night clerk gave me the wallet, which he had noticed on the counter, he told me, moments after we left.

I opened the wallet. The credit cards were all in the name of Jackson Anderton.

It took me half an hour to find my way back, as the sky grayed into full dawn. The tow truck was gone. The rear window of the red Honda Accord was broken, and the driver's-side door hung open. I wondered if it was a different car, if I had driven the wrong way to the wrong place; but there were the tow truck driver's cigarette stubs crushed on the road, and in the ditch nearby I found a gaping briefcase, empty, and beside it, a manilla folder containing a fifteen-page typescript, a prepaid hotel reservation at a Marriott in New Orleans in the name of Jackson Anderton, and a packet of three condoms, ribbed for extra pleasure.

On the title page of the typescript was printed:

"'This was the way Zombies are spoken of: They are the bodies without souls. The living dead. Once they were dead, and after that they were called back to life again.' Hurston. Tell My Horse."

I took the manilla folder but left the briefcase where it was. I drove south under a pearl-colored sky.

People come into your life for a reason. Right.

I could not find a radio station that would hold its signal. Eventually I pressed the scan button on the radio and just left it on, left it scanning from channel to channel in a relentless quest for signal, scurrying from gospel to oldies to Bible talk to sex talk to country, three seconds a station with plenty of white noise in between.

. . . Lazarus, who was dead, you make no mistake about that, he was dead, and Jesus brought him back to show us, I say to show us . . .

What I call a Chinese dragon, can I say this on the air? Just as you, y'know, get your rocks off, you whomp her round the backatha head, it all spurts outta her nose, I damn near laugh my ass off . . .

If you come home tonight I'll be waiting in the darkness for my woman with my bottle and my gun . . .

When Jesus says will you be there will you be there? No man knows the day or the hour so will you be there . . .

President unveiled an initiative today . . .

Fresh-brewed in the morning. For you, for me. For every day. Because every day is freshly ground . . .

Over and over. It washed over me, driving through the day, on the backroads. Just driving and driving.

They become more personable as you head south, the

people. You sit in a diner and, along with your coffee and your food, they bring you comments, questions, smiles, and nods.

It was evening, and I was eating fried chicken and collard greens and hush puppies, and a waitress smiled at me. The food seemed tasteless, but I guessed that might have been my problem, not theirs.

I nodded at her, politely, which she took as an invitation to come over and refill my coffee cup. The coffee was bitter, which I liked. At least it tasted of something.

"Looking at you," she said, "I would guess that you are a professional man. May I inquire as to your profession?" That was what she said, word for word.

"Indeed you may," I said, feeling almost possessed by something, and affably pompous, like W. C. Fields or the Nutty Professor (the fat one, not the Jerry Lewis one, although I am actually within pounds of the optimum weight for my height), "I happen to be . . . an anthropologist, on my way to a conference in New Orleans, where I shall confer, consult, and otherwise hobnob with my fellow anthropologists."

"I knew it," she said. "Just looking at you. I had you figured for a professor. Or a dentist, maybe."

She smiled at me one more time. I thought about stopping forever in that little town, eating in that diner every morning and every night. Drinking their bitter coffee and having her smile at me until I ran out of coffee and money and days.

Then I left her a good tip, and went south and west.

2. *"Tongue brought me here"*

There were no hotel rooms in New Orleans, or anywhere in the New Orleans sprawl. A Jazz Festival had eaten them, every one. It was too hot to sleep in my car, and, even if I'd cranked a window and been prepared to suffer the heat, I felt unsafe. New Orleans is a real place, which is more than I can say about most of the cities I've lived in, but it's not a safe place, not a friendly one.

I stank, and itched. I wanted to bathe, and to sleep, and for the world to stop moving past me.

I drove from fleabag motel to fleabag motel, and then, at the last, as I had always known I would, I drove into the parking lot of the downtown Marriott on Canal Street. At least I knew they had one free room. I had a voucher for it in the manilla folder.

"I need a room," I said to one of the women behind the counter.

She barely looked at me. "All rooms are taken," she said. "We won't have anything until Tuesday."

I needed to shave, and to shower, and to rest. *What's the worst she can say?* I thought. *I'm sorry, you've already checked in?*

"I have a room, prepaid by my university. The name's Anderton."

She nodded, tapped a keyboard, said "Jackson?" then gave me a key to my room, and I initialed the room rate. She pointed me to the elevators.

A short man with a ponytail and a dark, hawkish face dusted with white stubble cleared his throat as we stood beside the elevators. "You're the Anderton from Hopewell," he said. "We were neighbors in the *Journal of Anthropological Heresies.*" He wore a white T-shirt that said "Anthropologists Do It While Being Lied To."

"We were?"

"We were. I'm Campbell Lakh. University of Norwood and Streatham. Formerly North Croydon Polytechnic. England. I wrote the paper about Icelandic spirit-walkers and fetches."

"Good to meet you," I said, and shook his hand. "You don't have a London accent."

"I'm a Brummie," he said. "From Birmingham," he added. "Never seen you at one of these things before."

"It's my first conference," I told him.

"Then you stick with me," he said. "I'll see you're all right. I remember my first one of these conferences, I was scared shitless I'd do something stupid the entire time. We'll stop on the mezzanine, get our stuff, then get cleaned up. There must have been a hundred babies on my plane over, Isweartogod. They took it in shifts to scream, shit, and puke, though. Never less than ten of them screaming at a time."

We stopped on the mezzanine, collected our badges and programs. "Don't forget to sign up for the ghost walk," said the smiling woman behind the table. "Ghost walks of Old New Orleans each night, limited to fifteen people in each party, so sign up fast."

I bathed, and washed my clothes out in the basin, then hung them up in the bathroom to dry.

I sat naked on the bed and examined the former contents of Anderton's briefcase. I skimmed through the paper he had intended to present, without taking in the content.

On the clean back of page five he had written, in a tight, mostly legible, scrawl, "*In a perfect perfect world you could fuck people without giving them a piece of your heart. And every glittering kiss and every touch of flesh is another shard of heart you'll never see again.*

"*Until walking (waking? calling?) on your own is unsupportable.*"

When my clothes were pretty much dry I put them back on and went down to the lobby bar. Campbell was already there. He was drinking a gin and tonic, with a gin and tonic on the side.

He had out a copy of the conference program and had circled each of the talks and papers he wanted to see. ("Rule one, if it's before midday, fuck it unless you're the one doing it," he explained.) He showed me my talk, circled in pencil.

"I've never done this before," I told him. "Presented a paper at a conference."

"It's a piece of piss, Jackson," he said. "Piece of piss. You know what I do?"

"No," I said.

"I just get up and read the paper. Then people ask questions, and I just bullshit," he said. "Actively bullshit, as opposed to passively. That's the best bit. Just bullshitting. Piece of utter piss."

"I'm not really good at, um, bullshitting," I said. "Too honest."

"Then nod, and tell them that that's a really perceptive question, and that it's addressed at length in the longer version of the paper, of which the one you are reading is an edited abstract. If you get some nut job giving you a really difficult time about something you got wrong, just get huffy and say that it's not about what's fashionable to believe, it's about the truth."

"Does that work?"

"Christ yes, I gave a paper a few years back about the origins of the Thuggee sects in Persian military troops—it's why you could get Hindus and Muslims equally becoming Thuggee, you see, the Kali worship was tacked on later. It would have begun as some sort of Manichaean secret society—"

"Still spouting that nonsense?" She was a tall, pale woman with a shock of white hair, wearing clothes that looked both aggressively, studiedly Bohemian, and far too warm for the climate. I could imagine her riding a bicycle, the kind with a wicker basket in the front.

"Spouting it? I'm writing a fucking book about it," said the Englishman. "So, what I want to know is, who's coming with me to the French Quarter to taste all that New Orleans can offer?"

"I'll pass," said the woman, unsmiling. "Who's your friend?"

"This is Jackson Anderton, from Hopewell College."

"The Zombie Coffee Girls paper?" She smiled. "I saw

it in the program. Quite fascinating. Yet another thing we owe Zora, eh?"

"Along with *The Great Gatsby*," I said.

"Hurston knew F. Scott Fitzgerald?" said the bicycle woman. "I did not know that. We forget how small the New York literary world was back then, and how the color bar was often lifted for a Genius."

The Englishman snorted. "Lifted? Only under sufferance. The woman died in penury as a cleaner in Florida. Nobody knew she'd written any of the stuff she wrote, let alone that she'd worked with Fitzgerald on *The Great Gatsby*. It's pathetic, Margaret."

"Posterity has a way of taking these things into account," said the tall woman. She walked away.

Campbell stared after her. "When I grow up," he said, "I want to be her."

"Why?"

He looked at me. "Yeah, that's the attitude. You're right. Some of us write the bestsellers, some of us read them, some of us get the prizes, some of us don't. What's important is being human, isn't it? It's how good a person you are. Being alive."

He patted me on the arm.

"Come on. Interesting anthropological phenomenon I've read about on the Internet I shall point out to you tonight, of the kind you probably don't see back in Dead Rat, Kentucky. *Id est,* women who would, under normal circumstances, not show their tits for a hundred quid, who will be only too pleased to get 'em out for the crowd for some cheap plastic beads."

"Universal trading medium," I said. "Beads."

"Fuck," he said. "There's a paper in that. Come on. You ever had a Jell-O shot, Jackson?"

"No."

"Me neither. Bet they'll be disgusting. Let's go and see."

We paid for our drinks. I had to remind him to tip.

"By the way," I said. "F. Scott Fitzgerald. What was his wife's name?"

"Zelda? What about her?"

"Nothing," I said.

Zelda. Zora. Whatever. We went out.

3. "Nothing, like something, happens anywhere"

Midnight, give or take. We were in a bar on Bourbon Street, me and the English anthropology prof, and he started buying drinks—real drinks, this place didn't do Jell-O shots—for a couple of dark-haired women at the bar. They looked so similar they could have been sisters. One wore a red ribbon in her hair, the other wore a white ribbon. Gauguin could have painted them, only he would have painted them bare-breasted and without the silver mouse skull earrings. They laughed a lot.

We had seen a small party of academics walk past the bar at one point, being led by a guide with a black umbrella. I pointed them out to Campbell.

The woman with the red ribbon raised an eyebrow. "They go on the Haunted History tours, looking for ghosts, you want to say, dude, this is where the ghosts come, this is where the dead stay. Easier to go looking for the living."

"You saying the tourists are *alive?*" said the other, mock-concern on her face.

"When they *get* here," said the first, and they both laughed at that.

They laughed a lot.

The one with the white ribbon laughed at everything Campbell said. She would tell him, "Say fuck again," and he would say it, and she would say "Fook! Fook!" trying to copy him, and he'd say "It's not *fook,* it's *fuck,*" and she couldn't hear the difference, and would laugh some more.

After two drinks, maybe three, he took her by the hand and walked her into the back of the bar, where music was playing, and it was dark, and there were a couple of people already, if not dancing, then moving against each other.

I stayed where I was, beside the woman with the red ribbon in her hair.

She said, "So you're in the record company, too?"

I nodded. It was what Campbell had told them we did. "I hate telling people I'm a fucking academic," he had said, reasonably, when they were in the ladies' room. Instead he had told them that he had discovered Oasis.

"How about you? What do you do in the world?"

She said, "I'm a priestess of Santeria. Me, I got it all in my blood, my papa was Brazilian, my momma was Irish-Cherokee. In Brazil, everybody makes love with everybody and they have the best little brown babies. Everybody got black slave blood, everybody got Indian blood, my poppa even got some Japanese blood. His brother, my uncle, he looks Japanese. My poppa, he just a good-looking man. People think it was my poppa I got the Santeria from, but no, it was my grandmomma, said she was Cherokee, but I had her figgered for mostly high yaller when I saw the old photographs. When I was three I was talking to dead folks, when I was five I watched a huge black dog, size of a Harley Davidson, walking behind a man in the street, no one could see it but me, when I told my mom, she told my grandmomma, they said, she's got to know, she's got to learn. There's people to teach me, even as a little girl.

"I was never afraid of dead folk. You know that? They never hurt you. So many things in this town can hurt you, but the dead don't hurt you. Living people hurt you. They hurt you so bad."

I shrugged.

"This is a town where people sleep with each other, you know. We make love to each other. It's something we do to show we're still alive."

I wondered if this was a come-on. It did not seem to be.
She said, "You hungry?"

I said, a little.

She said, "I know a place near here they got the best
bowl of gumbo in New Orleans. Come on."

I said, "I hear it's a town you're best off not walking
on your own at night."

"That's right," she said. "But you'll have me with you.
You're safe, with me with you."

Out on the street college girls were flashing their
breasts to the crowds on the balconies. For every glimpse
of nipple the onlookers would cheer and throw plastic
beads. I had known the red-ribbon woman's name earlier in the evening, but now it had evaporated.

"Used to be they only did this shit at Mardi Gras," she
said. "Now the tourists expect it, so it's just tourists doing it for the tourists. The locals don't care. When you
need to piss," she added, "you tell me."

"Okay. Why?"

"Because most tourists who get rolled, get rolled
when they go into the alleys to relieve themselves. Wake
up an hour later in Pirate's Alley with a sore head and
an empty wallet."

"I'll bear that in mind."

She pointed to an alley as we passed it, foggy and deserted. "Don't go there," she said.

The place we wound up in was a bar with tables. A
TV on above the bar showed the *Tonight Show* with the
sound off and subtitles on, although the subtitles kept
scrambling into numbers and fractions. We ordered the
gumbo, a bowl each.

I was expecting more from the best gumbo in New
Orleans. It was almost tasteless. Still, I spooned it down,
knowing that I needed food, that I had had nothing to
eat that day.

Three men came into the bar. One sidled, one strutted,
one shambled. The sidler was dressed like a Victorian

undertaker, high top hat and all. His skin was fishbelly pale; his hair was long and stringy; his beard was long and threaded with silver beads. The strutter was dressed in a long black leather coat, dark clothes underneath. His skin was very black. The last one, the shambler, hung back, waiting by the door. I could not see much of his face, nor decode his race: what I could see of his skin was a dirty gray. His lank hair hung over his face. He made my skin crawl.

The first two men made straight to our table, and I was, momentarily, scared for my skin, but they paid no attention to me. They looked at the woman with the red ribbon, and both of the men kissed her on the cheek. They asked about friends they had not seen, about who did what to whom in which bar and why. They reminded me of the fox and the cat from *Pinocchio*.

"What happened to your pretty girlfriend?" the woman asked the black man.

He smiled, without humor. "She put a squirrel tail on my family tomb."

She pursed her lips. "Then you better off without her."

"That's what I say."

I glanced over at the one who gave me the creeps. He was a filthy thing, junkie-thin, gray-lipped. His eyes were downcast. He barely moved. I wondered what the three men were doing together: the fox and the cat and the ghost.

Then the white man took the woman's hand and pressed it to his lips, bowed to her, raised a hand to me, in a mock salute, and the three of them were gone.

"Friends of yours?"

"Bad people," she said. "Macumba. Not friends of anybody."

"What was up with the guy by the door? Is he sick?"

She hesitated, then she shook her head. "Not really. I'll tell you when you're ready."

"Tell me now."

On the TV, Jay Leno was talking to a thin, blonde woman. IT&S NOT .UST T½E MOVIE said the caption. SO H.VE SS YOU SE¾N THE AC ION F!GURE? He picked up a small toy from his desk, pretended to check under its skirt to make sure it was anatomically correct. [LAUGHTER], said the caption.

She finished her bowl of gumbo, licked the spoon with a red, red tongue, and put it down in the bowl. "A lot of kids they come to New Orleans. Some of them read Anne Rice books and figure they learn about being vampires here. Some of them have abusive parents, some are just bored. Like stray kittens living in drains, they come here. They found a whole new breed of cat living in a drain in New Orleans, you know that?"

"No."

SLAUGHTER S] said the caption, but Jay was still grinning, and the *Tonight Show* went to a car commercial.

"He was one of the street kids, only he had a place to crash at night. Good kid. Hitchhiked from L.A. to New Orleans. Wanted to be left alone to smoke a little weed, listen to his Doors cassettes, study up on Chaos magick and read the complete works of Aleister Crowley. Also get his dick sucked. He wasn't particular about who did it. Bright eyes and bushy tail."

"Hey," I said. "That was Campbell. Going past. Out there."

"Campbell?"

"My friend."

"The record producer?" She smiled as she said it, and I thought, *She knows. She knows he was lying. She knows what he is.*

I put down a twenty and a ten on the table, and we went out onto the street, to find him, but he was already gone.

"I thought he was with your sister," I told her.

"No sister," she said. "No sister. Only me. Only me."

We turned a corner and were engulfed by a crowd of noisy tourists, like a sudden breaker crashing onto the shore. Then, as fast as they had come, they were gone, leaving only a handful of people behind them. A teen-aged girl was throwing up in a gutter, a young man nervously standing near her, holding her purse and a plastic cup half full of booze.

The woman with the red ribbon in her hair was gone. I wished I had made a note of her name, or the name of the bar in which I'd met her.

I had intended to leave that night, to take the interstate west to Houston and from there to Mexico, but I was tired and two-thirds drunk, and instead I went back to my room, and when the morning came I was still in the Marriott. Everything I had worn the night before smelled of perfume and rot.

I put on my T-shirt and pants, went down to the hotel gift shop, picked out a couple more T-shirts and a pair of shorts. The tall woman, the one without the bicycle, was in there, buying some Alka-Seltzer.

She said, "They've moved your presentation. It's now in the Audubon Room, in about twenty minutes. You might want to clean your teeth first. Your best friends won't tell you, but I hardly know you, Mister Anderton, so I don't mind telling you at all."

I added a traveling toothbrush and toothpaste to the stuff I was buying. Adding to my possessions, though, troubled me. I felt I should be shedding them. I needed to be transparent, to have nothing.

I went up to the room, cleaned my teeth, put on the Jazz Festival T-shirt. And then, because I had no choice in the matter, or because I was doomed to confer, consult, and otherwise hobnob, or because I was pretty certain Campbell would be in the audience and I wanted to say good-bye to him before I drove away, I picked up the typescript and went down to the Audubon Room, where fifteen people were waiting. Campbell was not one of them.

I was not scared. I said hello, and I looked at the top of page one.

It began with another quote from Zora Neale Hurston:

Big Zombies who come in the night to do malice are talked about. Also the little girl Zombies who are sent out by their owners in the dark dawn to sell little packets of roasted coffee. Before sun-up their cries of "Café grillé" can be heard from dark places in the streets and one can only see them if one calls out for the seller to come with the goods. Then the little dead one makes herself visible and mounts the steps.

Anderton continued on from there, with quotations from Hurston's contemporaries, several extracts from old interviews with older Haitians, the man's paper leaping, as far as I was able to tell, from conclusion to conclusion, spinning fancies into guesses and suppositions and weaving those into facts.

Halfway through, Margaret, the tall woman without the bicycle, came in and simply stared at me. I thought, *She knows I'm not him. She knows.* I kept reading though. What else could I do?

At the end, I asked for questions.

Somebody asked me about Zora Neale Hurston's research practices. I said that was a very good question, which was addressed at greater length in the finished paper, of which what I had read was essentially an edited abstract.

Someone else, a short, plump woman, stood up and announced that the zombie girls could not have existed: Zombie drugs and powders numbed you, induced death-like trances, but still worked fundamentally on belief—the belief that you were now one of the dead and had no will of your own. How, she asked, could a child of four or five be induced to believe such a thing? No. The coffee girls were, she said, one with the Indian Rope Trick, just another of the urban legends of the past.

Personally I agreed with her, but I nodded and said that her points were well made and well taken. And that, from my perspective—which was, I hoped, a genuinely anthropological perspective—what mattered was not what it was easy to believe, but, much more importantly, the truth.

They applauded, and afterward a man with a beard asked me whether he might be able to get a copy of the paper for a journal he edited. It occurred to me that it was a good thing I had come to New Orleans, that Anderton's career would not be harmed by his absence from the conference.

The plump woman, whose badge said her name was Shanelle Gravely-King, was waiting for me at the door. She said, "I really enjoyed that. I don't want you to think that I didn't."

Campbell didn't turn up for his presentation. Nobody ever saw him again.

Margaret introduced me to someone from New York, and mentioned that Zora Neale Hurston had worked on *The Great Gatsby*. The man said yes, that was pretty common knowledge these days. I wondered if she had called the police, but she seemed friendly enough. I was starting to stress, I realized. I wished I had not thrown away my cell phone.

Shanelle Gravely-King and I had an early dinner in the hotel, at the beginning of which I said, "Oh, let's not talk shop," and she agreed that only the very dull talked shop at the table, so we talked about rock bands we had seen live, fictional methods of slowing the decomposition of a human body, and about her partner, who was a woman older than she was and who owned a restaurant, and then we went up to my room. She smelled of baby powder and jasmine, and her naked skin was clammy against mine.

Over the next couple of hours I used two of the three condoms. She was sleeping by the time I returned from the bathroom, and I climbed into the bed next to her. I thought about the words Anderton had written, hand-scrawled on the back of the typescript page, and I wanted to check them, but I fell asleep, a soft-fleshed jasmine-scented woman pressing close to me.

After midnight, I woke from a dream, and a woman's voice was whispering in the darkness.

She said, "So he came into town, with his Doors cassettes and his Crowley books, and his handwritten list of the secret URLs for Chaos magick on the Web, and everything was good, he even got a few disciples, runaways like him, and he got his dick sucked whenever he wanted, and the world was good.

"And then he started to believe his own press. He thought he was the real thing. That he was the dude. He thought he was a big mean tiger cat, not a little kitten. So he dug up . . . something . . . someone else wanted.

"He thought the something he dug up would look after him. Silly boy. And that night, he's sitting in Jackson Square, talking to the Tarot readers, telling them about Jim Morrison and the kabbalah, and someone taps him on the shoulder, and he turns, and someone blows powder into his face, and he breathes it in.

"Not all of it. And he is going to do something about it, when he realizes there's nothing to be done, because he's all paralyzed, there's fugu fish and toad skin and ground bone and everything else in that powder, and he's breathed it in.

"They take him down to emergency, where they don't do much for him, figuring him for a street rat with a drug problem, and by the next day he can move again, although it's two, three days until he can speak.

"Trouble is, he needs it. He wants it. He knows there's some big secret in the zombie powder, and he was almost there. Some people say they mixed heroin with it, some shit like that, but they didn't even need to do that. He wants it.

"And they told him they wouldn't sell it to him. But if he did jobs for them, they'd give him a little zombie powder, to smoke, to sniff, to rub on his gums, to swallow. Sometimes they'd give him nasty jobs to do no one else wanted. Sometimes they just humiliate him because they could—make him eat dog shit from the gutter, maybe. Kill for them, maybe. Anything but die. All skin and bones. He do anything for his zombie powder.

"And he still thinks, in the little bit of his head that's still him, that he's not a zombie. That he's not dead, that there's a threshold he hasn't stepped over. But he crossed it long time ago."

I reached out a hand, and touched her. Her body was hard, and slim, and lithe, and her breasts felt like breasts that Gauguin might have painted. Her mouth, in the darkness, was soft and warm against mine.

People come into your life for a reason.

4. *"Those people ought to know who we are and tell that we are here"*

When I woke, it was still almost dark, and the room was silent. I turned on the light, looked on the pillow for a ribbon, white or red, or for a mouse-skull earring, but there was nothing to show that there had ever been anyone in the bed that night but me.

I got out of bed and pulled open the drapes, looked out of the window. The sky was graying in the east.

I thought about moving south, about continuing to run, continuing to pretend I was alive. But it was, I knew now, much too late for that. There are doors, after all, between the living and the dead, and they swing in both directions.

I had come as far as I could.

There was a faint tap-tapping on the hotel room door.

I pulled on my pants and the T-shirt I had set out in and, barefoot, I pulled the door open.

The coffee girl was waiting for me.

Everything beyond the door was touched with light, an open, wonderful predawn light, and I heard the sound of birds calling on the morning air. The street was on a hill, and the houses facing me were little more than shanties. There was mist in the air, low to the ground, curling like something from an old black-and-white film, but it would be gone by noon.

The girl was thin and small; she did not appear to be more than six years old. Her eyes were cobwebbed with what might have been cataracts, her skin was as gray as it had once been brown. She was holding a white hotel cup out to me, holding it carefully, with one small hand on the handle, one hand beneath the saucer. It was half-filled with a steaming mud-colored liquid.

I bent to take it from her, and I sipped it. It was a very bitter drink, and it was hot, and it woke me the rest of the way.

I said, "Thank you."

Someone, somewhere, was calling my name.

The girl waited, patiently, while I finished the coffee. I put the cup down on the carpet, then I put out my hand and touched her shoulder.

She reached up her hand, spread her small gray fingers, and took hold of my hand. She knew I was with her. Wherever we were headed now, we were going there together.

I remembered something somebody had once said to me. "It's okay. Every day is freshly ground," I told her.

The coffee girl's expression did not change, but she nodded, as if she had heard me, and gave my arm an impatient tug. She held my hand tight with her cold cold fingers, and we walked, finally, side by side into the misty dawn.

OTHER PEOPLE

"Time is fluid here," said the demon.

He knew it was a demon the moment he saw it. He knew it, just as he knew the place was Hell. There was nothing else that either of them could have been.

The room was long, and the demon waited by a smoking brazier at the far end. A multitude of objects hung on the rock-gray walls, of the kind that it would not have been wise or reassuring to inspect too closely. The ceiling was low, the floor oddly insubstantial.

"Come close," said the demon, and he did.

The demon was rake thin and naked. It was deeply scarred, and it appeared to have been flayed at some time in the distant past. It had no ears, no sex. Its lips were thin and ascetic, and its eyes were a demon's eyes: they had seen too much and gone too far, and under their gaze he felt less important than a fly.

"What happens now?" he asked.

"Now," said the demon, in a voice that carried with it no sorrow, no relish, only a dreadful flat resignation, "you will be tortured."

"For how long?"

But the demon shook its head and made no reply. It walked slowly along the wall, eyeing first one of the devices that hung there, then another. At the far end of the wall, by the closed door, was a cat-o'-nine-tails made of frayed wire. The demon took it down with one three-fingered hand and walked back, carrying it reverently. It placed the wire tines onto the brazier, and stared at them as they began to heat up.

"That's inhuman."

"Yes."

The tips of the cat's tails were glowing a dead orange.

As the demon raised its arm to deliver the first blow, it said, "In time you will remember even this moment with fondness."

"You are a liar."

"No," said the demon. "The next part," it explained, in the moment before it brought down the cat, "is worse."

Then the tines of the cat landed on the man's back with a crack and a hiss, tearing through the expensive clothes, burning and rending and shredding as they struck, and, not for the last time in that place, he screamed.

There were two hundred and eleven implements on the walls of that room, and in time he was to experience each of them.

When, finally, the Lazarene's Daughter, which he had grown to know intimately, had been cleaned and replaced on the wall in the two hundred and eleventh position, then, through wrecked lips, he gasped, "Now what?"

"Now," said the demon, "the true pain begins."

It did.

Everything he had ever done that had been better left undone. Every lie he had told—told to himself, or told to others. Every little hurt, and all the great hurts. Each one was pulled out of him, detail by detail, inch by inch. The demon stripped away the cover of forgetfulness, stripped everything down to truth, and it hurt more than anything.

"Tell me what you thought as she walked out the door," said the demon.

"I thought my heart was broken."

"No," said the demon, without hate, "you didn't." It stared at him with expressionless eyes, and he was forced to look away.

"I thought, now she'll never know I've been sleeping with her sister."

The demon took apart his life, moment by moment, instant to awful instant. It lasted a hundred years, perhaps, or a thousand—they had all the time there ever was, in that gray room—and toward the end he realized that the demon had been right. The physical torture had been kinder.

And it ended.

And once it had ended, it began again. There was a self-knowledge there he had not had the first time, which somehow made everything worse.

Now, as he spoke, he hated himself. There were no lies, no evasions, no room for anything except the pain and the anger.

He spoke. He no longer wept. And when he finished, a thousand years later, he prayed that now the demon would go to the wall, and bring down the skinning knife, or the choke-pear, or the screws.

"Again," said the demon.

He began to scream. He screamed for a long time.

"Again," said the demon, when he was done, as if nothing had been said.

It was like peeling an onion. This time through his life he learned about consequences. He learned the results of things he had done; things he had been blind to as he did them; the ways he had hurt the world; the damage he had done to people he had never known, or met, or encountered. It was the hardest lesson yet.

"Again," said the demon, a thousand years later.

He crouched on the floor, beside the brazier, rocking gently, his eyes closed, and he told the story of his life, re-experiencing it as he told it, from birth to death, changing nothing, leaving nothing out, facing everything. He opened his heart.

When he was done, he sat there, eyes closed, waiting

for the voice to say, "Again," but nothing was said. He opened his eyes.

Slowly, he stood up. He was alone.

At the far end of the room, there was a door, and as he watched, it opened.

A man stepped through the door. There was terror in the man's face, and arrogance, and pride. The man, who wore expensive clothes, took several hesitant steps into the room, and then stopped.

When he saw the man, he understood.

"Time is fluid here," he told the new arrival.

KEEPSAKES AND TREASURES

*I am his Highness' dog at Kew
Pray tell me, sir, whose dog are you?*
ALEXANDER POPE,
On the Collar of a Dog Which I
Gave to His Royal Highness

You can call me a bastard if you like. It's true, which-
ever way you want to cut it. My mum had me two years
after being locked up "for her own protection"; this
was back in 1952, when a couple of wild nights out
with the local lads could be diagnosed as *clinical nym-
phomania,* and you could be put away "to protect
yourself and society" on the say-so of any two doctors.
One of whom was her father, my grandfather, the other
was his partner in the north London medical practice
they shared.

So I know who my grandfather was. But my father
was just somebody who shagged my mother somewhere
in the building or grounds of St. Andrews Asylum.
That's a nice word, isn't it? *Asylum.* With all its implica-
tions of a place of safety: somewhere that shelters you
from the bitter and dangerous old world outside. Nothing like the reality of that hole. I went to see it, before
they knocked it down in the late seventies. It still reeked
of piss and pine-scented disinfectant floor wash. Long,
dark badly lit corridors with clusters of tiny, cell-like

rooms off them. If you were looking for Hell and you found St. Andrews you'd not have been disappointed.

It says on her medical records that she'd spread her legs for anyone, but I doubt it. She was locked up back then. Anyone who wanted to stick his cock into her would have needed a key to her cell.

When I was eighteen I spent my last summer holiday before I went up to university hunting down the four men who were most likely to have been my father: two psychiatric nurses, the secure ward doctor, and the governor of the asylum.

My mum was only seventeen when she went inside. I've got a little black-and-white wallet photograph of her from just before she was put away. She's leaning against the side of a Morgan sports car parked in a country lane. She's smiling, sort of flirtily, at the photographer. She was a looker, my mum.

I didn't know which one of the four was my dad, so I killed all of them. They had each fucked her, after all: I got them to admit to it, before I did them in. The best was the governor, a red-faced fleshy old lech with an honest-to-goodness handlebar mustache, like I haven't seen for twenty years now. I garotted him with his Guards tie. Spit bubbles came from his mouth, and he went blue as an unboiled lobster.

There were other men around St. Andrews who might have been my father, but after those four the joy went out of it. I told myself that I'd killed the four likeliest candidates, and if I knocked off everyone who might have knocked up my mother it would have turned into a massacre. So I stopped.

I was handed over to the local orphanage to bring up. According to her medical records, they sterilized my mum immediately after I was born. Didn't want any more nasty little incidents like me coming along to spoil anybody's fun.

I was ten when she killed herself. This was 1964. I

was ten years old, and I was still playing conkers and knocking off sweet shops while she was sitting on the linoleum floor of her cell sawing at her wrists with a bit of broken glass she'd got from heaven-knows-where. Cut her fingers up, too, but she did it all right. They found her in the morning, sticky, red, and cold.

Mr. Alice's people ran into me when I was twelve. The deputy head of the orphanage had been using us kids as his personal harem of scabby-kneed love slaves. Go along with him and you got a sore bum and a Bounty bar. Fight back and you got locked down for a couple of days, a really sore bum and concussion. Old Bogey we used to call him, because he picked his nose whenever he thought we weren't looking.

He was found in his blue Morris Minor in his garage, with the doors shut and a length of bright green hosepipe going from the exhaust into the front window. The coroner said it was a suicide and seventy-five young boys breathed a little easier.

But Old Bogey had done a few favors for Mr. Alice over the years, when there was a chief constable or a foreign politician with a penchant for little boys to be taken care of, and he sent a couple of investigators out to make sure everything was on the up-and-up. When they figured out the only possible culprit was a twelve-year-old boy, they almost pissed themselves laughing.

Mr. Alice was intrigued, so he sent for me. This was back when he was a lot more hands-on than today. I suppose he hoped I'd be pretty, but he was in for a sad disappointment. I looked then like I do now: too thin, with a profile like a hatchet blade and ears like someone left the car doors open. What I remember of him mostly then is how big he was. Corpulent. I suppose he was still a fairly young man back then, although I didn't see it that way: he was an adult, and so he was the enemy.

A couple of goons came and took me after school, on my way back to the home. I was shitting myself, at first, but the goons didn't smell like the law—I'd had four years of dodging the Old Bill by then, and I could spot a plainclothes copper a hundred yards away. They took me to a little gray office, sparsely furnished, just off the Edgware Road.

It was winter, and it was almost dark outside, but the lights were dim, except for a little desk lamp casting a pool of yellow light on the desk. An enormous man sat at the desk, scribbling something in ballpoint pen on the bottom of a telex sheet. Then, when he was done, he looked up at me. He looked me over from head to toe.

"Cigarette?"

I nodded. He extended a Peter Stuyvesant soft pack, and I took a cigarette. He lit it for me with a gold-and-black cigarette lighter. "You killed Ronnie Palmerstone," he told me. There was no question in his voice.

I said nothing.

"Well? Aren't you going to say anything?"

"Got nothing to say," I told him.

"I only sussed it when I heard he was in the passenger seat. He wouldn't have been in the passenger seat, if he was going to kill himself. He would have been in the driver's seat. My guess is, you slipped him a mickey, then you got him into the Mini—can't have been easy, he wasn't a little bloke—here, mickey and Mini, that's rich— then you drove him home, drove into the garage, by which point he was sleeping soundly, and you rigged up the suicide. Weren't you scared someone would see you driving? A twelve-year-old boy?"

"It gets dark early," I said. "And I took the back way."

He chuckled. Asked me a few more questions, about school, and the home, and what I was interested in, things like that. Then the goons came and took me back to the orphanage.

Next week I was adopted by a couple named Jackson. He was an international business-law specialist. She was a self-defense expert. I don't think either of

them had ever met before Mr. Alice got them together
to bring me up.

I wonder what he saw in me at that meeting. It must
have been some kind of potential, I suppose. The potential for loyalty. And I'm loyal. Make no mistake about
that. I'm Mr. Alice's man, body and soul.

Of course, his name isn't really Mr. Alice, but I could
use his real name here just as easily. Doesn't matter.
You'd not have heard of him. Mr. Alice is one of the ten
richest men in the world. I'll tell you something: you
haven't heard of the other nine, either. Their names
aren't going to turn up on any lists of the hundred richest men in the world. None of your Bill Gateses, or
your Sultans of Brunei. I'm talking *real* money here.
There are people out there who are being paid more
than you will ever see in your life to make sure you
never hear a breath about Mr. Alice on the telly or in the
papers.

Mr. Alice likes to own things. And, as I've told you,
one of the things he owns is me. He's the father I didn't
have. It was him that got me the medical files on my
mum and the information on the various candidates for
my dad.

When I graduated (first class degrees in business studies and international law), as my graduation present to
myself, I went and found my-grandfather-the-doctor. I'd
held off on seeing him until then. It had been a sort of
incentive.

He was a year away from retirement, a hatchet-faced
old man with a tweed jacket. This was in 1978, and a
few doctors still made house calls. I followed him to a
tower block in Maida Vale. Waited while he dispensed
his medical wisdom, and stopped him as he came out,
black bag swinging by his side.

"Hullo Grandpa," I said. Not much point in trying to
pretend to be someone else, really. Not with my looks.
He was me, forty years on. Same fucking ugly face, but

with his hair thinning and sandy gray, not thick and mousy brown like mine. He asked what I wanted.

"Locking Mum away like that," I told him. "It wasn't very nice, was it?"

He told me to get away from him, or something like that.

"I've just got my degree." I told him. "You should be proud of me."

He said that he knew who I was, and I had better be off at once, or he would have the police down on me, and have me locked away.

I put the knife through his left eye and back into his brain, and while he made little choking noises I took his old calfskin wallet—as a keepsake, really, and to make it look more like a robbery. That was where I found the photo of my mum, in black-and-white, smiling and flirting with the camera, twenty-five years before. I wonder who owned the Morgan.

I had someone who didn't know me pawn the wallet. I bought it from the pawnshop when it wasn't redeemed. Nice clean trail. There's many a smart man who's been brought down by a keepsake. Sometimes I wonder if I killed my father that day, as well as my grandfather. I don't expect he'd have told me, even if I'd asked. And it doesn't really matter, does it?

After that I went to work full-time for Mr. Alice. I ran the Sri Lanka end of things for a couple of years, then spent a year in Bogotá on import-export, working as a glorified travel agent. I came back home to London as soon as I could. For the last fifteen years I've been working mainly as a troubleshooter, and as a smoother-over of problem areas. Troubleshooter. That's rich.

Like I said, it takes real money to make sure nobody's ever heard of you. None of that Rupert Murdoch cap-in-hand-to-the-merchant-bankers rubbish. You'll never see Mr. Alice in a glossy magazine, showing a photographer around his glossy new house.

Outside of business, Mr. Alice's main interest is sex, which is why I was standing outside Earl's Court station with forty million U.S. dollars' worth of blue-white diamonds in the inside pockets of my macintosh. Specifically, and to be exact, Mr. Alice's interest in sex is confined to relations with attractive young men. Now don't get me wrong, here: I don't want you thinking Mr. Alice is some kind of woofter. He's not a nancy or anything. He's a proper man, Mr. Alice. He's just a proper man who likes to fuck other men, that's all. Takes all sorts to make a world, I say, and leaves a lot more of what I like for me. Like at restaurants, where everyone gets to order something different from the menu. *Chacun à son goût*, if you'll pardon my French. So everybody's happy.

This was a couple of years ago, in July. I remember that I was standing in the Earls Court Road, in Earls Court, looking up at the Earl's Court Tube Station sign and wondering why the apostrophe was there in the station when it wasn't in the place, and then staring at the junkies and the winos who hang around on the pavement, and all the time keeping an eye out for Mr. Alice's Jag.

I wasn't worried about having the diamonds in my inside pocket. I don't look like the sort of bloke who's got anything you'd want to mug him for, and I can take care of myself. So I stared at the junkies and winos, killing time till the Jag arrived (stuck behind the road works in Kensington High Street, at a guess) and wondering why junkies and winos congregate on the pavement outside Earl's Court station.

I suppose I can sort of understand the junkies: they're waiting for a fix. But what the fuck are the winos doing there? Nobody has to slip you a pint of Guinness or a bottle of rubbing alcohol in a plain brown bag. It's not comfortable, sitting on the paving stones or leaning against the wall. If I were a wino, on a lovely day like this, I decided, I'd go down to the park.

Near me a little Pakistani lad in his late teens or early twenties was papering the inside of a glass phone box with hooker cards—CURVY TRANSSEXUAL and REAL BLONDE NURSE, BUSTY SCHOOLGIRL and STERN TEACHER NEEDS BOY TO DISCIPLINE. He glared at me when he noticed I was watching him. Then he finished up and went on to the next booth.

Mr. Alice's Jag drew up at the curb and I walked over to it and got in the back. It's a good car, a couple of years old. Classy, but not something you'd look twice at.

The chauffeur and Mr. Alice sat in the front. Sitting in the backseat with me was a pudgy man with a crew cut and a loud check suit. He made me think of the frustrated fiancé in a fifties film; the one who gets dumped for Rock Hudson in the final reel. I nodded at him. He extended his hand, and then, when I didn't seem to notice, he put it away.

Mr. Alice did not introduce us, which was fine by me, as I knew exactly who the man was. I'd found him, and reeled him in, in fact, although he'd never know that. He was a professor of ancient languages at a North Carolina university. He thought he was on loan to British Intelligence from the U.S. State Department. He thought this, because this was what he had been told by someone at the U.S. State Department. The professor had told his wife that he was presenting a paper to a conference on Hittite studies in London. And there was such a conference. I'd organized it myself.

"Why do you take the bloody tube?" asked Mr. Alice. "It can't be to save money."

"I would have thought the fact I've been standing on that corner waiting for you for the last twenty minutes demonstrates exactly why I didn't drive," I told him. He likes it that I don't just roll over and wag my tail. I'm a dog with spirit. "The average daytime speed of a vehicle through the streets of Central London has not changed in four hundred years. It's still under ten miles an hour. If the tubes are running, I'll take the tube, thanks."

"You don't drive in London?" asked the professor in the loud suit. Heavens protect us from the dress sense of American academics. Let's call him Macleod.

"I'll drive at night, when the roads are empty," I told him. "After midnight. I like driving at night."

Mr. Alice wound down the window and lit a small cigar. I could not help noticing that his hands were trembling. With anticipation, I guessed.

And we drove through Earls Court, past a hundred tall red-brick houses that claimed to be hotels, a hundred tattier buildings that housed guest-houses and bed-and-breakfasts, down good streets and bad. Sometimes Earls Court reminds me of one of those old women you meet from time to time who's painfully proper and prissy and prim until she's got a few drinks into her, when she starts dancing on the tables and telling everybody within earshot about her days as a pretty young thing, sucking cock for money in Australia or Kenya or somewhere.

Actually, that makes it sound like I like the place and, frankly, I don't. It's too transient. Things come and go and people come and go too damn fast. I'm not a romantic man, but give me South of the River, or the East End, any day. The East End is a proper place: it's where things begin, good and bad. It's the cunt and the arsehole of London; they're always close together. Whereas Earls Court is—I don't know what. The body analogy breaks down completely when you get out to there. I think that's because London is mad. Multiple personality problems. All these little towns and villages that grew and crashed into each other to make one big city, but never forget their old borders.

So the chauffeur pulled up in a road like any other, in front of a high, terraced house that might have been a hotel at one time. A couple of the windows were boarded over. "That's the house," said the chauffeur.

"Right," said Mr. Alice.

The chauffeur walked around the car and opened the door for Mr. Alice. Professor Macleod and I got out on our own. I looked up and down the pavement. Nothing to worry about.

I knocked on the door, and we waited. I nodded and smiled at the spyhole in the door. Mr. Alice's cheeks were flushed, and he held his hands folded in front of his crotch, to avoid embarrassing himself. Horny old bugger.

Well, I've been there, too. We all have. Only Mr. Alice, he can afford to indulge himself.

The way I look at it, some people need love, and some people don't. I think Mr. Alice is really a bit of a *don't*, all things considered. I'm a *don't* as well. You learn to recognize the type.

And Mr. Alice is, first and foremost, a connoisseur.

There was a bang from the door, as a bolt was drawn back, and the door was opened by an old woman of what they used to describe as "repulsive aspect." She was dressed in a baggy black one-piece robe. Her face was wrinkled and pouched. I'll tell you what she looked like. Did you ever see a picture of one of those cinnamon buns they said looked like Mother Teresa? She looked like that, like a cinnamon roll, with two brown raisin eyes peering out of her cinnamon roll face.

She said something to me in a language I did not recognize, and Professor Macleod replied, haltingly. She stared at the three of us, suspiciously, then she made a face and beckoned us in. She slammed the door behind us. I closed first one eye, then the other, encouraging them to adjust to the gloom inside the house.

The building smelled like a damp spice rack. I didn't like anything about the whole business; there's something about foreigners, when they're that foreign, that makes my skin crawl. As the old bat who'd let us in, whom I had begun to think of as the Mother Superior, led us up flight after flight of stairs, I could see more of the black-robed women, peering at us out of doorways and down the corridor. The stair carpet was frayed and the soles of my shoes made sticking noises as they pulled up from it; the plaster hung in crumbling chunks from the walls. It was a warren, and it drove me nuts. Mr. Alice shouldn't have to come to places like that, places he couldn't be protected properly.

More and more shadowy crones peered at us in silence as we climbed our way through the house. The old witch with the cinnamon bun face talked to Professor Macleod as we went, a few words here, a few words there; and he in return panted and puffed at her, from the effort of climbing the stairs, and answered her as best he could.

"She wants to know if you brought the diamonds," he gasped.

"Tell her we'll talk about that once we've seen the merchandise," said Mr. Alice. He wasn't panting, and if there was the faintest tremble in his voice, it was from anticipation.

Mr. Alice has fucked, to my personal knowledge, half a brat-pack of the leading male movie stars of the last two decades, and more male models than you could shake your kit at; he's had the prettiest boys on five continents; none of them knew precisely who they were being fucked by, and all of them were very well paid for their trouble.

At the top of the house, up a final flight of uncarpeted wooden stairs, was the door to the attic, and flanking each side of the door, like twin tree trunks, was a huge woman in a black gown. Each of them looked like she could have held her own against a sumo wrestler. Each of them held, I kid you not, a scimitar: they were guarding the Treasure of the Shahinai. And they stank like old horses. Even in the gloom, I could see that their robes were patched and stained.

The Mother Superior strode up to them, a squirrel facing up to a couple of pit-bulls, and I looked at their impassive faces and wondered where they originally came from. They could have been Samoan or Mongolian, could have been pulled from a freak farm in Turkey or India or Iran.

On a word from the old woman they stood aside from the door, and I pushed it open. It wasn't locked. I looked inside, in case of trouble, walked in, looked around, and gave the all-clear. So I was the first male in this generation to gaze upon the Treasure of the Shahinai.

He was kneeling beside a camp bed, his head bowed.

Legendary is a good word to use for the Shahinai. It means I'd never heard of them and didn't know anyone who had, and once I started looking for them even the people who had heard of them didn't believe in them.

"After all, my good friend," my pet Russian academic said, handing over his report, "you're talking about a race of people the sole evidence for the existence of which is half a dozen lines in Herodotus, a poem in the *Thousand and One Nights*, and a speech in the *Manuscrit Trouvé à Saragosse*. Not what we call reliable sources."

But rumors had reached Mr. Alice and he got interested. And what Mr. Alice wants, I make damned sure that Mr. Alice gets. Right now, looking at the Treasure of the Shahinai, Mr. Alice looked so happy I thought his face would break in two.

The boy stood up. There was a chamber pot half-sticking out from beneath the bed, with a cupful of vivid yellow piss in the bottom of it. His robe was white cotton, thin and very clean. He wore blue silk slippers.

It was so hot in that room. Two gas fires were burning, one on each side of the attic, with a low hissing sound. The boy didn't seem to feel the heat. Professor Macleod began to sweat profusely.

According to legend, the boy in the white robe—he was seventeen at a guess, no more than eighteen—was the most beautiful man in the world. I could easily believe it.

Mr. Alice walked over to the boy, and he inspected him like a farmer checking out a calf at a market, peering into his mouth, tasting the boy, and looking at the lad's eyes and his ears; taking his hands and examining his fingers and fingernails; and then, matter-of-factly, lifting up his white robe and inspecting his uncircumcised cock before turning him around and checking out the state of his arse.

And through it all the boy's eyes and teeth shone white and joyous in his face.

Finally Mr. Alice pulled the boy toward him and kissed him, slowly and gently, on the lips. He pulled back, ran his tongue around his mouth, nodded. Turned to Macleod. "Tell her we'll take him," said Mr. Alice.

Professor Macleod said something to the Mother Superior, and her face broke into wrinkles of cinnamon happiness. Then she put out her hands.

"She wants to be paid now," said Macleod.

I put my hands, slowly, into the inside pockets of my mac and pulled out first one, then two black velvet pouches. I handed them both to her. Each bag contained fifty flawless D or E grade diamonds, perfectly cut, each in excess of five carats. Most of them picked up cheaply from Russia in the mid-nineties. One hundred diamonds: forty million dollars. The old woman tipped a few into her palm and prodded at them with her finger. Then she put the diamonds back into the bag, and she nodded.

The bags vanished into her robes, and she went to the top of the stairs and as loud as she could, she shouted something in her strange language.

From all through the house below us there came a

wailing, like from a horde of banshees. The wailing continued as we walked downstairs through that gloomy labyrinth, with the young man in the white robe in the lead. It honestly made the hairs on the back of my neck prickle, that wailing, and the stink of wet-rot and spices made me gag. I fucking hate foreigners.

The woman wrapped him up in a couple of blankets, before they would let him out of the house, worried that he'd catch some kind of a chill despite the blazing July sunshine. We bundled him into the car.

I got a ride with them as far as the tube, and I went on from there.

I spent the next day, which was Wednesday, dealing with a mess in Moscow. Too many fucking cowboys. I was praying I could sort things out without having to personally go over there: the food gives me constipation.

As I get older, I like to travel less and less, and I was never keen on it in the first place. But I can still be hands-on whenever I need to be. I remember when Mr. Alice said that he was afraid that Maxwell was going to have to be removed from the playing field. I told him I was doing it myself, and I didn't want to hear another word about it. Maxwell had always been a loose cannon. Little fish with a big mouth and a rotten attitude.

Most satisfying splash I've ever heard.

By Wednesday night I was tense as a couple of wigwams, so I called a bloke I know, and they brought Jenny over to my flat in the Barbican. That put me in a better mood. She's a good girl, Jenny. Nothing sluttish about her at all. Minds her *P*s and *Q*s.

I was very gentle with her, that night, and afterward I slipped her a twenty-pound note.

"But you don't need to," she said. "It's all taken care of."

"Buy yourself something mad," I told her. "It's mad money." And I ruffled her hair, and she smiled like a schoolgirl.

Thursday I got a call from Mr. Alice's secretary to say that everything was satisfactory, and I should pay off Professor Macleod.

We were putting him up in the Savoy. Now, most people would have taken the tube to Charing Cross, or to Embankment, and walked up the Strand to the Savoy. Not me. I took the tube to Waterloo station and walked north over Waterloo Bridge. It's a couple of minutes longer, but you can't beat the view.

When I was a kid, one of the kids in the dorm told me that if you held your breath all the way to the middle of a bridge over the Thames and you made a wish there, the wish would always come true. I've never had anything to wish for, so I do it as a breathing exercise.

I stopped at the call box at the bottom of Waterloo Bridge (BUSTY SCHOOLGIRLS NEED DISCIPLINE. TIE ME UP TIE ME DOWN. NEW BLONDE IN TOWN). I phoned Macleod's room at the Savoy. Told him to come and meet me on the bridge.

His suit was, if anything, a louder check than the one he'd worn on Tuesday. He gave me a buff envelope filled with word-processed pages: a sort of homemade Shahinai-English phrase book. *"Are you hungry?"* *"You must bathe now."* *"Open your mouth."* Anything Mr. Alice might need to communicate.

I put the envelope in the pocket of my mac.

"Fancy a spot of sightseeing?" I asked, and Professor Macleod said it was always good to see a city with a native.

"This work is a philological oddity and a linguistic delight," said Macleod, as we walked along the Embankment. "The Shahinai speak a language that has points in common with both the Aramaic and the Finno-Ugric families of languages. It's the language that Christ might have spoken if he'd written the epistle to the primitive Estonians. Very few loanwords, for that matter. I have a theory that they must have been forced to make quite a few abrupt departures in their time. Do you have my payment on you?"

I nodded. Took out my old calfskin wallet from my jacket pocket, and pulled out a slip of brightly colored card. "Here you go."

We were coming up to Blackfriars Bridge. "It's real?"

"Sure. New York State Lottery. You bought it on a whim, in the airport, on your way to England. The numbers'll be picked on Saturday night. Should be a pretty good week, too. It's over twenty million dollars already."

He put the lottery ticket in his own wallet, black and shiny and bulging with plastic, and he put the wallet into the inside pocket of his suit. His hands kept straying to it, brushing it, absently making sure it was still there. He'd have been the perfect mark for any dip who wanted to know where he kept his valuables.

"This calls for a drink," he said. I agreed that it did but, as I pointed out to him, a day like today, with the sun shining and a fresh breeze coming in from the sea, was too good to waste in a pub. So we went into an off-licence. I bought him a bottle of Stoli, a carton of orange juice, and a plastic cup, and I got myself a couple of cans of Guinness.

"It's the men, you see," said the professor. We were sitting on a wooden bench looking at the South Bank across the Thames. "Apparently there aren't many of them. One or two in a generation. The Treasure of the Shahinai. The women are the guardians of the men. They nurture them and keep them safe.

"Alexander the Great is said to have bought a lover from the Shahinai. So did Tiberius, and at least two popes. Catherine the Great was rumored to have had one, but I think that's just a rumor."

I told him I thought it was like something in a storybook. "I mean, think about it. A race of people whose only asset is the beauty of their men. So every century they sell one of their men for enough money to keep the tribe going for another hundred years." I took a swig of the Guinness. "Do you think that was all of the tribe, the women in that house?"

"I rather doubt it."

He poured another slug of vodka into the plastic cup, splashed some orange juice into it, raised his glass to me. "Mr. Alice," he said. "He must be very rich."

"He does all right."

"I'm straight," said Macleod, drunker than he thought he was, his forehead prickling with sweat, "but I'd fuck that boy like a shot. He was the most beautiful thing I've ever seen."

"He was all right, I suppose."

"You wouldn't fuck him?"

"Not my cup of tea," I told him.

A black cab went down the road behind us. Its orange "For Hire" light was turned off, although there was nobody sitting in the back.

"So what is your cup of tea, then?" asked Professor Macleod.

"Little girls," I told him.

He swallowed. "How little?"

"Nine. Ten. Eleven or twelve, maybe. Once they've got real tits and pubes I can't get it up anymore. Just doesn't do it for me."

He looked at me as if I'd told him I liked to fuck dead dogs, and he didn't say anything for a bit. He drank his Stoli. "You know," he said, "back where I come from, that sort of thing would be illegal."

"Well, they aren't too keen on it over here."

"I think maybe I ought to be getting back to the hotel," he said.

A black cab came around the corner, its light on this time. I waved it down, and helped Professor Macleod into the back. It was one of our Particular Cabs. The kind you get into and you don't get out of.

"The Savoy, please," I told the cabbie.

"Righto, governor," he said, and took Professor Macleod away.

Mr. Alice took good care of the Shahinai boy. Whenever I went over for meetings or briefings the boy would be sitting at Mr. Alice's feet, and Mr. Alice would be twining and stroking and fiddling with his black-black hair. They doted on each other, you could tell. It was soppy and, I have to admit, even for a cold-hearted bastard like myself, it was touching.

Sometimes, at night, I'd have dreams about the Shahinai women—these ghastly, batlike, hag things, fluttering and roosting through this huge rotting old house, which was, at the same time, both human history and St. Andrews Asylum. Some of them were carrying men between them, as they flapped and flew. The men shone like the sun, and their faces were too beautiful to look upon.

I hated those dreams. One of them, and the next day was a write-off, and you can take that to the fucking bank.

The most beautiful man in the world, the Treasure of the Shahinai, lasted for eight months. Then he caught the flu.

His temperature went up to 106 degrees, his lungs filled with water and he was drowning on dry land. Mr. Alice brought in some of the best doctors in the world, but the lad flickered and went out like an old lightbulb, and that was that.

I suppose they just aren't very strong. Bred for something else, after all, not strength.

Mr. Alice took it really hard. He was inconsolable— wept like a baby all the way through the funeral, tears running down his face, like a mother who had just lost her only son. It was pissing with rain, so if you weren't standing next to him, you'd not have known. I ruined a perfectly good pair of shoes in that graveyard, and it put me in a rotten mood.

I sat around in the Barbican flat, practiced knife-throwing, cooked a spaghetti Bolognese, watched some football on the telly.

That night I had Alison. It wasn't pleasant.

The next day I took a few good men and we went down to the house in Earls Court, to see if any of the Shahinai were still about. There had to be more Shahinai young men somewhere. It stood to reason.

But the plaster on the rotting walls had been covered up with stolen rock posters, and the place smelled of dope, not spice.

The warren of rooms was filled with Australians and New Zealanders. Squatters, at a guess. We surprised a dozen of them in the kitchen, sucking narcotic smoke from the mouth of a broken R. White's Lemonade bottle.

We searched the house from cellar to attic, looking for some trace of the Shahinai women, something that they had left behind, some kind of clue, anything that would make Mr. Alice happy.

We found nothing at all.

And all I took away from the house in Earl's Court was the memory of the breast of a girl, stoned and oblivious, sleeping naked in an upper room. There were no curtains on the window.

I stood in the doorway, and I looked at her for too long, and it painted itself on my mind: a full, black-nippled breast, which curved disturbingly in the sodium yellow light of the street.

GOOD BOYS DESERVE FAVORS

My own children delight in hearing true tales from my childhood: The Time My Father Threatened to Arrest the Traffic Cop, How I Broke My Sister's Front Teeth Twice, When I Pretended to Be Twins, and even The Day I Accidentally Killed the Gerbil.

I have never told them this story. I would be hard put to tell you quite why not.

When I was nine the school told us that we could pick any musical instrument we wanted. Some boys chose the violin, the clarinet, the oboe. Some chose the timpani, the pianoforte, the viola.

I was not big for my age, and I, alone in the Junior School, elected to play the double bass, chiefly because I loved the incongruity of the idea. I loved the idea of being a small boy, playing, delighting in, carrying around an instrument much taller than I was.

The double bass belonged to the school, and I was deeply impressed by it. I learned to bow, although I had little interest in bowing technique, preferring to pluck the huge metal strings by hand. My right index finger was permanently puffed with white blisters until the blisters eventually became calluses.

I delighted in discovering the history of the double bass: that it was no part of the sharp, scraping family of the violin, the viola, the 'cello; its curves were gentler, softer, more sloping; it was, in fact, the final survivor of an extinct family of instruments, the viol family, and was, more correctly, the bass viol.

I learned this from the double bass teacher, an elderly musician imported by the school to teach me, and also to teach a couple of senior boys, for a few hours each week. He was a clean-shaven man, balding and intense, with long, callused fingers. I would do all I could to make him tell me about the bass, tell me of his experiences as a session musician, of his life cycling around the country. He had a contraption attached to the back of his bicycle, on which his bass rested, and he pedaled sedately through the countryside with the bass behind him.

He had never married. Good double bass players, he told me, were men who made poor husbands. He had many such observations. There were no great male cellists—that's one I remember. And his opinion of viola players, of either sex, was scarcely repeatable.

He called the school double bass she. "She could do with a good coat of varnish," he'd say. And "You take care of her, she'll take care of you."

I was not a particularly good double bass player. There was little enough that I could do with the instrument on my own, and all I remember of my enforced membership in the school orchestra was getting lost in the score and sneaking glances at the 'cellos beside me, waiting for them to turn the page, so I could start playing once more, punctuating the orchestral schoolboy cacophony with low, uncomplicated bass notes.

It has been too many years, and I have almost forgotten how to read music; but when I dream of reading music, I still dream in the bass clef. *All Cows Eat Grass. Good Boys Deserve Favors Always.*

After lunch each day, the boys who played instruments walked down to the music school and had music practice, while the boys who didn't lay on their beds and read their books and their comics.

I rarely practiced. Instead I would take a book down

to the music school and read it, surreptitiously, perched on my high stool, holding on to the smooth brown wood of the bass, the bow in one hand, the better to fool the casual observer. I was lazy and uninspired. My bowing scrubbed and scratched where it should have glided and boomed, my fingering was hesitant and clumsy. Other boys worked at their instruments. I did not. As long as I was sitting at the bass for half an hour each day, no one cared. I had the nicest, largest room to practice in, too, as the double bass was kept in a cupboard in the master music room.

Our school, I should tell you, had only one Famous Old Boy. It was part of school legend—how the Famous Old Boy had been expelled from the school after driving a sports car across the cricket pitch, while drunk, how he had gone on to fame and fortune—first as a minor actor in Ealing Comedies, then as the token English cad in any number of Hollywood pictures. He was never a true star but, during the Sunday afternoon film screening, we would cheer if ever he appeared.

When the door handle to the practice room clicked and turned, I put my book down on the piano and leaned forward, turning the page of the dog-eared *52 Musical Exercises for the Double Bass,* and I heard the headmaster say, "The music school was purpose-built of course. This is the master practice room . . ." and they came in.

They were the headmaster and the head of the music department (a faded, bespectacled man whom I rather liked) and the deputy head of the music department (who conducted the school orchestra, and disliked me cordially) and, there could be no mistaking it, the Famous Old Boy himself, in company with a fragrant fair woman who held his arm and looked as if she might also be a movie star.

I stopped pretending to play, and slipped off my high stool and stood up respectfully, holding the bass by the neck.

The headmaster told them about the soundproofing and the carpets and the fund-raising drive to raise the money to build the music school, and he stressed that the next stage of rebuilding would need significant further donations, and he was just beginning to expound upon the cost of double glazing when the fragrant woman said, "Just look at him. Is that cute or what?" and they all looked at me.

"That's a big violin—be hard to get it under your chin," said the Famous Old Boy, and everyone chortled dutifully.

"It's so big," said the woman. "And he's so small. Hey, but we're stopping you practicing. You carry on. Play us something."

The headmaster and the head of the music department beamed at me, expectantly. The deputy head of the music department, who was under no illusions as to my musical skills, started to explain that the first violin was practicing next door and would be delighted to play for them and—

"I want to hear *him*," she said. "How old are you, kid?"

"Eleven, Miss," I said.

She nudged the Famous Old Boy in the ribs. "He called me 'Miss,'" she said. This amused her. "Go on. Play us something." The Famous Old Boy nodded, and they stood there and they looked at me.

The double bass is not a solo instrument, really, not even for the competent, and I was far from competent. But I slid my bottom up onto the stool again and crooked my fingers around the neck and picked up my bow, heart pounding like a timpani in my chest, and prepared to embarrass myself.

Even twenty years later, I remember.

I did not even look at 52 *Musical Exercises for the Double Bass*. I played . . . *something*. It arched and boomed and sang and reverberated. The bow glided over strange and confident arpeggios, and then I put down the bow and plucked a complex and intricate pizzicato melody out of the bass. I did things with the bass that an experienced jazz bass player with hands as big as my head would not have done. I played, and I played, and I played, tumbling down into the four taut metal strings, clutching the instrument as I had never clutched a human being. And, in the end, breathless and elated, I stopped.

The blonde woman led the applause, but they all clapped, even, with a strange expression on his face, the deputy head of music.

"I didn't know it was such a versatile instrument," said the headmaster. "Very lovely piece. Modern, yet classical. Very fine. Bravo." And then he shepherded the four of them from the room, and I sat there, utterly drained, the fingers of my left hand stroking the neck of the bass, the fingers of my right caressing her strings.

Like any true story, the end of the affair is messy and unsatisfactory: the following day, carrying the huge instrument across the courtyard to the school chapel, for orchestra practice, in a light rain, I slipped on the wet bricks and fell forward. The wooden bridge of the bass was smashed, and the front was cracked.

It was sent away to be repaired, but when it returned it was not the same. The strings were higher, harder to pluck, the new bridge seemed to have been installed at the wrong angle. There was, even to my untutored ear, a change in the timbre. I had not taken care of her; she would no longer take care of me.

When, the following year, I changed schools, I did not continue with the double bass. The thought of changing to a new instrument seemed vaguely disloyal, while the dusty black bass that sat in a cupboard in my new school's music rooms seemed to have taken a dislike to me. I was marked another's. And I was tall enough now that there would be nothing incongruous about my standing behind the double bass.

And, soon enough, I knew, there would be girls.

THE FACTS IN THE CASE OF THE
DEPARTURE OF MISS FINCH

To begin at the end: I arranged the thin slice of pickled ginger, pink and translucent, on top of the pale yellow-tail flesh, and dipped the whole arrangement—ginger, fish, and vinegared rice—into the soy sauce, flesh-side down; then I devoured it in a couple of bites.

"I think we ought to go to the police," I said.

"And tell them what, exactly?" asked Jane.

"Well, we could file a missing persons report, or something. I don't know."

"And where did you last see the young lady?" asked Jonathan, in his most policemanlike tones. "Ah, I see. Did you know that wasting police time is normally considered an offense, sir?"

"But the whole circus . . ."

"These are transient persons, sir, of legal age. They come and go. If you have their names, I suppose I can take a report . . ."

I gloomily ate a salmon skin roll. "Well, then," I said, "why don't we go to the papers?"

"Brilliant idea," said Jonathan, in the sort of tone of voice which indicates that the person talking doesn't think it's a brilliant idea at all.

"Jonathan's right," said Jane. "They won't listen to us."

"Why wouldn't they believe us? We're reliable. Honest citizens. All that."

"You're a fantasy writer," she said. "You make up stuff like this for a living. No one's going to believe you."

"But you two saw it all as well. You'd back me up."

"Jonathan's got a new series on cult horror movies coming out in the autumn. They'll say he's just trying to get cheap publicity for the show. And I've got another book coming out. Same thing."

"So you're saying that we can't tell anyone?" I sipped my green tea.

"No," Jane said, reasonably, "we can tell anyone we want. It's making them believe us that's problematic. Or, if you ask me, impossible."

The pickled ginger was sharp on my tongue. "You may be right," I said. "And Miss Finch is probably much happier wherever she is right now than she would be here."

"But her name isn't Miss Finch," said Jane, "it's——" and she said our former companion's real name.

"I know. But it's what I thought when I first saw her," I explained. "Like in one of those movies. You know. When they take off their glasses and put down their hair. 'Why, Miss Finch. You're beautiful.' "

"She certainly was that," said Jonathan, "in the end, anyway." And he shivered at the memory.

There. So now you know: that's how it all ended, and how the three of us left it, several years ago. All that remains is the beginning, and the details.

For the record, I don't expect you to believe any of this. Not really. I'm a liar by trade, after all; albeit, I like to think, an honest liar. If I belonged to a gentlemen's club I'd recount it over a glass or two of port late in the evening as the fire burned low, but I am a member of no such club, and I'll write it better than ever I'd tell it. So here you will learn of Miss Finch (whose name, as you already know, was not Finch, nor anything like it, since I'm changing names here to disguise the guilty) and how it came about that she was unable to join us for sushi. Believe it or not, just as you wish. I am not even certain that I believe it anymore. It all seems such a long way away.

I could find a dozen beginnings. Perhaps it might be best to begin in a hotel room, in London, a few years ago. It was 11:00 AM. The phone began to ring, which surprised me. I hurried over to answer it.

"Hello?" It was too early in the morning for anyone in America to be phoning me, and there was no one in England who was meant to know that I was even in the country.

"Hi," said a familiar voice, adopting an American accent of monumentally unconvincing proportions. "This is Hiram P. Muzzledexter of Colossal Pictures. We're working on a film that's a remake of *Raiders of the Lost Ark* but instead of Nazis it has women with enormous knockers in it. We've heard that you were astonishingly well supplied in the trouser department and might be willing to take on the part of our male lead, Minnesota Jones . . ."

"Jonathan?" I said. "How on earth did you find me here?"

"You knew it was me," he said, aggrieved, his voice losing all trace of the improbable accent and returning to his native London.

"Well, it sounded like you," I pointed out. "Anyway, you didn't answer my question. No one's meant to know that I was here."

"I have my ways," he said, not very mysteriously. "Listen, if Jane and I were to offer to feed you sushi— something I recall you eating in quantities that put me in mind of feeding time at London Zoo's Walrus House— and if we offered to take you to the theater before we fed you, what would you say?"

"Not sure. I'd say 'Yes' I suppose. Or 'What's the catch?' I might say that."

"Not exactly a catch," said Jonathan. "I wouldn't exactly call it a *catch*. Not a real catch. Not really."

"You're lying, aren't you?"

Somebody said something near the phone, and then Jonathan said, "Hang on, Jane wants a word." Jane is Jonathan's wife.

"How are you?" she said.

"Fine, thanks."

"Look," she said, "you'd be doing us a tremendous favor—not that we wouldn't love to see you, because we would, but you see, there's someone . . ."

"She's your friend," said Jonathan, in the background.

"She's *not* my friend. I hardly know her," she said, away from the phone, and then, to me, "Um, look, there's someone we're sort of lumbered with. She's not in the country for very long, and I wound up agreeing to entertain her and look after her tomorrow night. She's pretty frightful, actually. And Jonathan heard that you were in town from someone at your film company, and we thought you might be perfect to make it all less awful, so please say yes."

So I said yes.

In retrospect, I think the whole thing might have been the fault of the late Ian Fleming, creator of James Bond. I had read an article the previous month, in which Ian Fleming had advised any would-be writer who had a book to get done that wasn't getting written to go to a hotel to write it. I had, not a novel, but a film script that wasn't getting written; so I bought a plane ticket to London, promised the film company that they'd have a finished script in three weeks' time, and took a room in an eccentric hotel in Little Venice.

I told no one in England that I was there. Had people known, my days and nights would have been spent seeing them, not staring at a computer screen and, sometimes, writing.

Truth to tell, I was bored half out of my mind and ready to welcome any interruption.

Early the next evening I arrived at Jonathan and Jane's house, which was more or less in Hampstead. There was a small green sports car parked outside. Up the stairs, and I knocked at the door. Jonathan answered it; he wore an impressive suit. His light brown hair was longer than I remembered it from the last time I had seen him, in life or on television.

"Hello," said Jonathan. "The show we were going to take you to has been canceled. But we can go to something else, if that's okay with you."

I was about to point out that I didn't know what we were originally going to see, so a change of plans would make no difference to me, but Jonathan was already leading me into the living room, establishing that I wanted fizzy water to drink, assuring me that we'd still be eating sushi and that Jane would be coming downstairs as soon as she had put the children to bed.

They had just redecorated the living room, in a style Jonathan described as Moorish brothel. "It didn't set out to be a Moorish brothel," he explained. "Or any kind of a brothel really. It was just where we ended up. The brothel look."

"Has he told you all about Miss Finch?" asked Jane. Her hair had been red the last time I had seen her. Now it was dark brown; and she curved like a Raymond Chandler simile.

"Who?"

"We were talking about Ditko's inking style," apologized Jonathan. "And the Neal Adams issues of *Jerry Lewis*."

"But she'll be here any moment. And he has to know about her before she gets here."

Jane is, by profession, a journalist, but had become a best-selling author almost by accident. She had written a companion volume to accompany a television series about two paranormal investigators, which had risen to the top of the best-seller lists and stayed there.

Jonathan had originally become famous hosting an evening talk show, and had since parlayed his gonzo charm into a variety of fields. He's the same person whether the camera is on or off, which is not always true of television folk.

"It's a kind of family obligation," Jane explained. "Well, not exactly *family.*"

"She's Jane's friend," said her husband, cheerfully.

"She is *not* my friend. But I couldn't exactly say no to them, could I? And she's only in the country for a couple of days."

And who Jane could not say no to, and what the obligation was, I never was to learn, for at the moment the doorbell rang, and I found myself being introduced to Miss Finch. Which, as I have mentioned, was not her name.

She wore a black leather cap, and a black leather coat, and had black, black hair, pulled tightly back into a small bun, done up with a pottery tie. She wore makeup, expertly applied to give an impression of severity that a professional dominatrix might have envied. Her lips were tight together, and she glared at the world through a pair of definite black-rimmed spectacles—they punctuated her face much too definitely to ever be mere glasses.

"So," she said, as if she were pronouncing a death sentence, "we're going to the theater, then."

"Well, yes and no," said Jonathan. "I mean, yes, we are still going out, but we're not going to be able to see *The Romans in Britain.*"

"Good," said Miss Finch. "In poor taste anyway. Why anyone would have thought that nonsense would make a musical I do not know."

"So we're going to a circus," said Jane, reassuringly. "And then we're going to eat sushi."

Miss Finch's lips tightened. "I do not approve of circuses," she said.

"There aren't any animals in this circus," said Jane.

"Good," said Miss Finch, and she sniffed. I was beginning to understand why Jane and Jonathan had wanted me along.

The rain was pattering down as we left the house, and the street was dark. We squeezed ourselves into the sports car and headed out into London. Miss Finch and I were in the backseat of the car, pressed uncomfortably close together.

Jane told Miss Finch that I was a writer, and told me that Miss Finch was a biologist.

"Biogeologist actually," Miss Finch corrected her. "Were you serious about eating sushi, Jonathan?"

"Er, yes. Why? Don't you like sushi?"

"Oh, I'll eat *my* food cooked," she said, and began to list for us all the various flukes, worms, and parasites that lurk in the flesh of fish and which are only killed by cooking. She told us of their life cycles while the rain pelted down, slicking night-time London into garish neon colors. Jane shot me a sympathetic glance from the passenger seat, then she and Jonathan went back to scrutinizing a handwritten set of directions to wherever we were going. We crossed the Thames at London Bridge while Miss Finch lectured us about blindness, madness, and liver failure; and she was just elaborating on the symptoms of elephantiasis as proudly as if she had invented them herself when we pulled up in a small back street in the neighborhood of Southwark Cathedral.

"So where's the circus?" I asked.

"Somewhere around here," said Jonathan. "They contacted us about being on the Christmas special. I tried to pay for tonight's show, but they insisted on comping us in."

"I'm sure it will be fun," said Jane, hopefully.

Miss Finch sniffed.

A fat, bald man, dressed as a monk, ran down the pavement toward us. "There you are!" he said. "I've been keeping an eye out for you. You're late. It'll be starting in a moment." He turned around and scampered back the way he had come, and we followed him. The rain splashed on his bald head and ran down his face, turning his Fester Addams makeup into streaks of white and brown. He pushed open a door in the side of a wall.

"In here."

We went in. There were about fifty people in there already, dripping and steaming, while a tall woman in bad vampire makeup holding a flashlight walked around checking tickets, tearing off stubs, selling tickets to anyone who didn't have one. A small, stocky woman immediately in front of us shook the rain from her umbrella and glowered about her fiercely. "This'd better be gud," she told the young man with her—her son, I suppose. She paid for tickets for both of them.

The vampire woman reached us, recognized Jonathan and said, "Is this your party? Four people? Yes? You're on the guest list," which provoked another suspicious stare from the stocky woman.

A recording of a clock ticking began to play. A clock struck twelve (it was barely eight by my watch), and the wooden double doors at the far end of the room creaked open. "Enter . . . of your own free will!" boomed a voice, and it laughed maniacally. We walked through the door into darkness.

It smelled of wet bricks and of decay. I knew then where we were: there are networks of old cellars that run beneath some of the overground train tracks—vast, empty, linked rooms of various sizes and shapes. Some of them are used for storage by wine merchants and used-car sellers; some are squatted in, until the lack of light and facilities drives the squatters back into the daylight; most of them stand empty, waiting for the inevitable arrival of the wrecking ball and the open air and the time when all their secrets and mysteries will be no more.

A train rattled by above us.

We shuffled forward, led by Uncle Fester and the vampire woman, into a sort of a holding pen where we stood and waited.

"I hope we're going to be able to sit down after this," said Miss Finch.

When we were all settled the flashlights went out, and the spotlights went on.

The people came out. Some of them rode motorbikes and dune buggies. They ran and they laughed and they swung and they cackled. Whoever had dressed them had been reading too many comics, I thought, or watched *Mad Max* too many times. There were punks and nuns and vampires and monsters and strippers and the living dead.

They danced and capered around us while the ringmaster—identifiable by his top hat—sang Alice Cooper's song "Welcome to My Nightmare," and sang it very badly.

"I know Alice Cooper," I muttered to myself, misquoting something half-remembered, "and you, sir, are no Alice Cooper."

"It's pretty naff," agreed Jonathan.

Jane shushed us. As the last notes faded away the ringmaster was left alone in the spotlight. He walked around our enclosure while he talked.

"Welcome, welcome, one and all, to the Theater of Night's Dreaming," he said.

"Fan of yours," whispered Jonathan.

"I think it's a *Rocky Horror Show* line," I whispered back.

"Tonight you will all be witnesses to monsters undreamed-of, freaks and creatures of the night, to displays of ability to make you shriek with fear—and laugh with joy. We shall travel," he told us, "from room to room—and in each of these subterranean caverns another nightmare, another delight, another display of wonder awaits you! Please—for your own safety—I must reiterate this!—Do not leave the spectating area marked out for you in each room—on pain of doom, bodily injury, and the loss of your immortal soul! Also, I must stress that the use of flash photography or of any recording devices is utterly forbidden."

And with that, several young women holding pencil flashlights led us into the next room.

"No seats then," said Miss Finch, unimpressed.

The First Room
In the first room a smiling blonde woman wearing a spangled bikini, with needle tracks down her arms, was chained by a hunchback and Uncle Fester to a large wheel.

The wheel spun slowly around, and a fat man in a red cardinal's costume threw knives at the woman, outlining her body. Then the hunchback blindfolded the cardinal, who threw the last three knives straight and true to outline the woman's head. He removed his blindfold. The woman was untied and lifted down from the wheel. They took a bow. We clapped.

Then the cardinal took a trick knife from his belt and pretended to cut the woman's throat with it. Blood spilled down from the knife blade. A few members of the audience gasped, and one excitable girl gave a small scream, while her friends giggled.

The cardinal and the spangled woman took their final bow. The lights went down. We followed the flashlights down a brick-lined corridor.

The Second Room
The smell of damp was worse in here; it smelled like a cellar, musty and forgotten. I could hear somewhere the

drip of rain. The ringmaster introduced the Creature—
"Stitched together in the laboratories of the night, the
Creature is capable of astonishing feats of strength."
The Frankenstein's monster makeup was less than con-
vincing, but the Creature lifted a stone block with fat
Uncle Fester sitting on it, and he held back the dune
buggy (driven by the vampire woman) at full throttle.
For his pièce de résistance he blew up a hot-water bottle,
then popped it.

"Roll on the sushi," I muttered to Jonathan.

Miss Finch pointed out, quietly, that in addition to the
danger of parasites, it was also the case that bluefin
tuna, swordfish, and Chilean sea bass were all being
overfished and could soon be rendered extinct, since
they were not reproducing fast enough to catch up.

The Third Room
went up for a long way into the darkness. The original
ceiling had been removed at some time in the past, and
the new ceiling was the roof of the empty warehouse far
above us. The room buzzed at the corners of vision with
the blue-purple of ultraviolet light. Teeth and shirts and
flecks of lint began to glow in the darkness. A low,
throbbing music began. We looked up to see, high above
us, a skeleton, an alien, a werewolf, and an angel. Their
costumes fluoresced in the UV, and they glowed like old
dreams high above us, on trapezes. They swung back
and forth, in time with the music, and then, as one, they
let go and tumbled down toward us.

We gasped, but before they reached us they bounced on
the air, and rose up again, like yo-yos, and clambered
back on their trapezes. We realized that they were attached to the roof by rubber cords, invisible in the darkness, and they bounced and dove and swam through the
air above us while we clapped and gasped and watched
them in happy silence.

The Fourth Room

was little more than a corridor: the ceiling was low, and the ringmaster strutted into the audience and picked two people out of the crowd—the stocky woman and a tall black man wearing a sheepskin coat and tan gloves—pulling them up in front of us. He announced that he would be demonstrating his hypnotic powers. He made a couple of passes in the air and rejected the stocky woman. Then he asked the man to step up onto a box.

"It's a setup," muttered Jane. "He's a plant."

A guillotine was wheeled on. The ringmaster cut a watermelon in half, to demonstrate how sharp the blade was. Then he made the man put his hand under the guillotine, and dropped the blade. The gloved hand dropped into the basket, and blood spurted from the open cuff.

Miss Finch squeaked.

Then the man picked his hand out of the basket and chased the Ringmaster around us, while the *Benny Hill Show* music played.

"Artificial hand," said Jonathan.

"I saw it coming," said Jane.

Miss Finch blew her nose into a tissue. "I think it's all in very questionable taste," she said. Then they led us to

The Fifth Room

and all the lights went on. There was a makeshift wooden table along one wall, with a young bald man selling beer and orange juice and bottles of water, and signs showed the way to the toilets in the room next door. Jane went to get the drinks, and Jonathan went to use the toilets, which left me to make awkward conversation with Miss Finch.

"So," I said, "I understand you've not been back in England long."

"I've been in Komodo," she told me. "Studying the dragons. Do you know why they grew so big?"

"Er . . ."

"They adapted to prey upon the pygmy elephants."

"There were pygmy elephants?" I was interested. This was much more fun than being lectured on sushi flukes.

"Oh yes. It's basic island biogeology—animals will naturally tend toward either gigantism or pygmyism. There are equations, you see . . ." As Miss Finch talked her face became more animated, and I found myself warming to her as she explained why and how some animals grew while others shrank.

Jane brought us our drinks; Jonathan came back from the toilet, cheered and bemused by having been asked to sign an autograph while he was pissing.

"Tell me," said Jane, "I've been reading a lot of cryptozoological journals for the next of the *Guides to the Unexplained* I'm doing. As a biologist—"

"Biogeologist," interjected Miss Finch.

"Yes. What do you think the chances are of prehistoric animals being alive today, in secret, unknown to science?"

"It's very unlikely," said Miss Finch, as if she were telling us off. "There is, at any rate, no 'Lost World' off on some island, filled with mammoths and Smilodons and aepyornis. . . ."

"Sounds a bit rude," said Jonathan. "A what?"

"Aepyornis. A giant flightless prehistoric bird," said Jane.

"I knew that really," he told her.

"Although of course, they're *not* prehistoric," said Miss Finch. "The last aepyornises were killed off by Portuguese sailors on Madagascar about three hundred years ago. And there are fairly reliable accounts of a pygmy mammoth being presented at the Russian court in the sixteenth century, and a band of something which from the descriptions we have were almost definitely some kind of saber-tooth—the Smilodon—brought in from North Africa by Vespasian to die in the circus. So these things aren't all prehistoric. Often, they're historic."

"I wonder what the point of the saber teeth would be," I said. "You'd think they'd get in the way."

"Nonsense," said Miss Finch. "Smilodon was a most efficient hunter. Must have been—the saber teeth are repeated a number of times in the fossil record. I wish with all my heart that there were some left today. But there aren't. We know the world too well."

"It's a big place," said Jane, doubtfully, and then the lights were flickered on and off, and a ghastly, disembodied voice told us to walk into the next room, that the latter half of the show was not for the faint of heart, and that later tonight, for one night only, the Theater of Night's Dreaming would be proud to present the Cabinet of Wishes Fulfill'd.

We threw away our plastic glasses, and we shuffled into

The Sixth Room

"Presenting," announced the ringmaster, "The Painmaker!"

The spotlight swung up to reveal an abnormally thin young man in bathing trunks, hanging from hooks through his nipples. Two of the punk girls helped him down to the ground, and handed him his props. He hammered a six-inch nail into his nose, lifted weights with a piercing through his tongue, put several ferrets into his bathing trunks, and, for his final trick, allowed the taller of the punk girls to use his stomach as a dartboard for accurately flung hypodermic needles.

"Wasn't he on the show, years ago?" asked Jane.

"Yeah," said Jonathan. "Really nice guy. He lit a firework held in his teeth."

"I thought you said there were no animals," said Miss Finch. "How do you think those poor ferrets feel about being stuffed into that young man's nether regions?"

"I suppose it depends mostly on whether they're boy ferrets or girl ferrets," said Jonathan, cheerfully.

The Seventh Room
contained a rock-and-roll comedy act, with some clumsy slapstick. A nun's breasts were revealed, and the hunchback lost his trousers.

The Eighth Room
was dark. We waited in the darkness for something to happen. I wanted to sit down. My legs ached, I was tired and cold, and I'd had enough.

Then someone started to shine a light at us. We blinked and squinted and covered our eyes.

"Tonight," an odd voice said, cracked and dusty. Not the ringmaster, I was sure of that. "Tonight, one of you shall get a wish. One of you will gain all that you desire, in the Cabinet of Wishes Fulfill'd. Who shall it be?"

"Ooh. At a guess, another plant in the audience," I whispered, remembering the one-handed man in the fourth room.

"Shush," said Jane.

"Who will it be? You sir? You madam?" A figure came out of the darkness and shambled toward us. It was hard to see him properly, for he held a portable spotlight. I wondered if he were wearing some kind of ape costume, for his outline seemed inhuman, and he moved as gorillas move. Perhaps it was the man who played the Creature. "Who shall it be, eh?" We squinted at him, edged out of his way.

And then he pounced. "Aha! I think we have our volunteer," he said, leaping over the rope barrier that separated the audience from the show area around us. Then he grabbed Miss Finch by the hand.

"I really don't think so," said Miss Finch, but she was being dragged away from us, too nervous, too polite, fundamentally too English to make a scene. She was pulled into the darkness, and she was gone to us.

Jonathan swore. "I don't think she's going to let us forget this in a hurry," he said.

The lights went on. A man dressed as a giant fish then proceeded to ride a motorbike around the room several times. Then he stood up on the seat as it went around. Then he sat down and drove the bike up and down the walls of the room, and then he hit a brick and skidded and fell over, and the bike landed on top of him.

The hunchback and the topless nun ran on and pulled the bike off the man in the fish-suit and hauled him away.

"I just broke my sodding leg," he was saying, in a dull, numb voice. "It's sodding broken. My sodding leg," as they carried him out.

"Do you think that was meant to happen?" asked a girl in the crowd near to us.

"No," said the man beside her.

Slightly shaken, Uncle Fester and the vampire woman ushered us forward, into

The Ninth Room
where Miss Finch awaited us.

It was a huge room. I knew that, even in the thick darkness. Perhaps the dark intensifies the other senses; perhaps it's simply that we are always processing more information than we imagine. Echoes of our shuffling and coughing came back to us from walls hundreds of feet away.

And then I became convinced, with a certainty bordering upon madness, that there were great beasts in the darkness, and that they were watching us with hunger.

Slowly the lights came on, and we saw Miss Finch. I wonder to this day where they got the costume.

Her black hair was down. The spectacles were gone. The costume, what little there was of it, fitted her perfectly. She held a spear, and she stared at us without emotion. Then the great cats padded into the light next to her. One of them threw its head back and roared.

Someone began to wail. I could smell the sharp animal stench of urine.

The animals were the size of tigers, but unstriped; they were the color of a sandy beach at evening. Their eyes were topaz, and their breath smelled of fresh meat and of blood.

I stared at their jaws: the saber teeth were indeed teeth, not tusks: huge, overgrown fangs, made for rending, for tearing, for ripping meat from the bone.

The great cats began to pad around us, circling slowly. We huddled together, closing ranks, each of us remembering in our guts what it was like in the old times, when we hid in our caves when the night came and the beasts went on the prowl; remembering when we were prey.

The Smilodons, if that was what they were, seemed uneasy, wary. Their tails switched whiplike from side to side impatiently. Miss Finch said nothing. She just stared at her animals.

Then the stocky woman raised her umbrella and waved it at one of the great cats. "Keep back, you ugly brute," she told it.

It growled at her and tensed back, like a cat about to spring.

The stocky woman went pale, but she kept her umbrella pointed out like a sword. She made no move to run in the torchlit darkness beneath the city.

And then it sprang, batting her to the ground with one huge velvet paw. It stood over her, triumphantly, and roared so deeply that I could feel it in the pit of my stomach. The stocky woman seemed to have passed out, which was, I felt, a mercy: with luck, she would not know when the bladelike fangs tore at her old flesh like twin daggers.

I looked around for some way out, but the other tiger was prowling around us, keeping us herded within the rope enclosure, like frightened sheep.

I could hear Jonathan muttering the same three dirty words, over and over and over.

"We're going to die, aren't we?" I heard myself say.

"I think so," said Jane.

Then Miss Finch pushed her way through the rope barrier, and she took the great cat by the scruff of its neck and pulled it back. It resisted, and she thwacked it on the nose with the end of her spear. Its tail went down between its legs, and it backed away from the fallen woman, cowed and obedient.

There was no blood, that I could see, and I hoped that she was only unconscious.

In the back of the cellar room light was slowly coming up. It seemed as if dawn were breaking. I could see a jungle mist wreathing about huge ferns and hostas; and I could hear, as if from a great way off, the chirp of crickets and the call of strange birds awaking to greet the new day.

And part of me—the writer part of me, the bit that has noted the particular way the light hit the broken glass in the puddle of blood even as I staggered out from a car crash, and has observed in exquisite detail the way that my heart was broken, or did not break, in moments of real, profound, personal tragedy—it was that part of me that thought, *You could get that effect with a smoke machine, some plants, and a tape track. You'd need a really good lighting guy, of course.*

Miss Finch scratched her left breast, unselfconsciously,

then she turned her back on us and walked toward the dawn and the jungle underneath the world, flanked by two padding saber-toothed tigers.

A bird screeched and chattered.

Then the dawn light faded back into darkness, and the mists shifted, and the woman and the animals were gone.

The stocky woman's son helped her to her feet. She opened her eyes. She looked shocked but unhurt. And when we knew that she was not hurt, for she picked up her umbrella, and leaned on it, and glared at us all, why then we began to applaud.

No one came to get us. I could not see Uncle Fester or the vampire woman anywhere. So unescorted we all walked on into

The Tenth Room

It was all set up for what would obviously have been the grand finale. There were even plastic seats arranged, for us to watch the show. We sat down on the seats and we waited, but nobody from the circus came on, and, it became apparent to us all after some time, no one was going to come.

People began to shuffle into the next room. I heard a door open, and the noise of traffic and the rain.

I looked at Jane and Jonathan, and we got up and walked out. In the last room was an unmanned table upon which were laid out souvenirs of the circus: posters and CDs and badges, and an open cash box. Sodium yellow light spilled in from the street outside, through an open door, and the wind gusted at the unsold posters, flapping the corners up and down impatiently.

"Should we wait for her?" one of us said, and I wish I could say that it was me. But the others shook their heads, and we walked out into the rain, which had by now subsided to a low and gusty drizzle.

After a short walk down narrow roads, in the rain

and the wind, we found our way to the car. I stood on the pavement, waiting for the back door to be unlocked to let me in, and over the rain and the noise of the city I thought I heard a tiger, for, somewhere close by, there was a low roar that made the whole world shake. But perhaps it was only the passage of a train.

STRANGE LITTLE GIRLS

THE GIRLS

New Age
She seems so cool, so focused, so quiet, yet her eyes remain fixed upon the horizon.

You think you know all there is to know about her immediately upon meeting her, but everything you think you know is wrong. Passion flows through her like a river of blood.

She only looked away for a moment, and the mask slipped, and you fell. All your tomorrows start here.

Bonnie's Mother
You know how it is when you love someone?

And the hard part, the bad part, the *Jerry Springer Show* part is that you never stop loving someone. There's always a piece of them in your heart.

Now that she is dead, she tries to remember only the love. She imagines every blow a kiss, the makeup that inexpertly covers the bruises, the cigarette burn on her thigh—all these things, she decides, were gestures of love.

She wonders what her daughter will do.

She wonders what her daughter will be.

She is holding a cake, in her death. It is the cake she was always going to bake for her little one. Maybe they would have mixed it together.

They would have sat and eaten it and smiled, all three of them, and the apartment would have slowly filled with laughter and with love.

Strange
There are a hundred things she has tried to chase away the things she won't remember and that she can't even let herself think about because that's when the birds scream and the worms crawl and somewhere in her mind it's always raining a slow and endless drizzle.

You will hear that she has left the country, that there was a gift she wanted you to have, but it is lost before it reaches you. Late one night the telephone will sing, and a voice that might be hers will say something that you cannot interpret before the connection crackles and is broken.

Several years later, from a taxi, you will see someone in a doorway who looks like her, but she will be gone by the time you persuade the driver to stop. You will never see her again.

Whenever it rains you will think of her.

Silence
Thirty-five years a showgirl that she admits to, and her feet hurt, day in, day out, from the high heels, but she can walk down steps with a forty-pound headdress in high heels, she's walked across a stage with a lion in high heels, she could walk through goddamn Hell in high heels if it came to that.

These are the things that have helped, that kept her walking and her head high: her daughter; a man from Chicago who loved her, although not enough; the national news anchor who paid her rent for a decade and didn't come to Vegas more than once a month; two bags of silicone gel; and staying out of the desert sun.

She will be a grandmother soon, very soon.

Love

And then there was the time that one of them simply wouldn't return her calls to his office. So she called the number he did not know that she had, and she said to the woman who answered that this was so embarrassing but as he was no longer talking to her could he be told that she was still waiting for the return of her lacy black underthings, which he had taken because, he said, they smelled of her, of both of them. Oh, and that reminded her, she said, as the woman on the other end of the phone said nothing, could they be laundered first, and then simply posted back to her. He has her address. And then, her business joyfully concluded, she forgets him utterly and forever, and she turns her attention to the next.

One day she won't love you, too. It will break your heart.

Time

She is not waiting. Not quite. It is more that the years mean nothing to her anymore, that the dreams and the street cannot touch her.

She remains on the edges of time, implacable, unhurt, beyond, and one day you will open your eyes and see her; and after that, the dark.

It is not a reaping. Instead, she will pluck you, gently, like a feather, or a flower for her hair.

Rattlesnake

She doesn't know who owned the jacket originally. Nobody claimed it after a party, and she figured it looked good on her.

It says KISS, and she does not like to kiss. People, men and women, have told her that she is beautiful, and she has no idea what they mean. When she looks in the mirror she does not see beauty looking back at her. Only her face.

She does not read, watch TV, or make love. She listens to music. She goes places with her friends. She rides roller coasters but never screams when they plummet or twist and plunge upside down.

If you told her the jacket was yours she'd just shrug and give it back to you. It's not like she cares, not one way or the other.

Heart of Gold

—sentences.

Sisters, maybe twins, possibly cousins. We won't know unless we see their birth certificates, the real ones, not the ones they use to get ID.

This is what they do for a living. They walk in, take what they need, walk out again.

It's not glamorous. It's just business. It may not always be strictly legal. It's just business.

They are too smart for this, and too tired.

They share clothes, wigs, makeup, cigarettes. Restless and hunting, they move on. Two minds. One heart.

Sometimes they even finish each other's—

Monday's Child

Standing in the shower, letting the water run over her, washing it away, washing everything away, she realizes that what made it hardest was that it had smelled just like her own high school.

She had walked through the corridors, heart beating raggedly in her chest, smelling that school smell, and it all came back to her.

It was only, what, six years, maybe less, since it had been her running from locker to classroom, since she had watched her friends crying and raging and brooding over the taunts and the names and the thousand hurts that plague the powerless. None of them had ever gone this far.

She found the first body in a stairwell.

That night, after the shower, which could not wash what she had had to do away, not really, she said to her husband, "I'm scared."

"Of what?"

"That this job is making me hard. That it's making me someone else. Someone I don't know anymore."

He pulled her close and held her, and they stayed touching, skin to skin, until dawn.

Happiness

She feels at home on the range; ear protectors in position, man-shaped paper target up and waiting for her.

She imagines, a little, she remembers, a little and she sights and squeezes and as her time on the range begins she feels rather than sees the head and the heart obliterate. The smell of cordite always makes her think of the Fourth of July.

You use the gifts God gave you. That was what her mother had said, which makes their falling-out even harder, somehow.

Nobody will ever hurt her. She'll just smile her faint vague wonderful smile and walk away.

It's not about the money. It's never about the money.

Raining Blood

Here: an exercise in choice. Your choice. One of these tales is true.

She lived through the war. In 1959 she came to America. She now lives in a condo in Miami, a tiny Frenchwoman with white hair, with a daughter and a granddaughter. She keeps herself to herself and smiles rarely, as if the weight of memory keeps her from finding joy.

Or that's a lie. Actually the Gestapo picked her up during a border crossing in 1943, and they left her in a meadow. First she dug her own grave, then a single bullet to the back of the skull.

Her last thought, before that bullet, was that she was four months' pregnant, and that if we do not fight to create a future there will be no future for any of us.

There is an old woman in Miami who wakes, confused, from a dream of the wind blowing the wildflowers in a meadow.

There are bones untouched beneath the warm French earth which dream of a daughter's wedding. Good wine is drunk. The only tears shed are happy ones.

Real Men

Some of the girls were boys.

The view changes from where you are standing.

Words can wound, and wounds can heal.

All of these things are true.

HARLEQUIN VALENTINE

It is February the fourteenth, at that hour of the morning when all the children have been taken to school and all the husbands have driven themselves to work or been dropped, steambreathing and greatcoated at the rail station at the edge of the town for the Great Commute, when I pin my heart to Missy's front door. The heart is a deep dark red that is almost a brown, the color of liver. Then I knock on the door, sharply, *rat-a-tat-tat!*, and I grasp my wand, my stick, my oh-so-thrustable and beribboned lance and I vanish like cooling steam into the chilly air. . . .

Missy opens the door. She looks tired.

"My Columbine," I breathe, but she hears not a word. She turns her head, so she takes in the view from one side of the street to the other, but nothing moves. A truck rumbles in the distance. She walks back into the kitchen, and I dance, silent as a breeze, as a mouse, as a dream, into the kitchen beside her.

Missy takes a plastic sandwich bag from a paper box in the kitchen drawer, and a bottle of cleaning spray from under the sink. She pulls off two sections of paper towel from the roll on the kitchen counter. Then she walks back to the front door. She pulls the pin from the painted wood—it was my hatpin, which I had stumbled across . . . where? I turn the matter over in my head: in Gascony, perhaps? or Twickenham? or Prague?

The face on the end of the hatpin is that of a pale Pierrot.

She removes the pin from the heart, and puts the heart into the plastic sandwich bag. She wipes the blood from the door with a squirt of cleaning spray and a rub of paper towel, and she inserts the pin into her lapel, where the little white-faced August stares out at the cold world with his blind silver eyes and his grave silver lips. Naples. Now it comes back to me. I purchased the hatpin in Naples, from an old woman with one eye. She smoked a clay pipe. This was a long time ago.

Missy puts the cleaning utensils down on the kitchen table, then she thrusts her arms through the sleeves of her old blue coat, which was once her mother's, does up the buttons, one, two, three, then she places the sandwich bag with the heart in it determinedly into her pocket and sets off down the street.

Secret, secret, quiet as a mouse I follow her, sometimes creeping, sometimes dancing, and she never sees me, not for a moment, just pulls her blue coat more tightly around her, and she walks through the little Kentucky town, and down the old road that leads past the cemetery.

The wind tugs at my hat, and I regret, for a moment, the loss of my hatpin. But I am in love, and this is Valentine's Day. Sacrifices must be made.

Missy is remembering in her head the other times she has walked into the cemetery, through the tall iron cemetery gates: when her father died; and when they came here as kids at All Hallows', the whole school mob and caboodle of them, partying and scaring each other; and when a secret lover was killed in a three-car pileup on the interstate, and she waited until the end of the funeral, when the day was all over and done with, and she came in the evening, just before sunset, and laid a white lily on the fresh grave.

Oh Missy, shall I sing the body and the blood of you, the lips and the eyes? A thousand hearts I would give you, as your valentine. Proudly I wave my staff in the air and dance, singing silently of the gloriousness of me, as we skip together down Cemetery Road.

A low gray building, and Missy pushes open the door. She says Hi and How's it going to the girl at the desk who makes no intelligible reply, fresh out of school and filling in a crossword from a periodical filled with nothing but crosswords, page after page of them, and the girl would be making private phone calls on company time if only she had somebody to call, which she doesn't, and, I see, plain as elephants, she never will. Her face is a mass of blotchy acne pustules and acne scars and she thinks it matters, and talks to nobody. I see her life spread out before me: she will die, unmarried and unmolested, of breast cancer in fifteen years' time, and will be planted under a stone with her name on it in the meadow by Cemetery Road, and the first hands to have touched her breasts will have been those of the pathologist as he cuts out the cauliflowerlike stinking growth and mutters "Jesus, look at the size of this thing, why didn't she *tell* anyone?" which rather misses the point.

Gently, I kiss her on her spotty cheek, and whisper to her that she is beautiful. Then I tap her once, twice, *thrice,* on the head with my staff and wrap her with a ribbon.

She stirs and smiles. Perhaps tonight she will get drunk and dance and offer up her virginity upon Hymen's altar, meet a young man who cares more for her breasts than for her face, and will one day, stroking those breasts and suckling and rubbing them say "Honey, you seen anybody about that lump?" and by then her spots will be long gone, rubbed and kissed and frottaged into oblivion. . . .

But now I have mislaid Missy, and I run and caper down a dun-carpeted corridor until I see that blue coat pushing into a room at the end of the hallway and I follow her into an unheated room tiled in bathroom green.

The stench is unbelievable, heavy and rancid and

wretched on the air. The fat man in the stained lab coat wears disposable rubber gloves and has a thick layer of mentholatum on his upper lip and about his nostrils. A dead man is on the table in front of him. The man is a thin, old black man with callused fingertips. He has a thin mustache. The fat man has not noticed Missy yet. He has made an incision, and now he peels back the skin with a wet, sucking sound, and how dark the brown of it is on the outside, and how pink, pretty the pink of it is on the inside.

Classical music plays from a portable radio, very loudly. Missy turns the radio off, then she says, "Hello, Vernon."

The fat man says, "Hello Missy. You come for your old job back?"

This is the Doctor, I decide, for he is too big, too round, too magnificently well-fed to be Pierrot, too unselfconscious to be Pantaloon. His face creases with delight to see Missy, and she smiles to see him, and I am jealous: I feel a stab of pain shoot through my heart (currently in a plastic sandwich bag in Missy's coat pocket) sharper than I felt when I stabbed it with my hatpin and stuck it to her door.

And speaking of my heart, she has pulled it from her pocket, and is waving it at the pathologist, Vernon. "Do you know what this is?" she says.

"Heart," he says. "Kidneys don't have the ventricles, and brains are bigger and squishier. Where'd you get it?"

"I was hoping that you could tell me," she says. "Doesn't it come from here? Is it your idea of a Valentine's card, Vernon? A human heart stuck to my front door?"

He shakes his head. "Don't come from here," he says. "You want I should call the police?"

She shakes her head. "With my luck," she says, "they'll decide I'm a serial killer and send me to the chair."

The Doctor opens the sandwich bag and prods at the

heart with stubby fingers in latex gloves. "Adult, in pretty good shape, took care of his heart," he said. "Cut out by an expert."

I smile proudly at this, and bend down to talk to the dead black man on the table, with his chest all open and his callused string-bass-picking fingers. "Go 'way Harlequin," he mutters, quietly, not to offend Missy and his doctor. "Don't you go causing trouble here."

"Hush yourself. I will cause trouble wherever I wish," I tell him. "It is my function." But, for a moment, I feel a void about me: I am wistful, almost Pierrotish, which is a poor thing for a harlequin to be.

Oh Missy, I saw you yesterday in the street, and followed you into Al's Super-Valu Foods and More, elation and joy rising within me. In you, I recognized someone who could transport me, take me from myself. In you I recognized my Valentine, my Columbine.

I did not sleep last night, and instead I turned the town topsy and turvy, befuddling the unfuddled. I caused three sober bankers to make fools of themselves with drag queens from Madame Zora's Revue and Bar. I slid into the bedrooms of the sleeping, unseen and unimagined, slipping the evidence of mysterious and exotic trysts into pockets and under pillows and into crevices, able only to imagine the fun that would ignite the following day as soiled split-crotch fantasy panties would be found poorly hidden under sofa cushions and in the inner pockets of respectable suits. But my heart was not in it, and the only face I could see was Missy's.

Oh, Harlequin in love is a sorry creature.

I wonder what she will do with my gift. Some girls spurn my heart; others touch it, kiss it, caress it, punish it with all manner of endearments before they return it to my keeping. Some never even see it.

Missy takes the heart back, puts it in the sandwich bag again, pushes the snap-shut top of it closed.

"Shall I incinerate it?" she asks.

"Might as well. You know where the incinerator is," says the Doctor, returning to the dead musician on the table. "And I meant what I said about your old job. I need a good lab assistant."

I imagine my heart trickling up to the sky as ashes and smoke, covering the world. I do not know what I think of this, but, her jaw set, she shakes her head and she bids good-bye to Vernon the pathologist. She has thrust my heart into her pocket and she is walking out of the building and up Cemetery Road and back into town.

I caper ahead of her. Interaction would be a fine thing, I decide, and fitting word to deed I disguise myself as a bent old woman on her way to the market, covering the red spangles of my costume with a tattered cloak, hiding my masked face with a voluminous hood, and at the top of Cemetery Road I step out and block her way.

Marvelous, marvelous, marvelous me, and I say to her, in the voice of the oldest of women, "Spare a copper coin for a bent old woman dearie and I'll tell you a fortune will make your eyes spin with joy," and Missy stops. She opens her purse and takes out a dollar bill.

"Here," says Missy.

And I have it in my head to tell her all about the mysterious man she will meet, all dressed in red and yellow, with his domino mask, who will thrill her and love her and never, never leave her (for it is not a good thing to tell your Columbine the *entire* truth), but instead I find myself saying, in a cracked old voice, "Have you ever heard of Harlequin?"

Missy looks thoughtful. Then she nods. "Yes," she says. "Character in the commedia dell'arte. Costume covered in little diamond shapes. Wore a mask. I think he was a clown of some sort, wasn't he?"

I shake my head, beneath my hood. "No clown," I tell her. "He was . . ."

And I find that I am about to tell her the truth, so I

choke back the words and pretend that I am having the kind of coughing attack to which elderly women are particularly susceptible. I wonder if this could be the power of love. I do not remember it troubling me with other women I thought I had loved, other Columbines I have encountered over centuries now long gone.

I squint through old-woman eyes at Missy: she is in her early twenties, and she has lips like a mermaid's, full and well-defined and certain, and gray eyes, and a certain intensity to her gaze.

"Are you all right?" she asks.

I cough and splutter and cough some more, and gasp, "Fine, my dearie-duck, I'm just fine, thank you kindly."

"So," she said, "I thought you were going to tell me my fortune."

"Harlequin has given you his heart," I hear myself saying. "You must discover its beat yourself."

She stares at me, puzzled. I cannot change or vanish while her eyes are upon me, and I feel frozen, angry at my trickster tongue for betraying me. "Look," I tell her, "a rabbit!" and she turns, follows my pointing finger and as she takes her eyes off me I disappear, *pop!*, like a rabbit down a hole, and when she looks back there's not a trace of the old fortune-teller lady, which is to say me.

Missy walks on, and I caper after her, but there is no longer the spring in my step there was earlier in the morning.

Midday, and Missy has walked to Al's Super-Valu Foods and More, where she buys a small block of cheese, a carton of unconcentrated orange juice, two avocados, and on to the County One Bank where she withdraws two hundred and seventy-nine dollars and twenty-two cents, which is the total amount of money in her savings account, and I creep after her sweet as sugar and quiet as the grave.

"Morning Missy," says the owner of the Salt Shaker

Café, when Missy enters. He has a trim beard, more pepper than salt, and my heart would have skipped a beat if it were not in the sandwich bag in Missy's pocket, for this man obviously lusts after her and my confidence, which is legendary, droops and wilts. *I am Harlequin, I tell myself, in my diamond-covered garments, and the world is my harlequinade. I am Harlequin, who rose from the dead to play his pranks upon the living. I am Harlequin, in my mask, with my wand.* I whistle to myself, and my confidence rises, hard and full once more.

"Hey, Harve," says Missy. "Give me a plate of hash browns and a bottle of ketchup."

"That all?" he asks.

"Yes," she says. "That'll be perfect. And a glass of water."

I tell myself that the man Harve is Pantaloon, the foolish merchant that I must bamboozle, baffle, confusticate, and confuse. Perhaps there is a string of sausages in the kitchen. I resolve to bring delightful disarray to the world, and to bed luscious Missy before midnight: my Valentine's present to myself. I imagine myself kissing her lips.

There is a handful of other diners. I amuse myself by swapping their plates while they are not looking, but I have difficulty finding the fun in it. The waitress is thin, and her hair hangs in sad ringlets about her face. She ignores Missy, whom she obviously considers entirely Harve's preserve.

Missy sits at the table and pulls the sandwich bag from her pocket. She places it on the table in front of her.

Harve-the-pantaloon struts over to Missy's table, gives her a glass of water, a plate of hash-browned potatoes, and a bottle of Heinz 57 Varieties Tomato Ketchup. "And a steak knife," she tells him.

I trip him up on the way back to the kitchen. He curses, and I feel better, more like the former me, and I goose the waitress as she passes the table of an old man who is reading *USA Today* while toying with his salad. She gives the old man a filthy look. I chuckle, and then I find I am feeling most peculiar. I sit down upon the floor, suddenly.

"What's that, honey?" the waitress asks Missy.

"Health food, Charlene," says Missy. "Builds up iron." I peep over the tabletop. She is cutting up small slices of liver-colored meat on her plate, liberally doused in tomato sauce, and piling her fork high with hash browns. Then she chews.

I watch my heart disappearing into her rosebud mouth. My Valentine's jest somehow seems less funny.

"You anemic?" asks the waitress, on her way past once more, with a pot of steaming coffee.

"Not anymore," says Missy, popping another scrap of raw gristle cut small into her mouth, and chewing it, hard, before swallowing.

And as she finishes eating my heart, Missy looks down and sees me sprawled upon the floor. She nods. "Outside," she says. "Now." Then she gets up and leaves ten dollars beside her plate.

She is sitting on a bench on the sidewalk waiting for me. It is cold, and the street is almost deserted. I sit down beside her. I would caper around her, but it feels so foolish now I know someone is watching.

"You ate my heart," I tell her. I can hear the petulance in my voice, and it irritates me.

"Yes," she says. "Is that why I can see you?"

I nod.

"Take off that domino mask," she says. "You look stupid."

I reach up and take off the mask. She looks slightly disappointed. "Not much improvement," she says. "Now, give me the hat. And the stick."

I shake my head. Missy reaches out and plucks my hat

from my head, takes my stick from my hand. She toys with the hat, her long fingers brushing and bending it. Her nails are painted crimson. Then she stretches and smiles, expansively. The poetry has gone from my soul, and the cold February wind makes me shiver.

"It's cold," I tell her.

"No," she says, "it's perfect, magnificent, marvelous and magical. It's Valentine's Day, isn't it? Who could be cold upon Valentine's Day? What a fine and fabulous time of the year."

I look down. The diamonds are fading from my suit, which is turning ghost-white, Pierrot-white.

"What do I do now?" I ask her.

"I don't know," says Missy. "Fade away, perhaps. Or find another role . . . A lovelorn swain, perchance, mooning and pining under the pale moon. All you need is a Columbine."

"You," I tell her. "You are my Columbine."

"Not anymore," she tells me. "That's the joy of a harlequinade, after all, isn't it? We change our costumes. We change our roles."

She flashes me such a smile, now. Then she puts my hat, my own hat, my harlequin hat, up onto her head. She chucks me under the chin.

"And you?" I ask.

She tosses the wand into the air: it tumbles and twists in a high arc, red and yellow ribbons twisting and swirling about it, and then it lands neatly, almost silently, back into her hand. She pushes the tip down to the sidewalk, pushes herself up from the bench in one smooth movement.

"I have things to do," she tells me. "Tickets to take. People to dream." Her blue coat that was once her mother's is no longer blue, but is canary yellow, covered with red diamonds.

Then she leans over, and kisses me, full and hard upon the lips.

* * *

Somewhere a car backfired. I turned, startled, and when I looked back I was alone on the street. I sat there for several moments, on my own.

Charlene opened the door to the Salt Shaker Café. "Hey. Pete. Have you finished out there?"

"Finished?"

"Yeah. C'mon. Harve says your ciggie break is over. And you'll freeze. Back into the kitchen."

I stared at her. She tossed her pretty ringlets and, momentarily, smiled at me. I got to my feet, adjusted my white clothes, the uniform of the kitchen help, and followed her inside.

It's Valentine's Day, I thought. *Tell her how you feel. Tell her what you think.*

But I said nothing. I dared not. I simply followed her inside, a creature of mute longing.

Back in the kitchen a pile of plates was waiting for me: I began to scrape the leftovers into the pig bin. There was a scrap of dark meat on one of the plates, beside some half-finished ketchup-covered hash browns. It looked almost raw, but I dipped it into the congealing ketchup and, when Harve's back was turned, I picked it off the plate and chewed it. It tasted metallic and gristly, but I swallowed it anyhow, and could not have told you why.

A blob of red ketchup dripped from the plate onto the sleeve of my white uniform, forming one perfect diamond.

"Hey, Charlene," I called, across the kitchen. "Happy Valentine's Day." And then I started to whistle.

LOCKS

We owe it to each other to tell stories,
as people simply, not as father and daughter.
I tell it to you for the hundredth time:

"There was a little girl, called Goldilocks,
for her hair was long and golden,
and she was walking in the Wood and
*   she saw—"*

"—cows." You say it with certainty,
remembering the strayed heifers
    we saw in the woods
behind the house, last month.

"Well, yes, perhaps she saw cows,
but also she saw a house."

"—a great big house," you tell me.
"No, a little house, all painted, neat and tidy."

"A great big house."
You have the conviction of all two-year-olds.
I wish I had such certitude.

"Ah. Yes. A great big house.
And she went in . . ."

I remember, as I tell it, that the locks
of Southey's heroine had silvered with age.
The Old Woman and the Three Bears . . .
Perhaps they had been golden once,
    when she was a child.

And now, we are already up to the porridge,
"And it was too—"
"—hot!"
"And it was too—"
"—cold!"
And then it was, we chorus, *"just right."*

The porridge is eaten,
    the baby's chair is shattered,
Goldilocks goes upstairs,
    examines beds, and sleeps,
unwisely.
But then the bears return.
Remembering Southey still, I do the voices:
Father Bear's gruff boom scares you,
    and you delight in it.

When I was a small child and heard the tale,
if I was anyone I was Baby Bear,
my porridge eaten, and my chair destroyed,
my bed inhabited by some strange girl.

You giggle when I do the baby's wail,
*"Someone's been eating my porridge,
    and they've eaten it—"*

"All up," you say. A response it is,
Or an amen.

The bears go upstairs hesitantly,
their house now feels desecrated. They realize

what locks are for. They reach the bedroom.
"Someone's been sleeping in my bed."
And here I hesitate, echoes of old jokes,
soft-core cartoons, crude headlines, in my head.

One day your mouth will curl at that line.
A loss of interest, later, innocence.
Innocence, as if it were a commodity.
"And if I could," my father wrote to me,
huge as a bear himself, when I was younger,
"I would dower you with experience,
 without experience,"
and I, in my turn, would pass that on to you.
But we make our own mistakes. We sleep
unwisely.
The repetition echoes down the years.
When your children grow, when your
 dark locks begin to silver,
when you are an old woman,
 alone with your three bears,
what will you see? What stories will you tell?

*"And then Goldilocks jumped out of the window
and she ran—"*
Together, now: *"All the way home."*

And then you say, *"Again. Again. Again."*

We owe it to each other to tell stories.
These days my sympathy's with Father Bear.
Before I leave my house I lock the door,
and check each bed and chair on my return.

Again.

Again.

Again.

THE PROBLEM OF SUSAN

She has the dream again that night.

In the dream, she is standing, with her brothers and her sister, on the edge of the battlefield. It is summer, and the grass is a peculiarly vivid shade of green: a wholesome green, like a cricket pitch or the welcoming slope of the South Downs as you make your way north from the coast. There are bodies on the grass. None of the bodies are human; she can see a centaur, its throat slit, on the grass near her. The horse half of it is a vivid chestnut. Its human skin is nut-brown from the sun. She finds herself staring at the horse's penis, wondering about centaurs mating, imagines being kissed by that bearded face. Her eyes flick to the cut throat, and the sticky red-black pool that surrounds it, and she shivers.

Flies buzz about the corpses.

The wildflowers tangle in the grass. They bloomed yesterday for the first time in . . . how long? A hundred years? A thousand? A hundred thousand? She does not know.

All this was snow, she thinks, as she looks at the battlefield.

Yesterday, all this was snow. Always winter, and never Christmas.

Her sister tugs her hand, and points. On the brow of the green hill they stand, deep in conversation. The lion is golden, his arms folded behind his back. The witch is *dressed all in white. Right now she is shouting at the lion, who is simply listening. The children cannot make out any of their words, not her cold anger, nor the lion's thrum-deep replies. The witch's hair is black and shiny, her lips are red.*

In her dream she notices these things.

They will finish their conversation soon, the lion and the witch . . .

There are things about herself that the professor despises. Her smell, for example. She smells like her grandmother smelled, like old women smell, and for this she cannot forgive herself, so on waking she bathes in scented water and, naked and towel-dried, dabs several drops of Chanel toilet water beneath her arms and on her neck. It is, she believes, her sole extravagance.

Today she dresses in her dark brown dress suit. She thinks of these as her interview clothes, as opposed to her lecture clothes or her knocking-about-the-house clothes. Now she is in retirement, she wears her knocking-about-the-house clothes more and more. She puts on lipstick.

After breakfast, she washes a milk bottle, places it at her back door. She discovers that the next-door's cat has deposited a mouse head and a paw, on the doormat. It looks as though the mouse is swimming through the coconut matting, as though most of it is submerged. She purses her lips, then she folds her copy of yesterday's *Daily Telegraph,* and she folds and flips the mouse head and the paw into the newspaper, never touching them with her hands.

Today's *Daily Telegraph* is waiting for her in the hall, along with several letters, which she inspects, without opening any of them, then places on the desk in her tiny study. Since her retirement she visits her study only to write. Now she walks into the kitchen and seats herself at the old oak table. Her reading glasses hang about her neck on a silver chain, and she perches them on her nose and begins with the obituaries.

She does not actually expect to encounter anyone she knows there, but the world is small, and she observes that, perhaps with cruel humor, the obituarists have run a photograph of Peter Burrell-Gunn as he was in the early 1950s, and not at all as he was the last time the professor had seen him, at a *Literary Monthly* Christmas party several years before, all gouty and beaky and trembling, and reminding her of nothing so much as a caricature of an owl. In the photograph, he is very beautiful. He looks wild, and noble.

She had spent an evening once kissing him in a summer house: she remembers that very clearly, although she cannot remember for the life of her in which garden the summer house had belonged.

It was, she decides, Charles and Nadia Reid's house in the country. Which meant that it was before Nadia ran away with that Scottish artist, and Charles took the professor with him to Spain, although she was certainly not a professor then. This was many years before people commonly went to Spain for their holidays; it was an exotic and dangerous place in those days. He asked her to marry him, too, and she is no longer certain why she said no, or even if she had entirely said no. He was a pleasant-enough young man, and he took what was left of her virginity on a blanket on a Spanish beach, on a warm spring night. She was twenty years old, and had thought herself so old . . .

The doorbell chimes, and she puts down the paper, and makes her way to the front door, and opens it.

Her first thought is how young the girl looks.

Her first thought is how old the woman looks. "Professor Hastings?" she says. "I'm Greta Campion. I'm doing the profile on you. For the *Literary Chronicle*."

The older woman stares at her for a moment, vulnerable and ancient, then she smiles. It's a friendly smile, and Greta warms to her. "Come in, dear," says the professor. "We'll be in the sitting room."

"I brought you this," says Greta. "I baked it myself." She takes the cake tin from her bag, hoping its contents hadn't disintegrated en route. "It's a chocolate cake. I read on-line that you liked them."

The old woman nods and blinks. "I do," she says. "How kind. This way."

Greta follows her into a comfortable room, is shown to her armchair, and told, firmly, not to move. The professor bustles off and returns with a tray, on which are teacups and saucers, a teapot, a plate of chocolate biscuits, and Greta's chocolate cake.

Tea is poured, and Greta exclaims over the professor's brooch, and then she pulls out her notebook and pen, and a copy of the professor's last book, *A Quest for Meanings in Children's Fiction,* the copy bristling with Post-it notes and scraps of paper. They talk about the early chapters, in which the hypothesis is set forth that there was originally no distinct branch of fiction that was only intended for children, until the Victorian notions of the purity and sanctity of childhood demanded that fiction for children be made . . .

"Well, pure," says the professor.

"And sanctified?" asks Greta, with a smile.

"And sanctimonious," corrects the old woman. "It is difficult to read *The Water Babies* without wincing."

And then she talks about ways that artists used to draw children—as adults, only smaller, without considering the child's proportions—and how the Grimms' stories were collected for adults and, when the Grimms realized the books were being read in the nursery, were bowdlerized to make them more appropriate. She talks of Perrault's "Sleeping Beauty in the Wood," and of its original coda in which the Prince's cannibal ogre mother attempts to frame the Sleeping Beauty for having eaten her own children, and all the while Greta nods and takes notes, and nervously tries to contribute enough to the conversation that the professor will feel that it is a conversation or at least an interview, not a lecture.

"Where," asks Greta, "do you feel your interest in children's fiction came from?"

The professor shakes her head. "Where do any of our interests come from? Where does *your* interest in children's books come from?"

Greta says, "They always seemed the books that were most important to me. The ones that mattered. When I was a kid, and when I grew. I was like Dahl's *Matilda*. . . . Were your family great readers?"

"Not really. . . . I say that, it was a long time ago that they died. Were killed. I should say."

"All your family died at the same time? Was this in the war?"

"No, dear. We were evacuees, in the war. This was in a train crash, several years after. I was not there."

"Just like in Lewis's *Narnia* books," says Greta, and immediately feels like a fool, and an insensitive fool. "I'm sorry. That was a terrible thing to say, wasn't it?"

"Was it, dear?"

Greta can feel herself blushing, and she says, "It's just I remember that sequence so vividly. In *The Last Battle*. Where you learn there was a train crash on the way back to school, and everyone was killed. Except for Susan, of course."

The professor says, "More tea, dear?" and Greta knows that she should leave the subject, but she says, "You know, that used to make me so angry."

"What did, dear?"

"Susan. All the other kids go off to Paradise, and Susan can't go. She's no longer a friend of Narnia because she's too fond of lipsticks and nylons and invitations to parties. I even talked to my English teacher about it, about the problem of Susan, when I was twelve."

She'll leave the subject now, talk about the role of children's fiction in creating the belief systems we adopt as adults, but the professor says, "And tell me, dear, what did your teacher say?"

"She said that even though Susan had refused Paradise then, she still had time while she lived to repent."

"Repent *what?*"

"Not believing, I suppose. And the sin of Eve."

The professor cuts herself a slice of chocolate cake. She seems to be remembering. And then she says, "I doubt there was much opportunity for nylons and lipsticks after her family was killed. There certainly wasn't for me. A little money—less than one might imagine—from her parents' estate, to lodge and feed her. No luxuries . . ."

"There must have been something else wrong with Susan," says the young journalist, "something they didn't tell us. Otherwise she wouldn't have been damned like that—denied the Heaven of further up and further in. I mean, all the people she had ever cared for had gone on to their reward, in a world of magic and waterfalls and joy. And she was left behind."

"I don't know about the girl in the books," says the professor, "but remaining behind would also have meant that she was available to identify her brothers' and her little sister's bodies. There were a lot of people dead in that crash. I was taken to a nearby school—it was the first day of term, and they had taken the bodies there. My older brother looked okay. Like he was asleep. The other two were a bit messier."

"I suppose Susan would have seen their bodies, and thought, they're on holidays now. The perfect school holidays. Romping in meadows with talking animals, world without end."

"She might have done. I only remember thinking what a great deal of damage a train can do, when it hits another train, to the people who were traveling inside. I suppose you've never had to identify a body, dear?"

"No."

"That's a blessing. I remember looking at them and thinking, *What if I'm wrong, what if it's not him after all?* My younger brother was decapitated, you know. A god who would punish me for liking nylons and parties by making me walk through that school dining room, with the flies, to identify Ed, well . . . he's enjoying himself a bit too much, isn't he? Like a cat, getting the last ounce of enjoyment out of a mouse. Or a gram of enjoyment, I suppose it must be these days. I don't know, really."

She trails off. And then, after some time, she says, "I'm sorry dear. I don't think I can do any more of this today. Perhaps if your editor gives me a ring, we can set a time to finish our conversation."

Greta nods and says of course, and knows in her heart, with a peculiar finality, that they will talk no more.

That night, the professor climbs the stairs of her house, slowly, painstakingly, floor by floor. She takes sheets and blankets from the airing cupboard, and makes up a bed in the spare bedroom, at the back. It is empty but for a wartime austerity dressing table, with a mirror and drawers, an oak bed, and a dusty applewood wardrobe, which contains only coathangers and a cardboard box. She places a vase on the dressing table, containing purple rhododendron flowers, sticky and vulgar.

She takes from the box in the wardrobe a plastic shopping bag containing four old photographic albums. Then she climbs into the bed that was hers as a child, and lies there between the sheets, looking at the black-and-white photographs, and the sepia photographs, and the handful of unconvincing color photographs. She looks at her brothers, and her sister, and her parents, and she wonders how they could have been that young, how anybody could have been that young.

After a while she notices that there are several children's books beside the bed, which puzzles her slightly, because she does not believe she keeps books on the bedside table in that room. Nor, she decides, does she usually have a bedside table there. On the top of the pile is an old paperback book—it must be more than forty years old: the price on the cover is in shillings. It shows a lion, and two girls twining a daisy chain into its mane.

The professor's lips prickle with shock. And only then does she understand that she is dreaming, for she does not keep those books in the house. Beneath the paperback is a hardback, in its jacket, of a book that, in her dream, she has always wanted to read: *Mary Poppins Brings in the Dawn,* which P. L. Travers had never written while alive.

She picks it up and opens it to the middle, and reads the story waiting for her: Jane and Michael follow Mary Poppins on her day off, to Heaven, and they meet the boy Jesus, who is still slightly scared of Mary Poppins because she was once his nanny, and the Holy Ghost, who complains that he has not been able to get his sheet properly white since Mary Poppins left, and God the Father, who says, "There's no making her do anything. Not her. *She's* Mary Poppins."

"But you're God," said Jane. "You created everybody and everything. They have to do what you say."

"Not her," said God the Father once again, and he scratched his golden beard flecked with white. "I didn't create *her*. *She's* Mary Poppins."

And the professor stirs in her sleep, and afterward dreams that she is reading her own obituary. It has been a good life, she thinks, as she reads it, discovering her history laid out in black and white. Everyone is there. Even the people she had forgotten.

* * *

Greta sleeps beside her boyfriend, in a small flat in Camden, and she, too, is dreaming.

In the dream, the lion and the witch come down the hill together.

She is standing on the battlefield, holding her sister's hand. She looks up at the golden lion, and the burning amber of his eyes. "He's not a tame lion, is he?" she whispers to her sister, and they shiver.

The witch looks at them all, then she turns to the lion, and says, coldly, "I am satisfied with the terms of our agreement. You take the girls: for myself, I shall have the boys."

She understands what must have happened, and she runs, but the beast is upon her before she has covered a dozen paces.

The lion eats all of her except her head, in her dream. He leaves the head, and one of her hands, just as a housecat leaves the parts of a mouse it has no desire for, for later, or as a gift.

She wishes that he had eaten her head, then she would not have had to look. Dead eyelids cannot be closed, and she stares, unflinching, at the twisted thing her brothers have become. The great beast eats her little sister more slowly, and, it seems to her, with more relish and pleasure than it had eaten her; but then, her little sister had always been its favorite.

The witch removes her white robes, revealing a body no less white, with high, small breasts, and nipples so dark they are almost black. The witch lies back upon the grass, spreads her legs. Beneath her body, the grass becomes rimed with frost. "Now," she says.

The lion licks her white cleft with its pink tongue, until she can take no more of it, and she pulls its huge mouth to hers, and wraps her icy legs into its golden fur. . . .

Being dead, the eyes in the head on the grass cannot look away. Being dead, they miss nothing.

And when the two of them are done, sweaty and sticky and sated, only then does the lion amble over to the head on the grass and devour it in its huge mouth, crunching her skull in its powerful jaws, and it is then, only then, that she wakes.

Her heart is pounding. She tries to wake her boyfriend, but he snores and grunts and will not be roused.

It's true, Greta thinks, irrationally, in the darkness. *She grew up. She carried on. She didn't die.*

She imagines the professor, waking in the night and listening to the noises coming from the old applewood wardrobe in the corner: to the rustlings of all these gliding ghosts, which might be mistaken for the scurries of mice or rats, to the padding of enormous velvet paws, and the distant, dangerous music of a hunting horn.

She knows she is being ridiculous, although she will not be surprised when she reads of the professor's demise. *Death comes in the night,* she thinks, before she returns to sleep. *Like a lion.*

The white witch rides naked on the lion's golden back. Its muzzle is spotted with fresh, scarlet blood. Then the vast pinkness of its tongue wipes around its face, and once more it is perfectly clean.

INSTRUCTIONS

Touch the wooden gate in the wall
    you never saw before
Say "please" before you open the latch,
go through,
walk down the path.
A red metal imp hangs from the
    green-painted front door,
as a knocker,
do not touch it; it will bite your fingers.
Walk through the house. Take nothing.
    Eat nothing.
However,
if any creature tells you that it hungers,
feed it.
If it tells you that it is dirty,
clean it.
If it cries to you that it hurts,
if you can,
ease its pain.

From the back garden you will be able
    to see the wild wood.
The deep well you walk past leads down
    to Winter's realm;
there is another land at the bottom of it.
If you turn around here,

you can walk back, safely;
you will lose no face. I will think no less of you.

Once through the garden you will be
   in the wood.
The trees are old. Eyes peer
   from the undergrowth.
Beneath a twisted oak sits an old woman.
   She may ask for something;
give it to her. She
will point the way to the castle. Inside it
are three princesses.
Do not trust the youngest. Walk on.
In the clearing beyond the castle the
   twelve months sit about a fire,
warming their feet, exchanging tales.
They may do favors for you, if you are polite.
You may pick strawberries in December's frost.

Trust the wolves, but do not tell them
   where you are going.
The river can be crossed by the ferry.
   The ferryman will take you.
(The answer to his question is this:
If he hands the oar to his passenger, he
   will be free to leave the boat.
Only tell him this from a safe distance.)

If an eagle gives you a feather, keep it safe.
Remember: that giants sleep too soundly; that
witches are often betrayed by their appetites;
dragons have one soft spot, somewhere, always;
hearts can be well-hidden,
and you betray them with your tongue.
Do not be jealous of your sister:
know that diamonds and roses

are as uncomfortable when they tumble
    from one's lips as toads and frogs:
colder, too, and sharper, and they cut.

Remember your name.
Do not lose hope—what you seek will be found.
Trust ghosts. Trust those that you have
    helped to help you in their turn.
Trust dreams.
Trust your heart, and trust your story.

When you come back, return the way you came.
Favors will be returned, debts be repaid.
Do not forget your manners.
Do not look back.
Ride the wise eagle (you shall not fall)
Ride the silver fish (you will not drown)
Ride the gray wolf (hold tightly to his fur).

There is a worm at the heart of the tower;
    that is why it will not stand.

When you reach the little house, the
    place your journey started,
you will recognize it, although it will seem
    much smaller than you remember.
Walk up the path, and through the garden
    gate you never saw before but once.
And then go home. Or make a home.

Or rest.

HOW DO YOU THINK IT FEELS?

I am in bed, now. I can feel the linen sheets beneath me, warmed to body temperature, slightly rumpled. There is no one in bed with me. My chest no longer hurts. I feel nothing at all. I feel just fine.

My dreams are vanishing as I wake, overexposed by the glare of the morning sun through my bedroom window, and are being replaced, slowly, by memories; and now, with only a purple flower and the scent of her still on the pillow, my memories are all of Becky, and fifteen years drifts away like confetti or falling blossom through my hands.

She was just twenty. I was by far the older man, almost twenty-seven, with a wife, and a career, and twin little girls. And I was ready to give them all up for her.

We met at a conference, in Hamburg, in Germany. I had seen her performing in a presentation on the future of interactive entertainment, and had found her attractive and amusing. Her hair was long and dark, her eyes were a greenish blue. At first, I was certain that she reminded me of someone I knew, and then I realized that I had never actually met the person she reminded me of: it was Emma Peel, Diana Rigg's character in *The Avengers* television series. I had loved her and longed for her in black-and-white, before I ever reached my tenth birthday.

That evening, passing her in a corridor, on my way to

some software vendor's party, I congratulated her upon her performance. She told me that she was an actress, hired for the presentation ("after all, we can't all be in the West End, can we?") and that her name was Rebecca.

Later, I kissed her in a doorway, and she sighed as she pressed against me.

Becky slept in my hotel room for the rest of the conference. I was, head-over-heels, in love, and so, I liked to think, was she. Our affair continued when we returned to England: fizzy, funny, utterly delightful. It was love, I knew, and it tasted like champagne in my mind.

I spent all my free time with her, told my wife I was working late, needed in London, busy. Instead I was in Becky's Battersea flat with Becky.

I took joy in her body, the golden litheness of her skin, her blue-green eyes. She found it hard to relax during sex—she seemed to like the idea of it, but to be less impressed by the physical practicalities. She found oral sex faintly disgusting, giving or receiving it, and liked the sexual act best when it was over fastest. I hardly cared: the way she looked was enough for me, and the speed of her wit. I liked the way she made little doll-faces out of modeling clay, and the way the Plasticine crept in dark crescents under her fingernails. She had a beautiful voice, and sometimes, spontaneously, would begin to sing—popular songs, folk songs, snatches of opera, television jingles, whatever came into her mind. My wife did not sing, not even nursery rhymes to our girls.

Colors seemed brighter because Becky was there. I began to notice parts of life I had never seen before: I saw the elegant intricacy of flowers, because Becky loved flowers; I became a fan of silent movies, because Becky loved silent movies, and I watched *The Thief of Baghdad* and *Sherlock Junior* over and over; I began to accumulate CDs and tapes, because Becky loved music, and I loved her, and I loved to love what she loved. I had never heard music before; never understood the black-and-white grace of a silent clown before; never touched or smelled or properly looked at a flower, before I met her.

She told me that she needed to stop acting and to do something that would make her more money, and would bring that money in regularly. I put her in touch with a friend in the music business, and she became his personal assistant. I wondered, sometimes, if they were sleeping together, but I said nothing about it—I did not dare, although I brooded on it. I did not want to endanger what we had together, and I knew that I had no cause to reproach her.

"How do you think I feel?" she asked. We were walking back to her flat from the Thai restaurant around the corner. We ate there whenever I could be with her. "Knowing that you are going back to your wife, every night? How do you think it feels for me?"

I knew she was right. I did not want to hurt anyone, yet I felt as if I were tearing myself apart. My work, at the small computer company I owned, suffered. I began to nerve myself to tell my wife that I was leaving her. I envisioned Becky's joy at learning that I was to be only hers forevermore; it would be hard and hurtful to Caroline, my wife, and harder on the twins, but it would have to be done.

Each time I played with the twins, my two almost-identical girls (clue: look for the tiny mole above Amanda's lip, the rounder line of Jessica's jaw), their hair a lighter shade of Caroline's dark honey color, every time I took them to the park or bathed them or tucked them in at night, it hurt me inside. But I knew what I had to do; that the pain I was feeling would soon be replaced with the perfect joy that living with Becky, loving Becky, spending every waking moment with Becky, would bring me.

It was less than a week before Christmas, and the

days were as short as they were going to get. I took
Becky out to the Thai place for dinner, and, as she licked
the peanut sauce from a stick of chicken satay, I told her
that I would soon be leaving my wife and children for
her. I expected to see a smile on her face, but she said
nothing, and she did not smile.

In her flat, that night, she refused to sleep with me.
Instead, she told me it was over between us. I drank too
much, cried for the last time as an adult, begged and
pleaded with her to change her mind.

"You aren't any fun anymore," she said, simply and
flatly, as I sat, forlorn, on the floor of her living room,
my back resting against the side of her battered sofa.
"You used to be fun, and funny. Now you just mope
around all the time."

"I'm sorry," I said, pathetically. "Really, I'm sorry. I
can change."

"See?" she said. "Absolutely no fun at all."

Then she opened the door to her bedroom, and went
inside, closing it and locking it, finally, behind her; and I
sat on the floor and finished a bottle of whiskey, all on
my own, and then, maudlin drunk, I wandered about
her flat, touching her things and sniveling. I read her di-
ary. I went into the bathroom and pulled her soiled panties from the laundry basket, and buried my face in
them, breathing her scents. At one point I banged on her
bedroom door, calling her name, but she did not re-
spond, and she did not open the door.

I made the gargoyle for myself in the small hours of
the morning, out of gray modeling clay.

I remember doing it. I was naked. I had found a large
lump of Plasticine on the mantelpiece, and I thumbed
and kneaded it until it was soft and pliable, then, in a
place of drunken, horny, angry madness, I masturbated
into it, and kneaded my milky seed into the gray, shapeless mess.

I have never been a sculptor, but something took

shape beneath my fingers that night: blocky hands and
grinning head, stumpy wings and twisted legs: I made it
of my lust and self-pity and hatred, then I baptized it
with the last drops of Johnnie Walker Black Label and
placed it over my heart, my own little gargoyle, to protect me from beautiful women with blue-green eyes and
from ever feeling anything again.

I lay on the floor, with the gargoyle upon my chest;
and, in moments, I slept.

When I woke up, a few hours later, her door was still
locked, and it was still dark. I crawled to the bathroom,
and threw up all over the toilet bowl and the floor and
the scattered mess I had left of her underwear. And then
I went home.

I do not remember what I told my wife, when I got
home. Perhaps there were things she did not wish to
know. Don't ask, don't tell, all that. Perhaps Caroline
teased me about Christmas drinking. I can barely remember.

I did not ever return to the flat in Battersea.

I saw Becky every couple of years, in passing, on
the tube, or in the City, never comfortably. She seemed
brittle and awkward around me, as I was, I am sure,
around her. We would say hello, and she would con-
gratulate me on whatever my latest achievements were,
for I had taken my energies and channeled them into my
work, building something that was, if it was not (as it
was often called) an entertainment empire, at least a
small principality of music and drama and interactive
adventure.

Sometimes I would meet girls, smart, beautiful, wonderful girls and, as time went on, women for whom I
could have fallen; people I could have loved. But I did
not love them. I did not love anybody.

Heads and hearts: and in my head I tried not to think
about Becky, assured myself I did not love her, did not
need her, did not think about her. But when I did think

of her, memories of her smile, or of her eyes, then I felt pain. A sharp hurt inside my rib-cage, a perceptible, actual pain inside me, as if something were squeezing sharp fingers into my heart.

And it was at these times that I imagined that I could feel the little gargoyle in my chest. It would wrap itself, stone-cold, about my heart, protecting me, until I felt nothing at all; and I would return to my work.

Years passed: the twins grew up, and eventually they left home to go to college (one in the North of England, one in the South, my not-so-identical twins), and I left home too, leaving it with Caroline, and I moved into a large flat in Chelsea and lived on my own, and was, if not happy, then, at least content.

And then it was yesterday afternoon. Becky saw me first, in Hyde Park, where I was sitting on a bench, reading a paperback book in the springtime sun, and she ran over to me and touched my hand.

"Don't you remember your old friends?" she asked.

I looked up. "Hello, Becky."

"You haven't changed."

"Neither have you," I told her. I had silver-gray in my thick beard, and had lost most of my hair on the top, and she was a trim woman in her mid-thirties. I was not lying, though, and neither was she.

"You are doing very well," she said. "I read about you in the papers all the time."

"Just means that my publicity people are earning their keep. What are you doing these days?"

She was running the press office of an independent television network. She wished, she said, that she had stuck with acting, certain that she would, by now, have been on the West End stage. She ran her hand through her long, dark hair and smiled like Emma Peel, and I would have followed her anywhere. I closed my book and put it into the pocket of my jacket.

We walked through the park, hand in hand. The

spring flowers nodded their heads at us, yellow and orange and white, as we passed.

"Like Wordsworth," I told her. "Daffodils."

"Those are *narcissi*," she said. "Daffodils are a kind of *narcissus*."

It was spring in Hyde Park, and we were almost able to forget the city surrounding us. We stopped at an ice cream stand and bought two violently colored frozen ice cream confections.

"Was there someone else?" I asked her, eventually, as casually as I could, licking my ice cream. "Someone you left me for?"

She shook her head. "You were getting too serious," she said. "That was all. And I wasn't a homewrecker."

Later that night, much later, she repeated it. "I wasn't a homewrecker," she said, and she stretched, languorously, and added, "—then. Now, I don't care."

I had not actually told her that I was divorced. We had eaten sushi and sashimi in a restaurant in Greek Street, drunk enough sake to warm us and to cast a rice-wine glow over the evening. We took a golden-painted taxi back to my flat in Chelsea.

The wine was warm in my chest. In my bedroom we kissed and hugged and giggled. Becky examined my CD collection carefully, and then she put on the Cowboy Junkies' *The Trinity Sessions,* singing along in a quiet voice. This was only a few hours ago, but I cannot remember the point at which she removed her clothes. I remember her breasts, however, still beautiful, although they had lost the firmness and shape they had when she was little more than a girl: her nipples were deep red and pronounced.

I had put on some weight. She had not.

"Will you go down on me?" she whispered, when we reached my bed, and I did. Her labia were engorged, purple, full and long, and they opened like a flower to my mouth when I began to lick her. Her clitoris swelled beneath my tongue and the salty taste of her filled my world, and I licked and teased and sucked and nibbled at her sex for what felt like hours.

She came, once, spasmodically, under my tongue, and then she pulled my head up to hers, and we kissed some more, and then, finally, she guided me inside her.

"Was your cock that big fifteen years ago?" she asked.

"I think so," I told her.

"Mmm."

After a while she said, "I want you to come in my mouth." And, soon after, I did.

We lay in silence, side by side, and she said, "Do you hate me?"

"No," I said, sleepily. "I used to. I hated you for years. And I loved you, too."

"And now?"

"No, I don't hate you anymore. It's gone away. Floated off into the night, like a balloon." I realized as I said it that I was speaking the truth.

She snuggled closer to me, pressed her warm skin against my skin. "I can't believe I ever let you go. I won't make that mistake twice. I do love you."

"Thank you."

"Not, *thank you*, idiot. Try *I love you too*."

"I love you too," I echoed, and, sleepily, I kissed her still sticky lips.

And then I slept.

In my dream, I felt something uncurling inside me, something moving and changing. The cold of stone, a lifetime of darkness. A rending, and a ripping, as if my heart were breaking; a moment of utter pain. Blackness and strangeness and blood.

I must have dreamed the gray dawn as well. I opened my eyes, moving away from one dream but not entirely coming awake. My chest was open, a dark split that ran from my navel to my neck, and a huge, misshapen hand, Plasticine-gray, was pulling back into my chest. There was long dark hair caught between the stone fingers. The hand retreated into my chest as I watched, as an insect will vanish into a crack when the lights are turned on. And, as I squinted sleepily down at it, my acceptance of the strangeness of it all my only clue that this was truly another dream, the crack in my chest healed, knit and mended, and the cold hand vanished for good. I felt my eyes closing once more. I was tired, and I swam back into the comforting, sake-flavored dark.

I slept once more, but the rest of the dreams are now lost to me.

I awoke, completely, a few moments ago, the morning sun full on my face. There was nothing beside me in the bed but a purple flower on the pillow. I am holding it now. It reminds me of an orchid, although I know little enough of flowers, and its scent is strange, salty and female.

Becky must have placed it here for me to find when she left, while I slept.

Pretty soon now I shall have to get up. I shall get out of this bed and resume my life.

I wonder if I shall ever see her again, and I realize that I scarcely care. I can feel the sheets beneath me, and the cold air on my chest. I feel fine. I feel absolutely fine.

I feel nothing at all.

MY LIFE

"My life? Hell, you don't want to hear about
   my life. Jesus, my throat is dry. . . .
A drink? Well, since you're buying, and it's a
   hot day, sure. Why not. Just a little one.
Maybe a beer. And a whiskey chaser. It's
   good to drink, on a hot day. Only
Problem with drinking is it makes me
   remember. And sometimes I don't want
To remember. I mean, my mom: there was a
   woman. I never knew her as a woman
But I seen photographs of her, before the
   operation. She said I needed a father,
And seeing my own father had dumped her
   after he regained his eyesight (following
A blow on the head from a Burmese cat,
   which jumped from a penthouse apartment
   window and fell
Thirty stories, miraculously striking my father in
   exactly the right place to restore his sight,
And then landing uninjured on the sidewalk,
   proving it's true what they say about
Cats always landing on their feet) claiming he had
   thought he was marrying her twin sister
Who looked completely different, but had, through
   a miracle of biology, exactly the same voice
Which was why the judge granted the divorce,

closed his eyes and even he couldn't tell
   them apart.
So my father walked out a free man, and on the
   way from the court he was struck on the head
By detritus falling from the sky; there was folks
   said it was lavatorial waste from a plane
Though chemical examination revealed traces of
   elements unknown to science, and it said
In the papers that the fecal matter contained
   alien proteins, but then it was hushed up.
They took my father's body away for safekeeping.
   The government gave us a receipt
Though in a week it faded, I guess that it was
   something in the ink, but that's another story.
So then my mom announced I needed a man
   around the house and it was going to be her,
And she worked a deal with that doctor
   so when the two of them won the
   Underwater Tango contest
He agreed to change her sex for nothing. Growing
   up I called her Dad, and knew none of this.
Nothing else interesting has ever
   happened to me. Another drink?
Well, just to keep you company maybe, another
   beer, and don't forget the whiskey,
Hey, make it a double. It isn't that I drink, but
   it's a hot day, and even when you're
Not a drinking man. . . . You know,
It was just such a day as this my wife dissolved.
   I'd read about the people who blew up,
Spontaneous combustion, that's the words. But
   Mary-Lou—that was my wife's name,
We met the day she came out of her coma,
   seventy years asleep and hadn't aged a day,
It's scary what ball-lightning can do. And
   all the people on that submarine,

Like Mary-Lou, they all were froze in time,
    and after we were wed she'd visit them,
Sit by their bedsides, watch them while they
    slept. I drove a truck, back then.
And life was good. She coped well
    with the missing seven decades, and me,
    I like to think that if
The dishwasher had not been haunted—well,
    possessed, I guess, would be more accurate—
She'd still be here today. It preyed upon her mind,
    and the only exorcist that we could get
Turned out to be a midget from Utrecht
    and actually not a priest at all,
For all he had a candle, bell, and book. And
    by coincidence, the very day my wife,
All haunted by the washer, deliquesced—went
    liquid in our bed—my truck was stole.
That was when I left the States to travel round
    the world.
And life's been dull as ditchwater since then.
    Except . . . but no, my mind is going blank.
My memory's been swallowed by the heat.
    Another drink? Well, sure. . . ."

FIFTEEN PAINTED CARDS

FROM A VAMPIRE TAROT

0.

The Fool

"What do you want?"

The young man had come to the graveyard every night for a month now. He had watched the moon paint the cold granite and the fresh marble and the old moss-covered stones and statues in its cold light. He had started at shadows and at owls. He had watched courting couples and drunks and teenagers taking nervous shortcuts: all the people who come through the graveyard at night.

He slept in the day. Nobody cared. He stood alone in the night and shivered in the cold. It came to him then that he was standing on the edge of a precipice.

The voice came from the night all around him, in his head and out of it.

"What do you want?" it repeated.

He wondered if he dared to turn and look, realized he did not.

"Well? You come here every night, to a place where the living are not welcome. I have seen you. Why?"

"I wanted to meet you," he said, without looking around. "I want to live forever." His voice cracked as he said it.

He had stepped over the precipice. There was no going back. In his imagination, he could already feel the prick of needle-sharp fangs in his neck, a sharp prelude to eternal life.

The sound began. It was low and sad, like the rushing of an underground river. It took him several long seconds to recognize it as laughter.

"This is not life," said the voice.

It said nothing more, and after a while the young man knew he was alone in the graveyard.

1.

The Magician

They asked St. Germain's manservant if his master was truly a thousand years old, as it was rumored he had claimed.

"How would I know?" the man replied. "I have only been in the master's employ for three hundred years."

2.

The Priestess

Her skin was pale, and her eyes were dark, and her hair was dyed black. She went on a daytime talk show and proclaimed herself a vampire queen. She showed the cameras her dentally crafted fangs, and brought on ex-lovers who, in various stages of embarrassment, admitted that she had drawn their blood, and that she drank it.

"You can be seen in a mirror, though?" asked the talk show hostess. She was the richest woman in America, and had got that way by bringing the freaks and the hurt and the lost out in front of her cameras and showing their pain to the world.

The studio audience laughed.

The woman seemed slightly affronted. "Yes. Contrary to what people may think, vampires can be seen in mirrors and on television cameras."

"Well, that's one thing you finally got right, honey," said the hostess of the daytime talk show. But she put her hand over her microphone as she said it, and it was never broadcast.

5.

The Pope

This is my body, he said, two thousand years ago. *This is my blood.*

It was the only religion that delivered exactly what it promised: life eternal for its adherents.

There are some of us alive today who remember him. And some of us claim that he was a messiah, and some think that he was just a man with very special powers. But that misses the point. Whatever he was, he changed the world.

6.

The Lovers

After she was dead, she began to come to him in the night. He grew pale, and there were deep circles under his eyes. At first, they thought he was mourning her. And then, one night, he was gone.

It was hard for them to obtain permission to disinter her, but they got it. They hauled up the coffin and they unscrewed the lid. Then they prized what they found out of the box. There was six inches of water in the bottom; the iron had colored it a deep, orangish red. There were two bodies in the coffin: hers, of course, and his. He was more decayed than she was.

Later, someone wondered aloud how both of them had

fitted in a coffin built for one. Especially given her condition, he said; for she was very obviously very pregnant.

This caused some confusion, for she had not been noticeably pregnant when she was buried.

Still later they dug her up for one last time, at the request of the church authorities, who had heard rumors of what had been found in the grave. Her stomach was flat. The local doctor told them all that it had just been gas and bloating as the stomach swelled. The townsfolk nodded, almost as if they believed him.

7.

The Chariot

It was genetic engineering at its finest: they created a breed of human to sail the stars. They needed to be possessed of impossibly long life spans, for the distances between the stars were vast; space was limited, and their food supplies needed to be compact; they needed to be able to process local sustenance, and to colonize the worlds they found with their own kind.

The homeworld wished the colonists well and sent them on their way. They removed all traces of their location from the ships' computers first, however. To be on the safe side.

10.

The Wheel of Fortune

What did you do with the doctor? she asked, and laughed. I thought the doctor came in here ten minutes ago.

I'm sorry, I said. I was hungry.

And we both laughed.

I'll go find her for you, she said.

I sat in the doctor's office, picking my teeth. After a while the assistant came back.

I'm sorry, she said. The doctor must have stepped out for a while. Can I make an appointment for you for next week?

I shook my head. I'll call, I said. But, for the first time that day, I was lying.

11.

Justice

"It is not human," said the magistrate, "and it does not deserve the trial of a human thing."

"Ah," said the advocate. "But we cannot execute it without a trial: there are the precedents. A pig, that had eaten a child who had fallen into its sty. It was found guilty and hanged. A swarm of bees, found guilty of stinging an old man to death, was burned by the public hangman. We owe the hellish creature no less."

The evidence against the baby was incontestable. It amounted to this: a woman had brought the baby from the country. She said it was hers and that her husband was dead. She lodged at the house of a coach maker and his wife. The old coach maker complained of melancholia and lassitude, and was, with his wife and their lodger, found dead by their servant. The baby was alive in its cradle, pale and wide-eyed, and there was blood on its face and lips.

The jury found the little thing guilty beyond all doubt, and condemned it to death.

The executioner was the town butcher. In the sight of all the town he cut the babe in two, and flung the pieces onto the fire.

His own baby had died earlier that same week. Infant mortality in those days was a hard thing but common. The butcher's wife had been brokenhearted.

She had already left the town to see her sister in the city, and, within the week, the butcher joined her. The three of them—butcher, wife, and babe—made the prettiest family you ever did see.

14.

Temperance

She said she was a vampire. One thing I knew already, the woman was a liar. You could see it in her eyes. Black as coals they were, but she never quite looked at you, staring at invisibles over your shoulder, behind you, above you, two inches in front of your face.

"What does it taste like?" I asked her. This was in the parking lot, behind the bar. She worked the graveyard shift in the bar, mixed the finest drinks, but never drank anything herself.

"V8 juice," she said. "Not the low-sodium kind, but the original. Or a salty gazpacho."

"What's gazpacho?"

"A sort of vegetable soup."

"You're shitting me."

"No."

"So you drink blood? Just like I drink V8?"

"Not exactly," she said. "If *you* get sick of drinking V8 you can drink something else."

"Yeah," I said. "Actually, I don't like V8 much."

"See?" she said. "In China it's not blood we drink, it's spinal fluid."

"What's that taste like?"

"Nothing much. Clear broth."

"You've tried it?"

"I know people."

I tried to figure out if I could see her reflection in the wing mirror of the truck we were leaning against, but it was dark, and I couldn't tell.

15.

The Devil

This is his portrait. Look at his flat, yellow teeth, his ruddy face. He has horns, and he carries a foot-long wooden stake in one hand and his wooden mallet in the other.

Of course, there is no such thing as the devil.

16.

The Tower

The tower's built of spit and spite,
Without a sound, without a sight.
The biter bit, the bitter bite.
(It's better to be out at night.)

17.

The Star

The older, richer, ones follow the winter, taking the long nights where they find them. Still, they prefer the Northern Hemisphere to the South.

"You see that star?" they say, pointing to one of the stars in the constellation of Draco, the dragon. "We came from there. One day we shall return."

The younger ones sneer and jeer and laugh at this. Still, as the years become centuries, they find themselves becoming homesick for a place they have never been; and they find the northern climes reassuring, as long as Draco twines about the greater and lesser bears, up near chill Polaris.

19.

The Sun

"Imagine," she said, "that there was something in the sky that was going to hurt you, perhaps even kill you. A huge eagle or something. Imagine that if you went out in daylight the eagle would get you.

"Well," she said. "That's how it is for us. Only it's not a bird. It's bright, beautiful, dangerous daylight, and I haven't seen it now in a hundred years."

20.

Judgment

It's a way of talking about lust without talking about lust, he told them.

It is a way of talking about sex, and fear of sex, and death, and fear of death, and what else is there to talk about?

22.

The World

"You know the saddest thing," she said. "The saddest thing is that we're you."

I said nothing.

"In your fantasies," she said, "my people are just like you. Only better. We don't die or age or suffer from pain or cold or thirst. We're snappier dressers. We possess the wisdom of the ages. And if we crave blood, well, it is no more than the way you people crave food or affection or sunlight—and besides, it gets us out of the house. Crypt. Coffin. Whatever."

"And the truth is?" I asked her.

"We're you," she said. "We're you, with all your fuck-ups and all the things that make you human—all your fears and lonelinesses and confusions . . . none of that gets better.

"But we're colder than you are. Deader. I miss daylight and food and knowing how it feels to touch someone and care. I remember life, and meeting people as people and not just as things to feed on or control, and I remember what it was to *feel* something, anything, happy or sad or *anything . . .* " And then she stopped.

"Are you crying?" I asked.

"We don't cry," she told me. Like I said, the woman was a liar.

FEEDERS AND EATERS

This is a true story, pretty much. As far as that goes, and whatever good it does anybody.

It was late one night, and I was cold, in a city where I had no right to be. Not at that time of night, anyway. I won't tell you which city. I'd missed my last train, and I wasn't sleepy, so I prowled the streets around the station until I found an all-night café. Somewhere warm to sit.

You know the kind of place; you've been there: café's name on a Pepsi sign above a dirty plate-glass window, dried egg residue between the tines of all their forks. I wasn't hungry, but I bought a slice of toast and a mug of greasy tea, so they'd leave me alone.

There were a couple of other people in there, sitting alone at their tables, derelicts and insomniacs huddled over their empty plates, dirty coats and donkey jackets buttoned up to the neck.

I was walking back from the counter with my tray when somebody said, "Hey." It was a man's voice. "You," the voice said, and I knew he was talking to me, not to the room. "I know you. Come here. Sit over here."

I ignored it. You don't want to get involved, not with anyone you'd run into in a place like that.

Then he said my name, and I turned and looked at

him. When someone knows your name, you don't have any option.

"Don't you know me?" he asked. I shook my head. I didn't know anyone who looked like that. You don't forget something like that. "It's me," he said, his voice a pleading whisper. "Eddie Barrow. Come on mate. You know me."

And when he said his name I did know him, more or less. I mean, I knew Eddie Barrow. We had worked on a building site together, ten years back, during my only real flirtation with manual work.

Eddie Barrow was tall, and heavily muscled, with a movie star smile and lazy good looks. He was ex-police. Sometimes he'd tell me stories, true tales of fitting-up and doing-over, of punishment and crime. He had left the force after some trouble between him and one of the top brass. He said it was the Chief Superintendent's wife forced him to leave. Eddie was always getting into trouble with women. They really liked him, women.

When we were working together on the building site they'd hunt him down, give him sandwiches, little presents, whatever. He never seemed to *do* anything to make them like him; they just liked him. I used to watch him to see how he did it, but it didn't seem to be anything he did. Eventually, I decided it was just the way he was: big, strong, not very bright, and terribly, terribly good-looking.

But that was ten years ago.

The man sitting at the Formica table wasn't good-looking. His eyes were dull and rimmed with red, and they stared down at the tabletop without hope. His skin was gray. He was too thin, obscenely thin. I could see his scalp through his filthy hair. I said, "What happened to you?"

"How d'you mean?"

"You look a bit rough," I said, although he looked worse than rough; he looked dead. Eddie Barrow had been a big guy. Now he'd collapsed in on himself. All bones and flaking skin.

"Yeah," he said. Or maybe "Yeah?" I couldn't tell. Then, resigned, flatly, "Happens to us all in the end."

He gestured with his left hand, pointed at the seat opposite him. His right arm hung stiffly at his side, his right hand safe in the pocket of his coat.

Eddie's table was by the window, where anyone could see you walking past. Not somewhere I'd sit by choice, not if it was up to me. But it was too late now. I sat down facing him and I sipped my tea. I didn't say anything, which could have been a mistake. Small talk might have kept his demons at a distance. But I cradled my mug and said nothing. So I suppose he must have thought that I wanted to know more, that I cared. I didn't care. I had enough problems of my own. I didn't want to know about his struggle with whatever it was that had brought him to this state—drink, or drugs, or disease—but he started to talk, in a gray voice, and I listened.

"I came here a few years back, when they were building the bypass. Stuck around after, the way you do. Got a room in an old place around the back of Prince Regent's Street. Room in the attic. It was a family house, really. They only rented out the top floor, so there were just the two boarders, me and Miss Corvier. We were both up in the attic, but in separate rooms, next door to each other. I'd hear her moving about. And there was a cat. It was the family cat, but it came upstairs to say hello, every now and again, which was more than the family ever did.

"I always had my meals with the family, but Miss Corvier, she didn't ever come down for meals, so it was a week before I met her. She was coming out of the upstairs lavvy. She looked so old. Wrinkled face, like an old, old monkey. But long hair, down to her waist, like a young girl.

"It's funny, with old people, you don't think they feel things like we do. I mean, here's her, old enough to be my granny and . . ." He stopped. Licked his lips with a gray tongue. "Anyway . . . I came up to the room one night and there's a brown paper bag of mushrooms outside my door on the ground. It was a present, I knew that straight off. A present for me. Not normal mushrooms, though. So I knocked on her door.

"I says, are these for me?

"Picked them meself, Mister Barrow, she says.

"They aren't like toadstools or anything? I asked. Y'know, poisonous? Or funny mushrooms?

"She just laughs. Cackles even. They're for eating, she says. They're fine. Shaggy inkcaps, they are. Eat them soon now. They go off quick. They're best fried up with a little butter and garlic.

"I say, are you having some, too?

"She says, no. She says, I used to be a proper one for mushrooms, but not anymore, not with my stomach. But they're lovely. Nothing better than a young shaggy inkcap mushroom. It's astonishing the things that people don't eat. All the things around them that people could eat, if only they knew it.

"I said thanks, and went back into my half of the attic. They'd done the conversion a few years before, nice job really. I put the mushrooms down by the sink. After a few days they dissolved into black stuff, like ink, and I had to put the whole mess into a plastic bag and throw it away.

"I'm on my way downstairs with the plastic bag, and I run into her on the stairs, she says Hullo Mister B.

"I say, Hello Miss Corvier.

"Call me Effie, she says. How were the mushrooms?

"Very nice, thank you, I said. They were lovely.

"She'd leave me other things after that, little presents, flowers in old milk-bottles, things like that, then nothing. I was a bit relieved when the presents suddenly stopped.

"So I'm down at dinner with the family, the lad at the poly, he was home for the holidays. It was August. Really hot. And someone says they hadn't seen her for about a week, and could I look in on her. I said I didn't mind.

"So I did. The door wasn't locked. She was in bed. She had a thin sheet over her, but you could see she was naked under the sheet. Not that I was trying to see anything, it'd be like looking at your gran in the altogether. This old lady. But she looked so pleased to see me.

"Do you need a doctor? I says.

"She shakes her head. I'm not ill, she says. I'm hungry. That's all.

"Are you sure, I say, because I can call someone, it's not a bother. They'll come out for old people.

"She says, Edward? I don't want to be a burden on anyone, but I'm so hungry.

"Right. I'll get you something to eat, I said. Something easy on your tummy, I says. That's when she surprises me. She looks embarrassed. Then she says, very quietly, *Meat*. It's got to be fresh meat, and raw. I won't let anyone else cook for me. Meat. Please, Edward.

"Not a problem I says, and I go downstairs. I thought for a moment about nicking it from the cat's bowl, but of course I didn't. It was like, I knew she wanted it, so I had to do it. I had no choice. I went down to Safeways, and I bought her a packet of best ground sirloin.

"The cat smelled it. Followed me up the stairs. I said, you get down, puss. It's not for you, I said. It's for Miss Corvier and she's not feeling well, and she's going to need it for her supper, and the thing mewed at me as if it hadn't been fed in a week, which I knew wasn't true because its bowl was still half full. Stupid, that cat was.

"I knock on her door, she says Come in. She's still in the bed, and I give her the pack of meat, and she says Thank you Edward, you've got a good heart. And she starts to tear off the plastic wrap, there in the bed. There's a puddle of brown blood under the plastic tray, and it drips onto her sheet, but she doesn't notice. Makes me shiver.

"I'm going out the door, and I can already hear her starting to eat with her fingers, cramming the raw mince into her mouth. And she hadn't got out of bed.

"But the next day she's up and about, and from there on she's in and out at all hours, in spite of her age, and I think there you are. They say red meat's bad for you, but it did her the world of good. And raw, well, it's just steak tartare, isn't it? You ever eaten raw meat?"

The question came as a surprise. I said, "Me?"

Eddie looked at me with his dead eyes, and he said, "Nobody else at this table."

"Yes. A little. When I was a small boy—four, five years old—my grandmother would take me to the butcher's with her, and he'd give me slices of raw liver, and I'd just eat them, there in the shop, like that. And everyone would laugh."

I hadn't thought of that in twenty years. But it was true.

I still like my liver rare, and sometimes, if I'm cooking and if nobody else is around, I'll cut a thin slice of raw liver before I season it, and I'll eat it, relishing the texture and the naked, iron taste.

"Not me," he said. "I liked my meat properly cooked. So the next thing that happened was Thompson went missing."

"Thompson?"

"The cat. Somebody said there used to be two of them, and they called them Thompson and Thompson. I don't know why. Stupid, giving them both the same name. The first one was squashed by a lorry." He pushed at a small mound of sugar on the Formica top with a fingertip. His left hand, still. I was beginning to wonder whether he had a right arm. Maybe the sleeve was empty. Not that it was any of my business. Nobody gets through life without losing a few things on the way.

I was trying to think of some way of telling him I
didn't have any money, just in case he was going to ask
me for something when he got to the end of his story. I
didn't have any money: just a train ticket and enough
pennies for the bus ticket home.

"I was never much of a one for cats," he said suddenly. "Not really. I liked dogs. Big, faithful things. You
knew where you were with a dog. Not cats. Go off for
days on end, you don't see them. When I was a lad, we
had a cat, it was called Ginger. There was a family down
the street, they had a cat they called Marmalade. Turned
out it was the same cat, getting fed by all of us. Well, I
mean. Sneaky little buggers. You can't trust them.

"That was why I didn't think anything when Thompson went away. The family was worried. Not me. I knew
it'd come back. They always do.

"Anyway, a few nights later, I heard it. I was trying to
sleep, and I couldn't. It was the middle of the night, and
I heard this mewing. Going on, and on, and on. It wasn't
loud, but when you can't sleep these things just get on
your nerves. I thought maybe it was stuck up in the raf-
ters, or out on the roof outside. Wherever it was, there
wasn't any point in trying to sleep through it. I knew
that. So I got up, and I got dressed, even put my boots
on in case I was going to be climbing out onto the roof,
and I went looking for the cat.

"I went out in the corridor. It was coming from Miss
Corvier's room on the other side of the attic. I knocked
on her door, but no one answered. Tried the door. It
wasn't locked. So I went in. I thought maybe that the cat
was stuck somewhere. Or hurt. I don't know. I just wanted
to help, really.

"Miss Corvier wasn't there. I mean, you know sometimes if there's anyone in a room, and that room was
empty. Except there's something on the floor in the corner going *Mrie, Mrie. . . .* And I turned on the light to
see what it was."

He stopped then for almost a minute, the fingers of his left hand picking at the black goo that had crusted around the neck of the ketchup bottle. It was shaped like a large tomato. Then he said, "What I didn't understand was how it could still be alive. I mean, it was. And from the chest up, it was alive, and breathing, and fur and everything. But its back legs, its rib cage. Like a chicken carcass. Just bones. And what are they called, sinews? And, it lifted its head, and it looked at me.

"It may have been a cat, but I knew what it wanted. It was in its eyes. I mean." He stopped. "Well, I just knew. I'd never seen eyes like that. You would have known what it wanted, all it wanted, if you'd seen those eyes. I did what it wanted. You'd have to be a monster not to."

"What did you do?"

"I used my boots." Pause. "There wasn't much blood. Not really. I just stamped, and stamped on its head, until there wasn't really anything much left that looked like anything. If you'd seen it looking at you like that, you would have done what I did."

I didn't say anything.

"And then I heard someone coming up the stairs to the attic, and I thought I ought to do something, I mean, it didn't look good, I don't know what it must have looked like really, but I just stood there, feeling stupid, with a stinking mess on my boots, and when the door opens, it's Miss Corvier.

"And she sees it all. She looks at me. And she says, You killed him. I can hear something funny in her voice, and for a moment I don't know what it is, and then she comes closer, and I realize that she's crying.

"That's something about old people, when they cry like children, you don't know where to look, do you? And she says, He was all I had to keep me going, and you killed him. After all I've done, she says, making it so the meat stays fresh, so the life stays on. After all I've done.

"I'm an old woman, she says. I need my meat.

"I didn't know what to say.

"She's wiping her eyes with her hand. I don't want to be a burden on anybody, she says. She's crying now. And she's looking at me. She says, I never wanted to be a burden. She says, that was my meat. Now, she says, who's going to feed me now?"

He stopped, rested his gray face in his left hand, as if he was tired. Tired of talking to me, tired of the story, tired of life. Then he shook his head and looked at me and said, "If you'd seen that cat, you would have done what I did. Anyone would have done."

He raised his head then, for the first time in his story, looked me in the eyes. I thought I saw an appeal for help in his eyes, something he was too proud to say aloud.

Here it comes, I thought. This is where he asks me for money.

Somebody outside tapped on the window of the café. It wasn't a loud tapping, but Eddie jumped. He said, "I have to go now. That means I have to go."

I just nodded. He got up from the table. He was still a tall man, which almost surprised me: he'd collapsed in on himself in so many other ways. He pushed the table away as he got up, and as he got up he took his right hand out of his coat pocket. For balance, I suppose. I don't know.

Maybe he wanted me to see it. But if he wanted me to see it, why did he keep it in his pocket the whole time? No, I don't think he wanted me to see it. I think it was an accident.

He wasn't wearing a shirt or a jumper under his coat, so I could see his arm, and his wrist. Nothing wrong with either of them. He had a normal wrist. It was only when you looked below the wrist that you saw most of the flesh had been picked from the bones, chewed like chicken wings, leaving only dried morsels of meat, scraps and crumbs, and little else. He only had three fingers left, and most of a thumb. I suppose the other finger bones must have just fallen right off, with no skin or flesh to hold them on.

That was what I saw. Only for a moment, then he put his hand back in his pocket and pushed out of the door into the chilly night.

I watched him then, through the dirty plate-glass of the café window.

It was funny. From everything he'd said, I'd imagined Miss Corvier to be an old woman. But the woman waiting for him, outside, on the pavement, couldn't have been much over thirty. She had long, long hair, though. The kind of hair you can sit on, as they say, although that always sounds faintly like a line from a dirty joke. She looked a bit like a hippy, I suppose. Sort of pretty, in a hungry kind of way.

She took his arm and looked up into his eyes, and they walked away out of the café's light for all the world like a couple of teenagers who were just beginning to realize that they were in love.

I went back up to the counter and bought another cup of tea and a couple of packets of crisps to see me through until the morning, and I sat and thought about the expression on his face when he'd looked at me that last time.

On the milk train back to the big city I sat opposite a woman carrying a baby. It was floating in formaldehyde, in a heavy glass container. She needed to sell it, rather urgently, and although I was extremely tired we talked about her reasons for selling it, and about other things, for the rest of the journey.

DISEASEMAKER'S CROUP

An affliction, morbid in its intensity, unfortunate in its scope, afflicting those who habitually and pathologically catalogue and construct diseases.

Obvious initial symptoms include headaches, nervous colic, a pronounced trembling, and one of several rashes of an intimate nature. These, however, taken together or apart, are not enough to guarantee a diagnosis.

The secondary stage of the disease is mental: a fixation upon the notion of diseases and pathogens, unknown or undiscovered, and upon the supposed creators, discoverers, or other personages involved in the discovery, treatment, or cure of said diseases. Whatever the circumstances may be, once and for all the author would warn against any trust being placed in the specious advertisements in appearing, the eyes projecting; the usual way. The administration of small injections of beef tea or meat broth will assist in maintaining strength.

At these stages the disease may be treatable.

It is the tertiary stage of Diseasemaker's Croup, though, at which its true nature can be seen and a diagnosis confirmed. It is at this point that certain problems afflicting both speech and thought manifest themselves in the speech and writing of the patient—who, if not placed under immediate care, will rapidly find the condition deteriorating.

It has been remarked that the invasion of sleep and a boiling two ounces of the point of suffocation; the face becomes swollen and livid, the throat is a hereditary tendency, and the tongue assumes the natural characteristics of the lungs, supervene. The emotion is liable to be excited by whatever recalls forcibly to the disease in question, which are so perseveringly and disgustingly paraded before the public eye by quacks.

Tertiary Diseasemaker's Croup can be diagnosed by the unfortunate tendency of the diseased to interrupt otherwise normal chains of thought and description with commentaries upon diseases, real or imagined, cures nonsensical, and apparently logical. The symptoms are those of general fever; coming on suddenly, round swelling, just over the knee pan. When quite chronic, and finally, perhaps vomiting, offensive fogs. Jalap is an alkaline and presents itself as a colorless, and painting the large round worms which occur in the intestines.

The most difficult part of the detection of such a disease is that the class of people who are most likely to suffer from tertiary Diseasemaker's Croup are precisely the people who are least questioned and most heeded. Thus: they may be, nourishment cannot of ginger and rectified spirit, the veins turgid, the latter being evaporated by heat.

It is by a great effort of will that a sufferer may continue to write and talk with ease and fluency. Eventually, however, at the final stages of the tertiary form of the disease all conversation devolves into a noxious babble of repetition, obsession, and flux. Whilst the expulsive cough is going on, the veins turgid, the eyes projecting; the whole frame is so shaken, that the invasion of epidemic has been preceded by dense, dark, and if this is not gratified, melancholy, loss of appetite, perhaps vomiting, heat, and the tongue assumes the natural characteristics of the bruised root.

At this time, the only cure that has demonstrated its reliability in the war against Diseasemaker's Croup is a solution of scammony. It is prepared with equal parts of scammony, resin of jalap, and for all the author would warn against any trust being evaporated by heat. Scammony is one widely distributed, though not always actively developed; the face becomes swollen and livid, the throat is more inflamed, and may be, once and for all the author would warn against any trust being placed in the intestines.

Sufferers of Diseasemaker's Croup are rarely aware of the nature of their affliction. Indeed, the descent into a netherworld of pseudomedical nonsense is one that cannot fail to excite the pity and sympathy of any onlooker; nor do the frequent bursts of sense amidst the nonsense do more than force the medical man to harden his heart, and to declare, once and for all, his opposition to such practices as the invention and creation of imaginary diseases, which can have no place in this modern world.

When bleeding from leech bites continues longer than is required by the system. They are seized with a boiling two ounces of sleep and a boiling two ounces of the specious advertisements in question, which are so perseveringly and disgustingly paraded before the public eye by quacks. Scammony is liable to be excited by heat. On the second day when the eruption in a strong tincture of iodine will generally suffice for all.

This is not madness.

This is such pain.

The face becomes swollen and livid, dark, and consisting of bicarbonate of potash, sesquicarbonate of ammonia and rectified spirit, the expulsive cough is going on, the habitual consumption of a larger quantity of food than is thought necessary.

When the mind the beloved scenes.

Whilst the beloved scenes.

They may also become enlarged.

IN THE END

In the end, the Lord gave Mankind the world. All the world was Man's, save for one garden. *This is my garden,* said the Lord, *and here you shall not enter.*

There was a man and a woman who came to the garden, and their names were Earth and Breath.

They had with them a small fruit which the Man carried, and when they arrived at the gate to the garden, the Man gave the fruit to the Woman, and the Woman gave the fruit to the Serpent with the flaming sword who guarded the Eastern Gate.

And the Serpent took the fruit and placed it upon a tree in the center of the garden.

Then Earth and Breath knew their clothedness, and removed their garments, one by one, until they were naked; and when the Lord walked through the garden he saw the man and the woman, who no longer knew good from evil, but were satisfied, and He saw it was good.

Then the Lord opened the gates and gave Mankind the garden, and the Serpent raised up, and it walked away proudly on four strong legs; and where it went none but the Lord can say.

And after that there was nothing but silence in the Garden, save for the occasional sound of the man taking away its name from another animal.

GOLIATH

I suppose I could claim that I had always suspected that the world was a cheap and shoddy sham, a bad cover for something deeper and weirder and infinitely more strange, and that, in some way, I already knew the truth. But I think that's just how the world has always been. And even now that I know the truth—as you will, my love, if you're reading this—the world still seems cheap and shoddy. Different world, different shoddy, but that's how it feels.

They say, *Here's the truth,* and I say, *Is that all there is?* And they say, *Kind of. Pretty much. As far as we know.*

So. It was 1977, and the nearest I had come to computers was I'd recently bought a big, expensive calculator, and then I'd lost the manual that came with it, so I didn't know what it did anymore. I'd add, subtract, multiply, and divide, and was grateful I had no need to cos, sine, or find tangents or graph functions or whatever else the gizmo did, because, having recently been turned down by the RAF, I was working as a bookkeeper for a small discount carpet warehouse in Edgware, in north London, near the top of the Northern Line. I pretended that it didn't hurt whenever I'd see a plane overhead, that I didn't care that there was a world my size denied me. I just wrote down the numbers in a big double-entry book. I was sitting at the table at the back of the warehouse that served me as a desk when the world began to melt and drip away.

Honest. It was like the walls and the ceiling and the rolls of carpet and the *News of the World* topless calendar were all made of wax, and they started to ooze and run, to flow together and to drip. I could see the houses and the sky and the clouds and the road behind them, and then *that* dripped and flowed away, and behind it all was blackness.

I was standing in the puddle of the world, a weird, brightly colored thing that oozed and brimmed and didn't cover the tops of my brown leather shoes. (I have feet like shoeboxes. Boots have to be specially made for me. Costs me a fortune.) The puddle cast a weird light upward.

In fiction, I think I would have refused to believe it was happening, would've wondered if I'd been drugged or if I was dreaming. In reality, hell, I was there and it was real, so I stared up into the darkness, and then, when nothing more happened, I began to walk, splashing through the liquid world, calling out, seeing if anyone was about.

Something flickered in front of me.

"Hey fella," said a voice. The accent was American, although the intonation was odd.

"Hello," I said.

The flickering continued for a few moments, and then resolved itself into a smartly dressed man in thick horn-rimmed spectacles.

"You're a pretty big guy," he said. "You know that?"

Of course I knew that. I was nineteen years old and even then I was close to seven feet tall. I have fingers like bananas. I scare children. I'm unlikely to see my fortieth birthday: people like me die young.

"What's going on?" I asked. "Do you know?"

"Enemy missile took out a central processing unit," he said. "Two hundred thousand people, hooked up in parallel, blown to dead meat. We've got a mirror going of course, and we'll have it all up and running again in next to no time. You're just free-floating here for a couple of nanoseconds, while we get London processing once more."

"Are you God?" I asked. Nothing he had said had made any sense to me.

"Yes. No. Not really," he said. "Not as you mean it, anyway."

And then the world lurched and I found myself coming to work again that morning, poured myself a cup of tea, had the longest, strangest bout of *déjà vu* I've ever had. Twenty minutes, where I knew everything that anyone was going to do or say. And then it went, and time passed properly once more, every second following every other second just like they're meant to.

And the hours passed, and the days, and the years.

I lost my job in the carpet company and got a new job bookkeeping for a company that sold business machines. I got married to a girl called Sandra I met at the swimming baths and we had a couple of kids, both normal sized, and I thought I had the sort of marriage that could survive anything, but I hadn't, so she went away and she took the kiddies with her. I was in my late twenties, and it was 1986, and I got a job in a little shop on Tottenham Court Road selling computers, and I turned out to be good at it.

I liked computers.

I liked the way they worked. It was an exciting time. I remember our first shipment of ATs, some of them with 40-megabyte hard drives. . . . Well, I was impressed easily back then.

I still lived in Edgware, commuted to work on the Northern Line. I was on the tube one evening, going home—we'd just gone through Euston and half the passengers had got off—and I was looking at the other people in the carriage over the top of the *Evening Standard* and wondering who they were, who they really were, inside: the thin, black girl writing earnestly in her notebook, the little old lady with the green velvet hat on, the girl with the dog, the bearded man with the turban. . . .

The tube stopped in the tunnel.

That was what I thought happened, anyway: I thought the tube had stopped. Everything went very quiet.

And then we went through Euston, and half the passengers got off.

And then we went through Euston, and half the passengers got off. And I was looking at the other passengers and wondering who they really were inside when the train stopped in the tunnel, and everything went very quiet.

And then everything lurched so hard I thought we'd been hit by another train.

And then we went through Euston, and half the passengers got off, and then the train stopped in the tunnel, and then everything went—

(*Normal service will be resumed as possible,* whispered a voice in the back of my head.)

And this time as the train slowed and began to approach Euston I wondered if I was going crazy: I felt like I was jerking back and forth on a video loop. I knew it was happening, but there was nothing I could do to change anything, nothing I could do to break out of it.

The black girl sitting next to me passed me a note. ARE WE DEAD? it said.

I shrugged. I didn't know. It seemed as good an explanation as any.

Slowly, everything faded to white.

There was no ground beneath my feet, nothing above me, no sense of distance, no sense of time. I was in a white place. And I was not alone.

The man wore thick horn-rimmed spectacles, and a

suit that looked like it might have been an Armani. "You again?" he said. "The big guy. I just spoke to you."

"I don't think so," I said.

"Half an hour ago. When the missiles hit."

"In the carpet factory? That was years ago. Half a lifetime."

"About thirty-seven minutes back. We've been running in an accelerated mode since then, trying to patch and cover, while we've been processing potential solutions."

"Who sent the missiles?" I asked. "The U.S.S.R.? The Iranians?"

"Aliens," he said.

"You're kidding?"

"Not as far as we can tell. We've been sending out seed probes for a couple of hundred years now. Looks like something has followed one back. We learned about it when the first missiles landed. It's taken us a good twenty minutes to get a retaliatory plan up and running. That's why we've been processing in overdrive. Did it seem like the last decade went pretty fast?"

"Yeah. I suppose."

"That's why. We ran it through pretty fast, trying to maintain a common reality while coprocessing."

"So what are you going to do?"

"We're going to counterattack. We're going to take them out. I'm afraid it will take a while: we don't have the machinery yet. We have to build it."

The white was fading now, fading into dark pinks and dull reds. I opened my eyes. For the first time. I choked on it. It was too much to take in.

So. Sharp the world and tangled-tubed and strange and dark and somewhere beyond belief. It made no sense. Nothing made sense. It was real, and it was a nightmare. It lasted for thirty seconds, and each cold second felt like a tiny forever.

And then we went through Euston, and half the passengers got off. . . .

I started talking to the black girl with the notebook. Her name was Susan. Several weeks later she moved in with me.

Time rumbled and rolled. I suppose I was becoming sensitive to it. Maybe I knew what I was looking for—knew there *was* something to look for, even if I didn't know what it was.

I made the mistake of telling Susan some of what I believed one night—about how none of this was real. About how we were really just hanging there, plugged and wired, central processing units or just cheap memory chips for some computer the size of the world, being fed a consensual hallucination to keep us happy, to allow us to communicate and dream using the tiny fraction of our brains that weren't being used by them—whoever *they* were—to crunch numbers and store information.

"We're memory," I told her. "That's what we are. Memory."

"You don't really believe this stuff," she told me, and her voice was trembling. "It's a story."

When we made love, she always wanted me to be rough with her, but I never dared. I didn't know my own strength, and I'm so clumsy. I didn't want to hurt her.

I never wanted to hurt her, so I stopped telling her my ideas, tried to kiss it better, to pretend it had all been a joke, just not the funny kind. . . .

It didn't matter. She moved out the following weekend.

I missed her, deeply, painfully. But life goes on.

The moments of déjà vu were coming more frequently now. Moments would stutter and hiccup and falter and repeat. Sometimes whole mornings would repeat. Once I lost a day. Time seemed to be breaking down entirely.

And then I woke up one morning and it was 1975 again, and I was sixteen, and after a day of hell at school I was walking out of school, into the RAF recruiting office next to the kebab house in Chapel Road.

"You're a big lad," said the recruiting officer. I thought he was American at first, but he said he was Canadian. He wore big horn-rimmed glasses.

"Yes," I said.

"And you want to fly?"

"More than anything." It seemed like I half-remembered a world in which I'd forgotten that I wanted to fly planes, which seemed as strange to me as forgetting my own name.

"Well," said the horn-rimmed man, "we're going to have to bend a few rules. But we'll have you up in the air in no time." And he meant it, too.

The next few years passed really fast. It seemed like I spent all of them in planes of different kinds, cramped into tiny cockpits, in seats I barely fitted, flicking switches too small for my fingers.

I got Secret clearance, then I got Noble clearance, which leaves Secret clearance in the shade, and then I got Graceful clearance, which the Prime Minister himself doesn't have, by which time I was piloting flying saucers and other craft that moved with no visible means of support.

I started dating a girl called Sandra, and then we got married, because if we married we got to move into married quarters, which was a nice little semi-detached house near Dartmoor. We never had any children: I had been warned that it was possible I might have been exposed to enough radiation to fry my gonads, and it seemed sensible not to try for kids, under the circumstances: didn't want to breed monsters.

It was 1985 when the man with horn-rimmed spectacles walked into my house.

My wife was at her mother's that week. Things had got a bit tense, and she'd moved out to buy herself some "breathing room." She said I was getting on her nerves. But if I was getting on anyone's nerves, I think they must have been my own. It seemed like I knew what was go-

ing to happen all the time. Not just me: it seemed like
everyone knew what was going to happen. Like we were
sleepwalking through our lives for the tenth or the twen-
tieth or the hundredth time.

I wanted to tell Sandra, but somehow I knew better,
knew I'd lose her if I opened my mouth. Still, I seemed
to be losing her anyway. So I was sitting in the lounge
watching *The Tube* on Channel Four and drinking a
mug of tea, and feeling sorry for myself.

The man with the horn-rimmed specs walked into my
house like he owned the place. He checked his watch.

"Right," he said. "Time to go. You'll be piloting something pretty close to a PL-47."

Even people with Graceful clearance weren't meant to
know about PL-47s. I'd flown a prototype a dozen times.
Looked like a teacup, flew like something from *Star
Wars*.

"Shouldn't I leave a note for Sandra?" I asked.

"No," he said, flatly. "Now, sit down on the floor and
breathe deeply and regularly. In, out, in, out."

It never occurred to me to argue with him, or to dis-
obey. I sat down on the floor, and I began to breathe,
slowly, in and out and out and in and . . .

In.

Out.

In.

A wrenching. The worst pain I've ever felt. I was
choking.

In.

Out.

I was screaming, but I could hear my voice and I
wasn't screaming. All I could hear was a low bubbling
moan.

In.

Out.

It was like being born. It wasn't comfortable, or pleasant. It was the breathing carried me through it, through

all the pain and the darkness and the bubbling in my lungs. I opened my eyes. I was lying on a metal disk about eight feet across. I was naked, wet, and surrounded by a sprawl of cables. They were retracting, moving away from me, like scared worms or nervous brightly colored snakes.

I looked down at my body. No body hair, no scars, no wrinkles. I wondered how old I was, in real terms. Eighteen? Twenty? I couldn't tell.

There was a glass screen set into the floor of the metal disk. It flickered and came to life. I was staring at the man in the horn-rimmed spectacles.

"Do you remember?" he asked. "You should be able to access most of your memory for the moment."

"I think so," I told him.

"You'll be in a PL-47," he said. "We've just finished building it. Pretty much had to go back to first principles, come forward. Modify some factories to construct it. We'll have another batch of them finished by tomorrow. Right now we've only got one."

"So if this doesn't work, you've got replacements for me."

"If we survive that long," he said. "Another missile bombardment started about fifteen minutes ago. Took out most of Australia. We project that it's still a prelude to the real bombing."

"What are they dropping? Nuclear weapons?"

"Rocks."

"Rocks?"

"Uh-huh. Rocks. Asteroids. Big ones. We think that tomorrow, unless we surrender, they may drop the moon on us."

"You're joking."

"Wish I was." The screen went dull.

The metal disk I was riding had been navigating its way through a tangle of cables and a world of sleeping naked people. It had slipped over sharp microchip towers and softly glowing silicone spires.

The PL-47 was waiting for me at the top of a metal mountain. Tiny metal crabs scuttled across it, polishing and checking every last rivet and stud.

I walked inside on tree trunk legs that still trembled and shook from lack of use. I sat down in the pilot's chair and was thrilled to realize that it had been built for me. It fitted. I strapped myself down. My hands began to go through warm-up sequence. Cables crept over my arms. I felt something plugging into the base of my spine, something else moving in and connecting at the top of my neck.

My perception of the ship expanded radically. I had it in 360 degrees, above, below. I was the ship, while at the same time, I was sitting in the cabin, activating the launch codes.

"Good luck," said the horn-rimmed man on a tiny screen to my left.

"Thank you. Can I ask one last question?"

"I don't see why not."

"Why me?"

"Well," he said, "the short answer is that you were designed to do this. We've improved a little on the basic human design in your case. You're bigger. You're much faster. You have improved processing speeds and reaction times."

"I'm not faster. I'm big, but I'm clumsy."

"Not in real life," he said. "That's just in the world."

And I took off.

I never saw the aliens, if there were any aliens, but I saw their ship. It looked like fungus or seaweed: the whole thing was organic, an enormous glimmering thing, orbiting the moon. It looked like something you'd see growing on a rotting log, half-submerged under the sea. It was the size of Tasmania.

Two-hundred mile-long sticky tendrils were dragging asteroids of various sizes behind them. It reminded me a little of the trailing tendrils of a Portuguese Man O' War, that strange compound sea creature: four inseparable organisms that dream they are one.

They started throwing rocks at me as I got a couple of hundred thousand miles away.

My fingers were activating the missile bay, aiming at a floating nucleus, while I wondered what I was doing. I wasn't saving the world I knew. That world was imaginary: a sequence of ones and zeroes. If I was saving anything, I was saving a nightmare. . . .

But if the nightmare died, the dream was dead, too.

There was a girl named Susan. I remembered her from a ghost life long gone. I wondered if she was still alive. (Had it been a couple of hours ago? Or a couple of lifetimes?) I supposed she was dangling hairless from cables somewhere, with no memory of a miserable, paranoid giant.

I was so close I could see the ripples of the creature's skin. The rocks were getting smaller and more accurate. I dodged and wove and skimmed to avoid them. Part of me was just admiring the economy of the thing: no expensive explosives to build and buy, no lasers, no nukes. Just good old kinetic energy: big rocks.

If one of those things had hit the ship I would have been dead. Simple as that.

The only way to avoid them was to outrun them. So I kept running.

The nucleus was staring at me. It was an eye of some kind. I was certain of it.

I was less than a hundred yards away from the nucleus when I let the payload go. Then I ran.

I wasn't quite out of range when the thing imploded. It was like fireworks—beautiful in a ghastly sort of way. And then there was nothing but a faint trace of glitter and dust. . . .

"I did it!" I screamed. "I did it! I fucking well did it!"

The screen flickered. Horn-rimmed spectacles were staring at me. There was no real face behind them anymore. Just a loose approximation of concern and interest, like a blurred cartoon. "You did it," he agreed.

"Now, where do I bring this thing down?" I asked.

There was a hesitation, then, "You don't. We didn't design it to return. It was a redundancy we had no need for. Too costly, in terms of resources."

"So what do I do? I just saved the Earth. And now I suffocate out here?"

He nodded. "That's pretty much it. Yes."

The lights began to dim. One by one, the controls were going out. I lost my 360-degree perception of the ship. It was just me, strapped to a chair in the middle of nowhere, inside a flying teacup.

"How long do I have?"

"We're closing down all your systems, but you've got a couple of hours, at least. We're not going to evacuate the remaining air. That would be inhuman."

"You know, in the world I came from, they would have given me a medal."

"Obviously, we're grateful."

"So you can't come up with any more tangible way to express your gratitude?"

"Not really. You're a disposable part. A unit. We can't mourn you any more than a wasps' nest mourns the death of a single wasp. It's not sensible and it's not viable to bring you back."

"And you don't want this kind of firepower coming back toward the Earth, where it could potentially be used against you?"

"As you say."

And then the screen went dark, with not so much as a good-bye. *Do not adjust your set,* I thought. *Reality is at fault.*

You become very aware of your breathing, when you

only have a couple of hours of air remaining. In. Hold. Out. Hold. In. Hold. Out. Hold. . . .

I sat there strapped to my seat in the half-dark, and I waited, and I thought. Then I said, "Hello? Is anybody there?"

A beat. The screen flickered with patterns. "Yes?"

"I have a request. Listen. You—you people, machines, whatever you are—you owe me one. Right? I mean I saved all your lives."

"Continue."

"I've got a couple of hours left. Yes?"

"About fifty-seven minutes."

"Can you plug me back into the . . . the real world. The other world. The one I came from?"

"Mm? I don't know. I'll see." Dark screen once more.

I sat and breathed, in and out, in and out, while I waited. I felt very peaceful. If it wasn't for having less than an hour to live, I'd have felt just great.

The screen glowed. There was no picture, no pattern, no nothing. Just a gentle glow. And a voice, half in my head, half out of it, said, "You got a deal."

There was a sharp pain at the base of my skull. Then blackness, for several minutes.

Then this.

That was fifteen years ago: 1984. I went back into computers. I own my computer store on the Tottenham Court Road. And now, as we head toward the new millennium, I'm writing this down. This time around, I married Susan. It took me a couple of months to find her. We have a son.

I'm nearly forty. People of my kind don't live much longer than that, on the whole. Our hearts stop. When you read this, I'll be dead. You'll know that I'm dead. You'll have seen a coffin big enough for two men dropped into a hole.

But know this, Susan, my sweet: my true coffin is orbiting the moon. It looks like a flying teacup. They gave me back the world, and you, for a little while. Last time I told you, or someone like you, the truth, or what I knew of it, you walked out on me. And maybe that wasn't you, and I wasn't me, but I don't dare risk it again. So I'm going to write this down, and you'll be given it with the rest of my papers when I'm gone. Good-bye.

They may be heartless, unfeeling, computerized bastards, leeching off the minds of what's left of humanity. But I can't help feeling grateful to them.

I'll die soon. But the last twenty minutes have been the best years of my life.

PAGES FROM A JOURNAL FOUND IN A SHOEBOX LEFT IN A GREYHOUND BUS SOMEWHERE BETWEEN TULSA, OKLAHOMA, AND LOUISVILLE, KENTUCKY

Monday the 28th
I guess I've been following Scarlet for a long time now. Yesterday I was in Las Vegas. Walking across the parking lot of a casino, I found a postcard. There was a word written on it in crimson lipstick. One word: *Remember*. On the other side of the postcard was a highway in Montana.

I don't remember what it is I'm meant to remember. I'm on the road now, driving north.

Tuesday the 29th
I'm in Montana, or maybe Nebraska. I'm writing this in a motel. There's a wind gusting outside my room, and I drink black motel coffee, just like I'll drink it tomorrow night and the night after that. In a small-town diner today I heard someone say her name. "Scarlet's on the road," said the man. He was a traffic cop, and he changed the subject when I got close and listened.

He was talking about a head-on collision. The broken glass glittered on the road like diamonds. He called me "Ma'am," politely.

Wednesday the 30th

"It's not the work that gets to you so bad," said the woman. "It's the way that people stare." She was shivering. It was a cold night and she wasn't dressed for it.

"I'm looking for Scarlet," I told her.

She squeezed my hand with hers, then she touched my cheek, so gently. "Keep looking, hon," she said. "You'll find her when you're ready." Then she sashayed on down the street.

I wasn't in a small town any longer. Maybe I was in Saint Louis. How can you tell if you're in Saint Louis? I looked for some kind of arch, something linking East and West, but if it was there I missed it.

Later, I crossed a river.

Thursday the 31st

There were blueberries growing wild by the side of the road. A red thread was caught in the bushes. I'm scared that I'm looking for something that does not exist anymore. Maybe it never did.

I spoke to a woman I used to love today, in a café in the desert. She's a waitress there, a long time ago.

"I thought I was your destination," she told me. "Looks like I was just another stop on the line."

I couldn't say anything to make it better. She couldn't hear me. I should have asked if she knew where Scarlet was.

Friday the 32nd

I dreamed of Scarlet last night. She was huge and wild, and she was hunting for me. In my dream, I knew what she looked like. When I woke I was in a pickup truck

parked by the side of the road. There was a man shining
a flashlight in the window at me. He called me "Sir" and
asked me for ID.

I told him who I thought I was and who I was looking
for. He just laughed and walked away, shaking his head.
He was humming a song I didn't know. I drove the
pickup south, into the morning. Sometimes I fear this is
becoming an obsession. She's walking. I'm driving. Why
is she always so far ahead of me?

Saturday the 1st
I found a shoebox that I keep things in. In a Jacksonville
McDonald's I ate a quarter pounder with cheese and a
chocolate milkshake, and I spread everything I keep in
the shoebox out on the table in front of me: the red
thread from the blueberry bush; the postcard; a Pola-
roid photograph I found in some fennel-blown waste-
land beside Sunset Boulevard—it shows two girls
whispering secrets, their faces blurred; an audio cas-
sette; some golden glitter in a tiny bottle I was given in
Washington, D.C.; pages I've torn from books and magazines. A casino chip. This journal.

"When you die," says a dark-haired woman at the next
table, "they can make you into diamonds now. It's scien-
tific. That's how I want to be remembered. I want to shine."

Sunday the 2nd
The paths that ghosts follow are written on the land in
old words. Ghosts don't take the interstate. They walk.
Is that what I'm following here? Sometimes it seems like
I'm looking out through her eyes. Sometimes it feels like
she's looking out through mine.

I'm in Wilmington, North Carolina. I write this on an
empty beach, while the sunlight glitters on the sea, and I
feel so alone.

We make it up as we go along. Don't we?

Monday the 3rd

I was in Baltimore, standing on a sidewalk in the light fall rain, wondering where I was going. I think I saw Scarlet in a car, coming toward me. She was a passenger. I could not see her face, but her hair was red. The woman who drove the car, an elderly pickup truck, was fat and happy, and her hair was long and black. Her skin was dark.

I slept that night in the house of a man I did not know. When I woke, he said, "She's in Boston."

"Who?"

"The one you're looking for."

I asked how he knew, but he wouldn't talk to me. After a while he asked me to leave, and, soon enough, I did. I want to go home. If I knew where it was, I would. Instead I hit the road.

Tuesday the 4th

Passing Newark at midday, I could see the tip of New York, already smudged dark by dust in the air, now scumbled into night by a thunderstorm. It could have been the end of the world.

I think the world will end in black-and-white, like an old movie. (Hair as black as coal, sugar, skin as white as snow.) Maybe as long as we have colors we can keep going. (Lips as red as blood, I keep reminding myself.)

I made Boston in the early evening. I find myself looking for her in mirrors and reflections. Some days I remember when the white people came to this land, and when the black people stumbled ashore in chains. I remember when the red people walked to this land, when the land was younger.

I remember when the land was alone.

"How can you sell your mother?" That was what the first people said, when asked to sell the land they walked upon.

Wednesday the 5th

She spoke to me last night. I'm certain it was her. I passed a pay phone on the street in Metairie, LA. It rang, I picked up the handset.

"Are you okay?" said a voice.

"Who is this?" I asked. "Maybe you have a wrong number."

"Maybe I do," she said. "But are you okay?"

"I don't know," I said.

"Know that you are loved," she said. And I knew that it had to be her. I wanted to tell her that I loved her too, but by then she'd already put down the phone. If it was her. She was only there for a moment. Maybe it was a wrong number, but I don't think so.

I'm so close now. I buy a postcard from a homeless guy on the sidewalk with a blanket of stuff, and I write *Remember* on it, in lipstick, so now I won't ever forget, but the wind comes up and carries it away, and just for now I guess I'm going to keep on walking.

HOW TO TALK TO GIRLS

AT PARTIES

"Come on," said Vic. "It'll be great."

"No, it won't," I said, although I'd lost this fight hours ago, and I knew it.

"It'll be brilliant," said Vic, for the hundredth time. "Girls! Girls! Girls!" He grinned with white teeth.

We both attended an all-boys' school in south London. While it would be a lie to say that we had no experience with girls—Vic seemed to have had many girlfriends, while I had kissed three of my sister's friends—it would, I think, be perfectly true to say that we both chiefly spoke to, interacted with, and only truly understood, other boys. Well, I did, anyway. It's hard to speak for someone else, and I've not seen Vic for thirty years. I'm not sure that I would know what to say to him now if I did.

We were walking the backstreets that used to twine in a grimy maze behind East Croydon station—a friend had told Vic about a party, and Vic was determined to go whether I liked it or not, and I didn't. But my parents were away that week at a conference, and I was Vic's guest at his house, so I was trailing along beside him.

"It'll be the same as it always is," I said. "After an hour you'll be off somewhere snogging the prettiest girl at the party, and I'll be in the kitchen listening to somebody's mum going on about politics or poetry or something."

"You just have to *talk* to them," he said. "I think it's probably that road at the end here." He gestured cheerfully, swinging the bag with the bottle in it.

"Don't you know?"

"Alison gave me directions and I wrote them on a bit of paper, but I left it on the hall table. S'okay. I can find it."

"How?" Hope welled slowly up inside me.

"We walk down the road," he said, as if speaking to an idiot child. "And we look for the party. Easy."

I looked, but saw no party: just narrow houses with rusting cars or bikes in their concreted front gardens; and the dusty glass fronts of newsagents, which smelled of alien spices and sold everything from birthday cards and secondhand comics to the kind of magazines that were so pornographic that they were sold already sealed in plastic bags. I had been there when Vic had slipped one of those magazines beneath his sweater, but the owner caught him on the pavement outside and made him give it back.

We reached the end of the road and turned into a narrow street of terraced houses. Everything looked very still and empty in the Summer's evening. "It's all right for you," I said. "They fancy you. You don't actually *have* to talk to them." It was true: one urchin grin from Vic and he could have his pick of the room.

"Nah. S'not like that. You've just got to talk."

The times I had kissed my sister's friends I had not spoken to them. They had been around while my sister was off doing something elsewhere, and they had drifted into my orbit, and so I had kissed them. I do not remember any talking. I did not know what to say to girls, and I told him so.

"They're just girls," said Vic. "They don't come from another planet."

As we followed the curve of the road around, my hopes that the party would prove unfindable began to fade: a low pulsing noise, music muffled by walls and doors, could be heard from a house up ahead. It was eight in the evening, not that early if you aren't yet sixteen, and we weren't. Not quite.

I had parents who liked to know where I was, but I don't think Vic's parents cared that much. He was the youngest of five boys. That in itself seemed magical to me: I merely had two sisters, both younger than I was, and I felt both unique and lonely. I had wanted a brother as far back as I could remember. When I turned thirteen, I stopped wishing on falling stars or first stars, but back when I did, a brother was what I had wished for.

We went up the garden path, crazy paving leading us past a hedge and a solitary rosebush to a pebble-dashed facade. We rang the doorbell, and the door was opened by a girl. I could not have told you how old she was, which was one of the things about girls I had begun to hate: when you start out as kids you're just boys and girls, going through time at the same speed, and you're all five, or seven, or eleven, together. And then one day there's a lurch and the girls just sort of sprint off into the future ahead of you, and they know all about everything, and they have periods and breasts and makeup and God-only-knew-what-else—for I certainly didn't. The diagrams in biology textbooks were no substitute for being, in a very real sense, young adults. And the girls of our age were.

Vic and I weren't young adults, and I was beginning to suspect that even when I started needing to shave every day, instead of once every couple of weeks, I would still be way behind.

The girl said, "Hello?"

Vic said, "We're friends of Alison's." We had met Alison, all freckles and orange hair and a wicked smile, in Hamburg, on a German exchange. The exchange organizers had sent some girls with us, from a local girls' school, to balance the sexes. The girls, our age, more or less, were raucous and funny, and had more or less adult boyfriends with cars and jobs and motorbikes and—in the case of one girl with crooked teeth and a raccoon coat, who spoke to me about it sadly at the end of a party in Hamburg, in, of course, the kitchen—a wife and kids.

"She isn't here," said the girl at the door. "No Alison."

"Not to worry," said Vic, with an easy grin. "I'm Vic. This is Enn." A beat, and then the girl smiled back at him. Vic had a bottle of white wine in a plastic bag, removed from his parents' kitchen cabinet. "Where should I put this, then?"

She stood out of the way, letting us enter. "There's a kitchen in the back," she said. "Put it on the table there, with the other bottles." She had golden, wavy hair, and she was very beautiful. The hall was dim in the twilight, but I could see that she was beautiful.

"What's your name, then?" said Vic.

She told him it was Stella, and he grinned his crooked white grin and told her that that had to be the prettiest name he had ever heard. Smooth bastard. And what was worse was that he said it like he meant it.

Vic headed back to drop off the wine in the kitchen, and I looked into the front room, where the music was coming from. There were people dancing in there. Stella walked in, and she started to dance, swaying to the music all alone, and I watched her.

This was during the early days of punk. On our own record players we would play the Adverts and the Jam, the Stranglers and the Clash and the Sex Pistols. At other people's parties you'd hear ELO or 10cc or even Roxy Music. Maybe some Bowie, if you were lucky. During the German exchange, the only LP that we had all been able to agree on was Neil Young's *Harvest,* and his song "Heart of Gold" had threaded through the trip like a refrain: *I crossed the ocean for a heart of gold. . . .*

The music playing in that front room wasn't anything I recognized. It sounded a bit like a German electronic pop group called Kraftwerk, and a bit like an LP I'd been given for my last birthday, of strange sounds made by the BBC Radiophonic Workshop. The music had a beat, though, and the half-dozen girls in that room were moving gently to it, although I only looked at Stella. She shone.

Vic pushed past me, into the room. He was holding a can of lager. "There's booze back in the kitchen," he told me. He wandered over to Stella and he began to talk to her. I couldn't hear what they were saying over the music, but I knew that there was no room for me in that conversation.

I didn't like beer, not back then. I went off to see if there was something I wanted to drink. On the kitchen table stood a large bottle of Coca-Cola, and I poured myself a plastic tumblerful, and I didn't dare say anything to the pair of girls who were talking in the underlit kitchen. They were animated and utterly lovely. Each of them had very black skin and glossy hair and movie star clothes, and their accents were foreign, and each of them was out of my league.

I wandered, Coke in hand.

The house was deeper than it looked, larger and more complex than the two-up two-down model I had imagined. The rooms were underlit—I doubt there was a bulb of more than 40 watts in the building—and each room I went into was inhabited: in my memory, inhabited only by girls. I did not go upstairs.

A girl was the only occupant of the conservatory. Her hair was so fair it was white, and long, and straight, and she sat at the glass-topped table, her hands clasped together, staring at the garden outside, and the gathering dusk. She seemed wistful.

"Do you mind if I sit here?" I asked, gesturing with my cup. She shook her head, and then followed it up with a shrug, to indicate that it was all the same to her. I sat down.

Vic walked past the conservatory door. He was talking to Stella, but he looked in at me, sitting at the table, wrapped in shyness and awkwardness, and he opened and closed his hand in a parody of a speaking mouth. *Talk*. Right.

"Are you from around here?" I asked the girl.

She shook her head. She wore a low-cut silvery top, and I tried not to stare at the swell of her breasts.

I said, "What's your name? I'm Enn."

"Wain's Wain," she said, or something that sounded like it. "I'm a second."

"That's uh. That's a different name."

She fixed me with huge, liquid eyes. "It indicates that my progenitor was also Wain, and that I am obliged to report back to her. I may not breed."

"Ah. Well. Bit early for that anyway, isn't it?"

She unclasped her hands, raised them above the table, spread her fingers. "You see?" The little finger on her left hand was crooked, and it bifurcated at the top, splitting into two smaller fingertips. A minor deformity. "When I was finished a decision was needed. Would I be retained, or eliminated? I was fortunate that the decision was with me. Now, I travel, while my more perfect sisters remain at home in stasis. They were firsts. I am a second.

"Soon I must return to Wain, and tell her all I have seen. All my impressions of this place of yours."

"I don't actually live in Croydon," I said. "I don't come from here." I wondered if she was American. I had no idea what she was talking about.

"As you say," she agreed, "neither of us comes from here." She folded her six-fingered left hand beneath her right, as if tucking it out of sight. "I had expected it to be bigger, and cleaner, and more colorful. But still, it is a jewel."

She yawned, covered her mouth with her right hand, only for a moment, before it was back on the table again. "I grow weary of the journeying, and I wish sometimes that it would end. On a street in Río, at Carnival, I saw them on a bridge, golden and tall and insect-eyed and winged, and elated I almost ran to greet them, before I saw that they were only people in costumes. I said to Hola Colt, 'Why do they try so hard to look like us?' and Hola Colt replied, 'Because they hate themselves, all shades of pink and brown, and so small.' It is what I experience, even me, and I am not grown. It is like a world of children, or of elves." Then she smiled, and said, "It was a good thing they could not any of them see Hola Colt."

"Um," I said, "do you want to dance?"

She shook her head immediately. "It is not permitted," she said. "I can do nothing that might cause damage to property. I am Wain's."

"Would you like something to drink, then?"

"Water," she said.

I went back to the kitchen and poured myself another Coke, and filled a cup with water from the tap. From the kitchen back to the hall, and from there into the conservatory, but now it was quite empty.

I wondered if the girl had gone to the toilet, and if she might change her mind about dancing later. I walked back to the front room and stared in. The place was filling up. There were more girls dancing, and several lads I didn't know, who looked a few years older than me and Vic. The lads and the girls all kept their distance, but Vic was holding Stella's hand as they danced, and when the song ended he put an arm around her, casually, almost proprietorially, to make sure that nobody else cut in.

I wondered if the girl I had been talking to in the conservatory was now upstairs, as she did not appear to be on the ground floor.

I walked into the living room, which was across the hall from the room where the people were dancing, and I sat down on the sofa. There was a girl sitting there already. She had dark hair, cut short and spiky, and a nervous manner.

Talk, I thought. "Um, this mug of water's going spare," I told her, "if you want it?"

She nodded, and reached out her hand and took the mug, extremely carefully, as if she were unused to taking things, as if she could trust neither her vision nor her hands.

"I love being a tourist," she said, and smiled hesitantly. She had a gap between her two front teeth, and she sipped the tap water as if she were an adult sipping a fine wine. "The last tour, we went to sun, and we swam in sunfire pools with the whales. We heard their histories and we shivered in the chill of the outer places, then we swam deepward where the heat churned and comforted us.

"I wanted to go back. This time, I wanted it. There was so much I had not seen. Instead we came to world. Do you like it?"

"Like what?"

She gestured vaguely to the room—the sofa, the armchairs, the curtains, the unused gas fire.

"It's all right, I suppose."

"I told them I did not wish to visit world," she said. "My parent-teacher was unimpressed. 'You will have much to learn,' it told me. I said, 'I could learn more in sun, again. Or in the deeps. Jessa spun webs between galaxies. I want to do that.'

"But there was no reasoning with it, and I came to world. Parent-teacher engulfed me, and I was here, embodied in a decaying lump of meat hanging on a frame of calcium. As I incarnated I felt things deep inside me, fluttering and pumping and squishing. It was my first experience with pushing air through the mouth, vibrating the vocal cords on the way, and I used it to tell parent-teacher that I wished that I would die, which it acknowledged was the inevitable exit strategy from world."

There were black worry beads wrapped around her wrist, and she fiddled with them as she spoke. "But knowledge is there, in the meat," she said, "and I am resolved to learn from it."

We were sitting close at the center of the sofa now. I decided I should put an arm around her, but casually. I would extend my arm along the back of the sofa and eventually sort of creep it down, almost imperceptibly, until it was touching her. She said, "The thing with the liquid in the eyes, when the world blurs. Nobody told me, and I still do not understand. I have touched the folds of the Whisper and pulsed and flown with the tachyon swans, and I still do not understand."

She wasn't the prettiest girl there, but she seemed nice enough, and she was a girl, anyway. I let my arm slide down a little, tentatively, so that it made contact with her back, and she did not tell me to take it away.

Vic called to me then, from the doorway. He was standing with his arm around Stella, protectively, waving at me. I tried to let him know, by shaking my head, that I was onto something, but he called my name and, reluctantly, I got up from the sofa and walked over to the door. "What?"

"Er. Look. The party," said Vic, apologetically. "It's not the one I thought it was. I've been talking to Stella and I figured it out. Well, she sort of explained it to me. We're at a different party."

"Christ. Are we in trouble? Do we have to go?"

Stella shook her head. He leaned down and kissed her, gently, on the lips. "You're just happy to have me here, aren't you darlin'?"

"You know I am," she told him.

He looked from her back to me, and he smiled his

white smile: roguish, lovable, a little bit Artful Dodger, a little bit wide-boy Prince Charming. "Don't worry. They're all tourists here anyway. It's a foreign exchange thing, innit? Like when we all went to Germany."

"It is?"

"Enn. You got to *talk* to them. And that means you got to listen to them, too. You understand?"

"I *did*. I already talked to a couple of them."

"You getting anywhere?"

"I was till you called me over."

"Sorry about that. Look, I just wanted to fill you in. Right?"

And he patted my arm and he walked away with Stella. Then, together, the two of them went up the stairs.

Understand me, all the girls at that party, in the twilight, were lovely; they all had perfect faces but, more important than that, they had whatever strangeness of proportion, of oddness or humanity it is that makes a beauty something more than a shop window dummy. Stella was the most lovely of any of them, but she, of course, was Vic's, and they were going upstairs together, and that was just how things would always be.

There were several people now sitting on the sofa, talking to the gap-toothed girl. Someone told a joke, and they all laughed. I would have had to push my way in there to sit next to her again, and it didn't look like she was expecting me back, or cared that I had gone, so I wandered out into the hall. I glanced in at the dancers, and found myself wondering where the music was coming from. I couldn't see a record player or speakers.

From the hall I walked back to the kitchen.

Kitchens are good at parties. You never need an excuse to be there, and, on the good side, at this party I couldn't see any signs of someone's mum. I inspected the various bottles and cans on the kitchen table, then I poured a half an inch of Pernod into the bottom of my plastic cup, which I filled to the top with Coke. I dropped in a couple of ice cubes and took a sip, relishing the sweet-shop tang of the drink.

"What's that you're drinking?" A girl's voice.

"It's Pernod," I told her. "It tastes like aniseed balls, only it's alcoholic." I didn't say that I only tried it because I'd heard someone in the crowd ask for a Pernod on a live Velvet Underground LP.

"Can I have one?" I poured another Pernod, topped it off with Coke, passed it to her. Her hair was a coppery auburn, and it tumbled around her head in ringlets. It's not a hair style you see much now, but you saw it a lot back then.

"What's your name?" I asked.

"Triolet," she said.

"Pretty name," I told her, although I wasn't sure that it was. She was pretty, though.

"It's a verse form," she said, proudly. "Like me."

"You're a poem?"

She smiled, and looked down and away, perhaps bashfully. Her profile was almost flat—a perfect Grecian nose that came down from her forehead in a straight line. We did *Antigone* in the school theater the previous year. I was the messenger who brings Creon the news of Antigone's death. We wore half-masks that made us look like that. I thought of that play, looking at her face, in the kitchen, and I thought of Barry Smith's drawings of women in the *Conan* comics: five years later I would have thought of the Pre-Raphaelites, of Jane Morris and Lizzie Siddall. But I was only fifteen then.

"You're a poem?" I repeated.

She chewed her lower lip. "If you want. I am a poem, or I am a pattern, or a race of people whose world was swallowed by the sea."

"Isn't it hard to be three things at the same time?"

"What's your name?"

"Enn."

"So you are Enn," she said. "And you are a male. And

you are a biped. Is it hard to be three things at the same time?"

"But they aren't different things. I mean, they aren't contradictory." It was a word I had read many times but never said aloud before that night, and I put the stresses in the wrong places. *Contradictory.*

She wore a thin dress made of a white, silky fabric. Her eyes were a pale green, a color that would now make me think of tinted contact lenses; but this was thirty years ago; things were different then. I remember wondering about Vic and Stella, upstairs. By now, I was sure that they were in one of the bedrooms, and I envied Vic so much it almost hurt.

Still, I was talking to this girl, even if we were talking nonsense, even if her name wasn't really Triolet (my generation had not been given hippie names: all the Rainbows and the Sunshines and the Moons, they were only six, seven, eight years old back then). She said, "We knew that it would soon be over, and so we put it all into a poem, to tell the universe who we were, and why we were here, and what we said and did and thought and dreamed and yearned for. We wrapped our dreams in words and patterned the words so that they would live forever, unforgettable. Then we sent the poem as a pattern of flux, to wait in the heart of a star, beaming out its message in pulses and bursts and fuzzes across the electromagnetic spectrum, until the time when, on worlds a thousand sun systems distant, the pattern would be decoded and read, and it would become a poem once again."

"And then what happened?"

She looked at me with her green eyes, and it was as if she stared out at me from her own Antigone half-mask; but as if her pale green eyes were just a different, deeper, part of the mask. "You cannot hear a poem without it changing you," she told me. "They heard it, and it colonized them. It inherited them and it inhabited them, its rhythms becoming part of the way that they thought; its images permanently transmuting their metaphors; its verses, its outlook, its aspirations becoming their lives. Within a generation their children would be born already knowing the poem, and, sooner rather than later, as these things go, there were no more children born. There was no need for them, not any longer. There was only a poem, which took flesh and walked and spread itself across the vastness of the known."

I edged closer to her, so I could feel my leg pressing against hers. She seemed to welcome it: she put her hand on my arm, affectionately, and I felt a smile spreading across my face.

"There are places that we are welcomed," said Triolet, "and places where we are regarded as a noxious weed, or as a disease, something immediately to be quarantined and eliminated. But where does contagion end and art begin?"

"I don't know," I said, still smiling. I could hear the unfamiliar music as it pulsed and scattered and boomed in the front room.

She leaned into me then and—I suppose it was a kiss. . . . I suppose. She pressed her lips to my lips, anyway, and then, satisfied, she pulled back, as if she had now marked me as her own.

"Would you like to hear it?" she asked, and I nodded, unsure what she was offering me, but certain that I needed anything she was willing to give me.

She began to whisper something in my ear. It's the strangest thing about poetry—you can tell it's poetry, even if you don't speak the language. You can hear Homer's Greek without understanding a word, and you still know it's poetry. I've heard Polish poetry, and Inuit poetry, and I knew what it was without knowing. Her whisper was like that. I didn't know the language, but her words washed through me, perfect, and in my mind's eye I saw towers of glass and diamond; and people with eyes of the palest green; and, unstoppable, beneath every syllable, I could feel the relentless advance of the ocean.

Perhaps I kissed her properly. I don't remember. I know I wanted to.

And then Vic was shaking me violently. "Come on!" he was shouting. "Quickly. Come on!"

In my head I began to come back from a thousand miles away.

"Idiot. Come on. Just get a move on," he said, and he swore at me. There was fury in his voice.

For the first time that evening I recognized one of the songs being played in the front room. A sad saxophone wail followed by a cascade of liquid chords, a man's voice singing cut-up lyrics about the sons of the silent age. I wanted to stay and hear the song.

She said, "I am not finished. There is yet more of me."

"Sorry love," said Vic, but he wasn't smiling any longer. "There'll be another time," and he grabbed me by the elbow and he twisted and pulled, forcing me from the room. I did not resist. I knew from experience that Vic could beat the stuffing out me if he got it into his head to do so. He wouldn't do it unless he was upset or angry, but he was angry now.

Out into the front hall. As Vic pulled open the door, I looked back one last time, over my shoulder, hoping to see Triolet in the doorway to the kitchen, but she was not there. I saw Stella, though, at the top of the stairs. She was staring down at Vic, and I saw her face.

This all happened thirty years ago. I have forgotten much, and I will forget more, and in the end I will forget everything; yet, if I have any certainty of life beyond death, it is all wrapped up not in psalms or hymns, but in this one thing alone: I cannot believe that I will ever forget that moment, or forget the expression on Stella's face as she watched Vic hurrying away from her. Even in death I shall remember that.

Her clothes were in disarray, and there was makeup smudged across her face, and her eyes—

You wouldn't want to make a universe angry. I bet an angry universe would look at you with eyes like that.

We ran then, me and Vic, away from the party and the tourists and the twilight, ran as if a lightning storm was on our heels, a mad helter-skelter dash down the confusion of streets, threading through the maze, and we did not look back, and we did not stop until we could not breathe; and then we stopped and panted, unable to run any longer. We were in pain. I held on to a wall, and Vic threw up, hard and long, into the gutter.

He wiped his mouth.

"She wasn't a—" He stopped.

He shook his head.

Then he said, "You know . . . I think there's a thing. When you've gone as far as you dare. And if you go any further, you wouldn't be *you* anymore? You'd be the person who'd done *that*? The places you just can't go. . . . I think that happened to me tonight."

I thought I knew what he was saying. "Screw her, you mean?" I said.

He rammed a knuckle hard against my temple, and twisted it violently. I wondered if I was going to have to fight him—and lose—but after a moment he lowered his hand and moved away from me, making a low, gulping noise.

I looked at him curiously, and I realized that he was crying: his face was scarlet; snot and tears ran down his cheeks. Vic was sobbing in the street, as unselfconsciously and heartbreakingly as a little boy. He walked away from me then, shoulders heaving, and he hurried down the road so he was in front of me and I could no longer see his face. I wondered what had occurred in that upstairs room to make him behave like that, to scare him so, and I could not even begin to guess.

The streetlights came on, one by one; Vic stumbled on ahead, while I trudged down the street behind him in the dusk, my feet treading out the measure of a poem that, try as I might, I could not properly remember and would never be able to repeat.

THE DAY THE SAUCERS CAME

That day, the saucers landed.
   Hundreds of them, golden,
Silent, coming down from the sky
   like great snowflakes,
And the people of Earth stood and
   stared as they descended,
Waiting, dry-mouthed, to find what waited
   inside for us
And none of us knowing if we would
   be here tomorrow
But you didn't notice it because

That day, the day the saucers came,
   by some coincidence,
Was the day that the graves gave up their dead
And the zombies pushed up through soft earth
or erupted, shambling and dull-eyed, unstoppable,
Came towards us, the living,
   and we screamed and ran,
But you did not notice this because

On the saucer day, which was the zombie day, it was
Ragnarok also, and the television screens showed us
A ship built of dead-men's nails, a serpent, a wolf,
All bigger than the mind could hold,
   and the cameraman could

Not get far enough away, and then
   the Gods came out
But you did not see them coming because

On the saucer-zombie-battling-gods
   day the floodgates broke
And each of us was engulfed by genies and sprites
Offering us wishes and wonders and eternities
And charm and cleverness and true
   brave hearts and pots of gold
While giants feefofummed across
   the land, and killer bees,
But you had no idea of any of this because

That day, the saucer day the zombie day
The Ragnarok and fairies day, the
   day the great winds came
And snows, and the cities turned
   to crystal, the day
All plants died, plastics dissolved, the day the
Computers turned, the screens telling
   us we would obey, the day
Angels, drunk and muddled,
   stumbled from the bars,
And all the bells of London
   were sounded, the day
Animals spoke to us in Assyrian, the Yeti day,
The fluttering capes and arrival of
   the Time Machine day,
You didn't notice any of this because
you were sitting in your room,
   not doing anything
not even reading, not really, just
looking at your telephone,
wondering if I was going to call.

SUNBIRD

They were a rich and a rowdy bunch at the Epicurean Club in those days. They certainly knew how to party. There were five of them:

There was Augustus TwoFeathers McCoy, big enough for three men, who ate enough for four men and who drank enough for five. His great-grandfather had founded the Epicurean Club with the proceeds of a tontine, which he had taken great pains, in the traditional manner, to ensure that he had collected in full.

There was Professor Mandalay, small and twitchy and gray as a ghost (and perhaps he was a ghost; stranger things have happened) who drank nothing but water, and who ate doll-portions from plates the size of saucers. Still, you do not need the gusto for the gastronomy, and Mandalay always got to the heart of every dish placed in front of him.

There was Virginia Boote, the food and restaurant critic, who had once been a great beauty but was now a grand and magnificent ruin, and who delighted in her ruination.

There was Jackie Newhouse, the descendant (on the left-handed route) of the great lover, gourmand, violinist, and duelist Giacomo Casanova. Jackie Newhouse had, like his notorious ancestor, both broken his share of hearts and eaten his share of great dishes.

And there was Zebediah T. Crawcrustle, who was the

only one of the Epicureans who was flat-out broke: he shambled in unshaven from the street when they had their meetings, with half a bottle of rotgut in a brown paper bag, hatless and coatless and, too often, partly shirtless, but he ate with more of an appetite than any of them.

Augustus TwoFeathers McCoy was talking—

"We have eaten everything that can be eaten," said Augustus TwoFeathers McCoy, and there was regret and glancing sorrow in his voice. "We have eaten vulture, mole, and fruitbat."

Mandalay consulted his notebook. "Vulture tasted like rotten pheasant. Mole tasted like carrion slug. Fruitbat tasted remarkably like sweet guinea pig."

"We have eaten kakopo, aye-aye, and giant panda—"

"Oh, that broiled panda steak," sighed Virginia Boote, her mouth watering at the memory.

"We have eaten several long-extinct species," said Augustus TwoFeathers McCoy. "We have eaten flash-frozen mammoth and Patagonian giant sloth."

"If we had but gotten the mammoth a little faster," sighed Jackie Newhouse. "I could tell why the hairy elephants went so fast, though, once people got a taste of them. I am a man of elegant pleasures, but after only one bite, I found myself thinking only of Kansas City barbecue sauce, and what the ribs on those things would be like, if they were fresh."

"Nothing wrong with being on ice for a millennium or two," said Zebediah T. Crawcrustle. He grinned. His teeth may have been crooked, but they were sharp and strong. "Even so, for real taste you had to go for honest-to-goodness mastodon every time. Mammoth was always what people settled for, when they couldn't get mastodon."

"We've eaten squid, and giant squid, and humongous squid," said Augustus TwoFeathers McCoy. "We've eaten lemmings and Tasmanian tigers. We've eaten bower bird and ortolan and peacock. We've eaten the dolphin fish (which is not the mammal dolphin) and the giant sea turtle and the Sumatran rhino. We've eaten everything there is to eat."

"Nonsense. There are many hundreds of things we have not yet tasted," said Professor Mandalay. "Thousands, perhaps. Think of all the species of beetle there are, still untasted."

"Oh Mandy," sighed Virginia Boote. "When you've tasted one beetle, you've tasted them all. And we all tasted several hundred species. At least the dung-beetles had a real kick to them."

"No," said Jackie Newhouse, "that was the dung-beetle balls. The beetles themselves were singularly unexceptional. Still, I take your point. We have scaled the heights of gastronomy, we have plunged down into the depths of gustation. We have become cosmonauts exploring undreamed-of worlds of delectation and gourmanderie."

"True, true, true," said Augustus TwoFeathers McCoy. "There has been a meeting of the Epicureans every month for over a hundred and fifty years, in my father's time, and my grandfather's time, and my great-grandfather's time, and now I fear that I must hang it up for there is nothing left that we, or our predecessors in the club, have not eaten."

"I wish I had been here in the twenties," said Virginia Boote, "when they legally had Man on the menu."

"Only after it had been electrocuted," said Zebediah T. Crawcrustle. "Half-fried already it was, all char and crackling. It left none of us with a taste for long pig, save one who was already that way inclined, and he went out pretty soon after that anyway."

"Oh, Crusty, *why* must you pretend that you were there?" asked Virginia Boote, with a yawn. "Anyone can see you aren't that old. You can't be more than sixty, even allowing for the ravages of time and the gutter."

"Oh, they ravage pretty good," said Zebediah T. Crawcrustle. "But not as good as you'd imagine. Anyway there's a host of things we've not eaten yet."

"Name one," said Mandalay, his pencil poised precisely above his notebook.

"Well, there's Suntown Sunbird," said Zebediah T. Crawcrustle. And he grinned his crookedy grin at them, with his teeth ragged but sharp.

"I've never heard of it," said Jackie Newhouse. "You're making it up."

"I've heard of it," said Professor Mandalay, "but in another context. And besides, it is imaginary."

"Unicorns are imaginary," said Virginia Boote, "but gosh, that unicorn flank tartare was tasty. A little bit horsy, a little bit goatish, and all the better for the capers and raw quail eggs."

"There's something about the Sunbird in one of the minutes of the Epicurean Club from bygone years," said Augustus TwoFeathers McCoy. "But what it was, I can no longer remember."

"Did they say how it tasted?" asked Virginia.

"I do not believe that they did," said Augustus, with a frown. "I would need to inspect the bound proceedings, of course."

"Nah," said Zebediah T. Crawcrustle. "That's only in the charred volumes. You'll never find out about it from there."

Augustus TwoFeathers McCoy scratched his head. He really did have two feathers, which went through the knot of black-hair-shot-with-silver at the back of his head, and the feathers had once been golden although by now they were looking kind of ordinary and yellow and ragged. He had been given them when he was a boy.

"Beetles," said Professor Mandalay. "I once calculated that, if a man such as myself were to eat six different species of beetle each day, it would take him more than twenty years to eat every beetle that has been identified.

And over that twenty years enough new species of beetle might have been discovered to keep him eating for another five years. And in those five years enough beetles might have been discovered to keep him eating for another two and a half years, and so on, and so on. It is a paradox of inexhaustibility. I call it Mandalay's Beetle. You would have to enjoy eating beetles, though," he added, "or it would be a very bad thing indeed."

"Nothing wrong with eating beetles if they're the right kind of beetle," said Zebediah T. Crawcrustle. "Right now, I've got a hankering on me for lightning bugs. There's a kick from the glow of a lightning bug that might be just what I need."

"While the lightning bug or firefly (*Photinus pyralis*) is more of a beetle than it is a glowworm," said Mandalay, "it is by no stretch of the imagination edible."

"They may not be edible," said Crawcrustle. "But they'll get you into shape for the stuff that is. I think I'll roast me some. Fireflies and habañero peppers. Yum."

Virginia Boote was an eminently practical woman. She said, "Suppose we did want to eat Suntown Sunbird. Where should we start looking for it?"

Zebediah T. Crawcrustle scratched the bristling seventh-day beard that was sprouting on his chin (it never grew any longer than that; seventh-day beards never do). "If it was me," he told them, "I'd head down to Suntown of a noon in midsummer, and I'd find somewhere comfortable to sit—Mustapha Stroheim's coffeehouse, for example—and I'd wait for the Sunbird to come by. Then I'd catch him in the traditional manner, and cook him in the traditional manner as well."

"And what would the traditional manner of catching him be?" asked Jackie Newhouse.

"Why, the same way your famous ancestor poached quails and wood grouse," said Crawcrustle.

"There's nothing in Casanova's memoirs about poaching quail," said Jackie Newhouse.

"Your ancestor was a busy man," said Crawcrustle. "He couldn't be expected to write everything down. But he poached a good quail nonetheless."

"Dried corn and dried blueberries, soaked in whiskey," said Augustus TwoFeathers McCoy. "That's how my folk always did it."

"And that was how Casanova did it," said Crawcrustle, "although he used barley grains mixed with raisins, and he soaked the raisins in brandy. He taught me himself."

Jackie Newhouse ignored this statement. It was easy to ignore much that Zebediah T. Crawcrustle said. Instead, Jackie Newhouse asked, "And where is Mustapha Stroheim's coffeehouse in Suntown?"

"Why, where it always is, third lane after the old market in the Suntown district, just before you reach the old drainage ditch that was once an irrigation canal, and if you find yourself outside One-eye Khayam's carpet shop you have gone too far," began Crawcrustle. "But I see by the expressions of irritation upon your faces that you were expecting a less succinct, less accurate description. Very well. It is in Suntown, and Suntown is in Cairo, in Egypt, where it always is, or almost always."

"And who will pay for an expedition to Suntown?" asked Augustus TwoFeathers McCoy. "And who will be on this expedition? I ask the question although I already know the answer, and I do not like it."

"Why, you will pay for it, Augustus, and we will all come," said Zebediah T. Crawcrustle. "You can deduct it from our Epicurean membership dues. And I shall bring my chef's apron and my cooking utensils."

Augustus knew that Crawcrustle had not paid his Epicurean Club membership in much too long a time, but the Epicurean Club would cover him; Crawcrustle had been a member of the Epicureans in Augustus's father's day. He simply said, "And when shall we leave?"

Crawcrustle fixed him with a mad old eye and shook

his head in disappointment. "Why, Augustus," he said. "We're going to Suntown, to catch the Sunbird. When else should we leave?"

"Sunday!" sang Virginia Boote. "Darlings, we'll leave on a Sunday!"

"There's hope for you yet, young lady," said Zebediah T. Crawcrustle. "We shall leave Sunday indeed. Three Sundays from now. And we shall travel to Egypt. We shall spend several days hunting and trapping the elusive Sunbird of Suntown, and, finally, we shall deal with it in the traditional way."

Professor Mandalay blinked a small gray blink. "But," he said. "I am teaching a class on Monday. On Mondays I teach mythology, on Tuesdays I teach tap dancing, and on Wednesdays, woodwork."

"Get a teaching assistant to take your course, Mandalay O Mandalay. On Monday you'll be hunting the Sunbird," said Zebediah T. Crawcrustle. "And how many other professors can say that?"

They went, one by one, to see Crawcrustle, in order to discuss the journey ahead of them, and to announce their misgivings.

Zebediah T. Crawcrustle was a man of no fixed abode. Still, there were places he could be found, if you were of a mind to find him. In the early mornings he slept in the bus terminal, where the benches were comfortable and the transport police were inclined to let him lie; in the heat of the afternoons he hung in the park by the statues of long-forgotten generals, with the dipsos and the winos and the hopheads, sharing their company and the contents of their bottles, and offering his opinion, which was, as that of an Epicurean, always considered and always respected, if not always welcomed.

Augustus TwoFeathers McCoy sought out Crawcrustle in the park; he had with him his daughter, Hollyberry

NoFeathers McCoy. She was small, but she was sharp as a shark's tooth.

"You know," said Augustus, "there is something very familiar about this."

"About what?" asked Zebediah.

"All of this. The expedition to Egypt. The Sunbird. It seemed to me like I heard about it before."

Crawcrustle merely nodded. He was crunching something from a brown paper bag.

Augustus said, "I went to the bound annals of the Epicurean Club, and I looked it up. And there was what I took to be a reference to the Sunbird in the index for forty years ago, but I was unable to learn anything more."

"And why was that?" asked Zebediah T. Crawcrustle, swallowing noisily.

Augustus TwoFeathers McCoy sighed. "I found the relevant page in the annals," he said, "but it was burned away, and afterward there was some great confusion in the administration of the Epicurean Club."

"You're eating lightning bugs from a paper bag," said Hollyberry NoFeathers McCoy. "I seen you doing it."

"I am indeed, little lady," said Zebediah T. Crawcrustle.

"Do you remember the days of great confusion, Crawcrustle?" asked Augustus.

"I do indeed," said Crawcrustle. "And I remember you. You were only the age that young Hollyberry is now. But there is always confusion, Augustus, and then there is no confusion. It is like the rising and the setting of the sun."

Jackie Newhouse and Professor Mandalay found Crawcrustle that evening, behind the railroad tracks. He was roasting something in a tin can over a small charcoal fire.

"What are you roasting, Crawcrustle?" asked Jackie Newhouse.

"More charcoal," said Crawcrustle. "Cleans the blood, purifies the spirit."

There was basswood and hickory, cut up into little chunks at the bottom of the can, all black and smoking.

"And will you actually eat this charcoal, Crawcrustle?" asked Professor Mandalay.

In response, Crawcrustle licked his fingers and picked out a lump of charcoal from the can. It hissed and fizzed in his grip.

"A fine trick," said Professor Mandalay. "That's how fire-eaters do it, I believe."

Crawcrustle popped the charcoal into his mouth and crunched it between his ragged old teeth. "It is indeed," he said. "It is indeed."

Jackie Newhouse cleared his throat. "The truth of the matter is," he said, "Professor Mandalay and I have deep misgivings about the journey that lies ahead."

Zebediah merely crunched his charcoal. "Not hot enough," he said. He took a stick from the fire and nibbled off the orange-hot tip of it. "That's good," he said.

"It's all an illusion," said Jackie Newhouse.

"Nothing of the sort," said Zebediah T. Crawcrustle, primly. "It's prickly elm."

"I have extreme misgivings about all this," said Jackie Newhouse. "My ancestors and I have a finely tuned sense of personal preservation, one that has often left us shivering on roofs and hiding in rivers—one step away from the law, or from gentlemen with guns and legitimate grievances—and that sense of self-preservation is telling me not to go to Suntown with you."

"I am an academic," said Professor Mandalay, "and thus have no finely developed senses that would be comprehensible to anyone who has not ever needed to grade papers without actually reading the blessed things. Still, I find the whole thing remarkably suspicious. If this Sunbird is so tasty, why have I not heard of it?"

"You have, Mandy old fruit. You have," said Zebediah T. Crawcrustle.

"And I am, in addition, an expert on geographical features from Tulsa, Oklahoma, to Timbuktu," continued Professor Mandalay. "Yet I have never seen a mention in any book of a place called Suntown in Cairo."

"Seen it mentioned? Why, you've taught it," said Crawcrustle, and he doused a lump of smoking charcoal with hot pepper sauce before popping it in his mouth and chomping it down.

"I don't believe you're really eating that," said Jackie Newhouse. "But even being around the trick of it is making me uncomfortable. I think it is time that I was elsewhere."

And he left. Perhaps Professor Mandalay left with him: that man was so gray and so ghostie it was always a toss-up whether he was there or not.

Virginia Boote tripped over Zebediah T. Crawcrustle while he rested in her doorway, in the small hours of the morning. She was returning from a restaurant she had needed to review. She got out of a taxi, tripped over Crawcrustle, and went sprawling. She landed nearby. "Whee!" she said. "That was some trip, wasn't it?"

"Indeed it was, Virginia," said Zebediah T. Crawcrustle. "You would not happen to have such a thing as a box of matches on you, would you?"

"I have a book of matches on me somewhere," she said, and she began to rummage in her purse, which was very large and very brown. "Here you are."

Zebediah T. Crawcrustle was carrying a bottle of purple methylated spirits, which he proceeded to pour into a plastic cup.

"Meths?" said Virginia Boote. "Somehow you never struck me as a meths drinker, Zebby."

"Nor am I," said Crawcrustle. "Foul stuff. It rots the guts and spoils the taste buds. But I could not find any lighter fluid at this time of night."

He lit a match, then dipped it near the surface of the cup of spirits, which began to burn with a flickery light. He ate the match. Then he gargled with the flaming liquid, and blew a sheet of flame into the street, incinerating a sheet of newspaper as it blew by.

"Crusty," said Virginia Boote, "that's a good way to get yourself killed."

Zebediah T. Crawcrustle grinned through black teeth. "I don't actually drink it," he told her. "I just gargle and breathe it out."

"You're playing with fire," she warned him.

"That's how I know I'm alive," said Zebediah T. Crawcrustle.

Virginia said, "Oh, Zeb. I *am* excited. I am so excited. What do you think the Sunbird tastes like?"

"Richer than quail and moister than turkey, fatter than ostrich and lusher than duck," said Zebediah T. Crawcrustle. "Once eaten it's never forgotten."

"We're going to Egypt," she said. "I've never been to Egypt." Then she said, "Do you have anywhere to stay the night?"

He coughed, a small cough that rattled around in his old chest. "I'm getting too old to sleep in doorways and gutters," he said. "Still, I have my pride."

"Well," she said, looking at the man, "you could sleep on my sofa."

"It is not that I am not grateful for the offer," he said, "but there is a bench in the bus station that has my name on it."

And he pushed himself away from the wall and tottered majestically down the street.

There really *was* a bench in the bus station that had his name on it. He had donated the bench to the bus station back when he was flush, and his name was attached to the back of it, engraved upon a small brass plaque. Zebediah T. Crawcrustle was not always poor. Sometimes he was rich, but he had difficulty in holding on to his wealth, and whenever he had become wealthy he discovered that the world frowned on rich men eating in hobo jungles at the back of the railroad, or consorting with the winos in the park, so he would fritter his wealth away as best he could. There were always little bits of it here and there that he had forgotten about, and sometimes he would forget that he did not like being rich, and then he would set out again and seek his fortune, and find it.

He had needed a shave for a week, and the hairs of his seven-day beard were starting to come through snow white.

They left for Egypt on a Sunday, the Epicureans. There were five of them there, and Hollyberry NoFeathers McCoy waved good-bye to them at the airport. It was a very small airport, which still permitted waves good-bye.

"Good-bye, Father!" called Hollyberry NoFeathers McCoy.

Augustus TwoFeathers McCoy waved back at her as they walked along the asphalt to the little prop plane, which would begin the first leg of their journey.

"It seems to me," said Augustus TwoFeathers McCoy, "that I remember, albeit dimly, a day like this long, long ago. I was a small boy, in that memory, waving good-bye. I believe it was the last time I saw my father, and I am struck once more with a sudden presentiment of doom." He waved one last time at the small child at the other end of the field, and she waved back at him.

"You waved just as enthusiastically back then," agreed Zebediah T. Crawcrustle, "but I think she waves with slightly more aplomb."

It was true. She did.

They took a small plane and then a larger plane, then

a smaller plane, a blimp, a gondola, a train, a hot-air balloon, and a rented Jeep.

They rattled through Cairo in the Jeep. They passed the old market, and they turned off on the third lane they came to (if they had continued on they would have come to a drainage ditch that was once an irrigation canal). Mustapha Stroheim himself was sitting outside in the street, perched on an elderly wicker chair. All of the tables and chairs were on the side of the street, and it was not a particularly wide street.

"Welcome, my friends, to my *Kahwa*," said Mustapha Stroheim. "*Kahwa* is Egyptian for café, or for coffeehouse. Would you like tea? Or a game of dominoes?"

"We would like to be shown to our rooms," said Jackie Newhouse.

"Not me," said Zebediah T. Crawcrustle. "I'll sleep in the street. It's warm enough, and that doorstep over there looks mighty comfortable."

"I'll have coffee, please," said Augustus TwoFeathers McCoy.

"Of course."

"Do you have water?" asked Professor Mandalay.

"Who said that?" said Mustapha Stroheim. "Oh, it was you, little gray man. My mistake. When I first saw you I thought you were someone's shadow."

"I will have *ShaySokkar Bosta*," said Virginia Boote, which is a glass of hot tea with the sugar on the side. "And I will play backgammon with anyone who wishes to take me on. There's not a soul in Cairo I cannot beat at backgammon, if I can remember the rules."

Augustus TwoFeathers McCoy was shown to his room. Professor Mandalay was shown to his room. Jackie Newhouse was shown to his room. This was not a lengthy procedure; they were all in the same room, after all.

There was another room in the back where Virginia would sleep, and a third room for Mustapha Stroheim and his family.

"What's that you're writing?" asked Jackie Newhouse.

"It's the procedures, annals, and minutes of the Epicurean Club," said Professor Mandalay. He was writing in a large leather-bound book with a small black pen. "I have chronicled our journey here, and all the things that we have eaten on the way. I shall keep writing as we eat the Sunbird, to record for posterity all the tastes and textures, all the smells and the juices."

"Did Crawcrustle say how he was going to cook the Sunbird?" asked Jackie Newhouse.

"He did," said Augustus TwoFeathers McCoy. "He says that he will drain a beer can, so it is only a third full. And then he will add herbs and spices to the beer can. He will stand the bird up on the can, with the can in its inner cavity, and place it up on the barbecue to roast. He says it is the traditional way."

Jackie Newhouse sniffed. "It sounds suspiciously modern to me."

"Crawcrustle says it is the traditional method of cooking the Sunbird," repeated Augustus.

"Indeed I did," said Crawcrustle, coming up the stairs. It was a small building. The stairs weren't that far away, and the walls were not thick ones. "The oldest beer in the world is Egyptian beer, and they've been cooking the Sunbird with it for over five thousand years now."

"But the beer can is a relatively modern invention," said Professor Mandalay, as Zebediah T. Crawcrustle came through the door. Crawcrustle was holding a cup of Turkish coffee, black as tar, which steamed like a kettle and bubbled like a tarpit.

"That coffee looks pretty hot," said Augustus Two-Feathers McCoy.

Crawcrustle knocked back the cup, draining half the

contents. "Nah," he said. "Not really. And the beer can isn't really that new an invention. We used to make them out of an amalgam of copper and tin in the old days, sometimes with a little silver in there, sometimes not. It depended on the smith, and what he had to hand. You needed something that would stand up to the heat. I see that you are all looking at me doubtfully. Gentlemen, consider: of course the Ancient Egyptians made beer cans; where else would they have kept their beer?"

From outside the window, at the tables in the street, came a wailing, in many voices. Virginia Boote had persuaded the locals to start playing backgammon for money, and she was cleaning them out. That woman was a backgammon shark.

Out back of Mustapha Stroheim's coffeehouse there was a courtyard containing a broken-down old barbecue, made of clay bricks and a half-melted metal grating, and an old wooden table. Crawcrustle spent the next day rebuilding the barbecue and cleaning it, oiling down the metal grille.

"That doesn't look like it's been used in forty years," said Virginia Boote. Nobody would play backgammon with her any longer, and her purse bulged with grubby piasters.

"Something like that," said Crawcrustle. "Maybe a little more. Here, Ginnie, make yourself useful. I've written a list of things I need from the market. It's mostly herbs and spices and wood chips. You can take one of the children of Mustapha Stroheim to translate for you."

"My pleasure, Crusty."

The other three members of the Epicurean Club were occupying themselves in their own way. Jackie Newhouse was making friends with many of the people of the area, who were attracted by his elegant suits and his skill at playing the violin. Augustus TwoFeathers McCoy went for long walks. Professor Mandalay spent time translating the hieroglyphics he had noticed were incised upon the clay bricks in the barbecue. He said that a foolish man might believe that they proved the barbecue in Mustapha Stroheim's backyard was once sacred to the Sun. "But I, who am an intelligent man," he said, "I see immediately that what has happened is that bricks that were once, long ago, part of a temple, have, over the millennia, been reused. I doubt that these people know the value of what they have here."

"Oh, they know all right," said Zebediah T. Crawcrustle. "And these bricks weren't part of any temple. They've been right here for five thousand years, since we built the barbecue. Before that we made do with stones."

Virginia Boote returned with a filled shopping basket. "Here," she said. "Red sandalwood and patchouli, vanilla beans, lavender twigs and sage and cinnamon leaves, whole nutmegs, garlic bulbs, cloves, and rosemary: everything you wanted and more."

Zebediah T. Crawcrustle grinned with delight. "The Sunbird will be so happy," he told her.

He spent the afternoon preparing a barbecue sauce. He said it was only respectful, and besides, the Sunbird's flesh was often slightly on the dry side.

The Epicureans spent that evening sitting at the wicker tables in the street out front, while Mustapha Stroheim and his family brought them tea and coffee and hot mint drinks. Zebediah T. Crawcrustle had told the Epicureans that they would be having the Sunbird of Suntown for Sunday lunch, and that they might wish to avoid food the night before, to ensure that they had an appetite.

"I have a presentiment of doom upon me," said Augustus TwoFeathers McCoy that night, in a bed that was far too small for him, before he slept. "And I fear it shall come to us with barbecue sauce."

* * *

They were all so hungry the following morning. Zebediah T. Crawcrustle had a comedic apron on, with the words KISS THE COOK written upon it in violently green letters. He had already sprinkled the brandy-soaked raisins and grain beneath the stunted avocado tree behind the house, and he was arranging the scented woods, the herbs, and the spices on the bed of charcoal. Mustapha Stroheim and his family had gone to visit relatives on the other side of Cairo.

"Does anybody have a match?" Crawcrustle asked.

Jackie Newhouse pulled out a Zippo lighter, and passed it to Crawcrustle, who lit the dried cinnamon leaves and dried laurel leaves beneath the charcoal. The smoke drifted up into the noon air.

"The cinnamon and sandalwood smoke will bring the Sunbird," said Crawcrustle.

"Bring it from where?" asked Augustus TwoFeathers McCoy.

"From the Sun," said Crawcrustle. "That's where he sleeps."

Professor Mandalay coughed discreetly. He said, "The Earth is, at its closest, 91 million miles from the Sun. The fastest dive by a bird ever recorded is that of the peregrine falcon, at 273 miles per hour. Flying at that speed, from the Sun, it would take a bird a little over thirty-eight years to reach us—if it could fly through the dark and cold and vacuum of space, of course."

"Of course," agreed Zebediah T. Crawcrustle. He shaded his eyes and squinted and looked upward. "Here it comes," he said.

It looked almost as if the bird was flying out of the sun; but that could not have been the case. You could not look directly at the noonday sun, after all.

First it was a silhouette, black against the sun and against the blue sky, then the sunlight caught its feathers, and the watchers on the ground caught their breath. You have never seen anything like sunlight on the Sunbird's feathers; seeing something like that would take your breath away.

The Sunbird flapped its wide wings once, then it began to glide in ever-decreasing circles in the air above Mustapha Stroheim's coffeehouse.

The bird landed in the avocado tree. Its feathers were golden, and purple, and silver. It was smaller than a turkey, larger than a rooster, and had the long legs and high head of a heron, though its head was more like the head of an eagle.

"It is very beautiful," said Virginia Boote. "Look at the two tall feathers on its head. Aren't they lovely?"

"It is indeed quite lovely," said Professor Mandalay.

"There is something familiar about that bird's head-feathers," said Augustus TwoFeathers McCoy.

"We pluck the headfeathers before we roast the bird," said Zebediah T. Crawcrustle. "It's the way it's always done."

The Sunbird perched on a branch of the avocado tree, in a patch of sun. It seemed almost as if it were glowing, gently, in the sunlight, as if its feathers were made of sunlight, iridescent with purples and greens and golds. It preened itself, extending one wing in the sunlight. It nibbled and stroked at the wing with its beak until all the feathers were in their correct position, and oiled. Then it extended the other wing, and repeated the process. Finally, the bird emitted a contented chirrup, and flew the short distance from the branch to the ground.

It strutted across the dried mud, peering from side to side short-sightedly.

"Look!" said Jackie Newhouse. "It's found the grain."

"It seemed almost that it was looking for it," said Augustus TwoFeathers McCoy. "That it was expecting the grain to be there."

"That's where I always leave it," said Zebediah T. Crawcrustle.

"It's so lovely," said Virginia Boote. "But now I see it

closer, I can see that it's much older than I thought. Its eyes are cloudy and its legs are shaking. But it's still lovely."

"The Bennu bird is the loveliest of birds," said Zebediah T. Crawcrustle.

Virginia Boote spoke good restaurant Egyptian, but beyond that she was all at sea. "What's a Bennu bird?" she asked. "Is that Egyptian for Sunbird?"

"The Bennu bird," said Professor Mandalay, "roosts in the Persea tree. It has two feathers on its head. It is sometimes represented as being like a heron, and sometimes like an eagle. There is more, but it is too unlikely to bear repeating."

"It's eaten the grain and the raisins!" exclaimed Jackie Newhouse. "Now it's stumbling drunkenly from side to side—such majesty, even in its drunkenness!"

Zebediah T. Crawcrustle walked over to the Sunbird, which, with a great effort of will, was staggering back and forth on the mud beneath the avocado tree, not tripping over its long legs. He stood directly in front of the bird, and then, very slowly, he bowed to it. He bent like a very old man, slowly and creakily, but still he bowed. And the Sunbird bowed back to him, then it toppled to the mud. Zebediah T. Crawcrustle picked it up reverently, and placed it in his arms, carrying it as one would carry a child, and he took it back to the plot of land behind Mustapha Stroheim's coffeehouse, and the others followed him.

First he plucked the two majestic headfeathers, and set them aside.

And then, without plucking the bird, he gutted it, and placed the guts on the smoking twigs. He put the half-filled beer can inside the body cavity, and placed the bird upon the barbecue.

"Sunbird cooks fast," warned Crawcrustle. "Get your plates ready."

The beers of the ancient Egyptians were flavored with

cardamom and coriander, for the Egyptians had no hops; their beers were rich and flavorsome and thirst-quenching. You could build pyramids after drinking that beer, and sometimes people did. On the barbecue the beer steamed the inside of the Sunbird, keeping it moist. As the heat of the charcoal reached them, the feathers of the bird burned off, igniting with a flash like a magnesium flare, so bright that the Epicureans were forced to avert their eyes.

The smell of roast fowl filled the air, richer than peacock, lusher than duck. The mouths of the assembled Epicureans began to water. It seemed like it had been cooking for no time at all, but Zebediah lifted the Sunbird from the charcoal bed and put it on the table. Then, with a carving knife, he sliced it up and placed the steaming meat on the plates. He poured a little barbecue sauce over each piece of meat. He placed the carcass directly onto the flames.

Each member of the Epicurean Club sat in the back of Mustapha Stroheim's coffeehouse, sat around an elderly wooden table, and they ate with their fingers.

"Zebby, this is amazing!" said Virginia Boote, talking as she ate. "It melts in your mouth. It tastes like heaven."

"It tastes like the sun," said Augustus TwoFeathers McCoy, putting his food away as only a big man can. He had a leg in one hand, and some breast in the other. "It is the finest thing I have ever eaten, and I do not regret eating it, but I do believe that I shall miss my daughter."

"It is perfect," said Jackie Newhouse. "It tastes like love and fine music. It tastes like truth."

Professor Mandalay was scribbling in the bound annals of the Epicurean Club. He was recording his reaction to the meat of the bird, and recording the reactions of the other Epicureans, and trying not to drip on the page while he wrote, for with the hand that was not writing he was holding a wing, and, fastidiously, he was nibbling the meat off it.

"It is strange," said Jackie Newhouse, "for as I eat it, it gets hotter and hotter in my mouth and in my stomach."

"Yup. It'll do that. It's best to prepare for it ahead of time," said Zebediah T. Crawcrustle. "Eat coals and flames and lightning bugs to get used to it. Otherwise it can be a trifle hard on the system."

Zebediah T. Crawcrustle was eating the head of the bird, crunching its bones and beak in his mouth. As he ate, the bones sparked small lightnings against his teeth. He just grinned and chewed the more.

The bones of the Sunbird's carcass burned orange on the barbecue, and then they began to burn white. There was a thick heat-haze in the courtyard at the back of Mustapha Stroheim's coffeehouse, and in it everything shimmered, as if the people around the table were seeing the world through water or a dream.

"It is so good!" said Virginia Boote as she ate. "It is the best thing I have ever eaten. It tastes like my youth. It tastes like forever." She licked her fingers, then picked up the last slice of meat from her plate. "The Sunbird of Suntown," she said. "Does it have another name?"

"It is the Phoenix of Heliopolis," said Zebediah T. Crawcrustle. "It is the bird that dies in ashes and flame, and is reborn, generation after generation. It is the Bennu bird, which flew across the waters when all was dark. When its time is come it is burned on the fire of rare woods and spices and herbs, and in the ashes it is reborn, time after time, world without end."

"Fire!" exclaimed Professor Mandalay. "It feels as if my insides are burning up!" He sipped his water, but seemed no happier.

"My fingers," said Virginia Boote. "Look at my fingers." She held them up. They were glowing inside, as if lit with inner flames.

Now the air was so hot you could have baked an egg in it.

There was a spark and a sputter. The two yellow feathers in Augustus TwoFeathers McCoy's hair went up like sparklers. "Crawcrustle," said Jackie Newhouse, aflame, "answer me truly. How long have you been eating the Phoenix?"

"A little over ten thousand years," said Zebediah. "Give or take a few thousand. It's not hard, once you master the trick of it; it's just mastering the trick of it that's hard. But this is the best Phoenix I've ever prepared. Or do I mean, 'this is the best I've ever cooked this Phoenix'?"

"The years!" said Virginia Boote. "They are burning off you!"

"They do that," admitted Zebediah. "You've got to get used to the heat, though, before you eat it. Otherwise you can just burn away."

"Why did I not remember this?" said Augustus Two-Feathers McCoy, through the bright flames that surrounded him. "Why did I not remember that this was how my father went, and his father before him, that each of them went to Heliopolis to eat the Phoenix? And why do I only remember it now?"

"Because the years are burning off you," said Professor Mandalay. He had closed the leather book as soon as the page he had been writing on caught fire. The edges of the book were charred, but the rest of the book would be fine. "When the years burn, the memories of those years come back." He looked more solid now, through the wavering burning air, and he was smiling. None of them had ever seen Professor Mandalay smile before.

"Shall we burn away to nothing?" asked Virginia, now incandescent. "Or shall we burn back to childhood and burn back to ghosts and angels and then come forward again? It does not matter. Oh Crusty, this is all such *fun!*"

"Perhaps," said Jackie Newhouse, through the fire,

"there might have been a little more vinegar in the sauce. I feel a meat like this could have dealt with something more robust." And then he was gone, leaving only an after-image.

"*Chacun à son goût,*" said Zebediah T. Crawcrustle, which is French for "each to his own taste," and he licked his fingers and he shook his head. "Best it's ever been," he said, with enormous satisfaction.

"Good-bye, Crusty," said Virginia. She put her flame-white hand out, and held his dark hand tightly, for one moment, or perhaps for two.

And then there was nothing in the courtyard back of Mustapha Stroheim's *Kahwa* (or coffeehouse) in Heliopolis (which was once the city of the Sun, and is now a suburb of Cairo) but white ash, which blew up in the momentary breeze, and settled like powdered sugar or like snow; and nobody there but a young man with dark, dark hair and even, ivory-colored teeth, wearing an apron that said KISS THE COOK.

A tiny golden-purple bird stirred in the thick bed of ashes on top of the clay bricks, as if it were waking for the first time. It made a high-pitched "peep!" and it looked directly into the sun, as an infant looks at a parent. It stretched its wings as if to dry them, and, eventually, when it was quite ready, it flew upward, toward the sun, and nobody watched it leave but the young man in the courtyard.

There were two long golden feathers at the young man's feet, beneath the ash that had once been a wooden table, and he gathered them up, and brushed the white ash from them and placed them, reverently, inside his jacket. Then he removed his apron, and he went upon his way.

Hollyberry TwoFeathers McCoy is a grown woman, with children of her own. There are silver hairs on her head, in there with the black, beneath the golden feathers in the bun at the back. You can see that once the feathers must have looked pretty special, but that would have been a long time ago. She is the president of the Epicurean Club—a rich and rowdy bunch—having inherited the position, many long years ago, from her father.

I hear that the Epicureans are beginning to grumble once again. They are saying that they have eaten everything.

(FOR HMG—A BELATED BIRTHDAY PRESENT)

INVENTING ALADDIN

In bed with him that night, like every night,
her sister at their feet, she ends her tale,
then waits. Her sister quickly takes her cue,
and says, "I cannot sleep. Another, please?"
Scheherazade takes one small nervous
    breath
and she begins, "In faraway Peking
there lived a lazy youth with his mama.
His name? Aladdin. His papa was dead. . . ."
She tells them how a dark magician came,
claiming to be his uncle, with a plan:
He took the boy out to a lonely place,
gave him a ring he said would keep him safe,
dropped in a cavern filled with precious stones,
"Bring me the lamp!" and when Aladdin won't,
in darkness he's abandoned and entombed. . . .

There now.

Aladdin locked beneath the earth,
she stops, her husband hooked for one
    more night.
Next day
she cooks
she feeds her kids
she dreams. . . .

Knowing Aladdin's trapped,
and that her tale
has bought her just one day.
What happens now?
She wishes that she knew.

It's only when that evening comes around
and husband says, just as he always says,
"Tomorrow morning, I shall have your head,"
when Dunyazade, her sister, asks, "But please,
what of Aladdin?" only then, she knows. . . .

And in a cavern hung about with jewels
Aladdin rubs his lamp. The Genie comes.
The story tumbles on. Aladdin gets
the princess and a palace made of pearls.
Watch now, the dark magician's coming back:
"New lamps for old," he's singing in the street.
Just when Aladdin has lost everything,
she stops.

He'll let her live another night.

Her sister and her husband fall asleep.
She lies awake and stares up in the dark
Playing the variations in her mind:
the ways to give Aladdin back his world,
his palace, his princess, his everything.
And then she sleeps. The tale will need an end,
but now it melts to dreams inside her head.

She wakes,
She feeds the kids
She combs her hair
She goes down to the market
Buys some oil
The oil-seller pours it out for her,

decanting it
from an enormous jar.
She thinks,
What if you hid a man in there?
She buys some sesame as well, that day.

Her sister says, "He hasn't killed you yet."
"Not yet." Unspoken waits the phrase, "He will."

In bed she tells them of the magic ring
Aladdin rubs. Slave of the Ring appears. . . .
Magician dead, Aladdin saved, she stops.
But once the story's done, the teller's dead,
her only hope's to start another tale.
Scheherazade inspects her store of words,
half-built, half-baked ideas and dreams combine
with jars just big enough to hide a man,
and she thinks, *Open Sesame,* and smiles.
"Now, Ali Baba was a righteous man,
but he was poor . . ." she starts, and she's away,
and so her life is safe for one more night,
until she bores him, or invention fails.

She does not know where any tale waits
before it's told. (No more do I.)
But forty thieves sounds good, so forty
thieves it is. She prays she's bought
    another clutch of days.

We save our lives in such unlikely ways.

THE MONARCH OF THE GLEN

An American Gods Novella

> "She herself is a haunted house. She does not possess
> herself; her ancestors sometimes come and peer out of
> the windows of her eyes and that is very frightening."
> ANGELA CARTER,
> "The Lady of the House of Love"

I

"If you ask me," said the little man to Shadow, "you're
something of a monster. Am I right?"

They were the only two people, apart from the barmaid, in the bar of a hotel in a town on the north coast
of Scotland. Shadow had been sitting there on his own,
drinking a lager, when the man came over and sat at his
table. It was late summer, and it seemed to Shadow that
everything was cold and small and damp. He had a
small book of Pleasant Local Walks in front of him, and
was studying the walk he planned to do tomorrow,
along the coast, toward Cape Wrath.

He closed the book.

"I'm American," said Shadow, "if that's what you
mean."

The little man cocked his head to one side, and he
winked, theatrically. He had steel gray hair, and a gray

face, and a gray coat, and he looked like a small-town lawyer. "Well, perhaps that is what I mean, at that," he said. Shadow had had problems understanding Scottish accents in his short time in the country, all rich burrs and strange words and trills, but he had no trouble understanding this man. Everything the little man said was small and crisp, each word so perfectly enunciated that it made Shadow feel like he himself was talking with a mouthful of oatmeal.

The little man sipped his drink and said, "So you're American. Oversexed, overpaid, and over here. Eh? D'you work on the rigs?"

"Sorry?"

"An oilman? Out on the big metal platforms. We get oil people up here, from time to time."

"No. I'm not from the rigs."

The little man took out a pipe from his pocket, and a small penknife, and began to remove the dottle from the bowl. Then he tapped it out into the ashtray. "They have oil in Texas, you know," he said, after a while, as if he were confiding a great secret. "That's in America."

"Yes," said Shadow.

He thought about saying something about Texans believing that Texas was actually in Texas, but he suspected that he'd have to start explaining what he meant, so he said nothing.

Shadow had been away from America for the better part of two years. He had been away when the towers fell. He told himself sometimes that he did not care if he ever went back, and sometimes he almost came close to believing himself. He had reached the Scottish mainland two days ago, landed in Thurso on the ferry from the Orkneys, and had traveled to the town he was staying in by bus.

The little man was talking. "So there's a Texas oilman, down in Aberdeen, he's talking to an old fellow he meets in a pub, much like you and me meeting actually, and they get talking, and the Texan, he says, Back in Texas I get up in the morning, I get into my car—I won't try to do the accent, if you don't mind—I'll turn the key in the ignition, and put my foot down on the accelerator, what you call the, the—"

"Gas pedal," said Shadow, helpfully.

"Right. Put my foot down on the gas pedal at breakfast, and by lunchtime I still won't have reached the edge of my property. And the canny old Scot, he just nods and says, Aye, well, I used to have a car like that myself."

The little man laughed raucously, to show that the joke was done. Shadow smiled and nodded to show that he knew it was a joke.

"What are you drinking? Lager? Same again over here, Jennie love. Mine's a Lagavulin." The little man tamped tobacco from a pouch into his pipe. "Did you know that Scotland's bigger than America?"

There had been no one in the hotel bar when Shadow came downstairs that evening, just the thin barmaid, reading a newspaper and smoking her cigarette. He'd come down to sit by the open fire, as his bedroom was cold, and the metal radiators on the bedroom wall were colder than the room. He hadn't expected company.

"No," said Shadow, always willing to play straight man. "I didn't. How'd you reckon that?"

"It's all fractal," said the little man. "The smaller you look, the more things unpack. It could take you as long to drive across America as it would to drive across Scotland, if you did it the right way. It's like, you look on a map, and the coastlines are solid lines. But when you walk them, they're all over the place. I saw a whole program on it on the telly the other night. Great stuff."

"Okay," said Shadow.

The little man's pipe lighter flamed, and he sucked and puffed and sucked and puffed until he was satisfied that the pipe was burning well, then he put the lighter, the pouch, and the penknife back into his coat pocket.

"Anyway, anyway," said the little man. "I believe you're planning on staying here through the weekend."

"Yes," said Shadow. "Do you . . . are you with the hotel?"

"No, no. Truth to tell, I was standing in the hall when you arrived. I heard you talking to Gordon on the reception desk."

Shadow nodded. He had thought that he had been alone in the reception hall when he had registered, but it was possible that the little man had passed through. But still . . . there was a wrongness to this conversation. There was a wrongness to everything.

Jennie the barmaid put their drinks onto the bar. "Five pounds twenty," she said. She picked up her newspaper, and started to read once more. The little man went to the bar, paid, and brought back the drinks.

"So how long are you in Scotland?" asked the little man.

Shadow shrugged. "I wanted to see what it was like. Take some walks. See the sights. Maybe a week. Maybe a month."

Jennie put down her newspaper. "It's the arse-end of nowhere up here," she said, cheerfully. "You should go somewhere interesting."

"That's where you're wrong," said the little man. "It's only the arse-end of nowhere if you look at it wrong. See that map, laddie?" He pointed to a fly-specked map of Northern Scotland on the opposite wall of the bar. "You know what's wrong with it?"

"No."

"It's upside down!" the man said, triumphantly. "North's at the top. It's saying to the world that this is where things stop. Go no further. The world ends here. But you see, that's not how it was. This wasn't the north of Scotland. This was the southernmost tip of the Viking world. You know what the second most northern county in Scotland is called?"

Shadow glanced at the map, but it was too far away to read. He shook his head.

"Sutherland!" said the little man. He showed his teeth. "The South Land. Not to anyone else in the world it wasn't, but it was to the Vikings."

Jennie the barmaid walked over to them. "I won't be gone long," she said. "Call the front desk if you need anything before I get back." She put a log on the fire, then she went out into the hall.

"Are you a historian?" Shadow asked.

"Good one," said the little man. "You may be a monster, but you're funny. I'll give you that."

"I'm not a monster," said Shadow.

"Aye, that's what monsters always say," said the little man. "I was a specialist once. In St. Andrews. Now I'm in general practice. Well, I was. I'm semiretired. Go in to the surgery a couple of days a week, just to keep my hand in."

"Why do you say I'm a monster?" asked Shadow.

"Because," said the little man, lifting his whisky glass with the air of one making an irrefutable point, "I am something of a monster myself. Like calls to like. We are all monsters, are we not? Glorious monsters, shambling through the swamps of unreason. . . ." He sipped his whisky, then said, "Tell me, a big man like you, have you ever been a bouncer? 'Sorry mate, I'm afraid you can't come in here tonight, private function going on, sling your hook and get on out of it,' all that?"

"No," said Shadow.

"But you must have done something like that?"

"Yes," said Shadow, who had been a bodyguard once, to an old god; but that was in another country.

"You, uh, you'll pardon me for asking, don't take this the wrong way, but do you need money?"

"Everyone needs money. But I'm okay." This was not

entirely true; but it was a truth that, when Shadow needed money, the world seemed to go out of its way to provide it.

"Would you like to make a wee bit of spending money? Being a bouncer? It's a piece of piss. Money for old rope."

"At a disco?"

"Not exactly. A private party. They rent a big old house near here, come in from all over at the end of the summer. So last year, everybody's having a grand old time, champagne out of doors, all that, and there was some trouble. A bad lot. Out to ruin everybody's weekend."

"These were locals?"

"I don't think so."

"Was it political?" asked Shadow. He did not want to be drawn into local politics.

"Not a bit of it. Yobs and hairies and idiots. Anyway. They probably won't come back this year. Probably off in the wilds of nowhere demonstrating against international capitalism. But just to be on the safe side, the folk up at the house've asked me to look out for someone who could do a spot of intimidating. You're a big lad, and that's what they want."

"How much?" asked Shadow.

"Can you handle yourself in a fight, if it came down to it?" asked the man.

Shadow didn't say anything. The little man looked him up and down, and then he grinned again, showing tobacco-stained teeth. "Fifteen hundred pounds, for a long weekend's work. That's good money. And it's cash. Nothing you'd ever need to report to the tax man."

"This weekend coming?" said Shadow.

"Starting Friday morning. It's a big old house. Part of it used to be a castle. West of Cape Wrath."

"I don't know," said Shadow.

"If you do it," said the little gray man, "you'll get a

fantastic weekend in a historical house, and I can guarantee you'll get to meet all kinds of interesting people. Perfect holiday job. I just wish I was younger. And, uh, a great deal taller, actually."

Shadow said "Okay," and as soon as he said it, wondered if he would regret it.

"Good man. I'll get you more details as and when." The little gray man stood up, and gave Shadow's shoulder a gentle pat as he walked past. Then he went out, leaving Shadow in the bar on his own.

II

Shadow had been on the road for about eighteen months. He had backpacked across Europe and down into northern Africa. He had picked olives and fished for sardines and driven a truck and sold wine from the side of a road. Finally, several months ago, he had hitchhiked his way back to Norway, to Oslo, where he had been born thirty-five years before.

He was not sure what he had been looking for. He only knew that he had not found it, although there were moments, in the high ground, in the crags and waterfalls, when he was certain that whatever he needed was just around the corner: behind a jut of granite, or in the nearest pine wood.

Still, it was a deeply unsatisfactory visit, and when, in Bergen, he was asked if he would be half of the crew of a motor yacht on its way to meet its owner in Cannes, he said yes.

They had sailed from Bergen to the Shetlands, and then to the Orkneys, where they spent the night in a bed and breakfast in Stromness. Next morning, leaving the harbor, the engines had failed, ultimately and irrevocably, and the boat had been towed back to port.

Bjorn, who was the captain and the other half of the crew, stayed with the boat, to talk to the insurers and field the angry calls from the boat's owner. Shadow saw no reason to stay: he took the ferry to Thurso, on the north coast of Scotland.

He was restless. At night he dreamed of freeways, of entering the neon edges of a city where the people spoke English. Sometimes it was in the Midwest, sometimes it was in Florida, sometimes on the East Coast, sometimes on the West.

When he got off the ferry he bought a book of scenic walks, and picked up a bus timetable, and he set off into the world.

Jennie the barmaid came back, and started to wipe all the surfaces with a cloth. Her hair was so blonde it was almost white, and it was tied up at the back in a bun.

"So what is it people do around here for fun?" asked Shadow.

"They drink. They wait to die," she said. "Or they go south. That pretty much exhausts your options."

"You sure?"

"Well, think about it. There's nothing up here but sheep and hills. We feed off the tourists, of course, but there's never really enough of you. Sad, isn't it?" Shadow shrugged.

"Are you from New York?" she asked.

"Chicago, originally. But I came here from Norway."

"You speak Norwegian?"

"A little."

"There's somebody you should meet," she said, suddenly. Then she looked at her watch. "Somebody who came here from Norway, a long time ago. Come on."

She put her cleaning cloth down, turned off the bar lights, and walked over to the door. "Come on," she said, again.

"Can you do that?" asked Shadow.

"I can do whatever I want," she said. "It's a free country, isn't it?"

"I guess."

She locked the bar with a brass key. They walked into the reception hall. "Wait here," she said. She went through a door marked PRIVATE, and reappeared several minutes later, wearing a long brown coat. "Okay. Follow me."

They walked out into the street. "So, is this a village or a small town?" asked Shadow.

"It's a fucking graveyard," she said. "Up this way. Come on."

They walked up a narrow road. The moon was huge and a yellowish brown. Shadow could hear the sea, although he could not yet see it. "You're Jennie?" he said.

"That's right. And you?"

"Shadow."

"Is that your real name?"

"It's what they call me."

"Come on, then, Shadow," she said.

At the top of the hill, they stopped. They were on the edge of the village, and there was a gray stone cottage. Jennie opened the gate and led Shadow up a path to the front door. He brushed a small bush at the side of the path, and the air filled with the scent of sweet lavender. There were no lights on in the cottage.

"Whose house is this?" asked Shadow. "It looks empty."

"Don't worry," said Jennie. "She'll be home in a second."

She pushed open the unlocked front door, and they went inside. She turned on the light switch by the door. Most of the inside of the cottage was taken up by a kitchen sitting room. There was a tiny staircase leading up to what Shadow presumed was an attic bedroom. A CD player sat on the pine counter.

"This is your house," said Shadow.

"Home sweet home," she agreed. "You want coffee? Or something to drink?"

"Neither," said Shadow. He wondered what Jennie wanted. She had barely looked at him, hadn't even smiled at him.

"Did I hear right? Was Doctor Gaskell asking you to help look after a party on the weekend?"

"I guess."

"So what are you doing tomorrow and Friday?"

"Walking," said Shadow. "I've got a book. There are some beautiful walks."

"Some of them are beautiful. Some of them are treacherous," she told him. "You can still find winter snow here, in the shadows, in the summer. Things last a long time, in the shadows."

"I'll be careful," he told her.

"That was what the Vikings said," she said, and she smiled. She took off her coat and dropped it on the bright purple sofa. "Maybe I'll see you out there. I like to go for walks." She pulled at the bun at the back of her head, and her pale hair fell free. It was longer than Shadow had thought it would be.

"Do you live here alone?"

She took a cigarette from a packet on the counter, lit it with a match. "What's it to you?" she asked. "You won't be staying the night, will you?"

Shadow shook his head.

"The hotel's at the bottom of the hill," she told him. "You can't miss it. Thanks for walking me home."

Shadow said good night, and walked back, through the lavender night, out to the lane. He stood there for a little while, staring at the moon on the sea, puzzled. Then he walked down the hill until he got to the hotel. She was right: you couldn't miss it. He walked up the stairs, unlocked his room with a key attached to a short stick, and went inside. The room was colder than the corridor.

He took off his shoes, and stretched out on the bed in the dark.

III

The ship was made of the fingernails of dead men, and it lurched through the mist, bucking and rolling hugely and unsteadily on the choppy sea.

There were shadowy shapes on the deck, men as big as hills or houses, and as Shadow got closer he could see their faces: proud men and tall, each one of them. They seemed to ignore the ship's motion, each man waiting on the deck as if frozen in place.

One of them stepped forward, and he grasped Shadow's hand with his own huge hand. Shadow stepped onto the gray deck.

"Well come to this accursed place," said the man holding Shadow's hand, in a deep, gravel voice.

"Hail!" called the men on the deck. "Hail sun-bringer! Hail Baldur!"

The name on Shadow's birth certificate was Balder Moon, but he shook his head. "I am not him," he told them. "I am not the one you are waiting for."

"We are dying here," said the gravel-voiced man, not letting go of Shadow's hand.

It was cold in the misty place between the worlds of waking and the grave. Salt spray crashed on the bows of the gray ship, and Shadow was drenched to the skin.

"Bring us back," said the man holding his hand. "Bring us back or let us go."

Shadow said, "I don't know how."

At that, the men on the deck began to wail and howl. Some of them crashed the hafts of their spears against the deck, others struck the flats of their short swords against the brass bowls at the center of their leather shields, setting up a rhythmic din accompanied by cries that moved from sorrow to a full-throated berserker ululation. . . .

A seagull was screaming in the early-morning air. The bedroom window had blown open in the night and was banging in the wind. Shadow was lying on the top of his bed in his narrow hotel room. His skin was damp, perhaps with sweat.

Another cold day at the end of the summer had begun.

The hotel packed him a Tupperware box containing several chicken sandwiches, a hard-boiled egg, a small packet of cheese-and-onion crisps, and an apple. Gordon on the reception desk, who handed him the box, asked when he'd be back, explaining that if he was more than a couple of hours late they'd call out the rescue services, and asking for the number of Shadow's mobile phone.

Shadow did not have a mobile phone.

He set off on the walk, heading toward the coast. It was beautiful, a desolate beauty that chimed and echoed with the empty places inside Shadow. He had imagined Scotland as being a soft place, all gentle heathery hills, but here on the North Coast everything seemed sharp and jutting, even the gray clouds that scudded across the pale blue sky. It was as if the bones of the world showed through. He followed the route in his book, across scrubby meadows and past splashing burns, up rocky hills and down.

Sometimes he imagined that he was standing still and the world was moving underneath him, that he was simply pushing it past with his legs.

The route was more tiring than he had expected. He had planned to eat at one o'clock, but by midday his legs were tired and he wanted a break. He followed his path to the side of a hill, where a boulder provided a convenient windbreak, and he crouched to eat his lunch. In the distance, ahead of him, he could see the Atlantic.

He had thought himself alone.

She said, "Will you give me your apple?"

It was Jennie, the barmaid from the hotel. Her too-fair hair gusted about her head.

"Hello Jennie," said Shadow. He passed her his apple. She pulled a clasp knife from the pocket of her brown coat, and sat beside him. "Thanks," she said.

"So," said Shadow, "from your accent, you must have come from Norway when you were a kid. I mean, you sound like a local to me."

"Did I say that I came from Norway?"

"Well, didn't you?"

She speared an apple slice, and ate it, fastidiously, from the tip of the knife blade, only touching it with her teeth. She glanced at him. "It was a long time ago."

"Family?"

She moved her shoulders in a shrug, as if any answer she could give him was beneath her.

"So you like it here?"

She looked at him and shook her head. "I feel like a *hulder*."

He'd heard the word before, in Norway. "Aren't they a kind of troll?"

"No. They are mountain creatures, like the trolls, but they come from the woods, and they are very beautiful. Like me." She grinned as she said it, as if she knew that she was too pallid, too sulky, and too thin ever to be beautiful. "They fall in love with farmers."

"Why?"

"Damned if I know," she said. "But they do. Sometimes the farmer realizes that he is talking to a hulder woman, because she has a cow's tail hanging down behind, or worse, sometimes from behind there is nothing there, she is just hollow and empty, like a shell. Then the farmer says a prayer or runs away, flees back to his mother or his farm.

"But sometimes the farmers do not run. Sometimes they throw a knife over her shoulder, or just smile, and they marry the hulder woman. Then her tail falls off. But she is still stronger than any human woman could ever be. And she still pines for her home in the forests and the mountains. She will never be truly happy. She will never be human."

"What happens to her then?" asked Shadow. "Does she age and die with her farmer?"

She had sliced the apple down to the core. Now, with a flick of the wrist, she sent the apple core arcing off the side of the hill. "When her man dies . . . I think she goes back to the hills and the woods." She stared out at the hillside. "There's a story about one of them who was married to a farmer who didn't treat her well. He shouted at her, wouldn't help around the farm, he came home from the village drunk and angry. Sometimes he beat her.

"Now, one day she's in the farmhouse, making up the morning's fire, and he comes in and starts shouting at her, for his food is not ready, and he is angry, nothing she does is right, he doesn't know why he married her, and she listens to him for a while, and then, saying nothing, she reaches down to the fireplace, and she picks up the poker. A heavy black iron jobbie. She takes that poker and, without an effort, she bends it into a perfect circle, just like her wedding ring. She doesn't grunt or sweat, she just bends it, like you'd bend a reed. And her farmer sees this and he goes white as a sheet, and doesn't say anything else about his breakfast. He's seen what she did to the poker and he knows that at any time in the last five years she could have done the same to him. And until he died, he never laid another finger on her, never said one harsh word. Now, you tell me something, Mister everybody-calls-you-Shadow, if she could do that, why did she let him beat her in the first place? Why would she want to be with someone like that? You tell me."

"Maybe," said Shadow. "Maybe she was lonely."

She wiped the blade of the knife on her jeans.

"Doctor Gaskell kept saying you were a monster," she said. "Is it true?"

"I don't think so," said Shadow.

"Pity," she said. "You know where you are with monsters, don't you?"

"You do?"

"Absolutely. At the end of the day, you're going to be dinner. Talking about which, I'll show you something." She stood up, and led him to the top of the hill. "See. Over there? On the far side of that hill, where it drops into the glen, you can just see the house you'll be working at this weekend. Do you see it, over there?"

"No."

"Look. I'll point. Follow the line of my finger." She stood close to him, held out her hand and pointed to the side of a distant ridge. He could see the overhead sun glinting off something he supposed was a lake—or a loch, he corrected himself, he was in Scotland after all—and above that a gray outcropping on the side of a hill. He had taken it for rocks, but it was too regular to be anything but a building.

"That's the castle?"

"I'd not call it that. Just a big house in the glen."

"Have you been to one of the parties there?"

"They don't invite locals," she said. "And they wouldn't ask me. You shouldn't do it, anyway. You should say no."

"They're paying good money," he told her.

She touched him then, for the first time, placed her pale fingers on the back of his dark hand. "And what good is money to a monster?" she asked, and smiled, and Shadow was damned if he didn't think that maybe she *was* beautiful, at that.

And then she put down her hand and backed away. "Well?" she said. "Shouldn't you be off on your walk? You've not got much longer before you'll have to start heading back again. The light goes fast when it goes, this time of year."

And she stood and watched him as he hefted his rucksack, and began to walk down the hill. He turned around when he reached the bottom and looked up. She was still looking at him. He waved, and she waved back.

The next time he looked back she was gone.

He took the little ferry across the kyle to the cape, and walked up to the lighthouse. There was a minibus from the lighthouse back to the ferry, and he took it.

He got back to the hotel at eight that night, exhausted but feeling satisfied. It had rained once, in the late afternoon, but he had taken shelter in a tumbledown bothy, and read a five-year-old newspaper while the rain drummed against the roof. It had ended after half an hour, but Shadow had been glad that he had good boots, for the earth had turned to mud.

He was starving. He went into the hotel restaurant. It was empty. Shadow said "Hello?"

An elderly woman came to the door between the restaurant and the kitchen and said, "Aye?"

"Are you still serving dinner?"

"Aye." She looked at him disapprovingly, from his muddy boots to his tousled hair. "Are you a guest?"

"Yes. I'm in room eleven."

"Well . . . you'll probably want to change before dinner," she said. "It's kinder to the other diners."

"So you *are* serving."

"Aye."

He went up to his room, dropped his rucksack on the bed, and took off his boots. He put on his sneakers, ran a comb through his hair, and went back downstairs.

The dining room was no longer empty. Two people were sitting at a table in the corner, two people who seemed different in every way that people could be different: a small woman who looked to be in her late fifties, hunched and birdlike at the table, and a young man, big and awkward and perfectly bald. Shadow decided that they were mother and son.

He sat down at a table in the center of the room.

The elderly waitress came in with a tray. She gave both of the other diners a bowl of soup. The man began to blow on his soup, to cool it; his mother tapped him, hard, on the back of his hand, with her spoon. "Stop that," she said. She began to spoon the soup into her mouth, slurping it noisily.

The bald man looked around the room, sadly. He caught Shadow's eye, and Shadow nodded at him. The man sighed, and returned to his steaming soup.

Shadow scanned the menu without enthusiasm. He was ready to order, but the waitress had vanished again.

A flash of gray; Dr. Gaskell peered in at the door of the restaurant. He walked into the room, came over to Shadow's table.

"Do you mind if I join you?"

"Not at all. Please. Sit down."

He sat down, opposite Shadow. "Have a good day?"

"Very good. I walked."

"Best way to work up an appetite. So. First thing tomorrow they're sending a car out here to pick you up. Bring your things. They'll take you out to the house. Show you the ropes."

"And the money?" asked Shadow.

"They'll sort that out. Half at the beginning, half at the end. Anything else you want to know?"

The waitress stood at the edge of the room, watching them, making no move to approach. "Yeah. What do I have to do to get some food around here?"

"What do you want? I recommend the lamb chops. The lamb's local."

"Sounds good."

Gaskell said loudly, "Excuse me, Maura. Sorry to trouble you, but could we both have the lamb chops?"

She pursed her lips, and went back to the kitchen.

"Thanks," said Shadow.

"Don't mention it. Anything else I can help you with?"

"Yeah. These folk coming in for the party. Why don't they hire their own security? Why hire me?"

"They'll be doing that too, I have no doubt," said Gaskell. "Bringing in their own people. But it's good to have local talent."

"Even if the local talent is a foreign tourist?"

"Just so."

Maura brought two bowls of soup, put them down in front of Shadow and the doctor. "They come with the meal," she said. The soup was too hot, and it tasted faintly of reconstituted tomatoes and vinegar. Shadow was hungry enough that he'd finished most of the bowl off before he realized that he did not like it.

"You said I was a monster," said Shadow to the steel gray man.

"I did?"

"You did."

"Well, there's a lot of monsters in this part of the world." He tipped his head toward the couple in the corner. The little woman had picked up her napkin, dipped it into her water glass, and was dabbing vigorously with it at the spots of crimson soup on her son's mouth and chin. He looked embarrassed. "It's remote. We don't get into the news unless a hiker or a climber gets lost, or starves to death. Most people forget we're here."

The lamb chops arrived, on a plate with overboiled potatoes, underboiled carrots, and something brown and wet that Shadow thought might have started life as spinach. He started to cut at the chops with his knife. The doctor picked his up in his fingers, and began to chew.

"You've been inside," said the doctor.

"Inside?"

"Prison. You've been in prison." It wasn't a question.

"Yes."

"So you know how to fight. You could hurt someone, if you had to."

Shadow said, "If you need someone to hurt people, I'm probably not the guy you're looking for."

The little man grinned, with greasy gray lips. "I'm sure you are. I was just asking. You can't give a man a hard time for asking. Anyway. *He's* a monster," he said, gesturing across the room with a mostly chewed lamb chop. The bald man was eating some kind of white pudding with a spoon. "So's his mother."

"They don't look like monsters to me," said Shadow.

"I'm teasing you, I'm afraid. Local sense of humor. They should warn you about mine when you enter the village. Warning, loony old doctor at work. Talking about monsters. Forgive an old man. You mustn't listen to a word I say." A flash of tobacco-stained teeth. He wiped his hands and mouth on his napkin. "Maura, we'll be needing the bill over here. The young man's dinner is on me."

"Yes, Doctor Gaskell."

"Remember," said the doctor to Shadow. "Eight-fifteen tomorrow morning, be in the lobby. No later. They're busy people. If you aren't there, they'll just move on, and you'll have missed out on fifteen hundred pounds, for a weekend's work. A bonus, if they're happy."

Shadow decided to have his after-dinner coffee in the bar. There was a log fire there, after all. He hoped it would take the chill from his bones.

Gordon from reception was working behind the bar. "Jennie's night off?" asked Shadow.

"What? No, she was just helping out. She'll do it if we're busy, sometimes."

"Mind if I put another log on the fire?"

"Help yourself."

If this is how the Scots treat their summers, thought Shadow, remembering something Oscar Wilde had once said, *they don't deserve to have any.*

The bald young man came in. He nodded a nervous

greeting to Shadow. Shadow nodded back. The man had no hair that Shadow could see: no eyebrows, no eyelashes. It made him look babyish, and unformed. Shadow wondered if it was a disease, or if it was perhaps a side effect of chemotherapy. He smelled of damp.

"I heard what he said," stammered the bald man. "He said I was a monster. He said my ma was a monster too. I've got good ears on me. I don't miss much."

He did have good ears on him. They were a translucent pink, and they stuck out from the side of his head like the fins of some huge fish.

"You've got great ears," said Shadow.

"You taking the mickey?" The bald man's tone was aggrieved. He looked like he was ready to fight. He was only a little shorter than Shadow, and Shadow was a big man.

"If that means what I think it does, not at all."

The bald man nodded. "That's good," he said. He swallowed, and hesitated. Shadow wondered if he should say something conciliatory, but the bald man continued, "It's not my fault. Making all that noise. I mean, people come up here to get away from the noise. And the people. Too many damned people up here anyway. Why don't you just go back to where you came from and stop making all that bluidy noise?"

The man's mother appeared in the doorway. She smiled nervously at Shadow, then walked hurriedly over to her son. She pulled at his sleeve. "Now then," she said. "Don't you get yourself all worked up over nothing. Everything's all right." She looked up at Shadow, birdlike, placatory. "I'm sorry. I'm sure he didn't mean it." She had a length of toilet paper sticking to the bottom of her shoe, and she hadn't noticed yet.

"Everything's all right," said Shadow. "It's good to meet people."

She nodded. "That's all right then," she said. Her son looked relieved. *He's scared of her,* thought Shadow.

"Come on pet," said the woman to her son. She pulled at his sleeve, and he followed her to the door.

Then he stopped, obstinately, and turned. "You tell them," said the bald young man, "not to make so much noise."

"I'll tell them," said Shadow.

"It's just that I can hear everything."

"Don't worry about it," said Shadow.

"He really is a good boy," said the bald young man's mother, and she led her son by the sleeve, into the corridor and away, trailing a tag of toilet paper.

Shadow walked out into the hall. "Excuse me," he said.

They turned, the man and his mother.

"You've got something on your shoe," said Shadow.

She looked down. Then she stepped on the strip of paper with her other shoe, and lifted her foot, freeing it. She nodded at Shadow, approvingly, and walked away.

Shadow went to the reception desk. "Gordon, have you got a good local map?"

"Like an Ordnance Survey? Absolutely. I'll bring it into the lounge for you."

Shadow went back into the bar and finished his coffee. Gordon brought in a map. Shadow was impressed by the detail: it seemed to show every goat-track. He inspected it closely, tracing his walk. He found the hill where he had stopped and eaten his lunch. He ran his finger southwest.

"There aren't any castles around here, are there?"

"I'm afraid not. There are some to the east. I've got a guide to the castles of Scotland I could let you look at—"

"No, no. That's fine. Are there any big houses in this area? The kind people would call castles? Or big estates?"

"Well, there's the Cape Wrath Hotel, just over here," and he pointed to it on the map. "But it's a fairly empty area. Technically, for human occupation, what do they call it, for population density, it's a desert up here. Not even any interesting ruins, I'm afraid. Not that you could walk to."

Shadow thanked him, then asked him for an early-morning alarm call. He wished he had been able to find the house he had seen from the hill on the map, but perhaps he had been looking in the wrong place. It wouldn't be the first time.

The couple in the room next door were fighting, or making love. Shadow could not tell, but each time he began to drift off to sleep raised voices or cries would jerk him awake.

Later, he was never certain if it had really happened, if she had really come to him, or if it had been the first of that night's dreams: but in truth or in dreams, shortly before midnight by the bedside clock radio, there was a knock on his bedroom door. He got up. Called, "Who is it?"

"Jennie."

He opened the door, winced at the light in the hall.

She was wrapped in her brown coat, and she looked up at him hesitantly.

"Yes?" said Shadow.

"You'll be going to the house tomorrow," she said.

"Yes."

"I thought I should say good-bye," she said. "In case I don't get a chance to see you again. And if you don't come back to the hotel. And you just go on somewhere. And I never see you."

"Well, good-bye, then," said Shadow.

She looked him up and down, examining the T-shirt and the boxers he slept in, at his bare feet, then up at his face. She seemed worried. "You know where I live," she said, at last. "Call me if you need me."

She reached her index finger out and touched it gently to his lips. Her finger was very cold. Then she took a step back into the corridor and just stood there, facing him, making no move to go.

Shadow closed the hotel room door, and he heard her footsteps walking away down the corridor. He climbed back into bed.

He was sure that the next dream was a dream, though. It was his life, jumbled and twisted: one moment he was in prison, teaching himself coin tricks and telling himself that his love for his wife would get him through this. Then Laura was dead, and he was out of prison; he was working as a bodyguard to an old grifter who had told Shadow to call him Wednesday. And then his dream was filled with gods: old, forgotten gods, unloved and abandoned, and new gods, transient scared things, duped and confused. It was a tangle of improbabilities, a cat's cradle which became a web which became a net which became a skein as big as a world. . . .

In his dream he died on the tree.

In his dream he came back from the dead.

And after that there was darkness.

IV

The telephone beside the bed shrilled at seven. He showered, shaved, dressed, packed his world into his backpack. Then he went down to the restaurant for breakfast: salty porridge, limp bacon, and oily fried eggs. The coffee, though, was surprisingly good.

At ten past eight he was in the lobby, waiting.

At fourteen minutes past eight, a man came in, wearing a sheepskin coat. He was sucking on a hand-rolled cigarette. The man stuck out his hand, cheerfully. "You'll be Mister Moon," he said. "My name's Smith. I'm your lift out to the big house." The man's grip was firm. "You *are* a big feller, aren't you?"

Unspoken was, "But I could take you," although Shadow knew that it was there.

Shadow said, "So they tell me. You aren't Scottish."

"Not me, matey. Just up for the week to make sure that everything runs like it's s'posed to. I'm a London boy." A flash of teeth in a hatchet-blade face. Shadow guessed that the man was in his midforties. "Come on out to the car. I can bring you up to speed on the way. Is that your bag?"

Shadow carried his backpack out to the car, a muddy Land Rover, its engine still running. He dropped it in the back, climbed into the passenger seat. Smith pulled one final drag on his cigarette, now little more than a rolled stub of white paper, and threw it out of the open driver's-side window into the road.

They drove out of the village.

"So how do I pronounce your name?" asked Smith. "Bal-der or Borl-der, or something else? Like *Cholmondely* is actually pronounced *Chumley*."

"Shadow," said Shadow. "People call me Shadow."

"Right."

Silence.

"So," said Smith. "Shadow. I don't know how much old Gaskell told you about the party this weekend."

"A little."

"Right, well, the most important thing to know is this. Anything that happens, you keep *shtum* about. Right? Whatever you see, people having a little bit of fun, you don't say nothing to anybody, even if you recognize them, if you take my meaning."

"I don't recognize people," said Shadow.

"That's the spirit. We're just here to make sure that everyone has a good time without being disturbed. They've come a long way for a nice weekend."

"Got it," said Shadow.

They reached the ferry to the cape. Smith parked the Land Rover beside the road, took their bags, and locked the car.

On the other side of the ferry crossing, an identical

Land Rover waited. Smith unlocked it, threw their bags in the back, and started along the dirt track.

They turned off before they reached the lighthouse, drove for a while in silence down a dirt road that rapidly turned into a sheep track. Several times Shadow had to get out and open gates; he waited while the Land Rover drove through, closed the gates behind it.

There were ravens in the fields and on the low stone walls, huge black birds that stared at Shadow with implacable eyes.

"So you were in the nick?" said Smith, suddenly.

"Sorry?"

"Prison. Pokey. Porridge. Other words beginning with a P, indicating poor food, no nightlife, inadequate toilet facilities, and limited opportunities for travel."

"Yeah."

"You're not very chatty, are you?"

"I thought that was a virtue."

"Point taken. Just conversation. The silence was getting on my nerves. You like it up here?"

"I guess. I've only been here for a few days."

"Gives me the fucking willies. Too remote. I've been to parts of Siberia that felt more welcoming. You been to London yet? No? When you come down south I'll show you around. Great pubs. Real food. And there's all that tourist stuff you Americans like. Traffic's hell, though. At least up here, we can drive. No bloody traffic lights. There's this traffic light at the bottom of Regent Street, I swear, you sit there for five minutes on a red light, then you get about ten seconds on a green light. Two cars max. Sodding ridiculous. They say it's the price we pay for progress. Right?"

"Yeah," said Shadow. "I guess."

They were well off-road now, thumping and bumping along a scrubby valley between two high hills. "Your party guests," said Shadow. "Are they coming in by Land Rover?"

"Nah. We've got helicopters. They'll be in in time for dinner tonight. Choppers in, then choppers out on Monday morning."

"Like living on an island."

"I wish we were living on an island. Wouldn't get loony locals causing problems, would we? Nobody complains about the noise coming from the island next door."

"You make a lot of noise at your party?"

"It's not my party, chum. I'm just a facilitator. Making sure that everything runs smoothly. But yes. I understand that they can make a lot of noise when they put their minds to it."

The grassy valley became a sheep path, the sheep path became a driveway running almost straight up a hill. A bend in the road, a sudden turn, and they were driving toward a house that Shadow recognized. Jennie had pointed to it yesterday, at lunch.

The house was old. He could see that at a glance. Parts of it seemed older than others: there was a wall on one wing of the building built out of gray rocks and stones, heavy and hard. That wall jutted into another, built of brown bricks. The roof, which covered the whole building, both wings, was a dark gray slate. The house looked out onto a gravel drive and then down the hill onto the loch. Shadow climbed out of the Land Rover. He looked at the house and felt small. He felt as though he were coming home, and it was not a good feeling.

There were several other four-wheel-drive vehicles parked on the gravel. "The keys to the cars are hanging in the pantry, in case you need to take one out. I'll show you as we go past."

Through a large wooden door, and now they were in a central courtyard, partly paved. There was a small fountain in the middle of the courtyard, and a plot of grass, a ragged green, viperous swath bounded by gray flagstones.

"This is where the Saturday-night action will be," said Smith. "I'll show you where you'll be staying."

Into the smaller wing through an unimposing door, past a room hung with keys on hooks, each key marked with a paper tag, and another room filled with empty shelves. Down a dingy hall, and up some stairs. There was no carpeting on the stairs, nothing but whitewash on the walls. ("Well, this is the servants' quarters, innit? They never spent any money on it.") It was cold, in a way that Shadow was starting to become familiar with: colder inside the building than out. He wondered how they did that, if it was a British building secret.

Smith led Shadow to the top of the house and showed him into a dark room containing an antique wardrobe, an iron-framed single bed that Shadow could see at a glance would be smaller than he was, an ancient wash-stand, and a small window which looked out onto the inner courtyard.

"There's a loo at the end of the hall," said Smith. "The servants' bathroom's on the next floor down. Two baths, one for men, one for women, no showers. The supplies of hot water on this wing of the house are distinctly limited, I'm afraid. Your monkey suit's hanging in the wardrobe. Try it on now, see if it all fits, then leave it off until this evening, when the guests come in. Limited dry-cleaning facilities. We might as well be on Mars. I'll be in the kitchen if you need me. It's not as cold down there, if the Aga's working. Bottom of the stairs and left, then right, then yell if you're lost. Don't go into the other wing unless you're told to."

He left Shadow alone.

Shadow tried on the black tuxedo jacket, the white dress shirt, the black tie. There were highly polished black shoes, as well. It all fitted, as if it had been tailored for him. He hung everything back in the wardrobe.

He walked down the stairs, found Smith on the landing, stabbing angrily at a small silver mobile phone. "No bloody reception. The thing rang, now I'm trying to call back it won't give me a signal. It's the bloody Stone Age up here. How was your suit? All right?"

"Perfect."

"That's my boy. Never use five words if you can get away with one, eh? I've known dead men talk more than you do."

"Really?"

"Nah. Figure of speech. Come on. Fancy some lunch?"

"Sure. Thank you."

"Right. Follow me. It's a bit of a warren, but you'll get the hang of it soon enough."

They ate in the huge, empty kitchen: Shadow and Smith piled enameled tin plates with slices of translucent orange smoked salmon on crusty white bread, and slices of sharp cheese, accompanied by mugs of strong, sweet tea. The Aga was, Shadow discovered, a big metal box, part oven, part water heater. Smith opened one of the many doors on its side and shoveled in several large scoops of coal.

"So where's the rest of the food? And the waiters, and the cooks?" asked Shadow. "It can't just be us."

"Well spotted. Everything's coming up from Edinburgh. It'll run like clockwork. Food and party workers will be here at three, and unpack. Guests get brought in at six. Buffet dinner is served at eight. Talk a lot, eat, have a bit of a laugh, nothing too strenuous. Tomorrow there's breakfast from seven to midday. Guests get to go for walks, scenic views, all that in the afternoon. Bonfires are built in the courtyard. Then in the evening the bonfires are lit, everybody has a wild Saturday night in the north, hopefully without being bothered by our neighbors. Sunday morning we tiptoe around, out of respect for everybody's hangover, Sunday afternoon the choppers land and we wave everybody on their way. You collect your pay packet, and I'll drive you back to the hotel, or you can ride south with me, if you fancy a change. Sounds good?"

"Sounds just dandy," said Shadow. "And the folks who may show up on the Saturday night?"

"Just killjoys. Locals out to ruin everybody's good time."

"What locals?" asked Shadow. "There's nothing but sheep for miles."

"Locals. They're all over the place," said Smith. "You just don't see them. Tuck themselves away like Sawney Beane and his family."

Shadow said, "I think I've heard of him. The name rings a bell . . ."

"He's *historical*," said Smith. He slurped his tea, and leaned back in his chair. "This was, what, six hundred years back—after the Vikings had buggered off back to Scandinavia, or intermarried and converted until they were just another bunch of Scots, but before Queen Elizabeth died and James came down from Scotland to rule both countries. Somewhere in there." He took a swig of his tea. "So. Travelers in Scotland kept vanishing. It wasn't that unusual. I mean, if you set out on a long journey back then, you didn't always get home. Sometimes it would be months before anyone knew you weren't coming home again, and they'd blame the wolves or the weather, and resolve to travel in groups, and only in the summer.

"One traveler, though, he was riding with a bunch of companions through a glen, and there came over the hill, dropped from the trees, up from the ground, a swarm, a flock, a pack of children, armed with daggers and knives and bone clubs and stout sticks, and they pulled the travelers off their horses, and fell on them, and finished them off. All but this one geezer, and he was riding a little behind the others, and he got away. He was the only one, but it only takes one, doesn't it? He made it to the nearest town, and raised the hue and cry, and they gather a troop of townsfolk and soldiers and they go back there, with dogs.

"It takes them days to find the hideout, they're ready to give up, when, at the mouth of a cave by the seashore, the dogs start to howl. And they go down.

"Turns out there's caves, under the ground, and in the biggest and deepest of the caves is old Sawney Beane and his brood, and carcasses, hanging from hooks, smoked and slow-roast. Legs, arms, thighs, hands, and feet of men, women, and children are hung up in rows, like dried pork. There are limbs pickled in brine, like salt beef. There's money in heaps, gold and silver, with watches, rings, swords, pistols, and clothes, riches beyond imagining, as they never spent a single penny of it. Just stayed in their caves, and ate, and bred, and hated.

"He'd been living there for years. King of his own little kingdom, was old Sawney, him and his wife, and their children and grandchildren, and some of those grandchildren were also their children. An incestuous little bunch."

"Did this really happen?"

"So I'm told. There are court records. They took the family to Leith to be tried. The court decision was interesting—they decided that Sawney Beane, by virtue of his acts, had removed himself from the human race. So they sentenced him as an animal. They didn't hang him or behead him. They just got a big fire going and threw the Beanies onto it, to burn to death."

"All of his family?"

"I don't remember. They may have burned the little kids, or they may not. Probably did. They tend to deal very efficiently with monsters in this part of the world."

Smith washed their plates and mugs in the sink, left them in a rack to dry. The two men walked out into the courtyard. Smith rolled himself a cigarette expertly. He licked the paper, smoothed it with his fingers, lit the finished tube with a Zippo. "Let's see. What d'you need to know for tonight? Well, basics are easy: speak when you're spoken to—not that you're going to find that one a problem, eh?"

Shadow said nothing.

"Right. If one of the guests asks you for something, do your best to provide it, ask me if you're in any doubt, but do what the guests ask as long as it doesn't take you off what you're doing, or violate the prime directive."

"Which is?"

"Don't. Shag. The posh totty. There's sure to be some young ladies who'll take it into their heads, after half a bottle of wine, that what they really need is a bit of rough. And if that happens, you do a *Sunday People*."

"I have no idea what you're talking about."

"*Our reporter made his excuses and left.* Yes? You can look, but you can't touch. Got it?"

"Got it."

"Smart boy."

Shadow found himself starting to like Smith. He told himself that liking this man was not a sensible thing to do. He had met people like Smith before, people without consciences, without scruples, without hearts, and they were uniformly as dangerous as they were likeable.

In the early afternoon the servants arrived, brought in by a helicopter that looked like a troop carrier: they unpacked boxes of wine and crates of food, hampers and containers with astonishing efficiency. There were boxes filled with napkins and with tablecloths. There were cooks and waiters, waitresses and chambermaids.

But, first off the helicopter, there were the security guards: big, solid men with earpieces and what Shadow had no doubt were gun-bulges beneath their jackets. They reported one by one to Smith, who set them to inspecting the house and the grounds. Shadow was helping out, carrying boxes filled with vegetables from the chopper to the kitchen. He could carry twice as much as anyone else. The next time he passed Smith he stopped and said, "So, if you've got all these security guys, what am I here for?"

Smith smiled affably. "Look, son. There's people coming to this do who're worth more than you or I will ever see in a lifetime. They need to be sure they'll be looked after. Kidnappings happen. People have enemies. Lots of things happen. Only with those lads around, they won't. But having them deal with grumpy locals, it's like setting a landmine to stop trespassers. Yeah?"

"Right," said Shadow. He went back to the chopper picked up another box marked *baby aubergines* and filled with small, black eggplants, put it on top of a crate of cabbages and carried them both to the kitchen, certain now that he was being lied to. Smith's reply was reasonable. It was even convincing. It simply wasn't true. There was no reason for him to be there, or if there was it wasn't the reason he'd been given.

He chewed it over, trying to figure out why he was in that house, and hoped that he was showing nothing on the surface. Shadow kept it all on the inside. It was safer there.

V

More helicopters came down in the early evening, as the sky was turning pink, and a score or more of smart people clambered out. Several of them were smiling and laughing. Most of them were in their thirties and forties. Shadow recognized none of them.

Smith moved casually but smoothly from person to person, greeting them confidently. "Right, now you go through there and turn left, and wait in the main hall. Lovely big log fire there. Someone'll come and take you up to your room. Your luggage should be waiting for you there. You call me if it's not, but it will be. 'Ullo your ladyship, you do look a treat—shall I 'ave someone carry your 'andbag? Looking forward to termorrer? Aren't we all."

Shadow watched, fascinated, as Smith dealt with each of the guests, his manner an expert mixture of familiarity and deference, of amiability and Cockney charm: aitches, consonants, and vowel sounds came and went and transformed according to who he was talking to.

A woman with short dark hair, very pretty, smiled at Shadow as he carried her bags inside. "Posh totty," muttered Smith, as he went past. "Hands off."

A portly man who Shadow estimated to be in his early sixties was the last person off the chopper. He walked over to Smith, leaned on a cheap wooden walking stick, said something in a low voice. Smith replied in the same fashion.

He's in charge, thought Shadow. It was there in the body language. Smith was no longer smiling, no longer cajoling. He was reporting, efficiently and quietly, telling the old man everything he should know.

Smith crooked a finger at Shadow, who walked quickly over to them.

"Shadow," said Smith. "This is Mister Alice."

Mr. Alice put out his hand, shook Shadow's big, dark hand with his pink, pudgy one. "Great pleasure to meet you," he said. "Heard good things about you."

"Good to meet you," said Shadow.

"Well," said Mr. Alice, "carry on."

Smith nodded at Shadow, a gesture of dismissal.

"If it's okay by you," said Shadow to Smith, "I'd like to take a look around while there's still some light. Get a sense of where the locals could come from."

"Don't go too far," said Smith. He picked up Mr. Alice's briefcase, and led the older man into the building.

Shadow walked the outside perimeter of the house. He had been set up. He did not know why, but he knew he was right. There was too much that didn't add up. Why hire a drifter to do security, while bringing in real security guards? It made no sense, no more than Smith introducing him to Mr. Alice, after two dozen other people had treated Shadow as no more human than a decorative ornament.

There was a low stone wall in front of the house. Behind the house, a hill that was almost a small mountain, in front of it a gentle slope down to the loch. Off to the side was the track by which he had arrived that morning. He walked to the far side of the house and found what seemed to be a kitchen garden, with a high stone wall and wilderness beyond. He took a step down into the kitchen garden, and walked over to inspect the wall.

"You doing a recce, then?" said one of the security guards, in his black tuxedo. Shadow had not seen him there, which meant, he supposed, that he was very good at his job. Like most of the servants, his accent was Scottish.

"Just having a look around."

"Get the lay of the land, very wise. Don't you worry about this side of the house. A hundred yards that way there's a river leads down to the loch, and beyond that just wet rocks for a hundred feet or so, straight down. Absolutely treacherous."

"Oh. So the locals, the ones who come and complain, where do they come from?"

"I wouldnae have a clue."

"I should head on over there and take a look at it," said Shadow. "See if I can figure out the ways in and out."

"I wouldnae do that," said the guard. "Not if I were you. It's really treacherous. You go poking around over there, one slip, you'll be crashing down the rocks into the loch. They'll never find your body, if you head out that way."

"I see," said Shadow, who did.

He kept walking around the house. He spotted five other security guards, now that he was looking for them. He was sure there were others that he had missed.

In the main wing of the house he could see, through the french windows, a huge, wood-paneled dining room, and the guests seated around a table, talking and laughing.

He walked back into the servants' wing. As each course was done with, the serving plates were put out on a sideboard, and the staff helped themselves, piling food high on paper plates. Smith was sitting at the wooden kitchen table, tucking into a plate of salad and rare beef.

"There's caviar over there," he said to Shadow. "It's Golden Osetra, top quality, very special. What the party officials used to keep for themselves in the old days. I've never been a fan of the stuff, but help yourself."

Shadow put a little of the caviar on the side of his plate, to be polite. He took some tiny boiled eggs, some pasta, and some chicken. He sat next to Smith and started to eat.

"I don't see where your locals are going to come from," he said. "Your men have the drive sealed off. Anyone who wants to come here would have to come over the loch."

"You had a good poke around, then?"

"Yes," said Shadow.

"You met some of my boys?"

"Yes."

"What did you think?"

"I wouldn't want to mess with them."

Smith smirked. "Big fellow like you? You could take care of yourself."

"They're killers," said Shadow, simply.

"Only when they need to be," said Smith. He was no longer smiling. "Why don't you stay up in your room? I'll give you a shout when I need you."

"Sure," said Shadow. "And if you don't need me, this is going to be a very easy weekend."

Smith stared at him. "You'll earn your money," he said.

Shadow went up the back stairs to the long corridor at the top of the house. He went into his room. He could hear party noises, and looked out of the small window. The french windows opposite were wide open, and the partygoers, now wearing coats and gloves, holding their glasses of wine, had spilled out into the inner courtyard. He could hear fragments of conversations that transformed and reshaped themselves; the noises were clear but the words and the sense were lost. An occasional phrase would break free of the susurrus. A man said, "I told him, judges like you, I don't own, I sell. . . ." Shadow heard a woman say, "It's a monster, darling. An absolute monster. Well, what can you do?" and another woman saying, "Well, if only I could say the same about my boyfriend's!" and a bray of laughter.

He had two alternatives. He could stay, or he could try to go.

"I'll stay," he said, aloud.

VI

It was a night of dangerous dreams.

In Shadow's first dream he was back in America, standing beneath a streetlight. He walked up some steps, pushed through a glass door, and stepped into a diner, the kind that had once been a dining car on a train. He could hear an old man singing, in a deep gravelly voice, to the tune of "My Bonnie Lies Over the Ocean,"

> *"My grandpa sells condoms to sailors*
> *He punctures the tips with a pin*
> *My grandma does back-street abortions*
> *My God how the money rolls in."*

Shadow walked along the length of the dining car. At a table at the end of the car, a grizzled man was sitting, holding a beer bottle, and singing, *"Rolls in, rolls in, my God how the money rolls in."* When he caught sight of Shadow his face split into a huge monkey grin, and he gestured with the beer bottle. "Sit down, sit down," he said.

Shadow sat down opposite the man he had known as Wednesday.

"So what's the trouble?" asked Wednesday, dead for almost two years, or as dead as his kind of creature was going to get. "I'd offer you a beer, but the service here stinks."

Shadow said that was okay. He didn't want a beer.

"Well?" asked Wednesday, scratching his beard.

"I'm in a big house in Scotland with a shitload of really rich folks, and they have an agenda. I'm in trouble, and I don't know what kind of trouble I'm in. But I think it's pretty bad trouble."

Wednesday took a swig of his beer. "The rich are different, m'boy," he said, after a while.

"What the hell does *that* mean?"

"Well," said Wednesday. "For a start, most of them are probably mortal. Not something *you* have to worry about."

"Don't give me that shit."

"But you *aren't* mortal," said Wednesday. "You died on the tree, Shadow. You died and you came back."

"So? I don't even remember how I did that. If they kill me this time, I'll still be dead."

Wednesday finished his beer. Then he waved his beer bottle around, as if he were conducting an invisible orchestra with it, and sang another verse:

"My brother's a missionary worker,
He saves fallen women from sin

For five bucks he'll save you a redhead,
My God how the money rolls in."

"You aren't helping," said Shadow. The diner was a train carriage now, rattling through a snowy night.

Wednesday put down his beer bottle, and he fixed Shadow with his real eye, the one that wasn't glass. "It's patterns," he said. "If they think you're a hero, they're wrong. After you die, you don't get to be Beowulf or Perseus or Rama any more. Whole different set of rules. Chess, not checkers. *Go,* not chess. You understand?"

"Not even a little," said Shadow, frustrated.

People, in the corridor of the big house, moving loudly and drunkenly, shushing each other as they stumbled and giggled their way down the hall.

Shadow wondered if they were servants, or if they were strays from the other wing, slumming. And the dreams took him once again. . . .

Now he was back in the bothy where he had sheltered from the rain, the day before. There was a body on the floor: a boy, no more than five years old. Naked, on his back, limbs spread. There was a flash of intense light, and someone pushed through Shadow as if he was not there and rearranged the position of the boy's arms. Another flash of light.

Shadow knew the man taking the photographs. It was Dr. Gaskell, the little steel-haired man from the hotel bar.

Gaskell took a white paper bag from his pocket, and fished about in it for something that he popped into his mouth.

"Dolly mixtures," he said to the child on the stone floor. "Yum yum. Your favorites."

He smiled and crouched down, and took another photograph of the dead boy.

Shadow pushed through the stone wall of the cottage, flowing through the cracks in the stones like the wind. He flowed down to the seashore. The waves crashed on the rocks and Shadow kept moving across the water, through gray seas, up the swells and down again, toward the ship made of dead men's nails.

The ship was far away, out at sea, and Shadow passed across the surface of the water like the shadow of a cloud.

The ship was huge. He had not understood before how huge it was. A hand reached down and grasped his arm, pulled him up from the sea onto the deck.

"Bring us back," said a voice as loud as the crashing of the sea, urgent and fierce. "Bring us back, or let us go." Only one eye burned in that bearded face.

"I'm not keeping you here."

They were giants, on that ship, huge men made of shadows and frozen sea-spray, creatures of dream and foam.

One of them, huger than all the rest, red-bearded, stepped forward. "We cannot land," he boomed. "We cannot leave."

"Go home," said Shadow.

"We came with our people to this southern country," said the one-eyed man. "But they left us. They sought other, tamer gods, and they renounced us in their hearts, and gave us over."

"Go home," repeated Shadow.

"Too much time has passed," said the red-bearded man. By the hammer at his side, Shadow knew him. "Too much blood has been spilled. You are of our blood, Baldur. Set us free."

And Shadow wanted to say that he was not theirs, was not anybody's, but the thin blanket had slipped from the bed, and his feet stuck out at the bottom, and thin moonlight filled the attic room.

There was silence, now, in that huge house. Something howled in the hills, and Shadow shivered.

He lay in a bed that was too small for him, and imagined time as something that pooled and puddled, wondered if there were places where time hung heavy, places where it was heaped and held—cities, he thought, must be filled with time: all the places where people congregated, where they came and brought time with them. And if that were true, Shadow mused, then there could be other places, where the people were thin on the ground, and the land waited, bitter and granite, and a thousand years was an eyeblink to the hills—a scudding of clouds, a wavering of rushes and nothing more, in the places where time was as thin on the ground as the people. . . .

"They are going to kill you," whispered Jennie, the barmaid.

Shadow sat beside her now, on the hill, in the moonlight. "Why would they want to do that?" he asked. "I don't matter."

"It's what they do to monsters," she said. "It's what they have to do. It's what they've always done."

He reached out to touch her, but she turned away from him. From behind, she was empty and hollow. She turned again, so she was facing him. "Come away," she whispered.

"You can come to me," he said.

"I can't," she said. "There are things in the way. The path there is hard, and it is guarded. But you can call. If you call me, I'll come."

Then dawn came, and with it a cloud of midges from the boggy land at the foot of the hill. Jennie flicked at them with her tail, but it was no use; they descended on Shadow like a cloud, until he was breathing midges, his nose and mouth filling with the tiny, crawling stinging things, and he was choking on the darkness. . . .

He wrenched himself back into his bed and his body and his life, into wakefulness, his heart pounding in his chest, gulping for breath.

VII

Breakfast was kippers, grilled tomatoes, scrambled eggs, toast, two stubby, thumblike sausages, and slices of something dark and round and flat that Shadow didn't recognize.

"What's this?" asked Shadow.

"Black pudden'," said the man sitting next to him. He was one of the security guards, and was reading a copy of yesterday's *Sun* as he ate. "Blood and herbs. They cook the blood until it congeals into a sort of a dark, herby scab." He forked some eggs onto his toast, ate it with his fingers. "I don't know. What is it they say, you should never see anyone making sausages or the law? Something like that."

Shadow ate the rest of the breakfast, but he left the black pudding alone.

There was a pot of real coffee now, and he drank a mug of it, hot and black, to wake him up and to clear his head.

Smith walked in. "Shadow-man. Can I borrow you for five minutes?"

"You're paying," said Shadow. They walked out into the corridor.

"It's Mr. Alice," said Smith. "He wants a quick word." They crossed from the dismal whitewashed servants' wing into the wood-paneled vastness of the old house. They walked up the huge wooden staircase and into a vast library. No one was there.

"He'll just be a minute," said Smith. "I'll make sure he knows you're waiting."

The books in the library were protected from mice and dust and people by locked doors of glass and wire mesh. There was a painting of a stag on the wall, and Shadow walked over to look at it. The stag was haughty and superior: behind it, a valley filled with mist.

"*The Monarch of the Glen,*" said Mr. Alice, walking in slowly, leaning on his stick. "The most reproduced picture of Victorian times. That's not the original, but it was done by Landseer in the late 1850s as a copy of his own painting. I love it, although I'm sure I shouldn't. He did the lions in Trafalgar Square, Landseer. Same bloke."

He walked over to the bay window, and Shadow walked with him. Below them in the courtyard, servants were putting out chairs and tables. By the pond in the center of the courtyard other people, party guests, were building bonfires out of logs and wood.

"Why don't they have the servants build the fires?" asked Shadow.

"Why should *they* have the fun?" said Mr. Alice. "It'd be like sending your man out into the rough some afternoon to shoot pheasants for you. There's something about building a bonfire, when you've hauled over the wood, and put it down in the perfect place, that's special. Or so they tell me. I've not done it myself." He turned away from the window. "Take a seat," he said. "I'll get a crick in my neck looking up at you."

Shadow sat down.

"I've heard a lot about you," said Mr. Alice. "Been wanting to meet you for a while. They said you were a smart young man who was going places. That's what they said."

"So you didn't just hire a tourist to keep the neighbors away from your party?"

"Well, yes and no. We had a few other candidates, obviously. It's just you were perfect for the job. And when I realized who you were. Well, a gift from the gods really, weren't you?"

"I don't know. Was I?"

"Absolutely. You see, this party goes back a very long way. Almost a thousand years, they've been having it. Never missed a single year. And every year there's a fight, between our man and their man. And our man wins. This year, our man is you."

"Who . . ." said Shadow. "Who are *they*? And who are *you*?"

"I am your host," said Mr. Alice. "I suppose. . . ." He stopped, for a moment, tapped his walking stick against the wooden floor. "*They* are the ones who lost, a long time ago. *We* won. We were the knights, and they were the dragons, we were the giant-killers, they were the ogres. We were the men and they were the monsters. And *we* won. They know their place now. And tonight is all about not letting them forget it. It's humanity you'll be fighting for, tonight. We can't let them get the upper hand. Not even a little. Us versus them."

"Doctor Gaskell said that I was a monster," said Shadow.

"Doctor Gaskell?" said Mr. Alice. "Friend of yours?"

"No," said Shadow. "He works for you. Or for the people who work for you. I think he kills children and takes pictures of them."

Mr. Alice dropped his walking stick. He bent down, awkwardly, to pick it up. Then he said, "Well, I don't think you're a monster, Shadow. I think you're a hero."

No, thought Shadow. *You think I'm a monster. But you think I'm your monster.*

"Now, you do well tonight," said Mr. Alice, "and I know you will—and you can name your price. You ever wondered why some people were film stars, or famous, or rich? Bet you think, *He's got no talent. What's he got that I haven't got*? Well, sometimes the answer is, he's got someone like me on his side."

"Are you a god?" asked Shadow.

Mr. Alice laughed then, a deep, full-throated chuckle. "Nice one, Mister Moon. Not at all. I'm just a boy from Streatham who's done well for himself."

"So who do I fight?" asked Shadow.

"You'll meet him tonight," said Mr. Alice. "Now, there's

stuff needs to come down from the attic. Why don't you lend Smithie a hand? Big lad like you, it'll be a doddle."

The audience was over and, as if on cue, Smith walked in.

"I was just saying," said Mr. Alice, "that our boy here would help you bring the stuff down from the attic."

"Triffic," said Smith. "Come on, Shadow. Let's wend our way upwards."

They went up, through the house, up a dark wooden stairway, to a padlocked door, which Smith unlocked, into a dusty wooden attic, piled high with what looked like . . .

"Drums?" said Shadow.

"Drums," said Smith. They were made of wood and of animal skins. Each drum was a different size. "Right, let's take them down."

They carried the drums downstairs. Smith carried one at a time, holding it as if it was precious. Shadow carried two.

"So what really happens tonight?" asked Shadow, on their third trip, or perhaps their fourth.

"Well," said Smith. "Most of it, as I understand, you're best off figuring out on your own. As it happens."

"And you and Mr. Alice. What part do you play in this?"

Smith gave him a sharp look. They put the drums down at the foot of the stairs, in the great hall. There were several men there, talking in front of the fire.

When they were back up the stairs again, and out of earshot of the guests, Smith said, "Mr. Alice will be leaving us late this afternoon. I'll stick around."

"He's leaving? Isn't he part of this?"

Smith looked offended. "He's the host," he said. "But." He stopped. Shadow understood. Smith didn't talk about his employer. They carried more drums down the stairs. When they had brought down all the drums, they carried down heavy leather bags.

"What's in these?" asked Shadow.

"Drumsticks," said Smith.

Smith continued, "They're old families. That lot downstairs. Very old money. They know who's boss, but that doesn't make him one of them. See? They're the only ones who'll be at tonight's party. They'd not want Mr. Alice. See?"

And Shadow did see. He wished that Smith hadn't spoken to him about Mr. Alice. He didn't think Smith would have said anything to anyone he thought would live to talk about it.

But all he said was, "Heavy drumsticks."

VIII

A small helicopter took Mr. Alice away late that afternoon. Land Rovers took away the staff. Smith drove the last one. Only Shadow was left behind, and the guests, with their smart clothes and their smiles.

They stared at Shadow as if he were a captive lion who had been brought for their amusement, but they did not talk to him.

The dark-haired woman, the one who had smiled at Shadow as she had arrived, brought him food to eat: a steak, almost rare. She brought it to him on a plate, without cutlery, as if she expected him to eat it with his fingers and his teeth, and he was hungry, and he did.

"I am not your hero," he told them, but they would not meet his gaze. Nobody spoke to him, not directly. He felt like an animal.

And then it was dusk. They led Shadow to the inner courtyard, by the rusty fountain, and they stripped him naked, at gunpoint, and the women smeared his body with some kind of thick yellow grease, rubbing it in.

They put a knife on the grass in front of him. A gesture with a gun, and Shadow picked the knife up. The hilt was black metal, rough and easy to hold. The blade looked sharp.

Then they threw open the great door, from the inner courtyard to the world outside, and two of the men lit the two high bonfires: they crackled and blazed.

They opened the leather bags, and each of the guests took out a single carved black stick, like a cudgel, knobbly and heavy. Shadow found himself thinking of Sawney Beane's children, swarming up from the darkness holding clubs made of human thigh-bones. . . .

Then the guests arranged themselves around the edge of the courtyard, and they began to beat the drums with the sticks.

They started slow, and they started quietly, a deep, throbbing pounding, like a heartbeat. Then they began to crash and slam into strange rhythms, staccato beats that wove and wound, louder and louder, until they filled Shadow's mind and his world. It seemed to him that the firelight flickered to the rhythms of the drums.

And then, from outside the house, the howling began.

There was pain in the howling, and anguish, and it echoed across the hills above the drumbeats, a wail of pain and loss and hate.

The figure that stumbled through the doorway to the courtyard was clutching its head, covering its ears, as if to stop the pounding of the drumbeats.

The firelight caught it.

It was huge, now: bigger than Shadow, and naked. It was perfectly hairless, and dripping wet.

It lowered its hands from its ears, and it stared around, its face twisted into a mad grimace. "Stop it!" it screamed. "Stop making all that noise!"

And the people in their pretty clothes beat their drums harder, and faster, and the noise filled Shadow's head and chest.

The monster stepped into the center of the courtyard.

It looked at Shadow. "You," it said. "I told you. I told you about the noise," and it howled, a deep throaty howl of hatred and challenge.

The creature edged closer to Shadow. It saw the knife, and stopped. "Fight me!" it shouted. "Fight me fair! Not with cold iron! Fight me!"

"I don't want to fight you," said Shadow. He dropped the knife on the grass, raised his hands to show them empty.

"Too late," said the bald thing that was not a man. "Too late for that."

And it launched itself at Shadow.

Later, when Shadow thought of that fight, he remembered only fragments: he remembered being slammed to the ground, and throwing himself out of the way. He remembered the pounding of the drums, and the expressions on the faces of the drummers as they stared, hungrily, between the bonfires, at the two men in the firelight.

They fought, wrestling and pounding each other.

Salt tears ran down the monster's face as it wrestled with Shadow. They were equally matched, it seemed to Shadow.

The monster slammed its arm into Shadow's face, and Shadow could taste his own blood. He could feel his own anger beginning to rise, like a red wall of hate.

He swung a leg out, hooking the monster behind the knee, and as it stumbled back Shadow's fist crashed into its gut, making it cry out and roar with anger and pain.

A glance at the guests: Shadow saw the bloodlust on the faces of the drummers.

There was a cold wind, a sea wind, and it seemed to Shadow that there were huge shadows in the sky, vast figures that he had seen on a ship made of the fingernails of dead men, and that they were staring down at him, that this fight was what was keeping them frozen on their ship, unable to land, unable to leave.

This fight was old, Shadow thought, older than even Mr. Alice knew, and he was thinking that even as the creature's talons raked his chest. It was the fight of man against monster, and it was old as time: it was Theseus battling the Minotaur, it was Beowulf and Grendel, it was the fight of every hero who had ever stood between the firelight and the darkness and wiped the blood of something inhuman from his sword.

The bonfires burned, and the drums pounded and throbbed and pulsed like the beating of a thousand hearts.

Shadow slipped on the damp grass, as the monster came at him, and he was down. The creature's fingers were around Shadow's neck, and it was squeezing; Shadow could feel everything starting to thin, to become distant.

He closed his hand around a patch of grass, and pulled at it, dug his fingers deep, grabbing a handful of grass and clammy earth, and he smashed the clod of dirt into the monster's face, momentarily blinding it.

He pushed up, and was on top of the creature, now. He rammed his knee hard into its groin, and it doubled into a fetal position, and howled, and sobbed.

Shadow realized that the drumming had stopped, and he looked up.

The guests had put down their drums.

They were all approaching him, in a circle, men and women, still holding their drumsticks, but holding them like cudgels. They were not looking at Shadow, though: they were staring at the monster on the ground, and they raised their black sticks and moved toward it in the light of the twin fires.

Shadow said, "Stop!"

The first club blow came down on the creature's head. It wailed and twisted, raising an arm to ward off the next blow.

Shadow threw himself in front of it, shielding it with

his body. The dark-haired woman who had smiled at him before now brought down her club on his shoulder, dispassionately, and another club, from a man this time, hit him a numbing blow in the leg, and a third struck him on his side.

They'll kill us both, he thought. *Him first, then me. That's what they do. That's what they always do.* And then, *She said she would come. If I called her.*

Shadow whispered, "Jennie?"

There was no reply. Everything was happening so slowly. Another club was coming down, this one aimed at his hand. Shadow rolled out of the way awkwardly, watched the heavy wood smash into the turf.

"Jennie," he said, picturing her too-fair hair in his mind, her thin face, her smile. "I call you. Come now. *Please.*"

A gust of cold wind.

The dark-haired woman had raised her club high, and brought it down now, fast, hard, aiming for Shadow's face.

The blow never landed. A small hand caught the heavy stick as if it were a twig.

Fair hair blew about her head, in the cold wind. He could not have told you what she was wearing.

She looked at him. Shadow thought that she looked disappointed.

One of the men aimed a cudgel blow at the back of her head. It never connected. She turned . . .

A rending sound, as if something was tearing itself apart . . .

And then the bonfires exploded. That was how it seemed. There was blazing wood all over the courtyard, even in the house. And the people were screaming in the bitter wind.

Shadow staggered to his feet.

The monster lay on the ground, bloodied and twisted. Shadow did not know if it was alive or not. He picked it up, hauled it over his shoulder, and staggered out of the courtyard with it.

He stumbled out onto the gravel forecourt, as the massive wooden doors slammed closed behind them. Nobody else would be coming out. Shadow kept moving down the slope, one step at a time, down toward the loch.

When he reached the water's edge he stopped, and sank to his knees, and let the bald man down onto the grass as gently as he could.

He heard something crash, and looked back up the hill.

The house was burning.

"How is he?" said a woman's voice.

Shadow turned. She was knee-deep in the water, the creature's mother, wading toward the shore.

"I don't know," said Shadow. "He's hurt."

"You're both hurt," she said. "You're all bluid and bruises."

"Yes," said Shadow.

"Still," she said. "He's not dead. And that makes a nice change."

She had reached the shore now. She sat on the bank, with her son's head in her lap. She took a packet of tissues from her handbag, and spat on a tissue, and began fiercely to scrub at her son's face with it, rubbing away the blood.

The house on the hill was roaring now. Shadow had not imagined that a burning house would make so much noise.

The old woman looked up at the sky. She made a noise in the back of her throat, a clucking noise, and then she shook her head. "You know," she said, "you've let them in. They'd been bound for so long, and you've let them in."

"Is that a good thing?" asked Shadow.

"I don't know, love," said the little woman, and she

shook her head again. She crooned to her son as if he were still her baby, and dabbed at his wounds with her spit.

Shadow was naked, at the edge of the loch, but the heat from the burning building kept him warm. He watched the reflected flames in the glassy water of the loch. A yellow moon was rising.

He was starting to hurt. Tomorrow, he knew, he would hurt much worse.

Footsteps on the grass behind him. He looked up.

"Hello Smithie," said Shadow.

Smith looked down at the three of them.

"Shadow," he said, shaking his head. "Shadow, Shadow, Shadow, Shadow, Shadow. This was not how things were meant to turn out."

"Sorry," said Shadow.

"This will cause real embarrassment to Mr. Alice," said Smith. "Those people were his guests."

"They were animals," said Shadow.

"If they were," said Smith, "they were rich and important animals. There'll be widows and orphans and God knows what to take care of. Mr. Alice will not be pleased." He said it like a judge pronouncing a death sentence.

"Are you threatening him?" asked the old lady.

"I don't threaten," said Smith, flatly.

She smiled. "Ah," she said. "Well, I do. And if you or that fat bastard you work for hurt this young man, it'll be the worse for both of you." She smiled then, with sharp teeth, and Shadow felt the hairs on the back of his neck prickle. "There's worse things than dying," she said. "And I know most of them. I'm not young, and I'm not one for idle talk. So if I were you," she said, with a sniff, "I'd look after this lad."

She picked up her son with one arm, as if he were a child's doll, and she clutched her handbag close to her with the other.

Then she nodded to Shadow and walked away, into the glass-dark water, and soon she and her son were gone beneath the surface of the loch.

"Fuck," muttered Smith.

Shadow didn't say anything.

Smith fumbled in his pocket. He pulled out the pouch of tobacco, and rolled himself a cigarette. Then he lit it. "Right," he said.

"Right?" said Shadow.

"We better get you cleaned up, and find you some clothes. You'll catch your death, otherwise. You heard what she said."

IX

They had the best room waiting for Shadow, that night, back at the hotel. And, less than an hour after Shadow returned, Gordon on the front desk brought up a new backpack, a box of new clothes, even new boots. He asked no questions.

There was a large envelope on top of the pile of clothes.

Shadow ripped it open. It contained his passport, slightly scorched, his wallet, and money: several bundles of new fifty-pound notes, wrapped in rubber bands.

My God, how the money rolls in, he thought, without pleasure, and tried, without success, to remember where he had heard that song before.

He took a long bath, to soak away the pain.

And then he slept.

In the morning he dressed, and walked up the lane next to the hotel, that led up the hill and out of the village. There had been a cottage at the top of the hill, he was sure of it, with lavender in the garden, a stripped pine countertop, and a purple sofa, but no matter where he looked there was no cottage on the hill, nor any evidence that there ever had been anything there but grass and a hawthorn tree.

He called her name, but there was no reply, only the wind coming in off the sea, bringing with it the first promises of winter.

Still, she was waiting for him, when he got back to the hotel room. She was sitting on the bed, wearing her old brown coat, inspecting her fingernails. She did not look up when he unlocked the door and walked in.

"Hello Jennie," he said.

"Hello," she said. Her voice was very quiet.

"Thank you," he said. "You saved my life."

"You called," she said dully. "I came."

He said, "What's wrong?"

She looked at him, then. "I could have been yours," she said, and there were tears in her eyes. "I thought you would love me. Perhaps. One day."

"Well," he said, "maybe we could find out. We could take a walk tomorrow together, maybe. Not a long one, I'm afraid, I'm a bit of a mess physically."

She shook her head.

The strangest thing, Shadow thought, was that she did not look human any longer: she now looked like what she was, a wild thing, a forest thing. Her tail twitched on the bed, under her coat. She was very beautiful, and, he realized, he wanted her, very badly.

"The hardest thing about being a hulder," said Jennie, "even a hulder very far from home, is that, if you don't want to be lonely, you have to love a man."

"So love me. Stay with me," said Shadow. "Please."

"You," she said, sadly and finally, "are not a man."

She stood up.

"Still," she said, "everything's changing. Maybe I can go home again now. After a thousand years I don't even know if I remember any *Norsk*."

She took his hands in her small hands, that could bend iron bars, that could crush rocks to sand, and she squeezed his fingers very gently. And she was gone.

He stayed another day in that hotel, and then he

caught the bus to Thurso, and the train from Thurso to Inverness.

He dozed on the train, although he did not dream.

When he woke, there was a man on the seat next to him. A hatchet-faced man, reading a paperback book. He closed the book when he saw that Shadow was awake. Shadow looked down at the cover: Jean Cocteau's *The Difficulty of Being*.

"Good book?" asked Shadow.

"Yeah, all right," said Smith. "It's all essays. They're meant to be personal, but you feel that every time he looks up innocently and says 'This is me,' it's some kind of double-bluff. I liked *Belle et la Bête*, though. I felt closer to him watching that than through any of these essays."

"It's all on the cover," said Shadow.

"How d'you mean?"

"The difficulty of being Jean Cocteau."

Smith scratched his nose.

"Here," he said. He passed Shadow a copy of the *Scotsman*. "Page nine."

At the bottom of page nine was a small story: retired doctor kills himself. Gaskell's body had been found in his car, parked in a picnic spot on the coast road. He had swallowed quite a cocktail of painkillers, washed down with most of a bottle of Lagavulin.

"Mr. Alice hates being lied to," said Smith. "Especially by the hired help."

"Is there anything in there about the fire?" asked Shadow.

"What fire?"

"Oh. Right."

"It wouldn't surprise me if there wasn't a terrible run of luck for the great and the good over the next couple of months, though. Car crashes. Train crash. Maybe a plane'll go down. Grieving widows and orphans and boyfriends. Very sad."

Shadow nodded.

"You know," said Smith, "Mr. Alice is very concerned about your health. He worries. I worry, too."

"Yeah?" said Shadow.

"Absolutely. I mean, if something happens to you while you're in the country. Maybe you look the wrong way crossing the road. Flash a wad of cash in the wrong pub. I dunno. The point is, if you got hurt, then whatsername, Grendel's mum, might take it the wrong way."

"So?"

"So we think you should leave the U.K. Be safer for everyone, wouldn't it?"

Shadow said nothing for a while. The train began to slow.

"Okay," said Shadow.

"This is my stop," said Smith. "I'm getting out here. We'll arrange the ticket, first class of course, to anywhere you're heading. One-way ticket. You just have to tell me where you want to go."

Shadow rubbed the bruise on his cheek. There was something about the pain that was almost comforting.

The train came to a complete stop. It was a small station, seemingly in the middle of nowhere. There was a large black car parked by the station building, in the thin sunshine. The windows were tinted, and Shadow could not see inside.

Mr. Smith pushed down the train window, reached outside to open the carriage door, and he stepped out onto the platform. He looked back in at Shadow through the open window. "Well?"

"I think," said Shadow, "that I'll spend a couple of weeks looking around the U.K. And you'll just have to pray that I look the right way when I cross your roads."

"And then?"

Shadow knew it, then. Perhaps he had known it all along.

"Chicago," he said to Smith, as the train gave a jerk,

and began to move away from the station. He felt older, as he said it. But he could not put it off forever.

And then he said, so quietly that only he could have heard it, "I guess I'm going home."

Soon afterward it began to rain: huge, pelting drops that rattled against the windows and blurred the world into grays and greens. Deep rumbles of thunder accompanied Shadow on his journey south: the storm grumbled, the wind howled, and the lightning made huge shadows across the sky, and in their company Shadow slowly began to feel less alone.

CREDITS

Some of the pieces appearing in this collection were first published elsewhere; permissions and copyright information as follows:

"Introduction" © 2006 by Neil Gaiman.

"A Study in Emerald" © 2003 by Neil Gaiman. First published in *Shadows Over Baker Street*.

"The Fairy Reel" © 2004 by Neil Gaiman. First published in *The Faery Reel*.

"October in the Chair" © 2002 by Neil Gaiman. First published in *Conjunctions* no. 39.

"The Hidden Chamber" © 2005 by Neil Gaiman. First published in *Outsiders*.

"Forbidden Brides of the Faceless Slaves in the Secret House of the Night of Dread Desire" © 2004 by Neil Gaiman. First published in *Gothic!*

"The Flints of Memory Lane" © 1997 by Neil Gaiman. First published in *Dancing with the Dark*.

"Closing Time" © 2002 by Neil Gaiman. First published

in *McSweeney's Mammoth Treasury of Thrilling Tales,* Issue 10.

"Going Wodwo" © 2002 by Neil Gaiman. First published in *The Green Man.*

"Bitter Grounds" © 2003 by Neil Gaiman. First published in *Mojo: Conjure Stories.*

"Other People" © 2001 by Neil Gaiman. First published in *The Magazine of Fantasy & Science Fiction* 101, nos. 4 and 5.

"Keepsakes and Treasures" © 1999 by Neil Gaiman. First published in 999.

"Good Boys Deserve Favors" © 1995 by Neil Gaiman. First published in *Overstreet's Fan Magazine* 1, no. 5.

"The Facts in the Case of the Departure of Miss Finch" © 1998 by Neil Gaiman. First published in *Frank Frazetta Fantasy Illustrated #3.*

"Strange Little Girls" © 2001 by Neil Gaiman. First published in Tori Amos's *Strange Little Girls* tour book.

"Harlequin Valentine" © 1999 by Neil Gaiman. First published in the World Horror Convention Book, 1999.

"Locks" © 1999 by Neil Gaiman. First published in *Silver Birch, Blood Moon.*

"The Problem of Susan" © 2004 by Neil Gaiman. First published in *Flights.*

"Instructions" © 2000 by Neil Gaiman. First published in *Wolf at the Door.*

"How Do You Think It Feels?" © 1998 by Neil Gaiman. First published in *In the Shadow of the Gargoyle.*

"My Life" © 2002 by Neil Gaiman. First published in *Sock Monkeys: 200 out of 1,863.*

"Fifteen Painted Cards from a Vampire Tarot" © 1998 by Neil Gaiman. First published in *The Art of the Vampire.*

"Feeders and Eaters" © 1990, 2002 by Neil Gaiman. First published as a comic book in *Revolver Horror Special.* First published in this form in *Keep Out the Night.*

"Diseasemaker's Croup" © 2002 by Neil Gaiman. First published in *The Thackery T. Lambshead Pocket Guide to Eccentric & Discredited Diseases.*

"In the End" © 1996 by Neil Gaiman. First published in *Strange Kaddish.*

"Goliath" by Neil Gaiman. Copyright © 1999 by Warner Bros. Studios, a division of Time Warner. First published online at www.whatisthematrix.com. Based on concepts by Larry and Andy Wachowski. Inspired by the motion picture *The Matrix,* written by Andy Wachowski and Larry Wachowski.

"Pages Found in a Shoebox Left in a Greyhound Bus Somewhere Between Tulsa, Oklahoma, and Louisville, Kentucky" © 2002 by Neil Gaiman. First published in Tori Amos's *Scarlet's Walk* tour book.

"How to Talk to Girls at Parties" © 2006. First publication.

"The Day the Saucers Came" © 2006. First published in the eZine *SpiderWords* 1, no. 2 (www.spiderwords.com).

"Sunbird" © 2005 by Neil Gaiman. First published in *Noisy Outlaws, Unfriendly Blobs, and Some Other Things That Aren't as Scary, Maybe, Depending on How You Feel About Lost Lands, Stray Cellphones, Creatures from the Sky, Parents Who Disappear in Peru, a Man Named Lars Farf, and One Other Story We Couldn't Quite Finish, So Maybe You Could Help Us Out.*

"Inventing Aladdin" © 2003 by Neil Gaiman. First published in *Swan Sister.*

"The Monarch of the Glen" © 2004 by Neil Gaiman. First published in *Legends II.*

Here is an excerpt from *Anansi Boys,*
the much-anticipated novel from
New York Times bestselling author
Neil Gaiman—a magnificent work
of literary magic that is
at once exciting, scary, and deeply funny . . .

Available wherever books are sold.

It begins, as most things begin, with a song.

In the beginning, after all, were the words, and they came with a tune. That was how the world was made, how the void was divided, how the lands and the stars and the dreams and the little gods and the animals, how all of them came into the world.

They were sung.

The great beasts were sung into existence, after the Singer had done with the planets and the hills and the trees and the oceans and the lesser beasts. The cliffs that bound existence were sung, and the hunting grounds, and the dark.

Songs remain. They last. The right song can turn an emperor into a laughingstock, can bring down dynasties. A song can last long after the events and the people in it are dust and dreams are gone. That's the power of songs.

There are other things you can do with songs. They do not only make worlds or re-create existence. Fat Charlie Nancy's father, for example, was simply using them to have what he hoped and expected would be a marvelous night out.

Before Fat Charlie's father had come into the bar, the barman had been of the opinion that the whole karaoke evening was going to be an utter bust. But then the little old man had sashayed into the room, walked past the table of several blonde women, with the fresh sun-burns and smiles of tourists, who were sitting by the little makeshift stage in the corner. He had tipped his hat to them, for he wore a hat, a spotless white fedora, and lemon-yellow gloves, and then he walked over to their table. They giggled.

"Are you enjoyin' yourselves, ladies?" he asked.

They continued to giggle and told him they were hav-ing a good time, thank you, and that they were here on vacation. He said to them, it gets better, just you wait.

He was older than they were, much, much older, but he was charm itself, like something from a bygone age when fine manners and courtly gestures were worth something. The barman relaxed. With someone like this in the bar, it was going to be a good evening.

There was karaoke. There was dancing. The old man got up to sing, on the makeshift stage, not once, that evening, but twice. He had a fine voice, and an excellent smile, and feet that twinkled when he danced. The first time he got up to sing, he sang "What's New Pussycat?" The second time he got up to sing, he ruined Fat Char-lie's life.

Fat Charlie was only ever fat for a handful of years, from shortly before the age of nine, when his mother announced to the world that if there was one thing she was over and done with and if he had any argument with it he could just stick it you know where it was her marriage to that elderly goat that she had made the un-fortunate mistake of marrying and she would be leaving in the morning for somewhere a long way away and he had better not try to follow, to the age of fourteen, when Fat Charlie grew a little and exercised a little more. He was not fat. Truth to tell, he was not really even chubby, simply a little soft-looking around the edges. But the name Fat Charlie clung to him, like chewing gum to the sole of a tennis shoe. He would introduce himself as Charles, or, in his early twenties, Chaz, or, in writing as C Nancy, but it was no use: the name would creep in, infiltrating the new part of his life just as cockroaches invade the cracks and the world behind the fridge in a brand-new kitchen, and like it or not—and he didn't—he would be Fat Charlie again.

It was, he knew, irrationally, because his father had given him the nickname, and when his father gave things names, they stuck.

There was a dog who had lived in the house across the way, in the street on which Fat Charlie had grown up. It was a chestnut-colored boxer, long-legged and pointy-eared with a face that looked like the beast had, as a puppy, run face-first into a wall. Its head was raised, its tail-nub erect. It was, unmistakably, an aristocrat amongst canines. It had entered dog-shows. It had rosettes for Best of Breed, and for Best in Class, and even one Rosette marked Best in Show. This dog rejoiced in the name of Campbell's Macinrory Arbuthnot the Seventh, and its owners, when they were feeling familiar, called it Kai. This lasted until the day that Fat Charlie's father, sitting out on their dilapidated porch-swing, sipping his beer, noticed the dog as it ambled back and forth across the neighbor's yard, on a leash that ran from a palm-tree to a fence-post.

"Hell of a goofy dog," said Fat Charlie's father. "Like that friend of Donald Duck's. Hey Goofy."

And what once had been Best In Show suddenly slipped and shifted. For Fat Charlie, it was as if he saw the dog through his father's eyes and darned if he *wasn't* a pretty goofy dog, all things considered. Almost rubbery.

It didn't take long for the name to spread up and down the street. Campbell's Macinrory Arbuthnot the Seventh's owners struggled with it, but they might as well have stood their ground and argued with a hurricane.

Total strangers would pat the once-proud boxer's head, and say "Hello Goofy. How's a boy?" The dog's owner's stopped entering him in dog shows soon after that. They didn't have the heart. "Goofy looking dog," said the judges.

Fat Charlie's father's names for things stuck. That was just how it was.

That was far from the worst thing about Fat Charlie's father.

There had been, during the years that he was growing up, a number of candidates for the worst thing about Fat Charlie's father: his roving eye and equally as adventurous fingers, at least according to the young ladies of the area, who would complain to Fat Charlie's mother, and then there would be trouble; the little black cigarillos, which he called cheroots, which he smoked, the smell of which clung to everything he touched; his fondness for a peculiar shuffling form of tap-dancing, fashionable, Fat Charlie suspected, for half an hour in Harlem in the 1920s; his total and invincible ignorance about current world affairs, combined with his apparent conviction that sitcoms were half-hour long insights into the lives and struggles of real people. These, individually, as far as Fat Charlie was concerned, were none of them the worst thing about Fat Charlie's father, although each of them had contributed to the worst thing.

The worst thing about Fat Charlie's father was simply this: he was embarrassing.

Of course, everyone's parents are embarrassing. It goes with the territory. The nature of parents is to embarrass merely by existing, just as it is the nature of children of a certain age to cringe with embarrassment, shame and mortification should their parents so much as speak to them on the street.

Fat Charlie's father, of course, had elevated this to an art-form, and he rejoiced in it, just as he rejoiced in practical jokes, from the simple—Fat Charlie would never forget the first time he had climbed into an apple-pie bed—to the unimaginably complex.

"Like what?" asked Rosie, Fat Charlie's fiancée, one evening, when Fat Charlie, who normally did not talk about his father, had attempted, stumblingly, to explain why he believed that simply inviting his father to their upcoming wedding would be a horrendously bad idea. They were in a wine bar in South London at the time. Fat Charlie had long been of the opinion that four thousand miles and the Atlantic Ocean were both good things to keep between himself and his father.

"Well . . ." said Fat Charlie, and he remembered a parade of indignities, each one of which made his toes curl involuntarily. He settled upon one of them. "Well, when I moved from the local junior school to the middle school, my Dad made a point of telling me how much he had always looked forward to Presidents' Day, when he was a boy, because it's the law that on Presidents' Day, the kids who go to school dressed as their favorite presidents get a big bag of candy."

"Oh. That's a nice law," said Rosie. "I wish we had something like that here." Rosie had never been out of England, if you didn't count a Club 18-30 holiday to an island in, she was fairly certain, the Mediterranean. She had warm brown eyes and a good heart, even if geography was not her strongest suit.

"It's not a nice law," said Fat Charlie. "It's not a law at all. He made it up. There is no tradition of going to school on Presidents' Day dressed as your favorite president. Kids dressed as presidents do not get big bags of candy by an Act of Congress, nor is your popularity in the years ahead, all through middle school and high school, decided entirely by which president you decided to dress as—the average kids dress as the obvious presidents, the Lincolns and Washingtons and Jeffersons, but the ones who would become popular, they dressed as John Quincy Adams or Warren Gamaliel Harding, or someone like that. And it's bad luck to talk about it before the day. Or rather it isn't, but he said it was."

"Boys *and* girls dress up as presidents?"

"Oh yes. Boys and girls. So I spent the week before Presidents' Day reading everything there was to read about Presidents in the World Book Encyclopedia, trying to choose the right one."

"Didn't you ever suspect that he was pulling your leg?"

Fat Charlie shook his head. "It's not something you think about, when my dad starts to work you over. He's the finest liar you'll ever meet. He's convincing."

Rosie took a sip of her Chardonnay. "So which President did you go to school as?"

"Taft. He was the 27th president. I wore a brown suit my father had found somewhere, with the legs all rolled up and a pillow stuffed down the front. I had a painted-on mustache. My dad took me to school himself that day. I walked in so proudly. The other kids just screamed and pointed, and somewhere in there I locked myself in a cubicle in the boys' room and cried. They wouldn't let me go home to change. I went through the day like that. It was Hell."

"You should have made something up," said Rosie. "You were going to a costume party afterward or something. Or just told them the truth."

"Yeah," said Fat Charlie meaningfully and gloomily, remembering.

"What did your dad say, when you got home?"

"Oh, he hooted with laughter. Chuckled and chortled and, and chittered and all that. Then he told me that maybe they didn't do that Presidents' Day stuff any more. Now, why didn't we go down to the beach together and look for mermaids?"

"Look for . . . mermaids?"

"We'd go down to the beach, and walk along it, and he'd be as embarrassing as any human being on the face of this planet has ever been—he'd start singing, and he'd start doing a shuffling sort of sand-dance on the sand, and he'd just talk to people as he went—white people—people he didn't even know, people he'd never met, and I hated it, except he told me there were mermaids out there in the Atlantic, and if I looked fast enough and sharp enough, I'd see one.

"'There!' he'd say. 'Did you see her? She was a big ol' redhead, with a green tail.' And I looked, and I looked, but I never did."

He shook his head. Then he took a handful of mixed nuts from the bowl on the table and began to toss them into his mouth, chomping down on them as if each nut was a twenty-year-old indignity that could never be erased.

"Well," said Rosie, brightly, "I think he sounds lovely, a real character! We have to get him to come over for the wedding He'd be the life and soul of the party."

Which, Fat Charlie explained, after briefly choking on a brazil nut, was really the last thing you wanted at your wedding after all, wasn't it, your father turning up and being the life and soul of the party. He said that his father was, he had no doubt, still the most embarrassing person on God's Green Earth. He added that he was perfectly happy not to have seen the old goat for several years, and that the best thing his mother ever did was to leave his father and come to England to stay with her Aunt Alanna. He buttressed this by stating categorically that he was damned, double-damned and quite possibly even thrice-damned if he was going to invite his father to their wedding. In fact, said Fat Charlie in closing, the best thing about getting married was not having to invite his dad to the reception.

And then Fat Charlie saw the expression on Rosie's face and the icy glint in her normally friendly eyes, and he corrected himself hurriedly, explaining that he meant the second-best, but it was already much too late.

"You'll just have to get used to the idea," said Rosie. "After all, a wedding is a marvelous opportunity for mending fences and building bridges. It's your opportunity to show him that there are no hard feelings."

"But there *are* hard feelings," said Fat Charlie. "Lots."

"Do you have an address for him?" asked Rosie. "Or a phone number? You probably ought to phone him. A letter's a bit impersonal when your only son is getting married . . . you are his only son, aren't you? Does he have e-mail?"

"Yes. I'm his only son. I have no idea if he has e-mail or not. Probably not," said Fat Charlie. Letters were good things, he thought. They could get lost in the post for a start.

"Well, you must have an address or a phone number."

"I don't," said Fat Charlie, honestly. Maybe his father had moved away. He could have left Florida and gone somewhere they didn't have telephones. Or addresses.

"Well," said Rosie, sharply, "who does?"

"Mrs. Higgler," said Fat Charlie, and all the fight went out of him.

Rosie smiled sweetly. "And who is Mrs. Higgler?" she asked.

"Friend of the family," said Fat Charlie. "When I was growing up, she used to live next door."

He had spoken to Mrs. Higgler several years before this, when his mother was dying. He had, at his mother's request, telephoned Mrs. Higgler to pass on the message to Fat Charlie's father, and to tell him to get in touch. And several days later there had been a message on Fat Charlie's ansaphone, left while he was at work, in a voice that was unmistakable his father's, even if it did sound rather older, and a little drunk.

His father said that it was not a good time, and that business affairs would be keeping him in America. And then he added that, for everything, Fat Charlie's mother was a damn fine woman. Several days later a vase of flowers had been delivered to the ward. Fat Charlie's mother had snorted, when she read the card.

"Thinks he can get around me that easily?" she said. "He's got another think coming, I can tell you that." But she had had the nurse put the flowers in a place of honor by her bed, and, several times since, had asked Fat Charlie if he had heard anything about his father coming and visiting her, before it was all over.

Fat Charlie said he hadn't. He grew to hate the question, and his answer, and the expression on her face when he told her that, no, his father wasn't coming.

The worst day, in Fat Charlie's opinion, was the day that the doctor, a gruff little man, had taken Fat Charlie aside and told him that it would not be long now, that his mother was fading fast, and it was a matter of keeping her comfortable until the end.

Fat Charlie had nodded, and gone in to his mother. She had held his hand, and was asking him whether or not he had remembered to pay her gas bill, when the noise began in the corridor—a clashing, parping, stomping, rattling, brass and bass and drum sort of noise, of the kind that tends not to be heard in hospitals, where signs in the stairwells request quiet and the icy glares of the nursing staff enforce it.

The noise was getting louder.

For one moment Fat Charlie thought it might be terrorists. His mother, though, smiled weakly at the cacophony. "Yellow bird," she whispered.

"What?" said Fat Charlie, scared that she had stopped making sense.

"*Yellow Bird,*" she said, louder and more firmly. "It's what they're playing."

Fat Charlie went to the door and looked out.

Coming down the hospital corridor, ignoring the protests of nurses, the stares of patients in pajamas and of their families, was what appeared to be a very small New Orleans jazz band. There was a saxophone, and a sousaphone and a trumpet. There was an enormous man with what appeared to be a double bass strung around his neck. There was a man with a bass drum, which he banged. And at the head of the pack, in a smart checked suit, with a porkpie hat and lemon yellow gloves, came Fat Charlie's father. He played no instrument, but was doing a soft-shoe-shuffle along the polished linoleum of the hospital floor, lifting his hat to each of the medical staff in turn, shaking hands with anyone who got close enough to talk or to attempt to complain.

Fat Charlie bit his lip, and prayed to anyone who might be listening that the Earth would open and swallow him up, or failing that, that he might suffer a brief, merciful and entirely fatal heart attack. No such luck. He remained among the living, the brass band kept coming, his father kept dancing, and shaking hands, and smiling.

If there is any justice in the world, thought Fat Charlie, my father will keep going down the corridor and he'll go straight past us and into the genito-urinary department; but there was no justice, and his father reached the door of the oncology ward and stopped.

"Fat Charlie," he said, loudly enough that everyone in the ward—on that floor—in the hospital—was able to comprehend that this was someone who knew Fat Charlie. "Fat Charlie, get out of the way. Your father is here."

Fat Charlie got out of the way.

The band, led by Fat Charlie's father, snaked their way through the ward to Fat Charlie's mother's bed. She looked up at them as they approached, and she smiled.

"Yellow bird," she said, weakly. "It's my favorite song."

"And what kind of man would I be if I forgot that?" asked Fat Charlie's father.

She shook her head slowly, and she reached out her hand and squeezed his hand in its lemon-yellow glove.

"Excuse me," said a woman with a clipboard, "are these people with you?"

"No," said Fat Charlie, his cheeks heating up. "They're not. Not really."

"But that is your mother, isn't it?" said the woman, with a basilisk glance. "I must ask you to make these people vacate the ward momentarily, and without incurring any further disturbance."

Fat Charlie muttered.

"What was that?"

"I said, I'm pretty sure I can't make them do anything," said Fat Charlie. He consoled himself that things could not possibly get any worse, when his father took a plastic carrier bag from the drummer, and began producing cans of brown ale and handing them out, to his band, to the nursing staff, to the patients. Then he lit a cheroot.

"Excuse me," said the woman with the clipboard, when she saw the smoke, and she launched herself across the room at Fat Charlie's father like a SCUD missile with its watch on upside down.

Fat Charlie took that moment to slip away. It seemed the wisest course of action.

He sat at home that night, waiting for the phone to ring or for a knock on the door, in much the same spirit that a man kneeling at the guillotine might wait for the blade to kiss his neck; but the doorbell did not ring.

He barely slept, and slunk in to the hospital the following afternoon, prepared for the worst.

His mother, in her bed, looked happier than she had looked in months. "He's gone back," she told Fat Charlie, when he came in. "He couldn't stay. I have to say, Charlie, I wish you hadn't just gone like that. We wound up having a party here. We had a fine old time."

Fat Charlie could think of nothing worse than having to attend a party in a cancer ward, thrown by his father with a jazz band. He didn't say anything.

"He's not a bad man," said Fat Charlie's mother, with a twinkle in her eye. Then she frowned. "Well, that's not exactly true. He's certainly not a good man. But he did me a power of good last night," and she smiled, a real smile and, for a moment, looked young again.

The woman with the clipboard was standing in the doorway, and she crooked her finger at him. Fat Charlie beetled down the ward toward her, apologizing before she was even properly within earshot. Her look, he realized, as he got closer to her, was no longer that of a basilisk with stomach cramps. Now she looked positively kittenish. "Your father," she said.

"I'm sorry," said Fat Charlie. It was what he always said, growing up, when his father was mentioned.

"No, no, no," said the former basilisk. "Nothing to apologize for. I was just wondering. Your father. In case we need to get in touch with him—we don't have a telephone number or an address on file. I should have asked him last night, but it completely got away from me."

"I don't think he has a phone number," said Fat Charlie. "And the best way to find him is to go to Miami, and to drive up Highway A1A—that's the coast road that runs up the east of Florida. In the afternoon you may find him fishing off a bridge. In the evening he'll be in a bar."

"Such a charming man," she said, wistfully. "What does he do?"

"I told you. He says it's the miracle of the loafs and the fishes."

She stared at him blankly, and he felt stupid. When his father said it, people would laugh. "Um. Like in the bible. The miracle of the loaves and the fishes. Dad used to say that he loafs and fishes, and it's a miracle that he still makes money. It was a sort of joke."

A misty look. "Yes. He told the funniest jokes." She clucked her tongue, and once more was all business. "Now, I need you back here at 5:30."

"Why?"

"To pick up your mother. And her belongings. Didn't Dr. Johnson tell you we were discharging her?"

"You're sending her home?"

"Yes, Mr. Nancy."

"What about the, about the cancer?"

"It seems to have been a false alarm."

Fat Charlie couldn't understand how it could have been a false alarm. Last week they'd been talking about sending his mother to a hospice. The doctor had been using phrases like "weeks not months" and "making her as comfortable as possible while we wait for the inevitable."

Still, Fat Charlie came back at 5:30 and picked up his mother, who seemed quite unsurprised to learn that she was no longer dying. On the way home she told Fat Charlie that she would be using her life-savings to travel around the world.

"The doctors were saying I had three months," she said. "And I remember I thought, if I get out of this hospital bed then I'm going to see Paris and Rome and places. I'm going back to Dominica. I may go to Africa. And China. I like Chinese food."

Fat Charlie wasn't sure what was going on, but whatever it was, he blamed his father. He accompanied his mother and a serious suitcase to Heathrow airport, and waved her goodbye at the International Departures gate. She was smiling hugely as she went through, clutching her passport and tickets, and she looked younger than he remembered her looking in many years.

She sent him postcards from Paris, and from Rome and from Athens, and from Lagos and Cape Town. Her postcard from Nanking told him that she didn't like the Chinese food in China, and that she couldn't wait to come back to London and eat *proper* Chinese food.

She died in her sleep, in a hotel in Roseau, on the island of Dominica.

At the funeral, at a South London Crematorium, Fat Charlie kept expecting to see his father: perhaps his father would make an entrance at the head of a jazz band, or followed down the aisle by a clown troupe or a half-dozen tricycle-riding cigar-puffing chimpanzees; and even during the service Fat Charlie kept glancing back, over his shoulder, toward the chapel door. But Fat Charlie's father was not there, only his mother's friends and relations, mostly big women in black hats, blowing their noses and dabbing at their eyes and shaking their heads.

It was during the final hymn, after the button had been pressed and Fat Charlie's mother had trundled off down the conveyor belt to her final reward, that Fat Charlie noticed a man of about his own age standing at the back of the chapel. It was not his father, obviously. It was someone he did not know, someone he might not even have noticed, at the back, in the shadows, had he not been darting troubled glances back . . . and then there was the stranger, in an elegant black suit, his eyes lowered, his hands folded.

Fat Charlie let his glance linger a moment too long, and the stranger looked at Fat Charlie and he flashed him a joyless smile, of the kind that suggested that they were both in this together. It was not the kind of expression you see on the faces of strangers, but Fat Charlie could not place the man. He turned his face back to the front of the chapel. They sang "Swing Low, Sweet Chariot," a song Fat Charlie was pretty sure his mother had always disliked, and the Reverend Wright invited them back to Fat Charlie's Great-Aunt Alanna's for something to eat.

There was nobody at his Great-Aunt Alanna's that he did not know. In the years since his mother had died, he sometimes wondered about that man: who he was, why he was there. Whether Fat Charlie had simply imagined him . . .

"So," said Rosie, draining her Chardonnay, "you'll

call your Mrs. Higgler, and give her my mobile number. Tell her about the wedding and the date . . . that's a thought: do you think we should invite her?"

"We can if we like," said Fat Charlie. "I don't think she'll come. She gets scared of flying. She's an old family friend. She knew my dad back in the dark ages."

"Well, sound her out. See if we should be sending her an invitation."

Rosie was a good person. There was in Rosie a little of the essence of Frances of Assisi, of Robin Hood, of Buddha and of Glinda the Good: the knowledge that she was about to bring together her true love and his estranged father gave her forthcoming wedding an extra dimension, she decided. It was not simply a wedding: it was practically a humanitarian mission, and Fat Charlie had known Rosie long enough to know never to stand between his fiancée and her need to do good.

"I'll call Mrs. Higgler tomorrow," he said.

"Tell you what," said Rosie, with an endearing wrinkle of her nose. "Call her tonight. It's not late in America, after all."

Fat Charlie nodded. They walked out of the wine bar together, Rosie with a spring in her step, Fat Charlie like a man going to the gallows. He told himself not to be silly: After all, perhaps Mrs. Higgler had moved, or had her phone disconnected. It was possible. Anything was possible. He came up with a plan.

They went up to Fat Charlie's place, the upstairs half of a smallish house off the Brixton Road.

"What time is it in Florida?" Rosie asked.

"Late afternoon," said Fat Charlie.

"Well. Go on then."

"Maybe we should wait a bit. In case she's out."

"And maybe we should call now, before she has her dinner."

Fat Charlie found his old paper address book, and under H was a scrap of an envelope, in his mother's handwriting, with a telephone number on it, and beneath that, Callyanne Higgler.

The phone rang and rang.

"She's not there," he said to Rosie, but at that moment the phone at the other end was answered, and a female voice said, "Yes? Who is this?"

"Um. Is that Mrs. Higgler?"

"Who is this?" said Mrs. Higgler. "If you're one of they damn telemarketers, you take me off your list right now or I sue. I know my rights."

"No. It's me. Charles Nancy. I used to live next door to you."

"Fat Charlie? If that don't beat all. I was looking for your number all this morning. I turned this place upside down, looking for it, and do you think I could find it? What I think happened was I had it written in my old accounts book, and it got thrown out by mistake. Upside down I turned the place. And I said to myself, Callyanne, this is a good time to just pray and hope the Lord hears you and sees you right, and I went down on my knees, well, my knees aren't what they were so I just put my hands together, but anyway, I still don't find your number, but I get you phoning me up, and that's even better from some points of view, particularly because I ain't made of money and I can't afford to go phoning no foreign countries even for something like this, although I was going to phone you, don't you worry, given the circumstances—"

And she stopped, suddenly, either to take a breath, or to take a sip from the huge mug of too-hot coffee she always carried in her hand, and during the brief quietus, Fat Charlie said, "I want to ask my dad to come to my wedding. Getting married." There was silence at the end of the line. "It's not till the end of the year, though," he said. Still silence. "Her name's Rosie," he added, helpfully. He was starting to wonder if they had been cut off; conversations with Mrs. Higgler were normally somewhere one-sided affairs, often with her doing your lines for you, and here she was, letting him say three whole things uninterrupted. He decided to go for a fourth. "You can come too if you want," he said.

"Lord, lord, lord," said Mrs. Higgler. "Nobody told you, did they?"

"Told me what?"

So she told him, at length and in detail, while he stood there and said nothing at all, and when she was done he said, "Thank you, Mrs. Higgler." He wrote something down on a scrap of paper, then he said, "Thanks. No, really, thanks," again, and he put down the phone.

"Well?" asked Rosie. "Have you got his number?"

Fat Charlie said, "Dad won't be coming to the wedding." Then he said, "I have to go to Florida." His voice was flat, and without emotion. He might have been saying, "I have to order a new checkbook."

"When?"

"Tomorrow."

"Why?"

"Funeral. My dad's. He's dead."

#1 *New York Times* Bestselling Author

NEIL GAIMAN

GOOD OMENS
with Terry Pratchett
978-0-06-085398-3

The nice and accurate prophecies of
Agnes Nutter, witch.

ANANSI BOYS
978-0-06-051519-5

Fat Charlie Nancy's normal life ended the
moment his father dropped dead. Charlie didn't
know his dad was a god. And he never
knew he had a brother.

AMERICAN GODS
978-0-380-78903-0

A perfectly wrought tale of a man
hired as a bodyguard to a grifter who becomes
enmeshed in a war between the old gods
and the new.

NEVERWHERE
978-0-380-78901-6

Richard Mayhew is a plain man with a
good heart and a dull job. One night he stumbles upon a
girl lying bleeding on the sidewalk, stops to
help her, and finds his life
changed forever.

STARDUST
978-0-380-80455-9

Young Tristran Thorn will do anything
to win the cold heart of beautiful Victoria—
and to prove it, one night he makes a rash promise
that sends him into the unexplored lands
east of their sleepy English village.

SHORT STORY
COLLECTIONS

SMOKE AND MIRRORS: Short Fictions and Illusions
978-0-06-145016-7
FRAGILE THINGS: Short Fictions and Wonders
978-0-06-051523-2

Visit www.AuthorTracker.com for exclusive
information on your favorite HarperCollins authors.

NG 0211

Available wherever books are sold or please call 1-800-331-3761 to order.